Hello and Goodbye

The Yellow Ribbon Chronicles: Volume One

A Novel

CARI SCHAEFFER

Published by Cari Schaeffer

This is a work of fiction. Names, characters, places, and incidents are the product of the author's imagination or are used fictitiously from real experiences and by permission. Any resemblance to actual events, locales, or persons, living or dead, is entirely coincidental.

This publication is protected under the US Copyright Act of 1976 and all other applicable international, federal, state and local laws, and all rights are reserved, including resale rights: you are not allowed to give or sell this publication to anyone else. If you received this publication from anyone other than Cari Schaeffer or her authorized retail sites, you've received a pirated copy. Please respect the hard work of this author.

Copyright © 2015 Cari Schaeffer. All rights reserved worldwide.

ISBN-13: 978-1514279960
ISBN-10: 1514279967

Read more at www.carischaeffer.com

Book Cover Design: Paper and Sage Design
Cover Photography: Susan Motluck

This book is available in print and as an e-book at most online retailers.
No part of this book may be used or reproduced in any manner whatsoever without written permission from the author except in the case of brief quotations embodied in critical articles and reviews. For more information, contact the author.

DEDICATION

This book is dedicated to the men and women who serve in our Armed Forces, especially to those who remain behind when loved ones in uniform work long hours or deploy. We rarely complain or ask for help, but need prayers and support. Loneliness should not be part of the territory.

Our sacrifice matters.
We matter.

Other books by Cari Schaeffer

Faith, Hope, Love, and Chocolate

Run, run, run...

Run away. That's what Faith Strauss has done for twenty years. She was destroyed by one tragic event. An event so horrific, she didn't share it with anyone, not even her husband. She buried it deep inside, where it can't hurt anyone.

If God is good, then where was He? Why didn't He stop it? How can she trust Him ever again?

Run, run, run...

She's not good enough. Never has been. Never will be. She could lose it all again, if she's not careful. She married, had children, and carved out a life for herself. But Fear is her ever-present companion, always reminding her never to reach too far, or too high.

Run, run, run...

God has another plan. A plan that she never saw, even though she has walked it her entire life. Will the unexpected exposure of her secret and the truth behind it restore her or destroy her all over again?

It's time to stop running.

FOREWARD

Even though this book was written this year, the story truly has its beginning decades ago. I am a veteran myself and the wife of a retired Air Force veteran. Many of the stories contained between these pages are real, even if the characters and locations themselves are not. By permission, I have collected stories from several spouses of military members with the understanding they may be fictionalized for this series.

You are going to read things that may make you shake your head and ask, "Could this *really* have happened?" More often than not, the answer is yes.

Because it did.

I hope you turn the last page of this book, and the series, with a greater understanding and appreciation for what it means to be a Military Spouse. As we walk this path along with our loved one in uniform, there are countless times over the years when we wonder if we are up to the task at hand. Many nights we fall on our knees knowing that we are not, and yet we go on.

You don't know what you don't know…yet.

Happy Reading,
Cari

Air Force Rank Structure

<u>Enlisted</u>

E-1 Airman Basic (no stripes)
E-2 Airman (one stripe)
E-3 Airman First Class (two stripes)
E-4 Senior Airman (three stripes)
E-5 Staff Sergeant (four stripes)
E-6 Technical Sergeant (five stripes)
E-7 Master Sergeant (six stripes)
E-8 Senior Master Sergeant (seven stripes)
E-9 Chief Master Sergeant (eight stripes)

<u>Officer</u>

O-1 Second Lieutenant (one gold bar)
O-2 First Lieutenant (one silver bar)
O-3 Captain (two silver bars)
O-4 Major (gold oak leaf)
O-5 Lieutenant Colonel (silver oak leaf)
O-6 Colonel (silver eagle)
O-7 Brigadier General (one silver star)
O-8 Major General (two silver stars)
O-9 Lieutenant General (three silver stars)
O-10 General (four silver stars)

PROLOGUE

2013

CARI SCHAEFFER

I hate musty, cluttered basements, especially my own. Unfortunately, they seem to end up that way. To be honest, my basement is more dusty than musty. I don't like coming down here and wouldn't without a good reason.

I scan the horde of boxes labeled "Rick's Military Stuff" that dominate the landscape, and frown. Finding one particular box is going to be daunting. It was Rick's idea to keep so much from his military life packed up in boxes. History, he called it.

It would have been a good idea to keep a few of the most important things, like his dress uniform. Rick chose to keep a copy of all of his orders from his numerous deployments and moves, a uniform with each stripe he earned, decades worth of old Leave and Earning Statements (the military version of a pay stub), every Personal Information File made on him at each duty station we were assigned to, and the squadron coins he collected over the years.

If a coin can't be spent, I don't see the point in keeping it. Old paper is for shredding once it's been saved for the obligatory seven years. It wasn't easy keeping all of it, considering the weight limits imposed on us by the military with each move. Rick insisted, so I gave in.

There is one good reason I didn't want to keep everything – there are some very dark days represented among these mementos. Leafing through and smiling about the good days doesn't make me want to revisit those memories that still carry a sting, even after all these years.

"Where is that box...?" I mutter, picking my way carefully toward the back of the room. The two bulbs that hang precariously from the ceiling cast enough light to elongate shadows, but not enough to illuminate.

Our daughter's wedding is coming up. I promised Elizabeth I would pull out my wedding gown for her by this weekend. She won't wear it as is; she's going to hand it over to a seamstress who will update it. When she asked my permission to make the alterations, I gladly gave it. It will save a ton of money not having to buy a new gown.

Through the corner of my eye, I spy a long shallow box poking out from under a stack of boxes. From the shape of it, it could very well hold a wedding gown.

"Aha!" Gingerly stepping over some boxes while moving others, I carefully make my way toward my goal. It takes five minutes to move twenty feet. Once I reach the desired stack, I pluck the boxes off one by one to uncover what I hope is my final and victorious destination. Once its bottom is no longer supported, however, the last box I lift promptly dumps its contents onto the floor at my feet.

"Perfect!" I grind my teeth. Various papers and trinkets are splayed around me in a three foot diameter. With a sigh, I realize they're some of Rick's military things.

Swiveling from side to side, there's no way I can pick up what I hope is the wedding gown box and walk safely across the floor with it. I have to clean up this mess first.

Resigning myself to the task, I squat down to gather it up. I proceed to stuff them back into the box. The papers flutter to my feet once again. Of course. I have to fix the box first.

Sighing impatiently, I examine the box in the shadowy light. The four bottom flaps hang limply from the useless cube. I interweave them to stabilize the bottom before realizing that was the problem in the first place. The box will need to be taped if it's going to be useful.

I throw the wobbly box as hard as I can toward the doorway. Due to its weightlessness, it lands well short of my target. Sighing again, I turn my attention back to the mess at my feet. There are a lot of papers, so I take care not to crush them as I pick them up. Eyeballing the stack, I know I'll have to make at least two trips.

Once the contents have been gathered, I march up the stairs and pile the trinkets on one corner of the dining room table with the papers stacked next to them. I repair the offending box and start the process of sifting through the papers to put them in some semblance of order before packing them away.

Most of the papers are typed in military jargon, which is gibberish to me. It always has been. I recognize most of them as orders for the various places that we not only lived as a couple and family, but also everywhere Rick went when the military took him away from me.

There are a lot of papers.

The date on one sheet catches my eye. It's from 1988 and has the name of the base my husband moved to two weeks after we got married. He had to leave me behind for a one year remote tour. Spouses are not allowed to accompany their military spouses on remote tours.

Technically, spouses *can* go on remote tours if they want to. But the military won't pay for you to move, and won't help you with housing or anything that you need to survive. You're on your own. So unless you're fabulously wealthy independent of military pay, it's not possible.

My lips press together, remembering that year. That is one of the many memories that still carries a sting. We were so young. I was very immature, and it was really hard. I can still remember the knot that welled up from my stomach into my throat when we drove to the airport to say goodbye...

PART ONE: INDUCTION

1988 – 1990

CHAPTER ONE

June, 1988

"You'll be okay. I promise," Rick assures me, keeping one hand on the wheel while squeezing my trembling hand with the other. "This year will go by really fast, you'll see. We'll be together at Christmas, and that's the halfway mark. Then it's into the home stretch, and I'll be back before you know it."

I keep my gaze averted, looking out the side window. Not trusting myself to speak, I nod and squeeze his hand harder. The city of San Antonio whizzes past me in a dreary gray blur. It's raining, which is unusual for this time of year, but very appropriate. The rain drops hit the glass like tears, mirroring the ones that cascade unchecked down my cheeks.

We married only two weeks ago, and I have to say goodbye to my new husband, my best friend, today. He's getting on a plane, flying halfway around the world, and leaving me for a whole year. Christmas is six months away. We barely had a honeymoon; he had to process out of his squadron while I had to get a dependent ID card and enroll in the military healthcare system. We spent most of our days bouncing from one office to another and waiting in one line or another.

Our wedding was a fabulous affair. His entire family flew in – I got to meet his parents and two brothers, Trent and Vance, for the first time. Rick's parents have interesting names – Skip and Lovey. Rick has his mother's sandy blond hair and his father's smile. They're a lovely family and got along well with mine. His parents are very wealthy. They insisted on paying not only for half the wedding, but the rehearsal dinner, as well. It was at the best steak house in the city. In spite of their wealth, they're very down-to-earth and welcomed me into their family.

We haven't even gotten our wedding photos back. The smile on my face at the memory of our wedding fades as reality crashes in.

Six months might as well be an eternity.

"Honey bun? You okay?" he asks.

I shake my head and turn toward him. "No, I'm not okay! How can they make you do this? We just got married, Rick!" I sob. I release his hand to dig into my purse for a tissue.

His expression is pained. He glances back and forth between the road and me. "I'm sorry, but we talked about this. I don't have a choice. I got orders and I have to go. This is military life. I don't want to leave you, but I'll be back. I promise."

"Then I hate military life." It sounds harsh, but it's the truth. This hurts so much.

He shakes his head in silence. I sob the rest of the way to the airport.

I didn't grow up in a military family. In fact, I never gave it a second thought. I grew up in one house in Oklahoma until I was about six. Then we moved to the second and only other house I ever lived in. This home is in the small town of Elmhurst, Texas which is about forty-five minutes away from Radley Air Force Base in San Antonio. That is where Rick is stationed. My parents still live in that house, and I will unfortunately continue living there.

I love my parents, but I'm a married woman now, and I want to live on my own with my husband.

We met at a gas station two years ago when I was eighteen and he was twenty-one. I was pumping gas into my super cool silver 1982 Honda Civic. My parents had purchased the used car for me as a high school graduation gift the year before. All I had to do was pay for car insurance, gas, and repairs. It took most of my paycheck, but I didn't mind. So what if the back seat had a tear in it and the window on the passenger side didn't roll down all the way? It was *mine*.

I spied Rick getting out of his candy apple red Chevy pick up truck at the pump in front of me. He was so handsome with his broad, muscled shoulders and sandy blond hair peeking out from under his military hat. I was distracted trying to catch a glimpse of the face that went with the physique that I forgot to pay attention to the gas I was pumping. It overflowed all over my car, the ground, and me. I screamed, dropped the nozzle, and jumped back.

He must have heard me and turned around. He calmly secured the nozzle for his own truck before sauntering my way.

I was mortified into open mouthed silence.

"You need some help?" he asked.

"Uh..." I blinked. Wow, did that face ever match the physique. I couldn't formulate words.

He chuckled, placed the dropped nozzle back into its cradle, pulled several paper towels from the window washing station next to the pump, and began wiping off my car.

I collected myself. "Uh...thank you. I...I can do that."

He shook his head and kept wiping, dumping the sopping paper towels into the trash can to exchange for new ones. "It's no trouble. I'm afraid you're going to need a car wash and a shower, though." He gestured to the bottom of my stone-washed jeans. They were soaked, as were my shoes. I loved those shoes; I had just bought them with my employee discount at Payless. Now they were ruined.

"Perfect," I grumbled.

"At least it didn't get in your eyes. That would really sting." He glanced up at me for a long moment. "Those eyes are too pretty to sting."

I felt my cheeks burn and gulped. "Uh...yeah. Thanks." Smooth.

He jerked his chin to the side of the gas station. "You might want to go wash your feet and legs at the water station. Otherwise, you'll get an awful headache from the fumes, and the inside of your car will stink."

"Okay." At least I didn't say "uh" this time. I walked woodenly toward the side of the gas station, glancing over my shoulder once I got there. He was staring at me as he wiped.

My cheeks burned hotter.

"Get a grip, Heather! This guy's cute *and* nice. At least introduce yourself! He probably thinks you're an idiot," I muttered under my breath while I hosed myself off. When I returned, he had finished wiping my car and even recapped the tank. He was leaning against my car with his arms crossed, studying me.

"Thank you," I squeaked. "That was...nice."

He extended his hand. "My name is Rick. What's yours?"

"Uh...Heather. My name is Heather." I felt giddy as his warm, strong hand enveloped mine. I giggled. I couldn't help myself. My cheeks were burning so hot they tingled.

He grinned, probably at my immature response. "It's nice to meet you, Heather."

It was indeed. He talked to me for awhile longer and eventually asked for my number, which I somehow remembered. On our first date, he took me hiking up a hill on the outskirts of the city to see the most amazing show – watching the stars come out in the desert sky while the sun set gently over the horizon. It was gorgeous beyond description. He introduced me to hiking and biking, which became a mutual passion. We did it as often as we could. As a matter of fact, most of our dates were unconventional. We didn't do a whole lot of movies and restaurants. We went hiking or biking and had picnics instead.

Now, two years later, he is leaving me. My parents and siblings came in a separate car to see him off. They linger a distance away at the departing gate so we can say our private goodbyes.

My eleven-year-old sister Debbie keeps stealing glances at us, giggling behind her hand. Jeff, my sixteen-year-old brother, allows his gaze to wander around the airport. His eyes land and remain on any attractive young girl that comes into view until she's well out of range.

Rick and I cling to each other. I bury my face in his shoulder, and he buries his face in my hair.

"I'll see you at Christmas. I'll call you once a month, I promise. I'll write every day, if I can," he whispers. He will only get one morale call a month.

I only get to hear his voice once a month.

"Rick..." My shoulders shake.

The final boarding call for his flight blares on the overhead speakers.

My husband has to leave right now.

"Oh, God..." I begin to hyperventilate.

My father's arms wrap around my shoulders and squeeze. "Heather, it's time. He's got to go."

I reach up and grab Rick's face in both my hands and kiss him hard. He kisses me with equal fervor. "I love you."

Debbie giggles. Mom reprimands her.

"I love you, too. I'll be back. I promise." He stares hard into my eyes, pecks me once more on the lips, and then he's gone. My final view of him is blurred through tears.

The tears flow all the way home. I'm thankful my parents came with us; I wouldn't have been able to drive. I ride in the car with my mother and Debbie. Dad drives Rick's truck with Jeff in tow. She reassures me all the way home, trying to engage me in distracting conversation.

It doesn't work.

CHAPTER TWO

September, 1988

The next few months are a blur. When our wedding photos arrived in August, I broke down in a crying fit trying to look at them. I had a hard time getting halfway through the album, but my mother insisted I look through the entire thing.

"What if there's something wrong with them? They may have another couple's picture in there or something. It could happen, you know," she said.

So I reluctantly trolled through the entire album, tears falling the entire time. There were no other couples' pictures in our album.

My heart aches every day and I lose my appetite, dropping ten pounds. I tried hiking to our favorite spots after work, but they only depress me. It is a reminder that Rick isn't here to share it.

Jeff and Debbie both make an effort to be nice. Debbie asks me to play dolls with her, which she hasn't done in a long time. She's pulling slowly away from childhood, making her first steps into adolescence. A Madonna poster is up on the wall in her room. I instead offer to paint her nails, and she accepts. I paint them blue with silver sparkles.

Jeff's idea of being nice to me includes punching me in the arm, or rubbing my head hard with his knuckles, which I've always hated. But he's taller than me and enjoys that very much.

Being the oldest sister is not all it's cracked up to be.

"I am twenty-one and a married woman now, Jeff! You should treat me like it!" I yell at him after having my head rubbed for the third time today.

"Hey, sis, you may be older, but you're not bigger," Jeff replies, taking a swing at my arm. Honestly, his punches don't hurt. They are infuriatingly annoying.

"Mom!" I stomp into the living room. "Will you tell Jeff to just leave me *alone?* I'm a grown up and married now!" I glare at my brother, who towers over me.

I can't help being only five feet four. Jeff may be a hulk at six feet, but he's still a twerp.

"Jeffrey Allen," Mom sighs. She only uses his whole name when she's had enough. "Leave her alone, young man. You know your sister is going through a difficult time. You don't need to make it worse."

In a glimmer of hope that may be the spark of adulthood for Jeff, he casts his glance sheepishly downward and thrusts his hands in the pockets of his Levi's.

"Sorry, Heather," he mutters, glancing at me sideways.

I glare up at him for a moment, searching his face for the devilish streak I know is in there. Not finding it, I grumble, "Thanks."

He shrugs and lopes out of the room.

I love my family, but I want to be with my husband. I want to finish growing up by moving *out*.

The only real light that shines is the once monthly phone calls from Rick as well as the letters I receive regularly. He sounds so distant on the phone; there's an echo and the occasional clicking sound on the line.

The first phone call I got from him upset me deeply. When he went in to meet the First Sergeant, along with the usual bundle of paperwork and mosquito repellent, Rick was given a box of condoms. He pushed them back across the First Sergeant's desk saying, "No, thank you. I'm married."

The First Sergeant pushed them right back across the desk. "I know. Don't take anything home to the wife."

I smacked the wall so hard with my fist that my parents hurried into the kitchen to see what happened. I shook my head. They retreated with worried expressions.

Rick reassured me he had thrown them away, and I was not to worry.

I was so angry and hurt at the assumption, and even endorsement, of my husband's infidelity that I cried myself to sleep that night. My parents were livid when I told them. There was nothing we could do.

I had to trust Rick.

Jeff and Debbie don't know about that incident, but they knew I was very upset. Jeff finally quit punching me and rubbing my head. I let Debbie paint my nails blue with silver sparkles this time.

"Don't you think it's romantic, Heather?" Debbie ventures dreamily. "I know it's hard that Rick is so far away, but you're like Romeo and Juliet pining for each other."

I look at her like she's lost her mind. "There's nothing romantic about this, Debbie. It really stinks."

She glances up at me apologetically for a moment before resuming the transformation of my nails. "I know, but still. I think it's sort of romantic," she mumbles.

I can't argue with the ideals of an eleven-year-old.

****

"Heather, why don't you take some college classes or go out and get a second job? You're just not getting a lot of hours at Payless. It'll make the time pass faster for you if you stay busy," Mom ventures one day over breakfast.

The Payless that I work at was sold and my hours have been cut to under ten hours a week. I don't want to take any classes – even though I graduated high school three years ago, I still don't know what I want to be when I grow up. Rick and I have a joint account and I can use his Senior Airman pay, but I still don't feel like it's "our" money. He made it clear that it is, but I feel funny using it. I apply at various retail sites around town. After multiple applications and rejections, I accept a part time job at the local pet store, cleaning fish tanks and rodent cages.

"Well, it's an honest living," Dad replies, trying to smother a chuckle with a cough while hiding behind his newspaper.

Debbie wants to know if she can get a free hamster out of the deal. I tell her no.

Working at both jobs occupies my time, but nothing occupies the empty space in my heart. I pour out my longing in page after page to Rick, who faithfully responds to each and every one. I once again hike or bike to some of our favorite spots in spite of the pain, stuffing a pen and notepad into a backpack to write letters to him where we used to have our picnics. Before I seal them, I spray my letters to him with his favorite perfume, and he sprays his letters to me with my favorite cologne. When his letters arrive, I close my eyes and inhale so deeply the paper presses stiffly up against my nose. It doesn't bother me a bit that the letters are often weeks old when they arrive.

****

November, 1988

Thanksgiving is right around the corner, and I can't wait to talk to Rick. I get to see him next month. I'm so excited, I drop another five pounds.

"You'll be nothing but a bag of bones when you see that boy!" my mother exclaims.

I wave her off. "I could use the extra room in my clothes. I'm so excited, Mom! He'll be here next month. It's been so long." My eyes glisten.

Mom's face softens and she holds my hands in hers. "I know, sweetheart. You're almost halfway done. I'm so proud of how well you're doing."

"Thanks." I wipe the tears from my eyes, and offer a weak smile. "This sucks."

Normally, my mother would frown at the use of that word and reprimand me. This time, however, she responds, "Yes, this does suck."

Hearing my mother use that word makes me laugh. I really need that.

****

December, 1988

Two weeks before Christmas, the phone rings. It's Rick.

"Hi, sweetie!" I grip the phone and squeal, yelling a bit to make sure he can hear me.

"How are you doing?" His voice crackles.

"Much better because I hear your voice. I miss you."

"I miss you, too."

"I can't wait to see you! You'll be the best Christmas present ever!"

There's a longer than usual pause on the other end. "Listen, honey, I hate to tell you this, but my leave got denied. I can't come home for Christmas. I should be able to get leave no problem in January, though. I'm really sorry."

I suck in a deep breath, and a knot sprouts in my stomach. "What?! How can they do this? I mean…you *promised*….you said you'd get leave after six months!"

He sighs deeply. "I know, Heather. I know. But I'm just a Senior Airman. The upper guys don't care about me. They just care about getting home to their own families. If it makes you feel any better, I'm not the only one that got denied. A lot of us are being pushed back to January."

I shake my head vehemently. "No. No! That doesn't make me feel better! I want you to come home for Christmas! This isn't fair!"

"I know. But being in the military isn't about what's fair. Believe me, there's nowhere on this earth I'd rather be than with you."

"When will you be home then? Will you get leave denied for January, too?!" I whine childishly.

"I doubt it. Everyone else will be back, and we lowly inmates will be given parole," he chuckles darkly. Even with the poor connection, I detect my own sarcasm echoed in his voice.

Our conversation ends with us declaring our love for each other, but my mood remains sullen. I can't hide my deep disappointment. We will miss our first Thanksgiving *and* our first Christmas together.

We will have missed our entire first year of marriage.

If this is what military life is like, I don't want it. Rick has told me he would like to make a career of this. I don't know if I am strong enough for that.

CHAPTER THREE

Christmas, 1988

"Aren't you going to try the ham? I made it with the brown sugar glaze you love," Mom interrupts my sulking over Christmas dinner.

I glance up from my plate that's filled with all of the traditional foods. I've just been pushing the food around. Any other Christmas, and my plate would have been licked clean. My heart hurts too much to enjoy it.

"Sorry," I mumble. "I'm not hungry." Sighing, I push my plate away, prop my elbows on the table and place my chin in my hands. "I'm just not in a Christmas mood."

"I'm really sorry, Heather," Dad says. "It's rotten to be separated from Rick on your first Christmas, but think of all the Christmases you have ahead of you."

"Do I?" I ask sullenly. "I mean, who's to say we'll be together for the next Christmas, or the next?"

"Heather, you are going to have to accept that you're a military wife. He wears the uniform, and this is part of the job," Mom replies.

I shake my head. "I didn't sign up for all this! I married Rick. I didn't marry the military."

"Yes, you did," Dad chides me. "When you marry a man that wears the uniform, you are signing up for this."

I don't like that he's probably right. It doesn't soften the pain of our separation. "Excuse me. I'm going to my room."

I close the door and throw myself on the bed, bitter thoughts on my mind.

This is so unfair. It's been six long months already. He didn't get to come home for Thanksgiving or Christmas. I wonder if he'll actually get to come home in January. Maybe somebody else will want to take leave again instead of letting him come home.

I rub the small golden heart attached to a delicate chain around my neck between my finger and thumb. It is Rick's Christmas present to me. It makes me feel slightly better to know that this delicate piece of jewelry passed through his hands before he sent it to me. The card he sent with it made me cry. Glancing over, I see the card sitting where I placed it this morning – on top of my dresser next to our wedding photo, along with every other card he has sent me.

Rolling off the bed, I pad over to the dresser and pick up our wedding photo. I finger his face gently before hugging the frame to my chest.

"I wish you were here, Rick," I whisper.

A gentle knock interrupts my thoughts. My mother peeks around the door.

"Are you okay?" she asks.

Shaking my head, I return the picture to my dresser. "Nothing about this is okay, Mom. This isn't what marriage is supposed to be, is it?"

Mom walks over and sits on my bed, patting the space next to her.

I sigh and plop down next to her. She rubs my back as she talks.

"Heather, the only thing you can plan on for certain is that marriage is a commitment. It isn't easy and it isn't always fun, but it is worth it. Your father and I don't know much about military things, but I suspect that your marriage is going to be even more difficult because Rick is in the military. We watched you and Rick while you were dating, and you guys are going to be just fine. Besides, doesn't the military look after its own?"

"I don't know. I haven't heard from anyone," I snort.

"Have you made an effort to talk to somebody on the base?" she asks.

"Mom, I wouldn't even know where to begin."

"Perhaps when you talk to Rick, you can ask him what you should do. Isn't he supposed to call today?"

"He said he would try, but he was scheduled to work. He's only got three stripes, Mom. That means he is nobody in the Air Force."

"Oh, I don't know about that. He's somebody to you, and to us," she replies, continuing to rub my back just like she did when I was little.

I turn my torso to face her. "Mom, do you really think this is worth it? Rick being in the military, I mean. He could get a job doing something else as a civilian, so do you really think he should stay in when his enlistment is done?"

Her brow puckers. "How many years does he have left on this enlistment?"

"Four years," I reply, feeling a little panicky. "He re-enlisted a few months before our wedding, remember?" I didn't have a problem with it at the time – it was before he received his remote tour orders. I had no idea such a thing could happen. We never discussed it. We were busy planning our life together, not apart. When the orders came down, he couldn't back out. They came a few weeks after his re-enlistment. There was nothing we could do because we were only engaged when he received them. Even if we had been married, the orders were not going to be cancelled. So here we are.

She searches my face before answering. "Sweetheart, I can't answer that for you, and you shouldn't answer that for Rick. You guys have plenty of time to work this out. That's a decision you'll both have to make when the time comes. You're young, and this is a really hard situation for you right now, but it won't last forever."

"He was supposed to come *home*. It's Christmas!" I pound the bed.

"But he couldn't," she shrugs. "There's nothing you can do about that, so try to move on. He said he'll be able to come home next month."

"I know. I sound like a whiny teenager, even to myself," I chuckle darkly. "Hopefully he'll be able to call today."

"Well, you're a twenty-year-old young bride, and you just want your husband home with you. That's understandable."

"Heather!" Dad's voice carries down the hallway. "Rick's on the phone!"

I leap from the bed, leaving Mom in my wake as I scramble down the hall into the kitchen, snatching the phone from my father. He smiles and retreats to give me privacy, pulling Debbie along with him. She poked her head in just as I grabbed the phone.

"Hello! Hello, Rick?" I cry into the phone.

"Merry Christmas!" his voice crackles. He's difficult to understand – his voice echoes three times with every word. It's like listening through a tunnel.

"Merry Christmas to you, too! This is a horrible connection," I yell into the phone.

"I know. It's Christmas and the lines are overloaded," he echoes. "Listen, I don't have much time. I just want you to know that I got my leave, and I'll be there in three weeks."

I scream into the phone, jumping up and down. "Seriously?! You'll be here in three weeks? Don't mess with me, Rick!"

His laughter echoes. "I'm not messing with you, Heather. I get to hold you in my arms in three weeks. I can hardly wait."

"Do you already have your flight information?" I ask hurriedly, knowing our connection could be dropped at any moment.

"Not yet. I just got my leave approved yesterday. I'll let you know as soon as I can," he crackles.

"I hope it goes by fast!"

"Me, too," he pauses. "I have to go. I love you and I'll see you soon. I'll call you when I…" His voice abruptly cuts off. Our connection is lost.

"I love you, too," I say into the deadness. I pull the phone away from my ear to look at it before replacing it on the cradle. "I'll see you soon."

I skip into the dining room where my parents have begun to clear the table. Jeff disappeared soon after dinner to go to his best friend's house and show off his new BB gun. I can hear the muffled sounds of music coming from Debbie's room; she got new cassette tapes. Dad has a bowl of mashed potatoes in one hand and a gravy boat in the other. Mom looks guilty; her finger is in her mouth and she is sucking it like a lollipop. She's standing in front of the bowl of cranberry chutney; she loves the stuff. I can't stand it.

"Good news?" Dad asks.

"Rick will be home in three weeks!"

Mom's pulls her finger out of her mouth with an audible *pop*. "Heather, that's wonderful!"

"Does he have his flight information?" Dad asks, smiling.

"No, not yet. He only got his leave approved yesterday. He said he'll call when he has it."

"How long will he be able to stay?" Mom asks.

"I didn't get the chance to ask. We got cut off." Our conversations get cut short occasionally, but this time it was really fast. Of course it happens on Christmas.

This experience saddens me. Our first year of marriage will be gone, and we will not have been able to spend more than a few weeks together when we celebrate our anniversary.

How often is this going to happen while we're married, especially if Rick decides to make the military a career? Only time will tell. I can change his mind – I have almost four years to do it. He's a smart man; he can get a good job. Of course he can! I may want to go to college someday, too. I really don't want to sell shoes or clean up after rodents the rest of my life. There's no real money to be made in the military anyway. I slowly begin to convince myself that he'll change his mind. He won't have to leave anymore – he'll just go to work and come home, like a normal person. We'll be just fine when he gets out.

We'll have to have a conversation about this. He'll agree with me.

Of course he will.

CHAPTER FOUR

January, 1989

The days before Rick comes home drag on. My excitement grows. At work, I have to force myself to focus, otherwise, there would have been some dead fish to account for and shoe boxes with two left feet. I whiz around our favorite trails on my bike to release nervous energy.

I become despondent as the sun rises and sets each day, and I still have no flight information from him. I don't get another phone call from him until one Tuesday morning almost three weeks later. He calls collect. He only has one morale call per month, and he used that on Christmas.

My parents graciously accept the charges.

"Hi, Heather! I can't wait to hear your voice in person. I don't want to stay on the line too long. This will cost your parents a fortune," Rick crackles.

I grip the phone tightly and press it to my ear. "I can't wait to see you. I've missed you so much. You're supposed to be here by now."

He chuckles. "I miss you too, Heather. I need to give you my flight information first, okay?"

"Hang on. Let me grab a pen and paper." I quickly yank the drawer next to the phone open and pull out a pen and paper. "Go ahead."

I meticulously write down the information he relays.

"Three days? You'll be here in three days!" I exclaim. "I can't wait. I wish you were coming home for good."

"Me, too," he replies. "We're over the halfway mark, though. I'll be home for good before you know it."

I press my lips together, fighting tears. "Yes."

If he gets out of the military, he *will* be home for good. I'll save that conversation for another time.

When we hang up, Dad pops in the kitchen.

"Did you get the flight information?"

I nod and hand him the paper. "He'll be here in three days," I smile, quickly punching in the numbers for both my jobs to let them know. They've been very supportive; both supervisors told me to just let them know when I would need the time off.

"Louise! Rick will be here in three days!" Dad yells into the hallway.

Mom's rapid footfalls echo down the hall as she hurries into the kitchen, gripping a partially folded towel. "I'm so glad! What time does he land?" She throws the towel over her shoulder and takes the paper from Dad, absorbing the information as her eyes scan the paper. "Holy moly! He lands at six in the morning?"

I finish the conversations with my supervisors and hang up before addressing my mother. "Yes, and I can't wait! I'm glad he's coming that early. I probably won't be able to sleep until then anyway, and I won't have to wait all day to see him."

Mom looks at Dad in a silent, significant way. I recognize their unspoken language.

"What?" I ask, perplexed.

"Should we tell her now, Leonard?" Mom asks.

"May as well," Dad shrugs.

Mom looks at me, smiling broadly. "Heather, your father and I wanted to surprise you. We paid for four days at the Hilton for you two. The reservations are flexible because we didn't know exactly when he'd be coming. You're still sort of on your honeymoon and, well, you need some time alone. It's a late Christmas present from both of us."

Dad squeezes my shoulders and kisses my forehead. "Merry Christmas, pumpkin."

"Thank you so much," I grin, and squeeze each of my parents in turn. "I can't wait to tell Rick! Wait. How can you guys afford four days at the Hilton? That's got to be expensive."

"Don't you worry about that. Just accept a gift from your old parents," Dad jokingly reprimands me.

"But still…" I reply.

"Heather, you guys go and have a good time," Mom interrupts.

My parents have never been wealthy, and Dad has always worked hard. He still does. Our lifestyle is comfortable, but not flashy. They've taught all of us the value of a dollar, and I know that this must have cost them. It makes me appreciate them, and the gift, even more.

"Mom, Dad, I love you guys. Thank you," I kiss them both on the cheek.

"You're welcome, pumpkin," Dad says, his voice a little choked. "Love you."

########

"I thought I could stay up all night," Jeff yawns, "But you take the cake, sis. I'm going to bed." He hauls himself slowly off the sofa and shuffles down the hallway, scratching his backside. It's almost one thirty in the morning, and Rick's flight will land in four and a half hours.

Jeff offered to stay up with me and watch movies to pass the time, but he fell asleep with his mouth open during the last thirty minutes of *Caddy Shack*, which is surprising. It's one of his favorite movies. He always shimmies to the music when the groundhog dances.

I pop the VHS tape out of the machine after rewinding it and slide it back into its case. There aren't a whole lot of other options to watch, so I flip on MTV and watch videos.

As predicted, I can't sleep. It's been almost seven months since Rick left. I will finally get to hold him again.

The Pink Floyd video ends and is replaced with Madonna. While Madonna gyrates, my thoughts float back to Rick.

What have I gotten myself into? Is this really what military life is like? Do I want to do this? I want to stay with Rick, of course, but if he has to be away all the time, I don't like how our lives will be separate. What will happen when we have children? I want them to know their father...

"Heather? It's time to wake up," Mom's soft voice fills my ear.

"Hmm? Wha?" I reply groggily. The only sound is the tick tock of the grandfather clock from the corner. Mom must have turned the television off.

"It's four thirty. We have to leave for the airport soon. I made coffee," Mom replies gently, moving my hair away from my face. She is partially illuminated in the soft light of the table lamp.

I frown and blink. Rubbing my face, I sit up. "I fell asleep?"

Mom chuckles. "Yes. Your heart may be wound up, but your body is exhausted."

Dad shuffles around the corner carrying two steaming mugs and offers one to me. "Coffee? Just the way you like it, extra sweet."

I grin, or rather grimace, up at him. "Thanks," I croak. I draw the mug to my face and inhale deeply before sipping. The warm liquid goes down smoothly and I exhale with a satisfied sigh.

"Do you want something to eat?" Mom asks.

"No, I don't think I can eat right now."

"Are you sure? I can pop some waffles in the toaster in a jiffy," she offers.

"You really should eat something," Dad chimes in.

I take another sip from the steaming mug before relenting. "Yeah, I guess. Just one, though," I yawn widely. "I need to get in the shower. I don't want to look hideous when Rick sees me for the first time."

Mom grins. "Oh, I don't think either of you will have to worry about that. You won't care what the other one looks like, just that you'll be together." She rises and heads into the kitchen.

I drop my head back on the sofa, forcing my eyes to stay open and sip more coffee.

Dad sits next to me, sipping from his own mug. "You'll make it," he says, patting my leg. "Go eat your waffle."

I yawn widely once more before joining Mom in the kitchen. Blinking at the bright fluorescent light, I grab my plate and slide into a chair at the Formica dinette that my parents have had since the seventies. It's a hideous color of olive green with silver flecks in it. I've always been embarrassed about it, but they don't see the point in replacing something that functions.

Mom joins me, taking the chair across from me. I pour syrup from the woman shaped bottle onto my waffle and slice it into neat, bite-sized squares.

"You still cut them into little squares, don't you?" Mom muses, sipping from her mug.

"It's the best way to eat it," I reply, popping one square into my mouth. "Nice and neat."

Mom rubs the mug back and forth between her hands. "You like things nice and neat, don't you?"

"Mm hmmm." I swirl another square around the syrup before popping it in my mouth.

"Well," she says softly. "Unfortunately, life isn't always nice and neat. It can be ugly and messy."

I stop chewing momentarily and stare at her. "I think I've figured that out already." I swallow. "I'm picking my new husband up from the airport this morning. I haven't seen him in seven months."

Mom nods, taking another sip of her coffee. I mirror her and do the same. Suddenly, she reaches across the table and covers my hand with her own. "I'm proud of you, Heather. You're strong."

"I don't feel like it."

She chuckles and withdraws her hand. "You are. Now, finish your breakfast and go get ready to pick up your husband."

Glancing at the clock, I make quick work of the remaining waffle by eating three squares at a time. I gulp down the last of my now lukewarm coffee before placing my dishes in the sink with a quick rinse.

The hot shower wakes me up. My stomach twists with excitement, making me thankful I ate. Otherwise, I would be nauseated.

I chose my reunion outfit with care two days before – a pair of stonewashed jeans and an ocean blue button down shirt with a chunky, gold-buckled belt. Rick always liked that color on me; he said it sets off my blue eyes perfectly. The golden heart pendant he gave me for Christmas sparkles against the blue. I haven't taken it off since I got it.

I rub the pendant, as I do several times a day, and regard my reflection in the mirror over my dresser. I quickly apply make up and style my hair.

"One more spritz ought to do it," I murmur as I apply one more squirt of hairspray to the roots of my hair for volume. I can't have flat hair on a day like this.

A knock on my bedroom door interrupts me. "Heather? We have to go," Dad mumbles from behind the door.

"I'm coming," I reply quickly, grabbing my purse. I jerk the door open and stare expectantly at my father. "How do I look?"

Dad's eyes crinkle as he grins. "As beautiful as the day you were born."

I roll my eyes. "Da-aaad…"

"Come on," he chuckles.

I bounce nervously in the seat on the way to the airport. The sun is not even on the horizon as we pull into the parking garage. Rick's flight will land in fifteen minutes. Fortunately, we find a parking spot close to the front. I don't wait until the car is in park before I open the door, ready to leap out.

"Hold on, Heather! At least let me get the car situated," Dad laughingly warns.

"Oh, Leonard. She's excited," Mom swivels in her seat. "Go on, honey. We'll catch up to you."

"Okay!" I leap out of the seat, clutching my purse and the flight information in one hand. As I walk quickly away, I call out over my shoulder. "I'll see you guys at the gate!"

"What's the flight number again?" Dad yells after me.

I call the information out over my shoulder, not even breaking my stride. I can't wait to see Rick.

When I enter the airport, I scan the arrivals screen for Rick's flight and gate number. Once I have it, I quickly make my way through the airport to the appointed gate. There are a number of people milling around awaiting the flight's arrival. I carefully pick my way through the crowd to get to the front. I want to be the first person Rick sees when he steps into the airport.

Bouncing on my heels, I glance at my watch. He should be here any minute. Suddenly, the overhead speaker announces his flight's arrival, and I yelp as someone grabs my arm. With a gasp, I turn toward the touch.

"It's just us," Dad laughs. "Just wanted you to know that we made it, in spite of your efforts to lose us."

"Leonard, don't tease her," Mom grins. "We'll get plenty of pictures for you. I've got a whole roll of film!" She jiggles her camera.

The gate attendant opens the door and secures it in position as the plane ever so slowly rolls toward the window. My heart hammers in my chest as my eyes fill with tears. I'm finally going to see Rick, feel his arms around me, and smell his scent. Butterflies work feverishly in my stomach. I twirl my wedding ring around and around my finger as I scan the long gangway for any sign of him. Finally, people begin to appear at the far end and work their way slowly to the front.

"Come on, come on..." I murmur, continuing to scan the line of people.

Five, ten, fifteen, twenty people walk in and disperse into the crowd.

Suddenly, a familiar sandy blond head bobs around the corner at the far end. I forget how to breathe. The head peers around the one in front of it and Rick's face explodes into a grin when he spies me.

"Rick!" I call out, jumping up and down. I don't care who is watching. "Rick!"

He waves and makes his way to the front as quickly as he can. As soon as he passes the threshold, I scream and run into his arms, burying my face in his neck, sobbing.

"Hi, honey bun," he murmurs, his breath hot in my ear. His arms are tight and warm. He smells of honey and sunshine and man. My man.

I'm home. This is where I belong. This is where I want to be. Always.

My surroundings disappear.

"I'm so glad you're home," I sob.

He turns my face up toward his and kisses me, ignoring my salty tears that season our kiss.

"I'm glad to be home. I've missed you so much," he murmurs, squeezing me so hard it takes my breath away. "You smell great."

I chuckle and my sobbing begins to ebb. "I was thinking the same thing about you."

"I probably smell horrible. I've been on a plane for almost twelve hours."

I shake my head, bury my face in his neck once more, and inhale deeply. "No. You smell like *you*." I kiss his neck and he sighs.

My father clears his throat; I suddenly become aware that the crowd is very thin around us. My parents are waiting patiently about twenty feet away. Mom is busily snapping pictures. I blush, pull apart from Rick, lace our fingers together and walk toward my parents. Mom continues to snap pictures.

"You remember my parents," I gesture toward them.

Rick stands tall, extending his hand toward my father. "Yes, sir. It's good to see you again."

Dad pumps his hand once before grabbing Rick in a bear hug, clapping him on the back. "Oh, son. It's our pleasure to look after your wife while you're away."

Mom stops taking pictures long enough to hug Rick, as well. Her chin quivers as she kisses him on the cheek. Rick blushes at the attention, but swells in pride at my father's choice of words.

"Well, I am glad to know she's in good hands." Rick smiles at me, wrapping his arm around my waist. Mom starts snapping pictures again.

"Mom," I hold my hand up, "It's okay. You can stop now. You don't have to use the whole roll at the airport."

Mom grins and puts the camera into her purse. "All right. But I'll be sure to get plenty while you're home, Rick."

"Let's get his luggage and get out of here. How was your flight?" Dad addresses Rick, leading the way.

Rick and I only let go of each other long enough for him to retrieve his duffel bag from the revolving belt. Dad insists on carrying Rick's bag. He doesn't say it, but I know it's so that Rick and I can hold hands, which we do.

The sun is just peeking over the horizon as we pick up speed on the highway heading home. Mom yawns loudly in the front seat.

"Need some more coffee, Sugar?" Dad asks her.

She shakes her head. "No, I need more sleep. I'll probably go back to bed for a bit when we get home. That okay with you kids?" She talks over her shoulder. "I'd love to visit with you, Rick, but we'll have plenty of time for that later."

"I'm pretty beat myself," I respond, snuggling into Rick. He wraps his arms around me and kisses my head.

"Yes, ma'am. We all need some sleep," he replies before murmuring something else for my ears only.

I blush crimson and stifle a giggle. He grins, chuckling quietly.

When we finally pull into the driveway, Rick slides out of his seat and smiles at me. I stifle another giggle.

Mom yawns widely and grunts her way out of the car, shoulders slumped. She had fallen asleep halfway home. "Whew, I am beat." She turns toward me. "Heather, honey. You guys make yourself at home. If Rick's hungry, just let him raid the fridge for anything he wants. I'll make a big lunch, okay?"

"Sure thing," I reply, ducking my head as my cheeks blush crimson again.

"I've got it, sir. Really. I'll just follow you inside," Rick assures my father. Dad capitulates after offering minor resistance. Once inside, Rick heads straight for my bedroom, placing the bag next to my dresser, before reappearing in the living room.

"Rick, I told Heather to let you raid the fridge for anything you want," Mom speaks softly; Jeff and Debbie are still fast asleep. It's Saturday. "I'll make us all a big lunch when we get up."

"Yes, ma'am. Thank you," Rick replies just as softly.

"Well, good night. Or good morning," Mom smiles and disappears down the hallway.

"I'm out, too," Dad replies, quick on Mom's heels. "Make yourself at home. See you two kids later."

Once their footfalls disappear with the click of their bedroom door at the far end, I turn toward Rick. My palms are sweaty and my heart is racing. The grandfather clock ticks loudly.

"Hi," I say shyly, suddenly unsure of myself.

Rick closes the distance between us in a few long strides and grabs my face in his hands, kissing me passionately. "God, I've missed you," he whispers hoarsely between kisses.

My hesitation and my heart melt. I kiss him back with equal passion.

He walks me quickly toward my, our, bedroom and closes the door softly behind him.

We do eventually go to sleep, but not before reuniting our hearts and bodies. It's like starving and then suddenly having a groaning buffet table before you; you just go for it.

Well…we go for it.

Many hours later, I awake feeling deeply satisfied and smiling like a Cheshire cat. My arm is draped over Rick's bare chest and my head is nestled in the crook of his shoulder. His arms are wrapped around me, his cheek resting on my head.

"Morning," I say thickly, twisting my face up to his.

He opens his eyes lazily and smiles. His lips are warm on mine. "Morning." He glances at my bedside clock. "Actually, afternoon."

"What time is it?" I ask, nestling into his shoulder again. I still can't believe he's here.

"Twelve thirty," he replies.

My eyes fly open. "Seriously? It's twelve thirty? Holy cow, we better get up." I flip the blankets off, forgetting I don't have a stitch of clothes on and immediately cover up, my cheeks flaming.

Rick chuckles. "Don't cover up. Please. I haven't seen you in seven months." He tugs at the blankets, but I cinch them up over my chest.

"It's so embarrassing, Rick!" I cry, grimacing.

"I'm your husband, Heather. There's nothing embarrassing about it." He grins, tugging harder, teasing me.

I tighten my grip. "Stop it," I hiss. I try to come off as fierce, but can't stop the corners of my mouth from turning up. It's just so ridiculous.

He notices. With a devilish glint in his eyes, in one fluid movement he flips onto his knees and tugs the blankets out from under my grasp, tossing them over the foot of the bed.

I gasp and scramble for something to cover myself with. I settle for grabbing his pillow and placing it in the best position for coverage.

He chokes out a throaty laugh, saying, "Oh, no you don't!" and snatches that from me, throwing it to the floor. I cover myself with my hands.

"Rick!" I hiss in protest. My whole face is crimson. "Stop it!"

"You look like Venus," he chuckles. "Even with the red face and skinny body. How much weight have you lost?" He bends down and kisses my cheeks and my forehead.

"About fifteen pounds, I think," I reply.

His eyebrows rise. "You were just fine, Heather. Why?"

"Because I missed you."

"Well, no more, okay? Plump back up to normal for me – I miss the rest of you." Then he kisses my lips and conversation stops.

We finally put our robes on and leave the room well after one thirty.

"Well, there they are! I thought you two would sleep the day away," Dad remarks when we enter the living room. "I told you not to stay up last night." Dad wags his finger at me.

"It's about time you guys got up," Jeff flashes a goofy grin. I have a deep urge to slap that grin right off his face. I settle for ducking my head and try to smooth my hair. I hope my cheeks don't burn too hotly.

"It was a long flight, sir," Rick replies, ignoring Jeff's comment. "I hope we didn't miss lunch. I'm famished!"

"We have plenty," Mom answers, rising. "Go ahead and have a seat. I kept it warm in the oven. Would you like some lemonade?"

"Yes, ma'am," Rick responds. We follow Mom into the kitchen and sit down at the dinette, holding hands.

Mom busies herself pulling out glasses, plates, and silverware. The smell of fried chicken permeates the air and my mouth waters. My stomach grumbles on cue.

When she puts our plates in front of us, Rick dives in heartily and I do the same. There's fried chicken, mashed potatoes with gravy, and buttered green beans.

"Mom, did you make your..." I start to ask, but as though she read my mind, a plate of biscuits appears. I look gratefully up at her. She smiles and squeezes my shoulder.

"Of course I did," she answers.

"Wow," Rick says, trying not to shovel the food in his mouth. "Mrs. Scott, this is the best thing I've had in a long time."

"Please, call me Louise."

"Yes, ma'am."

Mom rolls her eyes, amused. "Eat your fill, but save room for pie. I made cherry. Do you like cherry pie, Rick?"

"Yes, ma'am. There are only two kinds of pie I like: hot and cold." He grins.

Mom laughs.

"Make sure to give Heather an extra thick slice. She's gotten too skinny in my absence," Rick remarks. I glare at him.

Debbie peeks her head around the corner, smiling shyly at Rick. Rick spies her almost immediately.

"Well, hey there, squirt! Come on in here," he gestures to her.

She slowly comes around the corner, giggling behind her hand. She's always had a crush on Rick. It's cute. Rick gets along with everyone, even Jeff.

"How have you been?" Rick grins at Debbie, chucking her chin. She blushes crimson, just like me, and ducks behind her hand once more, giggling.

"Fine," she replies shyly.

"Do you want to join us?" I ask, patting the chair next to me.

She looks from me to Rick before shaking her head.

"No? Why not, squirt? You got somewhere else better to be than with us?" Rick teases.

She grins and shakes her head again, glancing at Mom.

"I told her not to bug you two. You need to have time to yourselves," Mom interjects.

"Oh, that's okay, Mom. She can sit and eat some pie with us," I reply, patting the seat next to me again.

Debbie smiles and happily plops down in the chair, staring dreamily at Rick. He winks at her. She smothers another giggle.

Once we finish our pie, I join the rest of the family in the living room while Rick calls his parents to let them know he arrived safely. They're in Florida at the moment — they own a condo down there. I'm so content I could burst, due in no small part to the delicious meal. I hope I can cook just as well when I'm on my own. I didn't spend a whole lot of time in the kitchen growing up. I regret that. Maybe I'll try to spend some time in the kitchen with Mom while Rick is gone. He'll come home to a wife who can cook.

There's a brief pain that pierces my heart — he'll have to leave again in two short weeks. I brush it aside; I won't dwell on that. I will enjoy every single moment with him. It's short enough.

Dad joins us a few minutes later and addresses Rick. "Did Heather share our surprise with you yet?"

Rick looks questioningly from me to my father. "No."

"We paid for four days at the Hilton for you guys. You can check in today at four o'clock sharp." Dad's always been big on punctuality, even when it really doesn't matter.

Rick's mouth falls open.

I squeeze his hand. "Isn't that sweet?"

"I, uh…" he starts. "I don't know what to say, sir. That is very generous of you. Wow." He turns toward me, grinning, before returning his attention to my father. "Thank you so much."

"It's our pleasure. We want you to enjoy your time together as much as possible," Mom chimes in. "As much fun as we are, I'm sure you'll have a better time with just you two. The Hilton has a great indoor pool, and your room has a gorgeous view from the balcony."

Jeff chortles. Dad throws him a stern look. Debbie's shoulders slump slightly; I think she was looking forward to staring at Rick for two weeks.

Dad coughs again. "Well, you two better get dressed. Your room will be ready by the time you get there. You don't want to be late." He taps his wristwatch.

"I'll go jump in the shower. I still have to pack." I kiss Rick quickly on the lips before rising.

"I can pack for you," Mom offers after me.

I shake my head. "That's okay, Mom. It won't take me long. It's only for a couple of days."

"Are you sure? I don't want you to be late," she offers again.

I turn to face her. "Mom, there is no *late* when it comes to checking into a hotel."

Mom chuckles. "Yes, I suppose you're right."

Once I finish my shower, Rick takes his turn. I pack my suitcase with the essentials, trying not to forget anything. I am sure to pack my bathing suit. The Hilton's pool is fantastic. At least that's what I have heard.

My father practically throws us out the door; we leave five minutes before four. Dad is sure they won't let us check in if we aren't there at four o'clock sharp. No amount of arguing will ever change his mind.

Climbing into Rick's truck, I scoot to the center and snuggle into the crook of his shoulder as he wraps his arm around me.

He kisses my head, "That was very kind of your parents, Heather. They're great people."

I smile and twist my head to kiss his lips. "Yes, they are."

Rick glances over my shoulder and chuckles. "Look at your father. I think he's shooing us away."

I glance over to see my father waving his arms at us, grimacing, like he's trying to push us down the driveway.

"You better get going or he may come over here and push on the tailgate," I laugh as Rick pulls away. "Dad hates to be late."

CHAPTER FIVE

January, 1989

When we arrive at the hotel, a crisply dressed bellhop trots over to greet us, followed by a valet. The bellhop opens my door, offers his gloved hand, and says, "Welcome to the Hilton. May I retrieve your luggage for you?"

"Thank you." I grin and take his hand, allowing him to help me out of the truck. Rick comes around the truck, handing the keys to the valet, and offers his arm to me. Addressing the bellhop, he says, "The luggage is in the jump seat. There are two bags."

"Yes, sir!" The bellhop responds cheerily. "I'll retrieve them and meet you at the front desk."

Rick escorts me to the front desk and gives our name to the smartly dressed receptionist. She looks at her computer screen, typing the information in.

"Yes, sir. Here you are. You are booked into the honeymoon suite. We also have something that was left here for when you checked in." She smiles and hands Rick a thick envelope.

We both look at each other, puzzled. Rick accepts the offered envelope and pulls it apart. A sheet of paper is wrapped around what appears to be money. Rick quickly stuffs it back into the envelope, placing it inside the chest pocket of his jacket, and murmurs to me, "Let's open it upstairs."

"Okay," I shrug.

Rick retrieves the key, and the bellhop happily escorts us to the elevator and our room. When Rick opens the door to our suite, I gasp.

The room is spacious to the point of having the footprint of an apartment. The entire suite is opulent in rich gold and ruby red. The bed is king sized with a mountain of pillows. I can just glimpse a Jacuzzi tub in the marbled bathroom. On the gorgeous round dining table stands a beautiful vase of fresh flowers, a dish of chocolate-covered strawberries, a bottle of champagne, and two fluted glasses.

The bellhop efficiently places our luggage on the racks near the antique-looking dressers and opens the curtains with a flourish. I gasp again. There's a sweeping view of the San Antonio skyline. It's going to be gorgeous when the sun goes down. Our balcony has a table and two chairs.

The bellhop is telling us about the features of the room, but I barely hear him. I walk slowly around the suite, drinking it all in. This must have cost my parents a small fortune.

"Here's your valet slip, sir." He hands a slip of paper to Rick. "If there's anything that we can do to help make your stay more enjoyable, please don't hesitate to let us know. We are at your service." He bows crisply.

"Thank you so much. We are going to have a wonderful time," Rick replies, handing the bellhop his tip. The bellhop bows again and retreats from the room, closing the door behind him.

"Rick, look at this place! This is incredible," I breathe. "I can't believe my parents could afford this. I mean, wow! Look!" I sweep my hand toward the balcony and the view.

Rick chuckles and embraces me. "Yes, I know. It's beautiful. But not as beautiful as you." His eyes smolder and he kisses me, but pulls back quickly. "Oh! I almost forgot." He pulls the thick envelope out of his jacket pocket.

"I wonder how much it is," I murmur.

Rick opens the envelope and pulls the bundle out. He removes the money and unfolds the sheet of paper, reading the message aloud. "To Rick and Heather. Have a great time. Mom and Dad."

As he starts to count the money, his eyes bug out. Once he's done, he turns to me, stunned. "Heather, there's four hundred dollars here."

"Are you serious?" I ask, snatching the money from him and counting it myself. "Oh, my gosh. I can't believe it."

"I guess they didn't want me to spend anything."

"Well, they did say it was our Christmas present," I reply excitedly.

"Do your parents think I can't afford it?" he asks warily.

"No. They just want to give us a gift. This is awesome, Rick!" I squeeze him hard and bounce up and down.

Rick chuckles. "Yeah, it is. Are you sure? I don't want them thinking I can't take care of you."

"Stop," I peck him on the lips. "Let's just enjoy their gift, all right?"

"All right," he murmurs, kissing me back. "We'll unpack later." He sweeps me off my feet and carries me to the giant bed.

I'm in heaven.

My parents couldn't have given us a better gift. Spending uninterrupted time with Rick for four whole days is going to be the best thing next to him coming back for good.

As dinner time approaches, our stomachs start to growl. We turn off the Jacuzzi we had migrated to and wrap ourselves in the lush robes provided by the hotel. I'm starting to get over being embarrassed around Rick. Not completely, however, as I didn't allow him to turn on the bathroom light.

"Should we order dinner and eat on the balcony?" Rick asks lazily, kissing the palm of my hand. "It's going to be a fantastic sunset. I have missed the stars over Texas."

"That sounds wonderful! But is it too cold outside? What should we order?" I ask, reaching for the room service menu.

"Order whatever you want. See if they have surf and turf on the menu," he replies. "I could go for some serious seafood. I'll go see if it's too cold out." He opens the sliding door and steps onto the balcony while I peruse the menu. I choose the grilled salmon. When Rick ducks back inside, closing the door behind him, he orders the steak and shrimp.

"It's a little chilly out. No balcony time right now," he laments.

"It's okay," I reassure him. "The dining table still has a great view of the sunset."

The prices on the menu are crazy, but Rick assures me it doesn't matter, thanks to my parents' generous gift.

"What about dessert?" I ask.

"Do you really want dessert? We already devoured most of the chocolate covered strawberries," Rick reminds me. I blush.

"Maybe not. You're all the dessert I need." I reach across the table and kiss him again. I am becoming rather bold.

****

A sharp knock on the door announces the arrival of dinner. We are sitting at the dining table, still dressed in robes, enjoying the champagne while watching the sun slowly retreat over the horizon. The gorgeous red velvet curtains frame the scene beautifully.

Rick rises to answer the door. I swivel in my chair to watch his retreating form. I can't get enough of even the sight of him. And he's mine. All mine. I twirl my wedding ring around my finger as I smile, savoring the thought.

"Good evening, sir. I have your dinner order. Shall I set the table for you?" The cheery attendant wheels the cart into the room.

"Yes, please," Rick replies, gesturing to the table.

The attendant makes quick work of setting the table for us, to include covering it with a white linen tablecloth. He places two domed dishes before us, sets the silverware just so, and finishes by setting a silver basket of bread, the condiments and a tiny crystal set of salt and pepper in the center of the table. With a flourish, he sweeps the silver domes up and away. I gasp at the beautiful food that appears in a swirl of steam.

Rick's shrimp are the size of small lobsters and are arranged into a tower with the tails pointing up, surrounding the steak. There are also herbed baby carrots and piped mashed potatoes with a pool of dark brown gravy in the middle. Two wedges of lemon and a sprinkle of chopped parsley around the edge finish the plate.

My salmon fillet is perfectly pink with a shiny glaze, surrounded by buttered broccoli florets and bright yellow saffron rice. It is finished the same as Rick's with the lemon and parsley.

"Will there be anything else?" the attendant asks politely.

"Uh…no. This is perfect! Thank you so much," Rick replies, thrusting a tip into the attendant's hand.

"Thank you, sir. When you're done, just call and let us know. I'll be happy to clear the table for you. Bon Appétit!" He quietly withdraws.

"Rick, this is too beautiful to eat," I breathe, my eyes taking in every detail. I lift the linen napkin from the bread basket to see an assortment of rolls. They're different shapes and colors. Even the butter has been molded into little hearts. I point at it. "Look at the butter!"

Rick laughs when he sees it. "That is awesome! They really think of every detail, don't they?"

After admiring the food, we devour it before it gets cold. It's as delicious as it looks. Our bites are interspersed with moans at the bursts of flavor with every forkful.

Midway through the meal, I gesture toward the balcony. "Rick, look at the sky line." The sun has just disappeared below the horizon and set the sky ablaze in crimson and orange. The city lights sparkle in the encroaching twilight.

"Do you stare up at the stars in Korea, Rick? Have you found anywhere to go hiking there?"

He nods, his eyes scanning the horizon. "Yeah, sort of. I mean, I can't go anywhere I want to, but there are some places I like to go on the base when the sun sets. I think of you and wonder if you see the same stars I do."

"I spend a lot of time going to our favorite spots and thinking the same thing about you. I write most of your letters there."

Rick's eyes continue to sweep over the horizon, drinking in the view. I do the same. The perfection of the moment touches a deep part of my heart. I reach across the table for Rick's hand. His large, warm hand engulfs mine.

"Rick, I've never been so happy. I get to enjoy the most delicious meal of my life with the most beautiful view I've ever seen. Most of all, I am here with the most handsome man in the world, and he's my husband."

Rick's eyes crinkle as he smiles my favorite broad smile. He kisses my hand twice. "Heather, even with all of this," he sweeps his arm out. "The most beautiful part of this evening is you. I love you."

We both stand and lean over the table to enjoy a long, lingering kiss. "Let's not waste the rest of this food or this view," he whispers in my ear.

I giggle. "I was thinking the same thing. I just didn't want to interrupt you."

"We have four days. Food will be one small part of it," he laughs. We sit back down to enjoy the rest of our meal.

Later that night, after we finish our meal and our dessert (which has nothing to do with the strawberries) I fall fast into the most blissful sleep of my life.

I wish life could always be just Rick, champagne, and chocolate-covered strawberries...

CHAPTER SIX

January, 1989

Our time at the hotel is better than I could've ever imagined. We make it to the indoor heated hotel pool. Once. It is crystal clear and beautiful. It would have been nice to swim in the outdoor pool, but even though we're in the southern United States, the water is too cold in January.

Mostly, we spend our time in the suite and order room service when we want to eat. Housekeeping must think we're crazy because we leave the Do Not Disturb sign on our door all the time.

I don't care; I can't get enough of Rick. Whether it's his attention, his body, or his conversation; I just want *more*. Knowing he has to leave after just two short weeks is a nagging itch in the back of my mind. I refuse to scratch it or even acknowledge it.

Rick mirrors my needs. We don't speak about him leaving, with the exception of one conversation on our last full day at the hotel.

"Heather, you know I will get to choose what base I am assigned to when I finish this tour, right?" he asks me as we finish our lunch at the dining table. I could get used to a white linen table cloth.

"Huh?" I blink, wiping my mouth on the linen napkin. "What do you mean?"

"The perk of doing a remote tour is that I get what's called 'base of preference' when I return. I can choose what base we move to. It's not guaranteed, but the chances are really good."

"So, you'll be coming back here then, right?" I ask confidently.

"Well," he places his fork down on his now empty plate. "I wanted to ask if maybe you'd like to go to Europe. We can go to England, Germany, Spain, or Italy. Would you like that?"

I pause for a moment. "I hadn't given it any thought, really. I just assumed you'd come back home. Don't you like living in Texas?"

"Of course I do. But would you like to do that? Think about it; we can get stationed in one place and travel all over Europe. We could even run into my parents occasionally," he chuckles.

"It sounds wonderful, but I don't think I want to leave just yet. I mean, sure I want to travel some time. But not yet. Do I have to decide right now?"

"Sort of," he sighs. "You don't have to decide right this minute. But I have to put my preference down as soon as I get back. Otherwise, who knows where we'll end up."

"Seriously? I have to decide this before you go back?" I ask.

"*We* have to decide this," he replies, reaching across the table for my hand. "I wanted to talk to you about it while we are face to face. Our phone connections are horrible and so spotty while I'm…over there."

We remain in silence, each lost in our own thoughts. Finally, Rick broaches the subject once more.

"I would love to take you to Europe, Heather," he says softly. "I hear great things about it from the guys I work with. Most of them have been to Germany and loved it. Another guy was stationed in Italy for three years and had a wonderful time. We could visit Paris and see the Eiffel Tower, and visit medieval castles in England."

"Rick…"

"Before you say no, please humor me and tell me you'll at least consider it." He comes around the table, kneels beside me, and pulls my chin up to stare into my eyes. "Please?"

He isn't playing fair; he knows I melt when he looks at me. I have since the day we met.

"Okay. I'll at least consider it."

"That's my girl," he kisses me.

Conversation stops.

****

I hate having to check out. As we close the door on the honeymoon suite, I have a sinking feeling. I'm waking up from a fabulous dream to face reality. Rick still has ten days left, but I won't have him all to myself. I have to share him, at least a little bit.

We also have to make a big decision before he leaves.

I'll miss the room service and the white linen tablecloths, too. I could so get used to that.

Sensing my melancholy, Rick puts the luggage down, kisses me on the cheek, and rubs my arms. "I'll miss it, too. It's been wonderful."

I nod and keep a firm grasp on his hand.

Rick retrieves the bags at his feet and we make our way to the front desk. The bellhop had offered to take care of our luggage, but the generous gift of money my parents had given us will be used up in room service. We have just enough to tip the valet.

"How was your stay?" the cheery receptionist inquires as we approach.

"It couldn't have been more perfect," Rick replies, squeezing my hand and smiling.

"Yes," I add. "Thank you so much. It has meant the world to us." Unable to help myself, a tear rolls down my cheek. I cup my free hand over my mouth, trying to gain control of my emotions.

The receptionist frowns sympathetically. "I'm sorry. Is something wrong?"

"Absolutely nothing," Rick quickly explains. "I'm only home on leave for a few weeks before I have to go back to Korea. My wife and I got married right before I left seven months ago. This is sort of our honeymoon."

The receptionist's eyebrows rise and her mouth twitches. "You've been apart for seven months?" she asks incredulously, looking from Rick to me. "And you have to go *back*?"

"Yeah," he nods. "It's a one year tour."

"Would you two excuse me for just a moment, please? I'll be right back." She smiles and disappears quickly around the corner.

I've regained my composure. Rick and I look at each other in bewilderment.

"I wonder what that's about," Rick murmurs.

The receptionist returns several moments later, followed by a portly, balding gentleman.

"Thank you for your patience," the receptionist introduces the gentleman, who nods and smiles at us. "This is my general manager, Mr. Blackwood. I told him about your situation."

Mr. Blackwood extends his hand first to Rick, and then to me.

"Mr. and Mrs. Johnson, we would like to thank you for choosing to spend your precious time together with us, and we also want to thank you for your service, sir," he nods to Rick. "In appreciation of your sacrifice, and as a small token of our gratitude, we would like to take care of your room service bill. Accept it as our gift to you from the Hilton family of hotels."

My mouth falls open, as does Rick's. We are both speechless. Finally, Rick recovers.

"Uh...thank you. That's more than generous of you. We can't," he looks to me. "We can't have you comp the bill, though. That's too much."

Mr. Blackwood shakes his head rapidly from side to side, causing his double chin to wobble. "No, sir. It's a very small price to pay for what you're doing. Please accept it with our gratitude. I hope you enjoyed your stay and will come again."

Rick looks at me briefly. "Well, thank you very much. We will certainly come again in the future. Thank you."

"Thank you," I blurt.

"It's truly our pleasure," Mr. Blackwood replies. "Brittany will complete your check out. You folks enjoy the rest of your time together." He nods and retreats back to his office.

"You didn't have to do that," I address the receptionist.

"My father served. My brother is serving right now," she replies solemnly. "He is a Marine and was in Beirut. He lost his best friend in the barracks attack in 1983. I know what your sacrifice is like, and I know what it means. It's the least we can do." She clears her throat and hands Rick a piece of paper. "Please sign here."

Rick signs where she directs him.

"You're all taken care of. Enjoy your time, folks!" she beams.

Rick extends his hand to her, which she accepts warmly. "Thank you very much. We will."

As we wait for the valet to retrieve Rick's truck, I turn to him. "Rick, I can't believe what just happened."

He shakes his head. "I know. I never expected that. It was very generous. We'll have to stay at a Hilton everywhere we go from now on." Rick means it; he's very loyal.

"Not just because of this gift, either. I loved that suite! I wish we could move in there, don't you?" I smile and slide my hands around his waist.

He bends down and kisses me just as his truck pulls up. "Absolutely."

The valet runs around the front of the truck, opening my door and handing Rick his keys with a smile. Rick hands a tip to the valet in exchange.

The valet stops just as he was about to run back to his booth when he sees the amount Rick gave him. He turns toward Rick with a frown, "Sir, I think you may have made a mistake." He offers the money back to Rick, who declines to take it.

"No, I didn't," Rick replies. "It's forty dollars, and I'd like you to have it."

The valet's eyes bug out and his jaw drops. "Thank…thank you, sir. Really. Thank you!" he stammers.

"You're very welcome," Rick smiles broadly, helping me into the truck after placing the bags in the back.

The valet runs back around the truck and opens Rick's door for him.

Once we are in the truck and the doors are closed, I ask, "Why did you do that?"

Rick glances at me as he clicks his seatbelt into place. "The tip, you mean? Because I want to be generous, too. When I'm given a gift, it's only fitting that I give a gift." He jerks his head toward the valet, who has returned to his booth, beaming. "Look at him. That probably made his day. It's a ripple."

"What?"

"You know," he shrugs. "A ripple. When you throw a stone into a pond, it ripples. One action causes another. It's a ripple."

Rick puts the truck in gear, pulls slowly out into the parking lot, and turns onto the street to head home.

I regard him for a few moments. "You know something, Mr. Johnson; I do believe I am the luckiest woman on earth."

"Why is that, Mrs. Johnson?" he responds formally.

"You are not only handsome, but you're kind, thoughtful, and generous, too."

His cheeks pink ever so slightly and he glances at me, smiling. "That was nothing."

My heart swells. "No, it was very generous. I love you, Rick." I lean over and kiss his cheek.

He chuckles and squeezes my hand, keeping his eyes on the road.

Rick is a really, really good person inside. Maybe I'm wrong to want him to get out of the military. Shouldn't I support what he wants? Can I do that? Can I be as generous as he is? What kind of ripple would that be? I sigh contentedly and enjoy the ride home.

Pulling into the driveway, we are met with a Welcome Home banner fixed across the front porch and red, white, and blue balloons secured to the mail box near the street.

"What's all this?" Rick asks, bewildered.

"I don't know. I had no idea they were going to do this," I shrug. "But it's really nice."

"It sure is," he replies. He parks the truck; we remove our seat belts and exit. Rick grabs our luggage and we make our way to the front door.

"Hello?" I call out as we enter. The smell of my mother's pot roast fills my nostrils.

Dad pokes his head around the corner from the kitchen. "Oh! You're home earlier than we thought. Louise!" he yells down the hall. "The kids are home!"

Debbie is the first to make her appearance. She heads straight for Rick and hugs him. He grabs her in a bear hug and spins her around once, making her giggle.

"Good to see you, too, squirt!" Rick exclaims.

Jeff follows closely on Mom's heels, grinning his goofy grin. When I make eye contact, he wags his eyebrows at me. I glare at him, slowly shaking my head from side to side.

He grins wider. It might be best to ignore him.

"Did you have a good time? Did you like the honeymoon suite? Wasn't it wonderful? How about the champagne? I wasn't sure what kind to get, but the hotel manager suggested it..." Mom asks questions too quickly to answer.

"Louise," Dad places his hand on her arm to stem the flow. "Let the kids get their bags in the door and maybe sit down first."

She places her hands on her cheeks. "Oh! Yes. Sorry. We're making a nice dinner for everyone. You two go ahead," she kisses each of us on the cheek. "Go unpack and relax."

"I'm sure they're plenty relaxed," Jeff jokes.

I shoot him a venomous look.

"Thank you, I'll just put these in the room for now," Rick replies, ignoring Jeff.

"I'll help you," Dad replies, grabbing one of the bags.

"Did you like the balloons and the banner?" Debbie asks. "I helped tape the balloons to the mailbox."

"They're wonderful!" I reply. Rick nods before disappearing down the hallway with my father. Their muted conversation fades with them.

"Jeff, you're in the kitchen with me." Mom pulls a reluctant Jeff along.

Debbie grins and grabs my hand, pulling me to the sofa. "Tell me all about the honeymoon suite. Mom said it's a very special hotel room." Her eyes grow wide. "She said it's for special occasions only. Did they have balloons in your room?"

"No, no balloons," I laugh. "But they did have a big bowl of chocolate covered strawberries waiting for us when we got there." I regale her with the details of the room decor, the view from the balcony, and the room service.

Her eyes take on the dreamy, far away look they get when she enters one of her fantasies.

"Oh," she sighs when I finish. "That sounds like heaven. I can't wait to get married and have a honeymoon suite, too."

Rick, who had joined us, pipes in. "I'm sure you'll have just as wonderful a time as we did with whoever is lucky enough to marry you." He reaches across and chucks her chin. Her cheeks flame and she giggles.

She always giggles with Rick. She is so tightly wrapped around his finger that it makes me smile. I am confident he will never let her down.

I am confident he will never let *me* down.

"Debbie, come help me with the salad, please," Mom calls. Debbie cheerfully rises to skip into the kitchen.

"She adores you, Rick," I whisper.

He chuckles. "I know. She's a good kid."

Dad reappears and plops into his easy chair with a groan.

"Thanks again, sir, for that wonderful welcome," Rick says. "We're also very, very thankful for the generous over-the-top gift you left. The room itself was gift enough."

Dad smiles and waves us off. "It was our pleasure."

"Did you tell him what the hotel did?" I ask.

Rick shakes his head. "No. I wanted to share that with your whole family over dinner."

Dad looks puzzled and leans forward. "What did they do? Did they take care of you? They promised they'd take care of you."

"They took very good care of us, Dad." I look at Rick. "We'll tell you about it at dinner."

Dad falls back in his chair. "All right. As long as they took care of you."

We continue in conversation until Mom calls us to the table for dinner. This time, along with her mouth-watering pot roast, she roasted potatoes, carrots, and pearl onions, made gravy, my favorite biscuits, salad, and peach cobbler. I'll gain back all the weight I've lost.

Rick inhales appreciatively. "That smells so good, ma'am," he winces comically as my mother gives him The Look, "I mean Louise. Thank you."

She nods and gestures at the table. "That's better. Please, let's sit down and eat."

We all take a seat at the table.

"I set the table," Debbie blurts, grinning at Rick.

"Yes, she did," Mom says proudly.

"I peeled the potatoes and carrots," Jeff interjects, not wanting to be left out.

"A fine job was done by all. This looks and smells amazing," compliments Rick.

We all bow our heads and Dad says grace, blessing the food and the people gathered at the table. As we fill our plates and start eating, Dad can't wait any longer and asks the question that has been burning. "Okay, kids. What did the hotel do?"

"What?" Mom asks, confused. "What do you mean, what did they do?"

Rick swallows before answering. "When we went to check out and settle our bill, they took care of our room service. They wiped it out and said it was their gift to us."

Mom gasps. "They did? Why?"

"We told them why we were there, and they wanted to thank Rick for his service," I reply.

"What's room service?" Debbie asks.

"It's when the hotel delivers food to your room because you don't want to leave it," Jeff remarks, grinning.

"Jeffrey Allen," Mom warns him.

Jeff ducks his head, but doesn't stop grinning.

"I wouldn't want to leave it, either," Debbie retorts innocently. "It sounds like heaven."

"It was, Debbie. It was absolutely gorgeous."

Jeff wisely remains silent. Whatever he was about to say, he keeps it to himself. Mom and Dad glaring at him may have something to do with it.

"Well, that was extremely generous of them," Dad exclaims. "I'll be sure to write a letter and thank them."

"That's a wonderful idea, Dad," I turn toward Rick. "I think we should write them a letter, too. Mom, can I use your electric typewriter?"

"Well, sure. But I think a handwritten one would be better, don't you?" Mom replies.

Mulling it over, I nod. "Yeah, I guess so."

"I have some beautiful blank cards you can use," Mom continues, spooning more gravy onto her pot roast.

I lean over and whisper to Rick, "Can I bring up your order thing?"

He looks at me, puzzled. "Now?"

I nod and turn my attention back to my family. "We also need to talk to you guys about something else." I glance at Rick, who is still staring at me. "Well, when Rick is done with his tour in Korea, he has to decide where he – where we – will get stationed. Since this is a remote tour, he will get his choice of where we go. I told him I want to stay here, but," I glance at Rick once more. "Rick wants to go to Europe."

Everyone freezes. Debbie actually drops her fork with a *clank* onto her plate.

After a minute of silence, Mom clears her throat, folds her napkin, and places it next to her plate before responding.

"Well, that would be an interesting place to go," she starts, looking meaningfully at my father.

Dad clears his throat exactly as my mother did. "Yes, that would be interesting," he looks at my mother and shrugs his shoulders. "But, how long would you be there?"

Rick places his fork on his half-empty plate and folds his hands in front of him. "Well, sir, it would be either a three or four year tour."

Debbie gasps. Jeff looks stunned.

"You mean," Debbie's voice cracks. "You would be gone for *years?*" She bites her lower lip.

I look mournfully at Rick, who avoids my gaze.

"If we went to Europe, yes. We would be gone for a couple of years. But," he glances at me. "We can come home for holidays and things. You can even come visit us there. You will still get to see us."

"That would be too cool! I could come and stay with you guys, and check out all the hot European babes!" Jeff crows.

"Jeff, that's enough," Dad warns him.

"It's true," Jeff laughs. "I think it would be awesome!"

"When will you find out where you're going?" Mom asks.

"You mean you *are* leaving?" Debbie asks, her eyes watery pools.

"No. No, it doesn't mean we are leaving, Debbie," I reply quickly. "We just have to decide what we are going to do before he goes back."

"We do want your input, of course," Rick squeezes my hand. "You are a wonderful family. You've made me feel so welcome, and I know how important you are to Heather. To us both. I want to go to Europe for the opportunity to travel and show Heather the world."

"What do you think?" I ask.

"I don't think we should tell you what we think," Mom says, placing her hand on Debbie's arm. Debbie is fighting back tears. "This is a decision that you two, as a married couple, need to make for yourselves."

Dad nods.

"Mom, we *want* your opinion," I answer hastily.

"All right," Dad starts, but Mom shoots him a look. "Louise, they are asking. Here's what I think," he clears his throat, squaring his shoulders. "I would prefer you stay close to home for now. When you get back, of course, you'll move into your own place. But military life isn't easy, and it would be good for Heather, for both of you, to have the support of her family close by to ease the transition."

Thank you, Dad.

"That's what I want too, Rick," I turn my face toward him. "I want to travel at some point, but just not right now."

Rick presses his lips together and looks at his hands. "All right," he casts his glance sideways at me. "If that's what you want."

"So you're not moving away?" Debbie asks hopefully.

"Most likely not, squirt. You're going to be stuck with me," Rick replies with a tight smile.

Her shoulders relax. She picks up her fork and resumes eating, as does everyone else but Rick.

He picks up his fork, moving the food around his plate. Eventually, he takes a few unenthusiastic bites.

****

"How could you ambush me like that?" Rick asks after closing the door to our room for the night. His voice is quiet but he's clearly upset.

"What do you mean ambush?" I ask innocently.

"Heather, you didn't need to bring up my orders in front of everybody over dinner the first night we get back," he replies evenly.

"I thought you wouldn't mind getting the opinion of my family."

"This is our first major decision together, and I think *we* should make it," he points with his index finger, moving his hand back and forth between us. "Together. As a married couple. That's what we are, right?"

"Of course, Rick," I move toward him, putting my arms around his waist. "But don't you think my parents can help?"

His jaw works. "Heather, the point is – we should make these decisions between *us* first. I didn't want to discuss it with your family the first night. Especially not before you and I have had a chance to talk about it."

"We did talk about it."

He pulls away from me. "No, I brought it up, but you didn't want to discuss it, remember?"

I don't like this. I look at him in what I hope is a seductive manner. "What I remember is you looking into my eyes in the way that makes me melt. The rest didn't involve conversation." I take a step toward him, but he takes a step back. "I don't want to fight about this."

Rick rubs his face. "Me, either."

I take a tentative step toward him again. This time he doesn't pull away, but his hold is loose.

"You brought it up without asking me."

"I did ask you," I remind him.

He eyes me for a moment, his jaw working. "It's getting late. We should get ready for bed." He turns away, opens the door, and leaves.

I am left standing there, mute and confused. What just happened?

Maybe I should've waited, but the input of my parents can really help. My father has always made really good decisions. Why shouldn't I include them? Rick is over-reacting. Why can't he be reasonable?

I hastily change into my over-sized T-shirt for bed. When Rick returns, I push past him without a word on my way to the bathroom, where I scrub my face and teeth a little too roughly.

My rest is fitful and I awaken after three, unable to fall back asleep.

"You okay?" Rick mumbles.

I turn toward him in the darkness. I am still bewildered by his reaction, but I don't want to waste any of our precious time being petulant.

"Yeah, I'm okay. I just can't sleep."

Rick wraps his arm around me, sighing deeply. "Just close your eyes. You'll drift off."

I kiss his warm cheek. "I love you."

Rick squeezes me. "Love you, too."

"Are we okay?" I ask.

"Yeah. Get some sleep." He snuggles closer. Within minutes, his breathing evens out and deepens.

I lie there, staring at the ceiling and mulling over the situation for a long while before drifting off.

****

Gradually, my mind rolls into consciousness. Stretching, I yawn widely and open my eyes, blinking at the sunlight streaming in through the lacy curtains on my window.

Searching for, but not finding, the heat of Rick's body next to me, I open my eyes and scowl around the brightness of the room.

He's not here.

Puzzled, I hoist myself up on my elbows and squint at the clock. It's past ten.

"Gah!" I exclaim, whipping the covers off.

Rick must have gotten up before me and just left me here. The sting of rejection pierces me; I had hoped to start our day off differently.

He's only got a week left, after all.

Lurching myself unsteadily out of the bed, I rearrange my over-sized T-shirt down over my hips and yank the door open, hurrying down the hallway in search of Rick.

The smell of cinnamon and coffee waft from the kitchen.

"That's crazy. They bury it in the *ground?*" my mother asks.

"Yup. In these huge clay pots," Rick replies.

My father is the first to spy me. "Well, look who decided to finally make an appearance!" he gestures with his coffee cup, grinning. "We saved you some cinnamon rolls. Are you hungry?"

"Rick was just regaling us with tales of Korean food. Have you ever heard of *kimchee?*" Mom asks. "It's this crazy fermented cabbage thing where they..."

"Mom," I interrupt her. "Please. I just woke up."

Rick rises and approaches me cautiously. "Morning, honey bun. Sleep okay?" he asks, kissing me lightly on the cheek.

"Why didn't you get me up?" I ask.

He smiles, escorting me to the chair next to him. "You looked so peaceful, I just couldn't."

Bologna. I narrow my eyes at him while I sit.

"Heather, can I get you a cinnamon roll?" Mom asks.

"Yes! I'm starving."

Rick's hand squeezes my thigh, trying to get my attention. I turn toward him, my eyes pleading. I really don't want to fight with such a short time left together.

He leans in and kisses me on the mouth this time, his expression telling me everything is okay.

I exhale audibly and my shoulders slump, the tension released.

"You all right, Heather?" Dad asks, brow furrowed.

"Yeah. I'm okay." I lean on Rick's shoulder and he rubs my back.

Mom places a large cinnamon roll in front of me; her cream cheese frosting oozes into the crevices and slowly melts down the sides. These gooey little treats have always been the favorite of my friends who begged her to make them for every sleepover.

"Coffee?" she asks.

"Mm hmmm," I reply, letting the cinnamon and sugar scents penetrate my nostrils and fill my lungs. "Please."

As large as the rolls are, I should use a knife and fork, but they're so much fun to eat with my fingers. I pull the outer coil of gooey dough away from the center slowly, savoring the experience. Once the piece is the length I'm looking for, I twist and tear it off, slowly fill my mouth. I close my eyes and enjoy.

"You look like you're having a religious experience there," Rick chuckles.

I lazily open my eyes and look at him, licking my fingers just as slowly. "Have you had one yet?"

"I've had two, actually," he says. He turns to my mother. "You'll have to share that recipe with Heather."

"No problem there," she replies proudly. "That's one thing she has helped me make on several occasions. She should already know."

"I don't think I could make them turn out the way you do," I reply, my mouth full. Once I swallow my second large bite, I sip my coffee which is more cream and sugar than coffee, before returning for a third bite, and a fourth.

My appetite has returned with a vengeance since Rick's arrival.

"Hopefully, you'll practice a lot and figure it out. I won't mind a bit." Rick reaches over and grabs his third roll. I don't know where he puts it; his stomach is flat as a wash board.

"So, what's your plan for today, kids?" Dad asks.

"I really need to get some laundry done. Other than that," I shrug, "I don't know."

"I want to go for a hike to one of our favorite spots. I thought we could have a picnic lunch, but after such a delicious late breakfast, there really is no point. Then I want to take Heather to the base and get her familiar with some of the services there. She's been on the base, but she didn't have an ID card before we got married, so she couldn't go in to a lot of the places."

"Sounds good. You guys do whatever you want and enjoy yourselves," Mom responds. "I can take care of your laundry for you, Heather. I don't want you wasting your time doing that while Rick is here."

"Mom, you don't have to do that," I protest.

Mom holds her hand up. "I won't hear of it. Now just leave it in a pile on the floor in front of the washer and I'll take care of it."

"Thanks, Mom," A swell of love washes over me. I hope we will be just as good to our own children. "I love you."

Mom looks at me over her coffee mug. "Love you, too."

Once we finish stuffing ourselves silly on cinnamon rolls, we retreat to our room to get dressed.

Closing the door quietly behind me, I turn to Rick.

"Are we really okay, Rick? I'm sorry about last night."

He wraps his arms around me, kissing the tip of my nose. "Yes, we really are all right. I just want you to be happy, and if you want to stay here when I am done in Korea, then we'll stay here."

I grin. "Really? You're okay with that?"

He nods and sighs, resignation in his eyes. "Yes. I'm okay with that."

"Good! I am so happy! We can go to Europe later."

He nods. "Yeah. Now let's get going. I really missed hiking with you and I want to get to the base, too."

I kiss him on the mouth. "Wouldn't you rather get undressed first? Besides, you already showed me around the base while we were dating."

He shakes his head. "Not everything. Now you can go inside the commissary and BX. I'm really surprised you haven't ventured over there while I've been gone."

I shrug. "I didn't really want to do it without you. Would you like to get undressed first anyway?"

"Normally, yes but," he chuckles, "I don't want to give Jeff more fuel for the day. We have a whole week, Heather." He winks and releases me.

I scowl. My stupid brother can make me so mad. Too bad he doesn't have school today like Debbie. I really can't wait to get our own place.

We hastily dress for the chill in the air as well as the hike. When we enter the living room, Jeff is grinning his stupid grin.

"Well, that was quick," he quips.

Suddenly, a hefty magazine whizzes and flaps through the air, smacking Jeff right on the head before landing on his lap. It's the *Reader's Digest*.

"Ouch!" he yells, rubbing the spot.

Dad points his finger at Jeff. "Jeffrey Allen, that is *enough*. I don't want to hear any more remarks from you. Is that clear?"

"Yes, sir," Jeff mumbles, scowling and rubbing his head. His cheeks are flaming and his eyes are misty. It must've really hurt.

Good. I hope it hurt enough to put an end to his comments.

Dad shakes his head and returns to reading his paper.

"Dad, we're heading out. We'll be back by dinner."

He looks up briefly, smiles, and nods. "Be good, kids." Dad loves his paper.

Once we're in the truck, Rick starts to snicker. It quickly becomes a full on belly laugh.

I look at him, puzzled. "What's so funny?"

"Are you kidding me?" he asks incredulously between laughs. "Your dad throwing the *Reader's Digest* at Jeff? Did you see the look on his face?" Rick guffaws even louder.

"Yeah," I smile. "It was pretty funny. I hope he'll stop making comments now."

Rick throws his head back in laughter. "Me, too. But it was all worth it just to see that." He shakes his head and starts the truck, putting it in gear. "Boy, I'll tell you what. Your family is a hoot!"

We enjoy hiking for over an hour, Rick marveling at the familiar sights. The landscape is asleep for the season and very peaceful. We encounter no other hikers on the trail.

Afterwards, we make several stops on base starting with the BX, which stands for Base Exchange, and the commissary. That's the military version of a grocery store.

Walking into the BX, I am floored at how big it is and what's for sale. It looks like a mini-mall and department store. There's even a food court.

A balding gentleman places his hand out to stop our advancement. "Excuse me; may I see your ID?"

Rick pulls his wallet out and flashes his ID. I follow suit.

"That's one thing I'll have to get used to," I remark.

"Yes, you will," Rick responds, tucking his wallet back into his pocket. "You have to show your ID to get into the commissary, too."

"I had no idea this was here," I breathe, my eyes sweeping over everything around me.

"I told you to come to the base and check it out, Heather."

"I would rather wait for you to come home and show me."

"Heather, I got you a sticker for your car so you can get on base, and you have your dependent ID card, too."

"Rick, look! There's even a make-up counter!" I pull Rick over to the cosmetic section, where a very made-up Asian woman wearing a black smock smiles at us.

"Can I help you?" she asks in a clipped accent I don't recognize.

"Yes, thank you. How much is this?" I point to a name brand moisturizer.

When she quotes the price, I'm floored. "Wow! That's so cheap." I pick up the box and make sure it's not a knock off brand. It isn't.

"I told you things are cheaper here," Rick replies, shaking his head. "You really need to check this place out while I'm gone."

The Asian woman continues to smile. "Would you like to have a complimentary facial? You have beautiful skin already, and this will make it glow." She gestures toward another box on the glass shelf.

"How long will that take?" I ask.

"Only about fifteen minutes," she replies.

I look hopefully at Rick. "Can I?"

He grins and nods. "Of course! I'll just go look at the televisions and be back in a bit." He jerks his head toward the back of the store.

I reach up and kiss him before turning my attention to the woman.

"Please, have a seat," she gestures toward a sleek black, high-backed stool surrounded by a mirror and more make-up than I've ever seen in one place.

I sit in the stool and release my face into her expert care.

"Are you newly married?" she asks as she begins gathering her supplies.

"Yes," I nod. "He's only home for two weeks, though. He's doing a remote tour in Korea right now."

She clucks her tongue. "I'm sorry. How much longer does he have?"

"He is supposed to be home in May."

"Tsk tsk tsk," she clucks again, rubbing cream all over my face. "I have done that, too, with my husband. It's not fun. I was here all by myself. I have my friends and they were helpful. My family is in the Philippines."

"Where are the Philippines?"

She gapes at me. "It's in the Pacific Ocean in Asia. You've never heard of the Philippines?"

"No, sorry," I shake my head.

"You weren't a military brat?" She wipes the cream off my face gently with a warm cloth.

"No. My family lives here, but we're not military."

"Ah, well there's an Air Force base in the Philippines, and that's how I met my husband. Do you usually wear make-up?" She dots another cream on my face and carefully rubs it in.

"Yes, I wear it most days," I reply.

She pulls open drawers and removes jars, tubes, and brushes, placing them on a white disposable cloth in front of her.

"How long have you been married?" I ask.

She squeezes some foundation onto a paper and dips a clean sponge into it, dabbing my face, before she answers. "Eleven years."

"How do you like the military life?"

She sighs, sweeping powder onto my face with a large brush. "Well, I like it because it has given me a life that I never would have had in the Philippines. There's not much opportunity there and it's very corrupt. I remember when Ferdinand and Imelda Marcos were in power. It was awful for most people."

"But it seems like it's not very fair. I mean, I don't like having to be away from my husband the entire first year we're married." I close my eyes for her to apply the eye make-up.

"Yes, things can be unfair. But it's still better for me and my family."

Puzzled, I ask, "I thought your family was still in the Philippines."

"Yes, they are. I send money every month to help them."

"Wow. Your husband must have a lot of rank for you to send enough money to support your family."

"Not really," she shakes her head. "He's a Tech Sergeant. But it's what's expected of me. I married an American. A dollar stretches very far there."

"How can you do that?" I press, still puzzled.

Her face goes blank and she shrugs. "It's what we do."

I can't respond; she's applying the lipstick. Her tone and expression convey that she can't fathom an alternative. I've never met or talked to a person from the Philippines before. Maybe it is just what they do. I'll have to ask Rick.

At that moment, Rick's face appears in my line of sight. He's grinning.

"Well, you look beautiful!" he exclaims.

The woman pulls back and smiles at her work. "I think so, too." She scribbles some notes on a card and hands the card to me. "These are all the products I used on you today. If you would like to purchase them, I would be happy to help. I do recommend you at least purchase the skin care products. It will keep your skin beautiful like it is now."

"Rick, what do you think?" I ask, peering at my reflection in the mirror. The make-up is a bit heavy-handed for me, but I like the technique.

"Whatever you'd like is fine," he replies.

The prices are cheaper than elsewhere, but I don't want to spend too much. I settle for a few of the skin care products she recommends.

While she tallies the total, I thank her for talking with me.

"It's my pleasure. Don't worry, it will be okay! You'll see." She smiles cheerily as I take the bag from her. "Good luck!"

I smile warmly. "Thank you."

Walking away, I turn to Rick. "Do you really like the make-up?"

He nods. "It's a bit too much, but it looks nice."

"I thought so, too. I want to ask you about something."

"Shoot."

"That woman is from the Philippines. She mentioned that she sends money home to her family every month to support them. Have you ever heard of that?"

Rick chuckles. "Yes, it happens all the time."

"What do you mean?"

"Look around you. There are a lot of not just Filipinos, but Koreans and Japanese, too married to military. It's an Asian invasion."

Confused, I look around as he suggests and notice that most of the workers in the BX are Asian. "Why is that?"

"We have a lot of bases over there and people meet. It's happens."

"Is that happening in Korea?" I ask, remembering his condom experience with the First Sergeant.

Rick glances at me. "Don't worry, Heather. I'm yours and yours alone."

Next, we walk over to the commissary located on the opposite end of the parking lot. It looks just like any other grocery store except we have to show our IDs to get in. Instead of individual lines for each register, there is one line that snakes along. At the head of the line, there is a man directing customers to each cashier, advancing the line slowly. It's quite the sight to see; he is bellowing out directions with flamboyant gestures and rapid speech like an auctioneer. He reminds me of traffic cops on TV.

"Is that how it always is?" I ask, gesturing to the man who is waving another customer in line with exaggerated movements.

Rick glances at the man. "No, I think it's just his style. He puts on quite a show, doesn't he?"

"It's incredible."

Just like the BX, the commissary prices are quite a bit lower, and they're all name brands.

"There are no store brands?" I ask, picking up a jar of pickles.

"Nope," he replies.

"I have to tell my mother about this. She won't believe it."

"Would you like to buy anything while we're here?" he asks.

"Do they have a bakery?"

"Of course there's a bakery; it's a grocery store," he chuckles.

We make our way over to the bakery and select a small sheet cake.

"Do we have to wait in that line?" I ask, pointing to the snaking line I noticed when we first walked in.

"No, we can go through the express line." He guides me to a smaller line on the side.

When Rick pays for the cake, I notice there's a gentleman in a white polo shirt placing our cake in a bag for us. There's a wooden box about the size of a Kleenex box nestled in the corner of the counter. The box is half full of an assortment of paper bills and coins.

"Rick," I lean over and whisper. "What's this?"

"The commissary baggers work for tips only," he replies and places three one dollar bills in the box, smiling at the gentleman, before gathering our bagged cake up with one hand.

The gentleman nods and smiles back. "Thank you."

I look at the end of all of the cashier lines and notice there is a sea of white polo shirts. There are two baggers at each line and they're feverishly bagging groceries that come toward them from the belt, placing them in short, two-tiered, upright carts. Once each customer is done, one of the two baggers pushes the strange carts out behind the customers, following them out of the commissary.

I hadn't noticed it before; I was too distracted by the frustrated auctioneer.

"You mean they bag all your groceries and take them out, too?"

"Yes," Rick nods. "It's really cool. They load your vehicle and everything. It's a great service and gives the baggers a source of income."

"How much do you have to tip? I saw you tipped him three dollars for just this little cake. It must be expensive."

"There's no amount that you *have* to tip, but I like to tip generously because they only work for tips. They're not employees of the commissary. I imagine it's not as easy as it looks. You try bending over, bagging, loading, and unloading groceries all day and see how your back and feet feel."

I study the baggers a bit longer; there are young, old, men, women, teens, adults, all manner of people that are wearing white polo shirts. There's no common theme among them.

"Honey? You ready?" Rick asks.

"Huh? Oh! Yes, sorry," I reply, following him outside.

The whole business fascinates me. I've never seen something like that. "Who hires them? Where do they apply?"

"I think you just have to be military-affiliated in some way. I have a guy that I work with that did it at his last base. He said there's a list you get your name on and they'll call you when there's an opening. Active duty personnel have first priority for call backs."

I'm even more puzzled. "But, why would anybody that's active duty want to be a bagger?"

"There are any number of reasons," Rick shrugs. "Obviously everyone does it to earn extra money. This guy did it because his wife had to quit her job; she was pregnant and ended up on bed rest. They needed the money to make ends meet."

"Wow. They make that much money just in tips?"

"I have no idea. I think what I was shocked to find out is how poorly they're treated by people," he shakes his head. "You should hear the stories this guy tells me. Some people give them a buck or just some change for a cartful of groceries, or insult them by saying 'here's your beer money.' Some people don't tip them at all. One guy even gave him some expired Burger King coupons as a tip. It's awful. So I always try to tip generously and treat them with respect."

"That's terrible! How can they get away with that?" I ask, feeling insulted for a guy I don't even know.

"I asked the same question. He said they're not allowed to say anything except thanks. I don't know that I could do that."

"Me, either," I reply, still awed and angry. "You should've given that bagger a five dollar bill."

Rick smiles at me. "From now on, I'll be sure to do that."

Our next stop is the housing office where Rick gathers information about the housing we are eligible for when he returns. All housing on base is assigned according to rank, so we will be in Junior Enlisted Housing. Being new to all of this, I didn't realize there was a waiting list for housing or that it was based on rank. I assumed we would look at the houses available, pick one, and move into a house that we like.

After I reveal my surprise, the stout receptionist at the housing office looks at me over her bifocals, which are suspended precariously on the tip of her nose, "Young lady, you have a lot to learn about military life." Her tone isn't condescending. If anything, it smacks of pity.

Her comment makes me bristle.

I'm about to open my mouth to reply, but Rick squeezes my hand.

"Do I need to have my orders in hand to get on the waiting list for housing?" he asks.

The woman turns her attention to Rick. "Yes, you do. We can't put you on the list without a copy of your official orders."

"I should have those within a month or two at the most, I think. How long is the waiting list?"

The woman glances down at the papers stacked side by side in front of her, scrolling with her finger to find the right stack. "Well, right now it's about seven to nine months long."

"What?" I blurt.

She glances at me. "Yes, Junior Enlisted is the longest because it's the one in the most demand."

I point to a list that looks very short. "What is this one for?"

"That's for Senior *Officers*," she answers with a sigh.

"How long is that wait?"

She presses her lips together and stares at me disapprovingly. "It's about a month at the most."

"That's not fair! Why do we have to wait so long when there are houses available to move into?"

The woman sighs exasperatingly and glares at Rick before answering me. "Honey, everything in the military is divided by rank. You need to get used to that."

"But…" I start before Rick interrupts me.

"Heather, it's not her fault and it's not her decision. It's just the way it is." He smiles at the woman. "Thank you, ma'am, for your help. How will I get a copy of my orders here to have us placed on the waiting list once I have them?"

"You can either fax them to me, which I don't recommend because that's not reliable; sometimes it doesn't arrive or gets sent who knows where, or you can mail them to your wife and she can come in and have you placed on the list. Just be sure her name is on your orders."

Rick glances at me; I'm still fuming. He addresses the woman again, "Thank you. You've been very helpful." He pulls me out of the office.

Once outside, I can't keep quiet anymore. "Rick, that's not fair! How come they make us wait when there are empty houses available now?"

Rick shakes his head, nodding at a passing man in uniform before answering me quietly. "Let's get in the truck first, all right?"

Once we're in the truck and the doors are closed, Rick turns his body to face me and speaks before I have a chance to get a word out. "Heather, you have to understand some things. First of all, the military isn't about what's fair, it's all about rank. I've only got three stripes. The more rank you have, the higher in priority you are for a lot of things on base. You'll have to accept that. Please don't go off on anybody about it, either. You never know who you're talking to, or who they know." He glances around the parking lot. "There will be times when things can be made more difficult if someone doesn't like you."

"Are you telling me I can't speak my mind about things when they're unfair and wrong?" I ask indignantly.

"Yes, I am, because it's not going to change anything. It will just make it worse for us," he replies, pointing his finger toward the housing office building. "That woman could be married to my future boss here. If you raise a stink about something that can't be changed and make her mad, she could remember us and make us wait even longer for housing, or make my life very difficult wherever I'm assigned to work."

My mouth falls open in disbelief. "Are you serious, Rick? That's absolutely ridiculous!"

"Ridiculous or not, that's the military way, Heather."

Righteous anger boils in me, making it difficult to control my tongue. "It's bad enough we have to be apart our first year of marriage, and you missed Thanksgiving *and* Christmas, but now you're telling me I have to pretend everything is perfect all the time? I don't know how to do that."

Rick stares at me for a moment, searching my face. Wordlessly, he adjusts himself in his seat, starts the truck, pulls out, and drives away.

As we exit the base, I turn to Rick. "I thought you were going to show me some other places, too."

Rick's jaw works. "Not today," he replies quietly.

The silence continues until we're almost home.

"Rick, what's wrong? Why are you so mad?"

He looks out his window a few times without answering. His jaw continues to work.

"Rick?"

Rick glances over my shoulder and suddenly swerves off the road, pulling onto a gravel road lined by low-lying trees.

"Where are we going?" I ask, gripping the door handle.

Rick remains silent, continuing to drive down the gravel road until we come to a small clearing where he pulls over and jerks the truck into park. He folds his arms over the steering wheel, staring stone-faced into the distance.

I'm stunned into silence. I have never seen him like this.

Long moments pass before Rick looks at me.

"Heather, I love you," he starts, his tone very low. "I want you to understand that. I really do love you. That's why I married you. But I also want you to understand that I want to make the military my career. That means that you will be by my side. I need you and I want you there. Being in the military is not easy, okay. I get that. But I need your support. I can't do this without you."

I gulp and nod. I am acting like a child and I know it. I just don't like things that are blatantly unfair.

Rick stares up at the ceiling for a moment before opening his door and getting out. He starts pacing back and forth, hands on his hips.

I exit my side of the truck and slowly make my way around to him. Instead of reaching for him, I stop short of his pacing path and fold my arms across my body.

"I'm sorry, Rick. I know this is what you want to do," I swallow hard, willing tears not to come. "Tell me again why, though."

Rick paces one more length of the truck before swiveling around to face me. "This is the career path I have chosen for myself. I told you that while we were dating. I love my job. I love working on the flight line and doing my part in the big picture. My job is important. If I don't do my job right, it *matters*. It lets me know that I matter..." He pauses and looks into the distance, gathering his thoughts. "My brothers both went to college straight out of high school. My parents expected the same from me. When I told them I wanted to join the military, they couldn't understand why. They were going to pay my way through college and had everything set. But I want to make my *own* way," he smacks his hand into his fist. "I don't want to take the easy way out. They respected my decision. Will you?"

"I will try. I promise. It's just hard for me to get used to this. It's just...unfair."

"I know, Heather. But life isn't fair. It's not an exclusive thing to the military, all right? You are going to have to let that go."

"I feel like I have to let *you* go, Rick. I miss you."

"I know, Heather. I miss you, too. This isn't permanent; it's just a few more months."

"Yes." I have nothing else to say.

Rick sighs and leans over his truck, gripping it with both hands. After a few moments, he pushes himself up and moves toward me. "Heather, you'll get used to it. It is a bewildering experience and I understand that. I wish I could make it easier, but I can't."

I force a smile. "I want you to be happy. I really do. I just don't understand how being apart and being told where we can live based on what you wear on your sleeve when you go to work fits into it." I slide my hands around his waist.

"That's not all it is or all that it's about. Yes, that is part of it. But I want you to think about the opportunities, too. I am very proud to serve my country by wearing the uniform. I know I can make a lasting difference by doing my part. I want to take you on wonderful travels all around the globe and show you cultures and foods that you never dreamed of. We can go biking and hiking all over Europe! There are some incredible trails there, you know. I want you to experience all I can offer you in life. The military will give us those opportunities like nothing else can. I also want to show my parents that I can do this and make a success of it. I plan to go all the way and make Chief."

"What's Chief?" I ask. I have a picture in my mind of a shirtless Rick wearing a long feathered headdress. It's not entirely unflattering, but I don't know what that has to do with the military.

Rick snorts. "It's the highest enlisted rank: Chief Master Sergeant." He pulls my hands up to his and kisses them. "I want to do it with you."

"I want to do life with you, too."

CHAPTER SEVEN

January, 1989

Returning home that evening, heaviness descends on my heart as I carry the cake into the house. It feels like Rick is already gone, even though I can feel his warm hand in mine. What is life going to be like for us?

My mother has always been very perceptive. She doesn't disappoint. As soon as we walk in the door, she takes one look at me and her brows knit together.

"Heather, honey. Are you all right?" she asks. She glances at my package. "What's that?"

"It's a cake. I'm okay," I whisper before shoving the bag into Rick's hands and run to my room, closing the door behind me. I fall on the bed and cry.

Eventually I hear the door click as someone enters. Expecting my mother, I roll over and am stunned to see Rick.

"Hey," he says softly, closing the door behind him and sliding onto the bed. He kisses the tip of my nose as I hiccup loudly.

"Why did you come?"

He wipes the tears from my cheeks. "Where else would I be?"

I hiccup again. "What did you tell my mother?"

"I told her what happened on base, and that you're upset about how unfair things are."

"Rick," I grimace and hiccup. "I'm scared."

"I know," he sighs. "But we are going to be fine, Heather. I promise."

I want to believe him. I *have* to believe him.

"Please remember you promised me that."

He cups my face in his hands. "I always keep my promises."

"That's all I need to hear."

We lay in each other's arms awhile longer in silence, holding tightly to one another. Our time together is so short.

"I almost forgot," I say, sitting up and wiping my face. I have to change the subject. "Our wedding pictures. Do you want to see them?"

Rick brightens. "Of course!"

I open my closet and pull the box down from the shelf. I lay it on the bed, carefully remove the lid and unfold the tissue paper. I pull the album out and sit next to him, linking my arm in his while he opens the cover. We look at each picture individually, slowly going through the pages.

"They came out great," Rick murmurs halfway through.

"I think so, too. You're so handsome."

Rick chuckles and turns the page.

Finally, when we've looked through the entire album, ending on the picture of us with our faces toward the setting sun, champagne flutes in the air for a toast, Rick studies it. "Life is going to be an adventure, Heather. You ready for it?"

"With you, yes." Whatever may come.

He smiles broadly. "Me, too."

"Rick! Heather! Dinner's ready!" Dad calls down the hallway.

We pack the album away and put it back in my closet. I catch a glimpse of my reflection on the dresser mirror and grimace. The beautiful make-up that nice Asian woman had applied is almost gone. There are only a few smudges left. My hair is pretty wild, too. I like it big, but not this big. "I need to go freshen up first. I'll meet you out there."

Rick slides off the bed and stretches. "Okay, even though you're always beautiful."

I reach over and kiss him lightly before disappearing down the hall. The smell of lasagna fills the air, making my mouth water.

When I emerge from the bathroom, Rick is placing garlic bread on the table. He glances up as I approach. He strides over, wrapping his arms around me. "You all right?" he whispers.

"I'm fine," I whisper, hugging him back.

We pull apart as Mom announces, "Dinner's ready. I hope you're hungry."

"Starving," Dad replies, appearing around the corner. He bends over the lasagna and inhales deeply before taking his seat. "Oh, boy, that smells good."

Rick and I sit down, and Debbie sits directly across from Rick, of course. It gives her the best view.

"Where's Jeff?" I ask.

"He's going out for pizza with his friends tonight," Dad replies, slicing the lasagna into squares and portioning them onto plates, which he proceeds to pass around the table.

Dad says grace. Once everyone has received their lasagna, salad, and garlic bread, we all dig in.

Mom glances at me occasionally, but doesn't pry.

Rick eats heartily and engages in the conversation, easily flipping from harmlessly flirting with Debbie until she hides her crimson, giggling face behind her hand to talking to Dad about the size of the base in Korea and the weather there in the winter.

Once during the meal, my eyes meet my mother's and her eyebrows rise in a wordless question. I smile and shake my head in reassurance. She shrugs, munching another bite of her garlic bread.

After enjoying the cake we brought home for dessert, I help clear the table while Rick engages in a game of Connect Four with Debbie on the coffee table in the living room. Her squeals of delight reverberate on the walls when she wins. Judging by the number of squeals, I suspect Rick lets her win a lot.

Dad has retreated to his recliner with the *Reader's Digest*, his reading glasses planted firmly on the bridge of his nose.

I absent-mindedly rinse the dishes in the sink.

"A penny for your thoughts," my mother says softly, placing the dirty glasses on the counter next to me.

Startled, I jerk and drop the plate into the sink with a *clank*. "Mom! You scared me."

"Sorry," she chuckles. "I didn't mean to."

I continue rinsing the dishes silently.

"It's okay if you don't want to talk about it."

I glance at her. "No, that's not it. I just," I sigh. "I don't know that I want Rick to make the military a career, and he is determined that it's what he wants to do."

"Why is that a problem for you?" she asks, grabbing a cloth and wiping the counter.

"He's already going to miss our first year of marriage, first of all. Don't you think that's a bad sign of things to come?"

"I don't believe in good or bad signs, Heather. It is difficult, certainly. But perhaps you can think of it this way; you're getting the worst of it out of the way early on," she smiles cheerily.

I roll my eyes. "Yes, mother."

She bumps me with her hip. "Oh, come on. It will all work out. Just be sure to make your decisions together and always remember the word compromise. It may save your marriage one day. I know it saved ours."

"Wait. What?" I ask, incredulous. "When was your and dad's marriage ever in trouble?"

She looks meaningfully at me. "Heather, trust me. *Every* marriage will face a crisis at one point or another. Anyone who has been married more than a couple of years will tell you so." She rips off a sheet of aluminum foil and wraps the remaining garlic bread.

My mouth falls open. I always thought my parents were the perfect couple. I have never even heard them raise their voices at each other. "What? When? What crisis?"

"Oh," she sighs. "It was a long time ago. You were only about five or six and Jeff was a toddler. Debbie, of course, wasn't even in the picture. She may never have shown up if we hadn't gotten through that." She shakes her head.

I'm stunned into silence, dishes forgotten.

Mom glances at me, picking up a towel to dry her hands. "What? You think we've never had problems? We're people, too, you know."

"But...but," I stutter. "What *happened*?"

Mom folds the towel neatly on the counter and pats it twice before walking over to the hideous dinette. "Why don't you sit down with me and I'll tell you the story."

I fall into the chair across from her.

Mom turns her head and looks out the window at the setting sun, her eyes taking on a very distant look.

She draws a deep breath before she begins. "Well, your father had taken a position with the largest ad agency in Tulsa. It was the big promotion he had been working toward since graduating from college a few years before. He worked so hard for that. We both knew that it meant some longer hours and things, but we had no idea the reality of it." The sadness that dominates her features is unsettling.

"He was a junior account executive, so he had to really hustle to get clients. We knew he would have to work hard, but... He was the gopher for all the higher ups. He worked from about seven in the morning until late at night. Sometimes he wouldn't get home until midnight and then he would be up doing some paperwork for a few more hours most nights. Half the time, he didn't even bother coming to bed. There were many times I would wake up to find him asleep on the sofa in his clothes. On the weekends, it was worse. He would have to entertain clients, take them out for breakfast, lunch, or dinner. He would even take them to and from the airport, if necessary. It was ridiculous!

"The few minutes I got to see him each week, I would ask how much longer this was going to go on. He always told me, 'not much longer' and that he was doing it for *us*. His paycheck was substantial. In the beginning it was nice. I could buy pretty clothes and expensive things, but the longer it continued, the lonelier I became. What's the point in having pretty clothes if there's nobody to see you or take you out? I began to want my husband more than the money. I would cry, beg, cajole, and even ignore him. I did whatever I could do to get his attention. None of it worked. I could tell he was worn out. So was our marriage." She pauses to look me in the eye. "Heather, we had moved to Tulsa for him to take that promotion, so I had no friends and no family to rely on. I was trying to raise two small children by myself. It was awful." She shudders.

I always knew my mom was strong, but never considered how she got that way.

She draws another deep breath. "I even started to wonder if your father had a mistress. His clothes smelled of cigarettes and cheap cologne, plus one time I saw a smudge of lipstick on his collar. I was doing laundry one day and had pulled out his shirt to inspect it for stains. That's when I saw it. I almost fell on the ground, thinking the worst. I began to believe that it was the real reason he was out late almost every night; he had someone else on the side. I didn't even get to see him enough to confront him. I couldn't sleep, I couldn't eat; I just couldn't function.

"After almost a year, I had enough. I left him a letter on the counter where I was sure he would see it when he got home. I wrote 'read now' on the envelope in big, bold letters, so he would be sure to open it. Then I packed you guys up and left. I drove straight home to my parents' house, nine hours away."

"You *left* daddy?" I ask, aghast.

Her shoulders slump back in the chair. "Yes. I'm not proud of it, but I was at the end of my rope. I saw no other way out. We didn't have a marriage, and my children didn't have a father. I didn't care that our bank account was padded nicely. I was miserable. I know now that your father was miserable, too. Would you believe he didn't open the letter that night? He didn't see it until the next night. He had fallen asleep on the sofa and went to work the next morning. He didn't even know we were gone."

"That's horrible! Why would daddy do that?"

She places her hand on mine. "Honey, he was a different man then. I was a different woman, too. He didn't know. He just didn't know." She pulls a napkin from the holder and dabs her eyes. "Well, he waited another two days to call me because he couldn't get away from work. When he finally did call, I was fit to be tied. From my perspective, he had ignored me. I thought maybe he would come rushing up to reclaim me, apologizing for what he'd done and we'd be a perfect family."

"What did he do?" I ask breathlessly.

"Well, he did apologize for not being home, but tried to explain to me why he couldn't help it. I told him that he would have to either quit his job or quit his marriage because I wasn't going to put up with it."

"Oh, my gosh. What did he say?"

"I don't remember the exact words, but it was a long conversation consisting mostly of me yelling at him, and him trying to make me understand his side. It wasn't pretty. Needless to say, I stayed with my parents for a few more weeks," she wadded the napkin in her hands. "Those were the worst weeks of my life. I thought for sure my marriage was over and I was going to be a single mother. My heart was shattered."

"Daddy didn't call back?" I remember staying with my grandparents, but I thought we were on vacation.

"Oh, yes. He called every couple of days, whenever he could get time. He sounded as miserable as I felt. The calls always ended with me in tears. Your father, too."

"Dad *cried*??"

"Yes, he did. Looking back now, I realize that his heart was just as broken. When two people are joined in marriage, their hearts become one. When they're pulled apart, they're going to shatter. It's inevitable. That's why you just don't do it."

"Did..." I don't want to ask, but I need to know. "Did he have a mistress?"

"No," Mom chuckles. "I fully expected him to deny it, which he did. I didn't believe him. It wasn't until later that I found out it was a harmless hug he had given to an older secretary at her retirement. I found that out from one of his co-workers, actually." She shakes her head. "A simple misunderstanding almost broke our marriage. I think lies break up more marriages than any truth ever could."

"Thank God," I say, relieved.

"Oh, trust me. I did!" she laughs. "If he had gone out and cheated on me, my father was going to have his head."

"What did Nana and Poppy say about all this?"

"They were really hurting for me, but didn't believe I should've left him. They think I should've stayed and dealt with it. But I couldn't. I was so hurt. So anyway," she sighs. "Your dad finally convinced me to come home. He said he had done some soul-searching and wanted to do whatever it took to make our marriage work. So I packed us all up again and drove the nine hours to come home. When we got there, he was waiting for us. He looked absolutely horrible, skinny with dark circles under his eyes. To say the house was a mess would be painting a pretty picture. Everything was a wreck. When we pulled up, he came right out of the house and pulled the car door open, yanked me out and into his arms. He started sobbing." She turns to me. "He was openly *sobbing*, Heather. I had never seen that before and haven't seen it since. Not even when his parents passed away. He kept telling me he loved me and missed me. You started crying, too, seeing your father like that. I don't think you remember that...?" She looks at me, concerned.

"No," I shake my head. "I don't remember that at all."

"Well, good. I wasn't sure if you would or not. I'm glad you don't. It was a hard time."

"So what happened with his job?" I want to erase the image of my father sobbing.

"Well, he and I had a long talk that night. I gave him an ultimatum; I told him that we couldn't continue like we were. If he couldn't get his hours to a reasonable amount each week, then he would have to find another job or we were gone for good. He agreed, but tried once more to bring up his paycheck. Heather, we were very well off. It basically comes down to this." She taps the table, speaking with deep conviction. "If your father had remained on that career path, we would be making enough money to purchase a new car almost every year and pay for all three of you to go to any college you wanted. He's *that* good at what he does. But the money isn't important. Relationships mean so much more than any paycheck."

I am speechless.

Mom looks around at her surroundings, the home that has heard laughter, crying, and lots of screaming from one whiny teenager. It's modest, but comfortable. My parents could in no way afford new cars or a fancy college education. A smile slowly spreads across her face. "Yes, we made the right choice. Your father made the right choice."

"So what happened with his job?"

"Well, he tendered his resignation that week. He asked if he could take a position that allowed him to have more time with his family." She lowers her head. "They practically laughed in his face. At that time, in the seventies, men were not encouraged to put their families first. It was understood and accepted that a hefty paycheck *was* putting your family first." She shrugs. "So he left and looked for a job with another agency. It was the same story all around. If he wasn't willing to work long and grueling hours, then he wasn't going to get anywhere. He finally found a job with a small printing press and we moved here."

"Do you regret any of that, Mom? Do you think Daddy would've eventually been able to have more time at home and still make good money?"

She shakes her head. "No. Money is just a way to buy stuff. Besides, I've seen over the years that all the executives he worked with have since divorced, some a few times over. Only one of them is still married, but he doesn't know his children or his wife. It's terrible. So you see; your father changed his dream to save our marriage. He made our marriage, and our family, his dream instead."

Stunned into silence, I stare at the floor while processing this revelation.

"I want you to remember that, Heather. Your father made a tremendous sacrifice for me and for our family. He was, and is, very good at what he does. He could've gone far, but he chose the better path. You're both very young, and Rick is just starting out. Give it some time. Don't pressure Rick to make any specific choice just because it's what you want, or think you want, right now. If you do, he may resent you for it. The military life is going to be challenging, but it will be rewarding, too."

"But you just told me that Daddy working long hours and always being gone almost cost you your marriage. It sounds to me like Rick should get out of the military right now if we don't want the same thing!" I feel vindicated hearing her story; Rick should definitely not make the military a career. It won't work.

Mom shakes her head vehemently. "No, no, no. That is not what I'm saying, Heather. I am telling you that we had to compromise in order to save our marriage. He gave up moving on the fast track in his career and I gave up a lot in terms of material wealth. But the point is that you can't dictate to him what he should do."

"You dictated to Daddy," I reply defensively. "You told him he had to choose his career or his marriage. How is that any different?"

Mom sighs heavily. "Yes, I did. I was very young and foolish. I am not saying that I regret the outcome, but I do regret the method I used to make it happen. Fortunately, your father was already miserable, too, but he thought the paycheck was enough to make up for it. Rick seems to really love being in the military. He has a heart to serve this country. Being by his side is also serving this country. Think about that. He certainly isn't doing it for the money. That's completely different. Don't force your husband to sacrifice something that means so much to him because you don't like it right *now*."

"Yeah. I guess you have a point."

Mom rises. "Heather, just don't think that the way things are now is the way they'll always be. Things, and people, change. You will, too." She bends over to kiss the top of my head, pats my shoulder, and walks out.

I prop my elbows on the table and rest my chin in my hands, watching the fading sunset through the kitchen window. I know compromise will be important, but it sounds like my father's job almost cost them their marriage. I can see how my marriage will be strained if Rick makes this a career. He's gone this whole year and when he gets back we have to wait to be told where we're going to live. It is going to be a difficult adjustment for me.

But Rick is worth it.

"You all right?" Dad asks, startling me. Both of my parents have a way of sneaking up.

I look up at my father's face; the crinkles around his eyes and the lines that frame his mouth. Although there are some furrows on his brow, they're not as deep as the lines that have been etched by years of laughter.

"Dad, I didn't know that Mom left you when I was little."

"Oh, that," he rolls his eyes. "Yeah, that was a pretty rough time. But we got through it."

"Mom says you gave up your career for her. For us."

Dad sits in the chair that was recently vacated. "Well," he starts. "It was just a job after all. No big deal."

"That's not what Mom says. She said you were making a lot of money, and you gave it all up because she told you to."

"It was something I knew I had to do; otherwise, I was going to lose her. I didn't want that."

"Have you ever regretted your decision?"

"Absolutely not," he responds without hesitation. "It was the right choice, and I figured that out pretty quickly. Your mom packing up and leaving helped me to realize that. Those were the worst weeks of my life." A hollowness flashes across his eyes.

I vacate my chair, walk around the small dinette and kiss my father's cheek. "Thanks for being a great dad."

He blinks a few times, clears his throat, and grins. "My pleasure." He pats my hand, rises, and leaves, clearing his throat one more time.

"I am the champion!" Debbie crows from the living room, followed by the crash of Connect Four pieces hitting the coffee table.

I finish loading the dishwasher and pad into the living room, plopping down in my mother's chair and folding my legs under me.

Rick glances up, smiles, and returns his attention to the game. He can easily win, but instead places his piece in a square that ensures Debbie's victory. She takes advantage of it and crows again, bouncing up and down excitedly.

"Well, squirt," Rick chuckles in mock defeat. "You bested me again! I think I'll call it a night."

"Ah! One more game; I promise to take it easy on you," she begs.

Rick shakes his head. "I know when I'm beat."

"It's getting late, bug," Dad quips, walking in from the hallway. "It's time to get your shower. You have school tomorrow."

Debbie sighs heavily and starts packing up the game.

Rick approaches me cautiously. "Ready for bed?"

I nod. He takes my hand and leads me down the hall.

Once he closes the door behind us, he turns to me, pulls me in and kisses me hard. When he releases me, my cheeks are tingling.

"What's that all about?" I ask breathlessly.

Wrapping his arms around me and holding me close, he whispers, "I don't have much time left, and I don't want to spend it arguing."

At the mention of our short time together, I grip him tighter. "Me, either."

We come together urgently, almost desperately. He has only a few more days left before he returns to Korea.

Four more long, lonely months apart.

Afterwards, lying in his arms, he asks, "What did you talk to your mom about for so long in the kitchen?"

I tell him the story of my parents' crisis. Once I finish, he is silent for so long, I wonder if he's fallen asleep.

"What did you take away from that?" he asks softly.

"The story? Well, that he…" I stop myself. "He made the right decision in the end."

"So he gave up his career to save his marriage?" There's a slight edge to his voice.

Choosing my words carefully, I reply, "Well, he had such a crazy job. It was insane. But my biggest take away is that sometimes we have to compromise. I will compromise for you, Rick. You're worth it."

Rick sighs deeply, kissing my head. "Let's get ready for bed."

Rising, I dress for bed and head to the bathroom to finish washing the remnants of my once beautiful make over away.

As we snuggle close that night, I both want and don't want to talk. I want reassurance that Rick will be with me, but I'm afraid of what compromises I will have to make.

How much of my heart will be chipped away as we walk his chosen path?

CHAPTER EIGHT

February, 1989

Rick's remaining days on leave are spent together, but not talking about *it*. The topic is taboo and neither of us brings it up. Our desire for each other is the glue that keeps us together.

It is enough.

Too quickly, the day arrives when we have to drive him to the airport. The military will take my husband away. Again.

I wake with dread and heaviness in my heart. It wasn't that long ago when I did this for the first time. It isn't any easier.

I don't want it to be. I never want it to be.

When I open my eyes this particular morning, Rick is propped on one elbow, staring at me. My eyes meet his.

"Morning," he says quietly. I'm glad he didn't pair it with the word "good." It doesn't fit. Not right now.

"Hi," I reply, reaching hungrily for him. His response mirrors my need.

In the end, I cry. It will be a very long time before I can kiss him again or feel his warmth next to me.

My heart throbs at the thought.

Glancing at the clock, Rick murmurs, "It's time. We have to get ready."

"No no no no..." I cry, clinging tighter to him, begging. "Please don't make me do this."

Rick hugs me tightly, rocking gently back and forth. "I don't want to, Heather. Believe me. I don't want to."

He holds me for a few moments longer before gently pulling at my arms. "Honey bun, we have to get moving."

I cry through my shower. Make-up is useless.

When we bring his duffel bag to the living room, my face is swollen from bawling.

Jeff's eyes grow wide when I come into view. For the first time ever, he is speechless. Debbie is nowhere to be seen.

Mom immediately rises and engulfs me in a hug, her eyes glassy with sympathetic tears. "I'm sorry, sweetheart. I'm so sorry," she whispers.

"That might be a good idea," Dad says quietly, clapping Rick on the shoulder. Rick pulls away from my father, his eyes full of concern as he regards me.

"What?" I hiccup. "What's a..." hiccup. "...good idea?"

"Maybe you shouldn't come to the airport, Heather. It's too much," my father says gently.

My heart squeezes. "I can't miss this," I protest, turning to Rick. "I don't want to miss a moment with you." I start bawling all over again.

"It's okay if you don't come. I don't think you can handle it," he says.

I shake my head. "No. I want to come." My mother rubs my back.

"Are you sure? This is really hard, for both of us. You don't have to."

"No," I protest. "I am coming."

Jeff shifts from foot to foot. Clearing his throat, he mutters, "I'll meet you guys in the car." He casts a sympathetic glance in my direction and disappears out the front door, scooping up Rick's duffel bag on the way.

"Where's Debbie?" I ask thickly, sniffing. Mom thrusts a tissue in my hand and I smile gratefully at her.

"She doesn't want to see him off," Dad replies.

Rick attempts to lighten the mood. "I never knew I had this much impact!"

Dad clears his throat and looks at his watch. "It's time."

I nod stoically, take a deep breath and follow Rick and my parents outside. Just as it was when we dropped him off the first time, I ride with Rick in his truck and my family follows behind in their car. My little Honda Civic has been sitting idle since Rick arrived.

"I'm really sorry about this, Heather," he says once we pick up speed on the freeway. "I wish I didn't have to leave you again."

"Me, too," I whisper quietly, swiping at my eyes.

"I won't be gone nearly as long this time. We're more than halfway through my tour."

I spend the remainder of our time together just being in the moment, not thinking about anything else. All I have is right now.

I hold it together for the most part until we walk him up to the boarding gate and his flight number is called out over the intercom.

As the line grows for those holding boarding passes, I start to hyperventilate.

Rick stands in front of me, rubbing my arms. "Keep it together. It's going to be all right." He grabs my face, kissing me hard before squeezing me. Just like when he arrived two short weeks ago, I bury my face in his neck and inhale his scent.

I do my best to imprint his scent into the deepest part of myself.

The final boarding call for his flight announces rudely overhead.

"I have to go," he whispers hoarsely, pulling back, away from me.

"Oh, God," I gasp. "No."

My parents wrap their arms around me, holding me up. Even Jeff comes over to hold my hand.

Rick reaches in for one final kiss. "I'll call as soon as I can and I'll be back. I promise." He takes two steps back, his eyes mahogany pools of pain, before turning to give his boarding pass to the flight attendant. He turns one final time toward me, waves, and disappears down the gangway.

Somehow, my family manages to get me to the parking garage. I insist on riding in Rick's truck.

When we arrive home, I lurch toward our, my, bedroom to collapse on the bed, holding tight to the pillow that so recently had cradled my husband's head. Burying my face in it, I inhale deeply searching for his scent.

It's still there. Faint, but still there.

****

Much later, I awaken with a throbbing head and heart, still clinging tightly to Rick's pillow. My arms ache.

Rolling slowly over to squint at the clock, I groan realizing I've slept for three hours.

I wish it could've been four months.

Rubbing my face, I crawl out of bed and go to the bathroom before stumbling into the living room. Upon spying me, my mother leans forward in her seat.

"Are you all right, honey?" she asks, searching my face.

"No," I shake my head, collapsing on the sofa next to her and dropping my head onto her shoulder. "I'll never be all right." I can't believe I have tears left to shed.

"Oh, sweetie," she sighs. "I'm so sorry."

"This hurts even more than when he left the first time, Mom," I cry.

"I know."

"How am I going to make it?"

"You will because you have to."

I cry harder. She's right.

****

My forehead is sore. Rick calls collect when he lands in Hawaii before his final flight back to Korea. The crackling line is a painful reminder of the increasing distance between us. We don't talk for very long because the charges are going to be outrageous.

I go back to work a few days later because I have to. Mom and Dad both think it will be good for me to occupy my time.

One afternoon a few weeks later, I am woodenly dragging the tiny green net around the fish tank at the pet store when a voice interrupts my reverie.

"You all right?" Tina, my co-worker, asks softly next to me.

"No."

"I'm really sorry, Heather," she says.

I'm tired of everybody apologizing to me.

"Thanks," I respond flatly.

"Anything I can do?" she asks, hooking up the tank vacuum.

"No."

She sighs. "Listen, my friends and I are going out for pizza on Friday night. Wanna come with?"

"No."

"Yes, you do. I am not going to let you just sit at home and mope." She nudges me with her elbow. I drop the tiny net into the tank. "Sorry."

I fish out the net. "I'm not going to mope."

"Yes, you are. You're moping now."

I finish with the net and take the vacuum from her to start cleaning the rocks at the bottom of the tank. "I'm not moping, Tina. I'm....my husband is halfway around the world. It's not easy."

Tina hugs me briefly. "Listen, I know it's hard. But you have to get through this somehow. Why not do it with some friends?"

I glance over at her freckled, smiling face. Tina is ninety pounds soaking wet with a head full of raging red curls. She reminds me of a grown up Pippy Longstocking, minus the braids.

Seeing the confidence on her face, I realize she could very well show up at my house and drag me out. "All right, I'll come. But don't expect me to be cheerful."

"Good!" She grins. "Are you working Friday?"

"Yes."

"Then we can just ride together after work. You'll be all right, Heather. You'll see!"

"Uh huh."

Mom and Dad are pleased to hear that I have plans on Friday night.

"Good for you!" Mom smiles. "Go out, have some fun. I know Rick would like you to."

****

The days drag on until Friday afternoon, still with no further call from Rick. I pour my heart and my pain out in letters to him every day, both at home and on the trails. I know he will call when he can.

Three weeks down, only thirteen more to go.

Eternity.

HELLO AND GOODBYE

****

"All right you two, finish up the last of the rabbit cages and get on outta here," the manager gestures with a flourish toward the glass tanks that house the bunnies along the back wall. It's almost five o'clock. He disappears toward the front of the store to help the few customers here on a Friday afternoon.

Tina is bent over at the waist, elbow deep in cedar shavings working on the first of the tanks. We're both wearing long green gloves that make our hands and forearms sweat.

"These little buggers really don't want a clean cage!" she laughs, trying to corner the little rabbits to put them in a cardboard box that has a towel nestled in the bottom. It will house them temporarily while we clean their tanks. They squeal and wriggle out of her hands.

"Try letting them climb onto your hand instead," I suggest.

"Ha!" she hoots, holding up three bunnies to me in triumph before carefully placing them in the prepared box. "Only two more to go." By the time she collects the remaining bunnies, she's practically in the tank with them.

The ridiculous scene makes me chuckle.

"How about you go ahead and start cleaning this cage out and I'll collect all the bunnies into the box?" Tina suggests, bending over the next cage.

"Just remember to keep them separate. We can't mingle them or we'll have more bunnies and Mr. Sikes won't appreciate that," I remind her.

"Oh! Yeah, thanks." She grabs two more cardboard boxes and prepares them with towels before wrestling with the creatures. They squeal and protest just as loudly as their peers. It takes awhile, but Tina prevails.

She wipes her arm across her forehead, attempting to tuck her wayward curls back into place. Placing her hands on her hips, she surveys her accomplishment. "Whew, they sure are fast! I'm working up a real appetite here. You?"

I scoop the soiled cedar shavings from the first tank into a plastic bag for disposal. "I don't have much of an appetite."

"Heather, it's *pizza*. How can you not want that?" she asks, reaching for a scoop and digging into the shavings in the second tank.

I glance at her and frown. "It's just pizza, Tina."

"It's my favorite food in the whole world. I love the chewy crust, melted gooey strings of cheese, pepperoni..." She shakes her head. "Let's hurry. I'm really getting hungry!"

She picks up her pace and we actually finish in under an hour. The bunnies are happily snuffling around in their clean homes while we drag the bags of soiled shavings out to the dumpster behind the store. We wave to Mr. Sikes on our way out.

"Good job, girls. Have a great weekend," he calls over the jingle of the bell on the door.

"Do you want to drive or do you want me to?" Tina asks.

"You can drive."

"Cool," she quips. "It's only ten minutes away. You'll like everybody."

Once we climb in her car and pull away, I ask, "How many people are coming?"

"Oh, about eight or so."

My mouth drops open. "Eight people? Do I even know any of them?"

She casts a sideways glance at me. "You might know a few of them. Lauren and Holly graduated from your high school. Same year as you, too."

I frown, trying to place the names with faces. "I don't think I know anyone named Lauren or Holly."

"It doesn't matter. I'm sure they'll all love you and you'll love them," she says cheerfully. "Here we are!"

She pulls into the Pizza Palace parking lot and slides into a space near the front. "Front row, no less! That's a good sign!"

The Pizza Palace was a popular hang out in high school. The pizza is decent; greasy the way teenagers like it. I haven't been there in a long time; I haven't really been in any of my old hang-outs since Rick and I started dating.

When we enter the restaurant, we're immediately blasted with music from the juke box and chatter all around. The familiar smell of pizza fills my nostrils. It's not appealing. As a matter of fact, my stomach rolls briefly when the aroma hits me. I swallow hard to keep from gagging.

Tina scans the space with her eyes before excitedly waving her hand at a group who wave back, gesturing for us to join them.

She grabs my arm and pulls me along, wedging between chairs and tables back to a large booth filled with unfamiliar faces. The group moves to make space for us. Fortunately, the booth is enormous. Three half-devoured pizzas are nested on stainless steel racks in the middle of the table. Pitchers of soda haphazardly take up more space. An empty beige plate and red cup are thrust in front of me. Some things will never change; these same beige plates and cups have been here for years.

"Soda?" a male voice asks. I glance toward the voice; the face attached to it flashes a grin.

"Uh, sure," I stammer. Tina is sitting on the other side of the booth, chatting to the girl next to her.

I didn't realize I sat next to a guy. I inch closer to the edge of the booth so that our legs don't touch.

"What's your poison? We have Coke, Diet Coke, and root beer," the guy gestures to the pitchers.

"I'll have root beer, please."

He fills my cup and passes it to me. "Pizza?"

"Cheese," I reply. He takes my plate and places two slices on it. "Just one," I protest.

He frowns momentarily. "Ah, don't be shy. There's plenty to go around."

I smile timidly, inching a little closer to the edge. I glance at Tina. She catches my eye and I glare at her.

"I'm John, by the way," the guy reaches his hand out to me, smiling confidently. He's not what I think of as handsome, but his body language exudes confidence.

I take the proffered hand and squeeze quickly. "I'm Heather. Nice to meet you."

"Sorry, Heather! Guys!" Tina yells over the noise. "This is my friend Heather. Heather, these are the guys." She grins.

The group enthusiastically greets me. I feel my cheeks burn and wave shyly around the table. I hate being the center of attention. This was a mistake. I don't know any of these people. But Tina drove, so I have no means of escape.

I choke down a bite of pizza and swallow some of the almost flat root beer while everyone goes back to their conversations.

Everyone except John, whose attention remains on me.

"So," he starts, stuffing another bite of pizza into his mouth. "You're from here?"

I nod, taking extra time sipping from my cup.

"I know your face!" a girl blurts from the back of the booth, pointing at me. My cheeks burn hotter. "We graduated together! I'm Holly. We used to be in trig together!" She grins, showing off pearly white and straight teeth.

"Oh, right. Nice to see you again." I have no clue who she is.

Holly nudges the girl next to her. "Lauren, don't you remember her? That's Heather, the one who sat in the front of the class. You were such a brainiac!" She rolls her eyes, laughing. "We all wanted to cheat off you during tests, but Mr. Waverly was always watching, and you sat so close to his desk."

Lauren squeals and smiles at me. "Yes! I remember you! Wow. You're still here, huh? I thought you'd be off to college or something."

Are my cheeks actually on fire? "Um, no. I am still here."

"College girl, huh?" John says, moving closer until our knees touch. "That's cool."

"Uh, no. I'm not a college girl." I move my knee away so that we're not in contact, trying to be nonchalant about it. He moves closer, closing the gap so that we're touching once again. If I inch any further away, I will be on the floor.

Panic sets in. I really want to get out of here. I try to catch Tina's attention, but she's engrossed in her pizza and laughing at something someone said.

Trying to ignore the offensive knee and the person attached to it, I engage in conversation with the two classmates I don't remember. "I always liked to sit up front in class, so I could see everything. Being in the back is too distracting for me."

"Yeah, I didn't care about that. I could never tear my eyes off of Nick," Lauren replies, rolling her eyes at Holly.

"Yeah, he was so *gorgeous*!" Holly squeals. Their childish laughter tinkles around the booth. "I wonder whatever happened to him."

"Dunno," Lauren shrugs. "The last I heard he went to college in Austin. He got a scholarship or something. So why are you still here, Heather? I thought for sure you would be out of this place."

I squeeze my legs together trying to put some space between John and me. He doesn't allow it; his knee follows mine.

I hold up my left hand and wiggle my fingers at them, showing off my wedding ring. "I got married, first of all. He's in the military and so I am waiting to see where we're going to be stationed before I decide anything."

The knee backs off. Thank God.

"Oh! That's cool! Is he working tonight?" Holly asks, sipping from her cup.

"He's actually in Korea for a year," I reply, choking down another bite of pizza. I won't cry here.

"Oh!" they reply in tandem cries of sympathy.

"That's awful!" Lauren cries, placing her hands across her chest. "How long has he been gone?"

"Eight months," I reply. "He was here for two weeks in January. We've got just under four months left."

The knee is back. This guy is a real creep. "That must be hard on you," John says, turning what he must think is a meaningful look in my direction.

"Yes, it is," I answer before turning my attention to John and his knee. "I'm sorry, would you mind moving over a little? I'm right on the edge of the booth." I smile imploringly.

He slides ever so slowly over, one whole inch. "Sorry. Is that better?"

"Actually a little more would be perfect." I smile broadly.

His shoulders slump slightly, and he moves over sufficiently for me to put my purse between us.

"Thank you. You're a real gentleman," I say, sipping my soda.

The conversation, and the evening, is filled with chatter reminiscent of high school. I'm not in high school anymore. At least John seems to accept my lack of interest and thankfully turns his attention elsewhere.

Finally, at eight thirty, I can't take anymore.

"Excuse me," I say, sliding out of the booth. "Tina, I am going to use the restroom and then would you mind taking me to my car? I really need to get going."

Tina blinks in surprise. "Oh. Sure. You're ready to go?"

"I hope you don't mind. I have to get up early," It's true – I have to work at Payless tomorrow. "It's not far, and if you want to come right back you can," I offer.

"Sure," she smiles.

I nod, pick up my purse, and make my way to the bathroom. When I get back, Tina is saying her goodbyes and hugging a few members of her group.

John's eyes follow me as I return to the table and say my goodbyes, as well.

"It was nice to meet all of you," I smile, careful not to look specifically at John. "It was nice to see you two again, Holly and Lauren. Thanks for letting me join you tonight."

"It was our pleasure!" Lauren says.

"It's good to see you, too," Holly adds. "Don't be such a stranger! We come here almost every Friday. You're welcome to join us any time."

"Thank you." I glance around the table one last time and smile.

Suddenly, John rises from his seat, takes my hand and kisses it, trying to hold my eyes. "It really was a pleasure to meet you," he murmurs.

It takes everything within me not to respond by ripping my hand away and wiping it on my jeans.

Instead, I politely withdraw my hand and smile tightly at him, addressing the whole group. Ignoring his gesture may be the best course of action. "Enjoy the rest of your night."

Once we are in Tina's car, I turn to her. "What was your friend John's problem?"

She laughs, twisting in her seat while she slowly backs out. "He really is taken with you."

"He's creepy!"

She puts the car in drive and pulls into the light Friday evening traffic. "Oh, he's not my friend. Let's get that straight, first of all," she chuckles. "He's a friend of Terry's. Terry was sitting between Holly and my friend Rachel."

I don't know who she's talking about. "Do you know him at all?"

"Eh," she shrugs. "He joins us occasionally when we do stuff. He's not really my type, though. When you went to the bathroom, he asked me if you really were married. He's totally into you. He watched you the whole time." She giggles.

"Ew! You told him I am, right? I mean, does that mean nothing to him?" I blurt.

"I did and I don't know," she replies. "Like I said, I don't really know him. What I do know, he seems like a decent guy."

"What kind of a decent guy flirts with a married woman?" I retort.

"Hey, hey, calm down. It's okay. I think it's flattering. There's no harm in it, right? You're not going to do anything, so don't worry about it. Just let it go."

I shake my head and stare into the dark night.

"Did you have fun otherwise?" she asks after a few minutes.

"Yes," I don't want to hurt her feelings. "Thanks for inviting me. I appreciate it."

"Cool. You can join us every Friday like Holly said, if you want. We usually go there, but we mix it up every now and then. Get Chinese or something," she says cheerfully.

I would rather not run into John again.

"No, that's okay."

"Oh," she replies quietly, pulling up behind my car.

"Please don't take it wrong, Tina. You're a good friend, and I appreciate you trying to cheer me up, but I just don't think that's really my thing. I'm more of a small group kind of girl." I smile gently at her.

She quickly rallies. "I understand. They can be a bit much. I'm glad I got you out of the house tonight, though! You need to do that more often, girl."

I gather my purse and open the door. "Thanks again," I call over my shoulder.

"No problem! I'll see you at work!"

Mom and Dad are sitting in the living room watching their favorite show when I walk in.

"You're home early," Dad glances at me, smiling.

"We thought you'd be out for another couple of hours," Mom adds.

"Did you have fun?" Dad asks.

"It was all right," I respond, dropping my purse and keys onto the hall table and plopping into a chair with a sigh. "Not really my thing, though."

"What do you mean?" Mom asks.

"Well, everyone talked about high school stuff. I graduated four years ago. I really don't want to re-hash it. It's like they haven't grown up yet."

"Did you know them from high school?" Dad asks.

"Two of them knew me, but I don't remember them. The others I have no clue."

"Well, at least you went out, Heather. That's a good thing." Mom smiles.

"How was your night?" I ask.

"Same old thing," Dad replies, patting Mom's knee. "Debbie is having a sleepover at Casey's house, and Jeff is out with his buddies. It's just your old Mom and Dad here at home."

"Oh, yeah. It's a rough life," Mom chuckles. "But we like it."

"The commercials are over," Dad nudges Mom. They both glue their attention back to the program.

I smile watching my parents. I always thought of them as sort of old fuddy duddies, but there's a certain comfort to be found in their companionship. I hope Rick and I will have that, too.

Loneliness creeps in. I miss him so much. I write him another letter before turning in for the night, keenly aware of the cold, empty space next to me.

CHAPTER NINE

February – March, 1989

Tina is cool toward me the following week. I didn't want to hurt her feelings. She was only trying to help.

I sidle up to her at the hamster cages. The tiny creatures are piled up like tan cotton balls, all napping. Tina efficiently dumps the food and water for fresh refills.

"Hi, Tina."

"Hi," she replies mechanically.

"Are you mad?"

"No," she sighs, glancing at me. "I'm just…bummed."

"What about?"

"Well, I went back to the pizza place and John was trying to pump me for information about you."

I'm aghast. "What? Why?"

She gathers her supplies and moves down the line of cages. I follow. "I think he's really into you, Heather."

"That guy is an absolute creep and I…"

"I told him to knock it off. Even Tony told him to back off." She hesitates, pressing her lips together.

"I hope you set him straight. That guy gives me the willies."

She frowns, her lips a thin line. There's something she's not telling me.

"What's wrong?"

"Well, I did mention that we work together here." She cringes, seeing my expression.

"You *what?* Do you think he'll show up here?" I glance around in horror.

"No," she shakes her head. "I really doubt it. I made it very clear that you're not available, so... He really made a bad impression on you, didn't he?" she asks.

"He's a total creep, Tina." I take the food from her, refill the dish and nestle it back into the cedar shavings. One puffball detaches itself from the pile, its whiskers twitching nervously in my direction.

"I'm really sorry, Heather. Please believe me."

"I do. You were trying to help. I just hope he doesn't show up here."

He doesn't show up until the following week. I am toward the back of the store when the bell rings over the door. I happen to glance up and recognize his face in profile.

Gasping, I practically drop the scoop in my hands. Ducking down before he sees me, I hobble toward the back room as fast as I can in a bent over position, closing the door quickly behind me.

In a few minutes, Mr. Sikes appears in the back room with a puzzled expression on his face, looking around. He spies me cowering behind the pallet of dog food bags in the corner, peering over the top.

"What are you doing hiding back here? I thought you were cleaning the..."

"I'm sorry, but are you looking for me?" I interrupt, rising to a standing position.

He frowns. "Yes. There's a young man here to see you." He turns to go.

"Wait! Tell him I'm not here and I'm not coming back." I cower back behind the pallet of dog food.

Mr. Sikes blinks in surprise. "What? Why would I do that?"

I quickly fill him in on the highlights of the story.

Mr. Sikes narrows his eyes, thinking. "All right. But just this one time, you understand. I don't like turning away customers."

"He's not a customer. He's only here to see me, right?"

His eyebrows rise. "True... Okay, I'll do it this once. But I hope he gets the hint. This is not the place for tom foolery." He wags his index finger sternly at me before disappearing, closing the door behind him.

Mr. Sikes doesn't like drama; he says it's not good for the animals.

I remain hunkered down behind the dog food for quite awhile before he reappears, his head popping around the corner of the door.

"He's gone. It took some doing, but I let him have it. He won't be back," he grins, proud of himself.

I rise with a sigh of relief. "What did you say?"

"I told him you weren't here and he argued with me because I had just told him you were. He asked why you were gone all of a sudden and I told him listen buddy, she doesn't want to see you. She's a married woman, and you would do well to leave her alone! I won't have this nonsense in my store!"

I snort a laugh. "You really said that?"

His cheeks pink and he nods decidedly. "I did. I'd do it again, too. Now get back to work," he replies gently. He opens the door wide for me to pass.

"Thanks, Mr. Sikes." I walk quickly out of the back room, glancing briefly at the front door before returning to my duty.

So much poop, so little time.

****

The phone rings that evening during dinner. As soon as I pick it up, I'm sure it's Rick. There's a crackle on the line.

"Hello?" I ask anxiously.

"Hey, honey bun! How are you?" his voice echoes.

"I'm glad to finally hear from you! I haven't even gotten a letter."

"I know. The mail here is squirrely. You should be getting some soon, though. I started mailing some as soon as I got back. I wanted to let you know that I put in for Radley as my base of preference. I should get my orders in the next month or two. Then I'll send you copies, so you can get us on the waiting list for housing, okay?"

"Okay," I nod. "I'm glad. I really miss you."

He's silent for a moment. "I know. I miss you, too. It really stinks being apart, but it won't be for much longer. Hang in there."

"I will," I reply, trying to control the waver in my voice. "It's just hard."

"Are you all right otherwise?"

"Yes, I'm just stressed with you being gone. My stomach isn't doing well."

"Try to relax. I'm all right and so are you. We'll be together before you know it."

I don't know how to answer. "I love you, Rick. I miss you."

"Miss you..." The line goes dead. We are cut off.

Well, at least we almost got to finish our conversation this time. Three more phone calls and we will be together. Perhaps that's a good way to think about it. My stomach roils.

"Did you have a good conversation?" Mom asks when I return to my seat.

"We got cut off." I push the food around my plate.

Dad reaches over and wraps his arm around my shoulder with a firm squeeze. "He'll be back before you know it."

"Yeah," I reply flatly, pushing my plate away. "I'm not very hungry."

"You barely touched it," Mom protests. "Heather, you're not looking well again."

"I know, I know," I sigh. "I can't help it."

"I think you look sick," Debbie pipes up. I glare at her and she quickly back tracks. "I don't mean you look really bad, you just don't look really *good*."

Surprisingly, Jeff remains silent, only occasionally glancing at me in sympathy. He has made a complete turn around since Rick left. I think having the *Reader's Digest* thrown at his head helped.

"I know what you mean. I don't feel very good, so I suppose I should look like it. I'm done." I rise and gather up my still full plate to take in the kitchen. Once I've scraped it into the garbage, I plod into the living room and dump myself onto the sofa, flipping aimlessly through the channels.

Quiet chatter and the clink of utensils on porcelain continue in the dining room. Eventually, dinner is done and the sound shifts to the kitchen, now intermingled with the splash of water in the sink.

"You ready for bed?" My mother's voice interrupts.

I blink up at her, confused. "What?" I squint around the room, orienting myself. "Did I fall asleep?"

"Yes," she chuckles. "A few hours ago."

I look at the television, confused. Dad is in his recliner, watching the news. I don't remember him even coming in the living room. "What time is it?"

"It's a little after nine," she sweeps the hair off my forehead.

I bolt upright. "What? Why didn't you wake me?"

"Why should I? You're tired, you can sleep."

I rub my face, yawning. "I guess. I'll just go to bed."

"Sleep good," Dad calls as I stumble down the hallway. I brush my teeth, wash my face, and fall onto the bed, exhausted.

My appetite continues to decline over the next couple of weeks and I can barely keep my eyes open some days. My hiking and biking adventures become shorter and less in number. I woodenly go through the motions of each day: shower, work, laundry, and writing letters to Rick. Mom thinks I might be depressed.

"Mom, I'm not depressed! Well," I amend my statement. "Not like *that* kind of depressed anyway. I just miss Rick."

"I know you do, but you just aren't yourself. You're not eating very well and you're sleeping a lot. It's worse than before. You know, I read in a magazine that sleeping a lot is one of the signs of medical depression."

"Mom, I'm okay, and I don't need to see a doctor for depression."

Her brow creases. "Are you sure? I really don't like how pale you are." She touches my cheek. "I worry about you."

I muster a smile, stifling a yawn at the same time. "I know. I will be all right."

"Do you think going out with some friends will help you?"

"No," I shake my head vehemently. "I don't want to and besides, I don't really have time for that. I am working two jobs, you know."

"All right. But I really hope you'll at least try to eat some more. You look unwell."

"I will." I mean it, but my appetite is just not there.

One afternoon the following week, I didn't eat breakfast and am in the middle of cleaning the bunny tanks when a severe wave of nausea rolls over me. I bolt for the bathroom which is, thankfully, unoccupied and dry heave into the toilet.

When I exit, Tina is waiting for me. "I heard that. It sounded awful. You okay?"

"Yes," I reassure her, wiping my forehead. "I just forgot to eat breakfast."

"And lunch, Heather. It's two o'clock." She thrusts a package of peanut butter crackers at me. "Here. Go sit in the break room and eat this. I'll finish the bunny tanks."

She frowns as I take the package. "Thanks."

"You're welcome." She turns and leaves.

I take a seat at the table in the break room, tearing into the package. My hands are shaking; I didn't realize it was so late. I finish the entire package and gulp down some water, too. Glancing at the clock on the wall, I fold my arms on the table and put my head down to rest for a few minutes.

"Heather? Heather, wake up," Tina shakes my arm.

I jerk my head up, peering at her. "What?" I ask, annoyed. I just wanted to rest for a second. Is that too much?

"Really? You've been back here for forty-five minutes is *what*. Are you all right?" She looks more alarmed than annoyed.

My eyes flick to the clock on the wall in disbelief. "Wow! I'm sorry!" I leap up and the room shifts. I grab the table to steady myself.

Tina grabs me around the waist. "Heather, don't pass out. You're white as a sheet. Sit."

I drop back into the chair. "I'm okay. Just give me a minute. I'm sorry; I didn't mean to fall asleep."

"Uh huh. Look, I think you need to go home. I'll tell Mr. Sikes you got sick." She looks genuinely worried. "I think you should see a doctor. You haven't looked like yourself for awhile. It's getting worse. Something's not right."

Wanting to just go home and go to bed, I nod and get up more slowly. The room doesn't shift this time. "Thanks for the crackers," I mumble, making my way out to gather my purse. I head to the front of the store with Tina in tow.

"Mr. Sikes, Heather needs to go home. She just got sick and, well, look at her!" She gestures to me.

Mr. Sikes peers at me, appraising my condition. "You do look rather peaked," he murmurs. "Go on home. I'll see you Thursday, if you're feeling better."

"Thanks," I mumble.

"You okay to drive home?" Tina asks, still worried.

"I'll be all right."

"You need to see a doctor!" she calls after me.

I wave, but don't turn around.

Once I walk in the front door, Mom's head pops around the corner from the kitchen, a confused expression on her face. "You're home early."

I nod. "I'm going to lie down. I don't feel good," I mumble, dumping my purse and keys on the table in the hall.

"Okay." She watches me go, drying her hands on a dish towel as I pass. "Want me to keep your dinner warm in the oven or wake you up?"

"I don't care," I reply, closing my bedroom door. I drop on my bed, curl up and immediately fall asleep.

The bed shivers and sinks on one side.

I take a deep breath and roll over, squinting. My mother is sitting on the edge of my bed, bathed in the glow of the light from the hallway. "Hey, Mom," I mumble, stretching. "What time is it?"

"About six. Are you hungry?" she asks.

"I slept for two and a half hours?" I sit up slowly, remembering my incident earlier. "Why does this keep happening? What's wrong with me?"

Mom rises, turns on the light, and closes the door. "Oh, I have a theory." She sighs and sits down again.

I squint in the brightness. "I'm not depressed, Mom."

"I know. How are you feeling?"

"I'm just really tired, a little dizzy, and not very hungry," I reply, rubbing my eyes.

"I have felt like that a few times myself," she answers quietly, eyeing me. "Anything else?"

"Not really. What are you getting at?"

"Heather, when was your last period?"

"My last period? What does...." Oh. My hands fly to my mouth as I calculate it in my head. It was before Rick came home. Almost two months ago.

I'm late. Really late.

"Oh...do you think I could...I could be *pregnant?*" I ask breathlessly. "Mom..."

Mom grins at me, nodding vigorously. "I do. Don't you?"

Stunned, I can only stare blankly into space. It hadn't even crossed my mind.

"I was thinking about how you've been acting lately, and I can't believe it didn't occur to me earlier," Mom begins, seeing that I've become mute. "It only makes sense. We should make an appointment soon. You need to know for sure."

Words still have not found their way into my head, much less my mouth.

"Heather, you'll need to make an appointment on the base soon," she repeats.

"But, how…"

"Heather, you know how," Mom chuckles. "Now, get up and let's get some food in you. If you are pregnant, then eating a little something will be good for you."

"But…"

Mom grabs me in a quick hug, before pulling back and looking me in the eye. "Deep down inside, you know it's true. Now, come on. Let's get going."

"But…"

"But what?" Mom asks, still grinning.

"Have you mentioned this to Dad?" I ask. Something else occurs to me and my cheeks pink. "Or Jeff, or Debbie?"

She frowns. "I mentioned it to your father, and he agrees with me. No, we haven't brought it up to Jeff or Debbie. Why would we?"

"When?"

Mom rises and smooths her skirt. "When what?"

"When did you bring this up to Dad?"

"Oh, a few days ago. I had my suspicions and wanted to know what he thought," she replies, placing her hands on her hips. "You're having the same symptoms I had when I was expecting all three of you."

My jaw drops. "A few *days* ago?"

"Yes," she replies matter-of-factly. "Now, let's get some dinner. I've kept yours warm."

I mutely follow my mother into the kitchen and fall into a chair at the little dinette. My food appears in front of me, startling me. Chicken and dumplings don't look appetizing, even though it is my favorite.

"Eat at least half, Heather. You need it," Mom encourages.

I swallow hard, grimacing. "It doesn't look good."

"I'm sure it doesn't, but eat anyway." She chuckles and joins me in an adjacent chair.

I dip the spoon in the steamy, cloudy broth and bring it to my lips. It doesn't taste bad, but it doesn't taste good, either. I take another spoonful, and another.

"Good. Keep going." Mom rises, busying herself at the sink.

I am able to finish just over half before I can't stand it anymore. I push the bowl away and sigh.

"Done?" Mom reaches for the bowl. I nod and she whisks it away. "Good. How do you feel?"

"Eh." I shrug.

"You don't like my chicken and dumplings anymore?" she jokes.

"Yes, but not right now." I smile wanly.

She brushes off my response, rinsing the bowl.

"Call and schedule your appointment tomorrow, all right?" Mom reminds me.

"What appointment?" Jeff's head pops into the kitchen. He grabs an apple from the fruit bowl on the counter, tearing a large crunchy chunk out of it between his teeth.

"Don't worry about that, Jeffrey Allen. It's not your business," Mom reprimands him.

His eyebrows rise in shock. "All right, gosh! I just asked a simple question, and I get hammered about it." He shakes his head and walks out, taking another chunk out of his apple.

Mom eyes me once more. "Call tomorrow," she whispers.

****

Thumbing through the booklet Rick gave me with all the numbers for various services on base, I discover the number for the clinic appointment line. It's not even noon and Mom has hounded me three times to make the appointment.

I am sure to have my ID card in front of me; Rick told me I would need that to schedule anything. It's one more thing I'm learning. He's considered my sponsor, and I'm his dependent. I don't particularly care for those terms.

Once I speak with the clerk, give her Rick's social security number, and schedule the appointment to have my blood drawn, I scribble it on a piece of paper and tuck it into my purse. The only thing I write on the calendar in the kitchen is "Heather – appointment 12:30" on the little square for this coming Friday.

Butterflies dance in my stomach. Could it be true? Could I be pregnant? Of course, we want to have children, but not this soon. Rick will come home to a ballooning wife. My heart sinks; if I am pregnant, how long will it be before I can tell him? He only gets to call once a month.

I relay the information to my mother, and she nods, smiling knowingly. Suddenly, she grabs me in a bear hug and kisses my cheek. "I'm so excited! Our first grandbaby!" she exclaims.

"Mom, we don't know for sure."

She waves her hand dismissively. "This is just a formality. I'm going to be a grandma!"

****

With the slightest pinch, the needle pricks the inner crease at my elbow. Slowly, thick burgundy liquid fills the slender tube. The sight of blood has never bothered me; on the contrary, I find the human body fascinating. Once the tube is full, the technician expertly and efficiently removes the tube followed by the needle, and places a cotton ball and a length of tape on the miniscule wound.

"All done!" he says, grinning at me.

"How long before I know the results?" I ask, bending my arm.

"You should know this afternoon, I would imagine."

"Thank you."

"Not a problem. Good luck."

I nod, gather my purse and enter the waiting room, where my mother waits anxiously.

"Well?" she asks excitedly.

I roll my eyes. "Mom, they said I should know this afternoon. Let's go."

"Will they call you or do you have to call them?"

"They'll call me, Mom."

"Did they say exactly what time?"

Exasperated, I stop walking and turn to her. "Mom, please. Stop. They'll call me and I don't know what time. All right?"

"I'm sorry, Heather. I am just so excited!"

"I can tell," I chuckle. "But keep a lid on it for now, will you? We still don't know if that's what it is."

She mutters, "Yes, we do."

The afternoon drags on, and the phone remains maddeningly silent. Finally, at 4:15, I can't stand it anymore. I pull the number out of my purse and dial the clinic. Five rings later, someone picks up.

"764th clinic, this is Airman Brown. How can I help you?"

"Hi, I had my blood drawn earlier for a pregnancy test. I was supposed to get a call today to find out the results, but I haven't heard from anyone."

"Hang on." There's a sigh followed by the sound of paper shuffling. "What's your name?"

"Heather Johnson."

"Who's your sponsor and what's his social?"

I bristle and give the information. More silence. I grip the phone tightly; my life may or may not change drastically at this moment.

"Yes, ma'am. I see that. I'm sorry, but there is nobody here to give you the results. They've all gone home for the day because it's a down day. You will be notified on Monday."

I blink, confused. "What? But I was told I would find out the results today. What is a down day?"

"I'm sorry, ma'am. But as I said, there's nobody here. A down day means that we are at minimum manning."

"But you're there," I blurt. "Can't you tell me what the results are?"

"No, ma'am. I am an airman, and I'm not authorized to read results over the phone. I'm sorry."

"What do you mean you can't read the results?! They're right there, aren't they?" Anger wells in me. My mother looks at me bewildered. I shake my head.

"Yes, ma'am, they're here, but as I told you – I'm not authorized to read results over the phone. It's against policy. You will be notified on Monday."

My mouth hangs open as I process this ludicrous situation. "But, but," I sputter. "But this is ridiculous! Isn't there anybody there who can *read?!* Just a simple yes or no! That's all I'm asking for!"

"No, ma'am," the airman repeats, exasperated. "I can't do it. I'm sorry. You'll find out on Monday."

Tears prick my eyes. "Great!" I slam the phone down on the wall, ending the conversation.

Mom's face registers shock; she worked hard to teach us manners and slamming the phone down to end a conversation is not good manners. "Heather, what in the world was that all about?"

"There's nobody there to tell me the results of the test because it's a 'down day'," I make air quotations. "The airman that answered the phone apparently can't read." I rub my face, letting the tears fall.

"What does that mean, for heaven's sake?"

I remove my hands, swiping the tears from my eyes. "It means there's nobody there to read my stupid results!" I wail.

"But, then who were you talking to?" Mom blinks, still bewildered.

"Some airman that can't *read.* She said she can't read results over the phone and nobody else is there to do it." I kick the floor. "I just want to know if I'm pregnant or not!"

Mom continues to blink, staring out the window. "That is the strangest thing I've ever heard. You're sure they told you they'd call you this afternoon? Maybe you misheard them?"

"I didn't mishear them, Mom. They lied to me, apparently."

"I'm sure it was just a mistake. I'm sorry, Heather. Well," she sighs. "I guess we'll wait until Monday, then. No sense in being upset over something we can't help. In the grand scheme of things, what's three days?"

"It's an eternity," I mutter, kicking the floor again.

"I understand how you feel, but," she shrugs. "There's nothing we can do. So let's just go about our business and enjoy the weekend. What do you want for dinner?"

"I don't care," I reply, rising. "I'm not hungry anyway. I'm going to lie down."

"Nap time?"

"Yeah."

Mom hugs me. "Don't let it get to you. It is what it is. How about shepherd's pie?"

"Sure," I mumble, disengaging myself and moping to my room.

I curl up on top of my comforter, hugging Rick's pillow tightly. His scent has completely disappeared even though I haven't washed the pillow case. Rather than sleep, my brain turns this event over and over. It's just not right; they said they would call me *today*. How could they not do that? This is a big deal to me, obviously not to them.

My mind wanders to the possibility of a positive pregnancy test and my stomach flips. I press my hand onto my belly; it's still flat and soft. What if there is a new life growing in there, one that is half me and half Rick? My stomach flips again.

Will it be a girl or a boy? I imagine a baby boy with Rick's sandy blond hair and my blue eyes. We could get a nice little seat to put on the back of my bike and take him biking with us. Maybe a baby girl with Rick's mahogany eyes and my dark hair; we could name her Snow White. My hair isn't black, but it's close enough.

I giggle at the thought of telling people we named our daughter Snow White. It would be pretty funny. Would Disney sue me for that? I'm not sure.

I bury my face into the pillow, inhaling deeply, searching for even the hint of Rick's scent. Nothing. It was worth a try. I wonder what Rick's reaction will be, if it's true. Will he be excited, scared, or both? Warming to the idea, I'm a little of both myself. I wish I could see his face when I tell him, if it's true. I picture the warmth in his eyes turning to liquid, and the crinkles that form around his eyes deepening when he smiles. He would hug me, kiss me, and tell me everything will be all right…

"Heather? Heather, wake up," Mom's soft voice interrupts my thoughts.

"Hm?" I stir. I look blankly at the emptiness next to me; I was sure Rick was there. My heart sinks; it was only a dream.

"Dinner's ready. Come on and get up. You need to eat something," Mom pulls me into a sitting position.

"All right," I yawn. "I was having a good dream."

"What about?"

"About telling Rick."

"I'm sure it was a good one."

"It was," I nod.

"Let's eat." Mom rises and I follow suit. I squint while my eyes adjust.

"Well, look who decided to join us!" Dad exclaims. "How are you feeling?"

Unable to stifle another yawn, I reply, "Tired."

"Well, you need to eat something. Your appetite isn't very good; that's why your energy level is so low," Dad says while filling a plate for me. Mom did indeed made shepherd's pie; the rich, brown gravy surrounding ground beef and vegetables oozes out of a crust of cheesy mashed potatoes.

Determined to eat whether my stomach likes it or not, I purposefully fill my fork and place it in my mouth. While the flavor is the same, the texture is unappealing. I gulp it down as quickly as I can with minimal chewing.

Debbie and Jeff make conversation with me; easy questions to answer and I try to be engaged. It's difficult.

When my plate is half empty, I push it away.

"Too much?" Mom asks.

I nod and place my hand over my mouth, trying to disguise the movement by pretending to wipe my mouth with a napkin.

"What's wrong, Heather?" Debbie asks, concerned. I glance at her and Jeff. He looks worried, too.

I lift my chin to keep from gagging and attempt a smile. "Nothing. I just…don't feel good. Excuse me," I reply tightly and rise. I barely make it to the bathroom and close the door before I can't contain it any longer; dinner makes a hasty reappearance in the toilet.

CHAPTER TEN

March, 1989

Blinking the sleep from my eyes, consciousness gradually replaces slumber like the sun chasing the moon from the sky at dawn. My thoughts come into alignment; it's Monday. I should hear the results of my test today. I spent the weekend with nothing else on my mind. During my shift at Payless on Saturday, I gave a large man a pair of pink ballet slippers to try on. In my own defense, they were in his size.

I will be surprised if the test comes up negative; I can't keep anything down or my eyes open.

I could tell Rick in a letter, but I would rather hear his reaction instead. I wish his calls were more frequent. I wish he didn't have to call at all; he should just be home. We have two months left. It had better go by fast.

Easing myself slowly into a sitting position, my stomach wakes up but doesn't send me bolting for the bathroom. A few deep breaths and I rise to greet the day. A scowl descends on my features and darkens my mood; I can't believe that airman wouldn't tell me the results on Friday.

"That's just dumb," I mutter, cinching my robe.

The scowl remains when I enter the kitchen and pour myself a cup of coffee. As the steaming liquid fills my mug, I continue muttering under my breath.

"Somebody woke up on the wrong side of the bed," Mom quips from the dinette. I glance in her direction; she regards me over the reading glasses that are perched on the end of her nose. Sections of the morning paper are scattered around the table. Her current piece of interest is the comics. My mother is quirky.

"I'm still mad about not hearing the results on Friday," I reply, taking residence in a chair across from her. I push a section of newspaper over to make room for my mug.

Mom removes her reading glasses, letting them drop onto her chest and hang by the beaded necklace they're attached to. "I agree," she sighs. "I don't understand that myself. But what is there to do but wait? Besides, I'm sure it's positive."

I take an unsteady sip. "Me, too."

"How are you feeling? Hungry?"

I shake my head. "Not in the slightest."

"Well, you know, eating a little something always helped me keep the nausea at bay. Soda crackers became my best friend for a few months."

I inhale the roasted richness of the coffee. That, at least, still smells good. "I'm afraid if I eat anything, it will just come right back up."

"At least try eating a few crackers," she says, retrieving some from the cupboard.

To appease my mother more than my stomach, I nibble on a few of them slowly in between sips of coffee.

"If I am pregnant, how should I tell Rick? Should I write him or wait for him to call?"

"How would you like to tell him?" she asks, refilling her own mug. "Do you want more coffee? I just took the last of it."

I shake my head. "No, thanks. I would like to tell him in person, but that's obviously not an option."

"So of your options, which would be better?"

"I don't know. Our conversations are always cut off and they're really bad connections. I'd like to hear his reaction. What do you think I should do?"

"It's up to you," she shrugs. "A letter may be the quickest way to get the news to him. Plus it's something you can save as a keepsake for the future."

"I suppose," I sigh. "I just would rather see and hear his reaction."

"Oh, that's all right. I'm sure you'll hear it in his voice when he does call. When is he supposed to call again?"

"He mentioned about the same time as last month, so another week and a half, I guess. But who knows. He'll call when he can."

"I don't think you'd want to wait that long to tell him, would you? Write the letter." She pats my hand.

"I will after I find out the results. I mean, there's still a chance I could have a horrible flu bug or something," I smile wryly.

"Of course." She returns her attention to the newspaper, placing the reading glasses back into position at the end of her nose.

****

The clock chimes two and my patience has gone. I still have not received the results of my test. Every time the phone rings, I dash over and answer only to be disappointed.

"Heather, go ahead and give them a call. This is utterly ridiculous!" My mother's patience has worn just as thin.

Not needing any convincing, I pick up the phone and dial the number. The phone is picked up on the third ring. A voice answers with the standard greeting.

Instead of waiting for them to ask for the information, I state why I'm calling immediately followed by Rick's social security number and my name. My fingers tap the wall impatiently while the person on the other end places me on hold.

Mom calmly walks over and gently removes my hand from the wall, rubbing it between both of hers. I smile gratefully at her.

When someone else picks up on the other end, I jerk and feel my heart rate accelerate.

This is it.

"Hello? Yes, I'm Heather Johnson and I'm calling to find out the results of my pregnancy test. My blood was drawn on Friday."

"One moment, please," the gentleman on the other end responds. I roll my eyes, anticipating. Papers shuffle for an eternity. "Yes, here we are. Your results are positive. So, yes, you are definitely pregnant. Congratulations, Mrs. Johnson."

For the briefest of moments, time stops. I actually feel the air entering my lungs, particle by particle. The tiny mauve flowers imprinted on the wallpaper behind the phone are suddenly in exquisite detail. I never noticed the little leaves; they're more yellow than green. Huh. I wonder why.

A tug on my hand brings me back into the passage of time. I blink and stare blankly at my mother. "Well?" she asks excitedly. I nod woodenly, unable to speak. She grins broadly and hugs me, crushing the phone into my ear.

"Ouch!" I exclaim. Mom pulls back apologetically. There's still a voice talking to me on the other end of the line.

"Hello? Mrs. Johnson? Are you still there?" he asks.

"Uh…yes. Yes, I'm here. What?"

He chuckles. "You didn't hear anything I said after I said you were pregnant, did you?"

I shake my head before realizing he can't see me. "No. Sorry, I didn't."

"It's all right. I get that reaction a lot. I was giving you the number of the OB/GYN clinic to set up your first prenatal appointment. I suggest you do that immediately. Do you have a pen and paper handy?"

"Uh, hang on," I gesture to my mother for a pen and paper, which she eagerly hands to me. "Go ahead. I'm ready." I scribble the information down with a shaky hand; it's barely legible. I cover the mouthpiece to address Mom, "Can you read this?"

She nods, still grinning.

"Did you get that, Mrs. Johnson? Do you need me to repeat it?"

"No, I got it. Thank you."

"Not a problem. Good luck and congratulations!"

"Thanks. Bye." I hang up and turn to fully face my mother. "Mom, I'm *pregnant*!" I yell and burst into tears.

Mom squeals like a teenager and grabs me in a fierce hug, jumping up and down. "My baby girl is going to have a baby! I'll be a *grandma*!!"

"Mom," I try to interrupt her. "Mom, stop. I'm..." I clap my hand over my mouth, pull away and run for the bathroom. I throw up the chicken noodle soup I had at lunch. It looks even nastier on the way up than it does coming out of the can.

Mom peers around the corner, still grinning. "Sorry, sweetie! I am just so excited!!" She squeals again, clapping her hands together while I continue heaving in the toilet, unable to answer. When I'm done, I stand upright and glare at my mother briefly. I know she can't help herself, but I hope this morning sickness thing will pass quickly. It's awful.

"I know you're excited, Mom. I'm...scared." Tears prick my eyes.

Mom stops her crazy dancing and her brow furrows. "What? Why are you scared?" she asks, coming to my side and hugging me with one arm. "What's to be scared about, sweetie?"

"I don't know. Everything! We...we didn't plan this and Rick's not even here. I hate throwing up and..." I start crying.

"Oh, Heather. Come on, let's go sit down." She leads me into the living room and onto the sofa. "Now, what are you really scared about?"

I take a deep breath, trying to collect my thoughts. What am I scared about? I don't know where to start. "I'm pregnant. Mom," I turn to her. "I'm pregnant. I'm going to....have a baby. Oh, my God. I'm going to have an actual *baby*. What am I going to do with a baby?" My voice becomes squeaky and high-pitched.

"You're going to love it and raise him or her to be a wonderful human being, just like you and Rick are." Mom smooths my hair and her eyes search my face, chin quivering with emotion. "You'll be wonderful parents, Heather. Don't worry."

My hands creep to my stomach, contemplating the ramifications. There's a brand new little person inside me; one that is half Rick and half me.

Wow. What a miracle.

Mom's hand covers mine and I look up, eyes shining. "I'm going to be a mother. Me; a mother," I whisper.

Mom nods, tears dribbling down her cheeks. "Yes, you are," she squeaks. She takes a ragged breath in and replies in a much stronger voice, "And I get to be a *grandma!* Yippee!!"

I can't help but laugh.

Once we collect ourselves, Mom reminds me to make my prenatal appointment. I had completely forgotten. We return to the kitchen, and I dial the number with shaky hands. Once I relay all the information to the person at the clinic, I am booked for an appointment in two weeks. The only special instructions are to be sure to have my dependent ID card with me and to have a full bladder for a urine test. I am warned the appointment may take up to two hours.

"Why so long?" I ask, perplexed.

"It's your first appointment, so you'll have paper work to fill out, a complete physical, have your blood drawn, and receive your prenatal vitamin prescription which you will fill at the pharmacy."

"All right," I answer uneasily.

I make note of the appointment on the calendar and fill Mom in on the details when I hang up.

"Well," She grins broadly again. "How do you want to tell the family?"

"I hadn't thought about it. I still don't know how to tell Rick he's going to be a father."

"A letter is a great way to find out, and he'll remember it and be able to read it over and over again," she reminds me.

Thinking for a moment, I slowly nod. "Yes, I'll go ahead and write. At least get a letter started." I turn to go into my room, mulling over how to word it.

"What about Dad, Jeff, and Debbie? How do you want to break it to them? What kind of cake should I make?" Mom asks before I can leave.

"I don't know. Do you have any ideas?"

She taps her lips with her finger, concentrating. "How about I bake a cake in the shape of an egg with blue and pink stripes on it?" Mom likes to be clever when sharing big news. This is Big News. Baking a cake is synonymous with celebrations and announcements in our house.

"Mom, it's almost three o'clock. You won't have time to get it done."

"You're right," she sighs. Suddenly, her face brightens and she stares past me. "I know! I'll just bake a sheet cake, but I'll put pink icing on one half and blue icing on the other with the words 'What will it be?' written on it! Yes!" she answers herself. She begins to mutter quietly, pulling flour and sugar out. I've been dismissed. I leave my mother in the kitchen, alone and talking excitedly. This should be interesting.

Staring at the sheet of paper in front of me, my mind goes blank. How do I do this? Should I try to be clever or just come right out with it? I pick up the pen and realize my hand is still shaking. I put the pen down, close my eyes, and take some slow deep breaths.

"It's okay," I mutter between breaths. "It's okay. Just tell him."

I open my eyes and pick up the pen. It touches the paper and I begin to tell Rick the biggest news of his life, of *our* life. My love, fear, longing, and excitement pour out in the words I ink. I intermittently cry and laugh while I write. In the end, the letter is five pages long. It's the longest letter I've ever written. I sign it with "To the Best Daddy in the World with all my love, Heather." Smiling, I fold it carefully, spray it with my perfume and seal it in the envelope.

"I wish I could be there when you read this, Rick," I murmur, hugging the bulky envelope to my chest.

The smell of baking cake wafts into my room. I brace myself for what it might do to my stomach, but thankfully all it does is make me smile. I have lost count of how many times over the years my mother has made one of her delicious cakes to celebrate one thing or another. The aroma alone will tip off the rest of the family that something is up.

When my parents wanted to announce her pregnancy with Debbie, she made a bunch of cupcakes and used them to spell the word "BABY" on a baking sheet and placed it in the middle of the table after dinner. I was nine and Jeff was only four at the time and he couldn't read, so he just grabbed a cupcake and started munching on it. It spelled "BABV" instead. They ended up just having to tell us what the news was because her cleverness was lost on her young children. The cupcakes were delicious.

Mom is just taking the cake out of the oven when I enter the kitchen. It's yellow.

"Yellow? Not chocolate?" I ask.

Mom removes her oven mitts, admiring her work. "Yes. The icing won't work with chocolate cake. It's too dark." I notice two bowls of frosting sitting on the counter, waiting to be slathered on the cake when it cools. One is baby blue and the other is a bright, almost fluorescent pink.

"Wow. That's a bright pink, Mom. Did you mean for it to come out like that?" I dip the tip of my pinkie finger in and taste it. It's cloyingly sweet, just like frosting should be.

"I was going for more of a pastel, but I put too many drops of food coloring in, and well, you know the number one rule of cooking," she says, looking at me expectantly, waiting for me to finish the sentence.

"Yes," I roll my eyes. "You can always add more, but you can't take out."

"Exactly. So, bright pink it is! Maybe that means it'll be a baby girl, huh? How are you feeling?"

"Okay, I guess. Not very hungry, but at least I'm not sick."

"That's good, that's good," Mom answers absently; she's busily pounding steaks to tenderize them. My guess is we're having Swiss steaks for dinner.

"Are you making mushroom gravy?" I ask.

"Mm hmm," she replies between whacks. "And rice this time instead of mashed potatoes. Dad wants rice. I think it might be better for your stomach, too; easier to keep down." She grins and whacks the meat once more.

"Want me to help?" I ask, hoping she says no.

"No. I don't think so. I don't want you to vomit all over dinner."

I flash a grateful smile and retreat.

****

"Is everyone ready for dessert?" Mom asks gleefully.

"Yeah, we want to know what the big news is," Jeff chuckles. "I could smell it when I walked in the door!"

"Is Rick home early?" Debbie asks hopefully.

I wince; if only it were true. "No, Rick's not home early," I reply. Debbie's shoulders slump.

Dad remains silent; he already knows.

"Well, I'll just go get it then, and we'll find out what it is," Mom grins at her own double meaning, places her napkin next to her plate and rises, practically skipping into the kitchen. I am glad she's happy about this; some women would cringe at the thought of being a grandma because it somehow suddenly makes them old. Mom has never been vain.

My heart beats furiously in my chest, and I press my hands into my stomach, hoping I don't have to make a leap for the bathroom. I ate mostly rice.

Mom appears around the corner, holding the pan high so that we can't see it. She stops at the table, grins at all of us with a wink toward me before she slowly, dramatically places it in the center of the table. Three sets of eyes dart around the cake, reading the words Mom carefully piped on.

"What will it be?" Debbie reads the words piped on the cake aloud. "What does that…"

"Woo hoo!! I knew it!!" Dad claps and laughs. He jumps up and grabs me in a hug. "Congratulations!"

Debbie's eyes are large and round. Jeff's face registers bewilderment before realization dawns. He grins his goofy grin at me. "Way to go, Rick!" he chortles.

"What is it? What happened?" Debbie asks, baffled.

Mom fills Debbie in. "Your sister is going to be a mother, Debbie. She's pregnant!"

Debbie jerks in surprise and her mouth falls open. "What? Really? I get to be an aunt?!" She leaps up and starts dancing around her chair.

I laugh nervously at their reactions. "Yeah, I guess you do."

"That's why you've been sick lately. I thought something was up," Jeff replies, trying to act knowledgeable.

"You had no clue, son, and you know it," Dad retorts jokingly, punching Jeff lightly in the arm.

Jeff casts a sideways glance at him, suppressing a smile. "Did, too," he mutters.

"I think it's going to be a girl. I want a niece," Debbie interjects, studying the cake.

Conversation centers on the gender of the baby, the excitement of adding a new member to the family, and my medical appointment while Mom slices the cake and passes wedges around. Finally, Dad asks the question nobody else will; when will Rick find out.

I gulp down my cake, and my emotions, before answering. "I wrote him a letter," I reply softly, pressing my fork into the crumbs on my plate. "I don't know when he'll be able to call, so…"

Jeff clears his throat. "I think that's a good idea. He'll be really excited."

I turn my gaze to Jeff and he actually looks older, more mature, these days. "Thanks, Jeff." I smile.

Suddenly embarrassed by his own reaction, Jeff shrugs and digs into his second piece of cake.

****

The next day on my way to work, I drop the letter into the mail box with a trembling hand and a silent prayer. I won't share the news with Mr. Sikes yet; I want to wait until I have my first doctor's appointment to share it officially. I don't even know when I'm due.

"Hello? Are you in outer space or something?" Tina interrupts me.

My hand stops in mid-air, suspending the scoop of food over the guinea pig cage. I turn toward her in surprise. "Excuse me?"

Tina snorts a laugh and rolls her eyes. "Since when do guinea pigs eat rabbit food?" She points at the bag grasped in my left hand.

I read the label and frown. "Oh. I didn't realize I grabbed the wrong one." I dump the scoop back into the bag and retrieve the correct bag from the rolling cart.

"What is up with you today? You're in the twilight zone or something," Tina quips, pushing the cart forward a few feet and sprinkling tiny, smelly flakes into the fish tank. Goldfish zip and dart around the water, their little mouths opening and closing.

Reading the label twice to be sure, I scoop out the dull brown pellets and fill the dish for the guinea pigs before answering. "I don't know; I just miss Rick, I guess."

"You really need to chill out, Heather. First you make yourself sick about it, and now you just check out. You don't want Mr. Sikes to find fish food in the hamster cage or crickets in the rabbit cage, do you?" She bursts into a brief hoot of laughter. "That would be pretty funny, though!"

I laugh politely. I look down the line, seeing the door that leads to the reptile section of the pet store getting closer and closer. I never cared much for that before, but I *really* don't want to go near it now. Bile rises in my throat and I swallow hard. I cannot see myself putting crickets in the frog cages today. My mind recoils at the thought of feeding the snakes. I flick a glance at the little cardboard box that holds about a dozen mice; it quivers and jumps every now and then. I squeeze my eyes shut and try unsuccessfully to block it out.

I barely manage a quick apology to Tina before bolting for the bathroom to reacquaint myself with breakfast.

When I emerge from the bathroom and take my place at the cart again, Tina's eyes are narrowed and she's frowning in concentration. "What's wrong, Heather? You never did say why you're sick. I don't think it's just because you miss Rick."

I keep my focus on placing the correct food in the correct cage. "Well, that's what it is."

Tina drops the scoop back into the bag she was working from, turns to face me, and crosses her arms across her flat chest. "I think you're lying." She juts her chin up in challenge. "I think there's more to it than that."

I try to push the cart further down the line, but she sticks her foot in front of the wheel to stop it. She places both hands on the edge of the cart and leans over it, putting her face right up to mine. I can see the cinnamon flecks of color in her eyes. "Heather. What's. Wrong?"

I stare at her for a moment, warring with myself. Finally, I sigh and look around to be sure nobody else is around within ear shot. "First, you have to promise not to say a word. All right?"

Her eyes widen and she nods slowly, holding her right hand up. "I promise."

"I had my blood drawn last week and…" I lower my voice. "I'm pregnant."

Tina's mouth and eyes pop wide open. "I *knew* it! I knew it!" she chortles and claps.

"You can't tell anybody, Tina. I mean it," I reprimand her. "I have my first appointment in a couple of weeks. I will let Mr. Sikes know after that. You promised."

Tina claps her hand over her mouth and nods enthusiastically. "I promise! Oh, that's so cool!" she hisses, trying to contain herself. "Does Rick know yet?"

I shake my head and her expression collapses. "I mailed a letter to tell him today."

She wrinkles her nose. "It stinks he has to find out like that."

"Yeah," I whisper. "Hey, listen. I really can't go in the reptile room today. Do you mind?"

"Oh! Sure, no problem. Go ahead and I'll take care of it." She waves me off.

"Thanks. I'll go inventory the dog food instead."

"Sounds good." She pushes the cart through the door of the reptile room and disappears into the darkness.

Tina keeps her word and my secret. Every time I see her at work, she doesn't say anything unless I bring it up. I am grateful for her help in covering for me. The queasiness and aversions get more pronounced. Changing the animal cages becomes more and more challenging with each passing day. I don't know that I'll be able to keep this job if it doesn't get better, even with Tina's help.

Finally, the day arrives for my first prenatal appointment.

I have no idea what I'm in for.

I enter the OB/GYN clinic and get in line at the registration desk with my mother in tow. Once it's my turn and I approach the desk, a young man in uniform addresses me. "May I have your ID, please?"

I give it to him; he looks it over and taps something into the computer. "Yes, Mrs. Johnson. You are here for your first prenatal appointment. Please fill these out, take a seat over there," he hands me my ID, a clipboard full of papers and a pen, and gestures to my left. "Your name will be called shortly. Thank you." He looks past me to the next person in line.

My mother and I find two empty seats in the cluster of chairs he indicated, and I begin the laborious process of filling out sheet after sheet of paper.

I've barely finished filling out the last sheet when a young uniformed woman carrying a clipboard emerges from a door near the front desk, and calls my name. My mother and I rise and approach her. She smiles, "Hello. Did you fill out your paperwork?" I nod. "Very good. Please follow me. Mrs. Johnson, we will need a urine sample. Follow the instructions posted in the bathroom very carefully; it must be a clean sample. Once you're done, please leave the specimen in the window inside the bathroom and take a seat in here. You will be called when a room is available." She takes the clipboard from me, adds it to her own, and thrusts three small paper squares of what appear to be wet wipes and a specimen cup into my suddenly emptied hands. I glance at the bathroom she indicates and notice it's at the end of another waiting room filled with women in various stages of pregnancy. Some of the women in more advanced stages of pregnancy are reading books or staring at the walls.

I look at my mother, bewildered. She shrugs and smiles. "I'll wait here for you. Go take care of business."

When I emerge from the bathroom, I scan the room and find my mother saving a seat for me in the corner. She gives me a little wave and I join her. "I wonder how long this will take. Did you notice most of the really pregnant women are reading books? Maybe they know something I don't," I whisper.

I wait in the second waiting room for forty-five minutes before my name is called. When I am brought into an exam room, I am told rather efficiently to remove all my clothing (I can leave my socks on, if I wish) and to wear a paper gown. Once the uniformed woman leaves, I pull the curtain and do as I am instructed. I leave my socks on.

"Is this going to be really bad, Mom?" I ask nervously.

"What do you mean?" she looks up from her magazine, perplexed.

"Why do I have to get *naked?*" I whisper.

"Heather, you will get a full physical exam to be sure you both are healthy. It's all right, honey." She reaches over and pats my knee.

I rub my hands together and pull the flimsy sheet up over my lap. I feel so exposed. After twenty minutes, there is a soft knock on the door. "Mrs. Johnson, may I come in?" A female voice asks.

I breathe a sigh of relief; at least it's a woman. "Yes," I reply.

An exhausted woman wearing drab green scrubs enters with another uniformed woman in tow. The exhausted woman thrusts her hand toward me and smiles. "I'm Dr. Burns, the Chief Resident in OB/GYN. How are you feeling?" After I shake her hand, she rolls a stool over, and sits on it with a sigh.

"I'm okay, just really queasy most of the time."

Dr. Burns turns toward my mother and repeats her introduction. "You're her mother, I presume? I see the resemblance."

"Yes," Mom chuckles. "I'm standing in for her husband. He's stationed in Korea."

"Oh," Dr. Burns' eyebrows rise and she smiles. "I assume he came home recently." She turns her attention back to me.

I blush and Dr. Burns' smile widens. "All right. First thing's first." She reaches wordlessly behind her to the other uniformed woman who promptly hands her a folder. Dr. Burns opens the folder and scans it. It's filled with the paperwork I recently filled out. "Mm hmm. Mm hmm. Your urine looks good, but you are a little dehydrated. So you've been throwing up a lot lately. Is that getting any better or worse?"

I answer her questions and relax as she explains things. The other uniformed woman remains silent, efficiently prepping for the upcoming exam. Finally, Dr. Burns rises. "Let's begin the exam. Would you like to hear the baby's heartbeat?" She pulls the curtain in front of the door closed.

"Really? You can hear the baby's heart beat this early?" I ask excitedly, glancing at my mother, who is on the edge of her seat.

Dr. Burns chuckles. "Yes." When she places the wand over my lower abdomen and begins moving it back and forth, I am tense waiting to hear something I've never heard before. Suddenly, a rhythmic flutter of a whisper fills the room. Dr. Burns' hand stops. "There it is."

Collectively, my mother and I gasp. I wish Rick could hear this.

"It sounds strong and healthy," Dr. Burns says. "Let's be sure everything else is going well, too. Place your feet here." She guides my feet into the stirrups.

Once the exam is done, Dr. Burns helps me rise to a sitting position. "Everything looks good." She pulls a circular tool from her pocket; it has two pieces attached in the center that slide back and forth. "Based on your last menstrual period, your due date is October twelfth. You're right on track."

After getting dressed, I am directed to get in the original line at the front desk to schedule my next appointment. I am disappointed to find out that I can't schedule my appointment with the same doctor that I just had.

"I'm sorry, Mrs. Johnson, but you'll just have to see whoever is on duty that day," the young uniformed man tells me for the third time, despite my protests and pleas.

"Young man, isn't there anything you can do?" Mom asks sweetly.

He shakes his head. "I'm sorry, but no. This is the way it is."

Realizing I won't get anywhere, I take the slip of paper he hands me reminding me of my next appointment and leave.

"That's strange. I had the same doctor with each of you."

"It's something else I have to get used to with military life," I mutter.

Fortunately, there is a large stack of letters from Rick jammed into our mailbox waiting for me when we get home. Whatever clog in the system that existed has flushed out.

"Go read the letters, Heather. I'll write your appointment on the calendar," Mom offers when she sees the volume of letters spilling out of our mailbox.

I grin and hurry into my bedroom, closing the door behind me. I carefully place the letters in the proper order by date so I can read them in sequence. They all smell like Rick and I smile, inhaling each one deeply before opening them. In every letter, he tells me how much he misses me and about the trivial things of his day. He echoes my sentiment of counting down the days until he gets home. Once I finish reading them all, I wonder if he has gotten my letter telling him he'll be a father yet. Will he be able to call me, or will he have to write me, as well?

****

"Heather! It's Rick!" Dad calls excitedly down the hall two weeks later.

I drop the pen and hurry to the phone as quickly as I can; I was just writing him another letter.

"Hello!" I blurt excitedly into the phone.

"Honey bun? Is that you?" Rick crackles into my ear; his voice is high pitched and very much not like himself. He must have received my letter.

"Yes! Did you get my letter?"

"I....I got it today. Is it really true? I'm going to be a father?" Even through the crackle, I can hear raw emotion.

Tears blur my vision. "Yes. It's true. You're going to be a father."

Silence reigns for a long moment followed by a loud yelling on the other end. "I'm going to be a father! Hey, I'm going to be a daddy!" Rick yells.

Relief floods my heart and mind. "Who are you talking to?" I ask.

Rick laughs. "Nobody! Everybody! I'm going to be a father! Woohoo!!" he yells again.

"I'm so glad you're happy about it, sweetie."

"What else would I be?! This is incredible! Do you know what we're having yet? No, of course you don't. It's too early!" His laughter crackles across the line. "How are you doing? You feeling all right?"

"I am throwing up and sleeping a lot, but otherwise I'm all right."

"Oh, I'm sorry. I wish I could be there to …" His sentence stops.

Did we get cut off already? "Rick? Are you there?" I ask anxiously.

"Yes, I'm here," he replies, his voice shaking. "I'm just…" He's crying.

"I know, sweetie. I wish you were here, too. I went to the doctor already for my first appointment and I heard the heart beat. Everything is fine. I'm due October twelfth." I rush to get everything in before we really are cut off.

"Oh…Oh, Heather. I love you. I can't wait to hear it for myself." His voice shakes.

"I'm counting down, sweetie. I love you and I miss you."

"I miss you, too. More than you can imagine. Please take good care of yourself and…our baby." His voice cracks; it has nothing to do with the connection.

"I will. I promise. I'm sure he or she can't wait until you come home, too." I swipe at the tears.

"Wow. I can't believe this. I'll call you as soon as I can and I'll keep writing every day. Are my letters getting through now?"

"Yes," I nod. "They've started coming through again. I love to smell them."

"I love smelling yours, too. Hey, thanks!"

"Thanks for what?" I ask, confused.

"The guys are congratulating me," he laughs.

"I'm doing all the work here!" I joke.

"Yeah, I know. I really can't wait to get home now!"

"I hope it flies by, Rick. It will be so nice not to have to count down until we are together again. Especially now."

Rick clears his throat. "I feel the same way. I am so done being over here. I wish I could come home today."

For once, our conversation isn't cut off, and we are able to say our goodbyes properly. Rick promises to try to call after my next appointment; I am able to relay the information to him in full. He got his orders and mailed some copies to me. He wants us to get on the base housing list so that hopefully we can get into housing before the baby is born.

****

April, 1989

A few weeks later, with Rick's orders in hand, I walk into the housing office on base and approach the counter. The same woman is working, but there's not even a hint of recognition in her eyes when she turns her gaze on me.

"Can I help you?" she asks.

"Yes, I need to put our name on the waiting list for housing, please." I can hear Rick's admonition ringing in my ears to *be nice.*

"Is your husband here?" she asks.

I push the stack of papers that are Rick's orders toward her on the counter. "He will be. Here are his orders."

She glances over them and a spark of recognition registers on her face. "Oh! Yes, I remember now. He's in Korea, isn't he? Junior Enlisted?"

Shame at my own behavior tints my cheeks pink. "Yes. We would like to be on the waiting list, please. I just found out we're expecting."

"Congrats and it's okay, honey," she says. "It's a hard thing to get used to. Currently, the wait time is about seven months, but we're moving along at a pretty good clip, so it could be sooner than that."

"Oh. That's good, right?"

"It sure is. No guarantees, but right now that's what it looks like." She removes a few papers from my stack, shuffles some things around and begins writing information down. A few moments later, she returns her gaze to me and smiles. "All done! You're on the list. Feel free to come in any time to see where your name is. Right now you're number seventy-six on the list."

My eyes grow wide. "There are seventy-five people ahead of us? That's a lot."

She shrugs. "It could be worse; I have seen it get to one hundred."

"Wow. Is there anything else I need to do?"

"No," she shakes her head. "You're on the list. Of course, if anything changes, let us know."

"Thank you." I collect my things and depart. That was easy and painless.

****

My morning sickness continues. I have developed a deep aversion to most things I formerly enjoyed like chicken, gravy, tomato sauce in any form, and chewing gum. The last time I tried chewing a piece of gum, there was something about the texture that caused me to spit it out within minutes and bolt for the bathroom.

When I told Mr. Sikes about my pregnancy, he mumbled his congratulations, but was concerned about my work schedule.

"You gonna be able to handle this? It's a stinky job, you know," he said, his arms folded across his barrel chest.

"I hope so," I answered honestly.

His shoulders drooped; he tries to put off a tough impression, but he's basically a nice man and a good boss. "Well, do what you can do and we'll work around you as best we can."

"Thank you, Mr. Sikes," I smiled gratefully. "I really appreciate that."

He cleared his throat and squared his shoulders. "You're a good employee," he said gruffly. "Now get back to work."

It isn't long before I can't continue cleaning the cages and tanks; everything about it is revolting. Tina is great about helping, but it comes to the point that she is doing everything because I can't stay out of the bathroom long enough to help. Even the smell of clean cedar shavings makes me take a deep breath, trying to keep whatever food I've eaten from coming up.

Mr. Sikes offers to switch me to the front of the store where all I have to do is run the register and inventory the supplies. Unfortunately, that only lasts about a week; the smell of the fish food, cedar shavings, and everything else pet-related smacks me in the face as soon as I walk in the door.

"I am sorry, Mr. Sikes. I really am, but I can't keep doing this," I tell him regretfully over the phone. "Even the smell of the store makes me sick to my stomach. Please forgive me, but I have to quit." My voice quavers; I really did enjoy this job.

Mr. Sikes takes a deep breath and exhales slowly. "Yeah, I kind of thought it was coming to this when you ran out on the customer the other day."

Blanching, I can still see the wiggly white mice with their twitchy noses and beady little eyes in the cardboard box; I had to count them. The customer bought five and I knew he had a pet snake. I couldn't finish the transaction.

"I'm really sorry, Mr. Sikes. I hope you know that."

"Ah hey, kiddo. It was bound to happen soon anyway. Your husband will be home and you guys need to set up housekeeping and such. If you ever need a job here, I'll be sure to have one for you. You take care."

"Thank you, Mr. Sikes."

When I tell Tina, she sounds mournful, but is not surprised. "I thought that was coming. You haven't really been able to do this for awhile. Hey, we'll still get together, though, right? We're still friends?"

"Yeah, yeah. Of course," I reply, trying to sound positive. "I just wanted to thank you for being so helpful while I've had morning sickness. You're very sweet and I appreciate you."

"No problem. You'd do the same for me!" she replies cheerfully. "Come on back when you're feeling better, okay?"

"Sure thing."

When I hang up the phone to end our conversation, I have a deep sense that I'm ending a friendship, too. Tina and I have only been friends because we work at the pet store. We only went out socially the one time. I don't think this friendship is one that will last. To tell her so would just be mean, so I don't. She's a good person and I wish her well.

****

"You are supposed to be *gaining* weight, young lady, not *losing* it," the elderly doctor glares at me over his glasses after reading through my chart.

I sit on the exam table wearing the paper gown and clutching the sheet that covers my lower half. My mother sits in the chair against the wall. "I have tried and tried to get her to eat more, doctor, but she just won't do it."

He nods. "According to this, you have lost a total of eight pounds in your first trimester. Is your nausea not getting better?"

"Not really. I just don't want to eat if I know it's going to come back up."

He shakes his head, adjusts himself on the stool and continues to glare at me. I feel like I'm in the principal's office, if the principal's office made you strip, pee in a cup and feel like you're in a herd of cattle being prodded through one waiting line to another. This time I ended up with a doctor old enough to be my grandfather. No sign of the female Dr. Burns anywhere. This doctor is accompanied by a young female in uniform, just like last time. Also like last time, she doesn't utter a word; she just does the doctor's bidding.

"Well, have you tried eating bland foods like crackers, oatmeal, rice, and bananas?" he offers, still glaring.

"Yes, I have. But I don't like them. I threw up oatmeal in the shower the other morning. It was disgusting."

He shakes his head and adjusts himself once more, this time with a grunt. "Well, young lady, you'll have to try harder because you shouldn't lose any more weight. Your baby won't suffer, but you will. Now, let's see how you're measuring and how the baby sounds." His exam is more old-school and less sensitive than last time. He's certainly very efficient; the exam only lasts five minutes. I barely have time to hear the heartbeat before he's moved on to the measuring tape which he stretches across my abdomen. He mutters the number to the lady who promptly writes it down.

"What does that measurement mean?" my mother asks.

"That tells us how far along she is based on the size of the womb. It should correlate to the week of gestation," he replies. "You're measuring right on track, so the baby is growing normally. But you still need to eat." He wags his finger at me.

"Yes, sir," I mumble, unable to shake the principal's office feeling.

Once again, when I approach the front desk to make my next

appointment, I ask if I can see Dr. Burns at my next appointment. "I'll even go a different day if I have to."

The young lady shakes her head. "I'm sorry, ma'am, but it doesn't work that way. You'll have to see whoever is on duty."

I sigh. I take the slip of paper and leave.

Remembering that Rick is supposed to call tonight, I smile on the way home.

Nine o'clock rolls around; the phone doesn't ring. I last until ten thirty and can't keep my eyes open any longer.

"Maybe the lines are down," Mom offers. Dad went to bed an hour ago; he has to get up early for work.

"Yeah," I yawn widely. "Maybe. Do you think I should stay up some more?"

"No," she shakes her head. "He knows what time it is here and he would've called by now if he could have. Maybe he'll call tomorrow. Let's get to bed."

Disappointment is my companion as I fall asleep that night, cradling my stomach.

CHAPTER ELEVEN

April, 1989

Five days pass before Rick's voice finally appears on the other end of the telephone.

"Rick! What happened? Why haven't you called? I've been worried sick, as if being pregnant doesn't make me sick enough! Are you all right? Did anything bad happen? Why couldn't you just call me real quick and let me know you're still there?" My rapid fire remarks don't allow him to get a word in. All the pent up anxiety boils over into the phone line.

"Heather, calm down..." he crackles.

"Don't tell me to calm down! You were supposed to call five days ago, Rick. Why didn't you call? Do you have any idea how worried I have been?" My voice reaches a pitch that only dogs could hear.

"Heather, *calm down*. I'm fine. I couldn't call because there was a glitch with the phone lines here. Nobody was making any unofficial calls. This is the first time I've been able to get a line out. Honey, I'm sorry. I really didn't want you to worry, but there was nothing I could do."

Sobs prevent me from answering coherently.

"Are you crying?"

"Yes," I manage to squeak.

"I'm sorry. Everything is all right."

I take some deep breaths, allowing relief to flood me. "Rick, I didn't know what was going on."

"I know," he sighs. "I can only imagine. I wanted to call you so bad and hear how the baby is doing. You had your appointment, right?"

"Yes, everything is fine. But I'm...well..."

"What? Is something wrong?"

"No, it's just...I'm still getting sick and don't like to eat. I've lost eight pounds and the doctor isn't happy."

"What? You've *lost* weight? That's not right, Heather."

I roll my eyes. "I don't like to throw up, so I don't want to eat."

Rick spends equal time chastising and imploring me to take care of myself for the baby's sake. I assure him that the doctor says the baby is growing normally and I'll try to do better.

"I can't wait to get home. I'll make sure you eat and take care of yourself and the baby."

"How much longer do we have? It feels like you've been gone forever."

"By my count, we only have about five or six weeks left."

"Thank God," I breathe.

"I have," he chuckles. "More so than I ever have before. I don't have a specific date yet, but of course I'll let you know as soon as I find out."

"It's been a long year, Rick. I don't want to do this again."

"Me, either. I only have to do one in my career, so this should be it."

Our conversation almost ends naturally; we get to express our love for each other before we're cut off. I never got the chance to talk to him about not seeing the same doctor from one appointment to the next.

"Is everything all right?" Mom asks, peering around the corner once I place the phone back into the cradle.

I can't answer. I just nod.

She embraces me. "What happened?"

"The phone lines were down for a few days. This is the first time he could call. Why am I crying about this?" I ask, angrily swiping tears that continue to spring up.

"You're pregnant. It goes along with the territory."

"That's one more thing that goes haywire, huh? Great."

With only one part time job to occupy my time, I spend most days biking slowly down the trails Rick and I frequented before he left. Texas heats up pretty quickly this time of year, so I stick to biking in the morning hours. I have some favorite rocks to sit on and write, or from which to just stare out at the landscape. Very few people pass through these areas, so I enjoy the solitude.

I spend the afternoons of my days off napping. Slowly, the morning sickness begins to recede.

"Have you and Rick thought about where you're going to live once he gets home? Before you move into base housing, I mean," Mom asks one morning after I return from a bike ride.

"Not really. I just thought we would stay at home because a house on base will probably come up pretty quickly."

"Well, you can stay with us or you can get an apartment if you'd like. But, how much stuff does Rick have anyway?" She casts a sideways glance in my direction. "We don't mind you staying in our house, but I don't want you two to feel crowded."

"Rick lived in the dorms before he went to Korea, so he doesn't have a whole lot of stuff. By my calculations, we will have about five months to wait before we get a house on base once he gets back. Don't you think we should just stay here?"

"Heather, we would love to have you two stay with us, but it would be best to discuss this with Rick first. He's your husband and you two need to do what's best for you two…er, *three*, first."

"But don't you think that's the wisest choice? I mean, otherwise we would end up moving twice in just a few months. With me being pregnant…"

"What I think shouldn't be as important to you as what your husband thinks."

I remember how Rick felt ambushed at dinner that one night. I don't want him feel that way again.

After I shower and get cleaned up from my bike ride, Mom treats me to ice cream at Flavors Ice Cream shop. I choose my favorite: vanilla with chocolate sauce. I don't have a strong sweet tooth, but am thankful that I can still enjoy a good bowl of ice cream despite the morning sickness. When we get home, I am exhausted.

"I'm going to take a nap before dinner, okay?" I yawn, dropping my purse onto the table in the hall.

"I thought you might," Mom chuckles. "You look like you need it."

I dump myself onto the bed, face down and feel a lump jutting into my stomach. I try to smooth the comforter under me, but quickly realize it's not the comforter. Scowling, I roll off the bed, looking for an offending pillow, perhaps. No pillow. Puzzled, I scan the bed to see what could have been jabbing at me. Nothing. The bed is flat and the comforter is smooth.

I plop face down onto the bed again, and am immediately met with a lump jabbing my stomach again. Reaching both hands under me, I gasp as I realize the lump *is* me. Rather, it's my stomach that's jabbing me. My stomach is no longer flat and soft.

"Holy smokes!" I roll onto my back and suck my stomach in, pressing my hands down onto my lower stomach. Normally, my stomach would flatten even further, but there's a distinct hard ball in my pelvis that doesn't retract.

Marveling, I slowly rub the hardness. "My baby," I whisper. "Our baby is in there, Rick." He'll be home in about three weeks. It can't come soon enough.

I close my eyes and savor the moment all by myself. For once, I want to let Rick know this before the rest of my family. I want to save something that is just us.

Eventually, I drift off to sleep with a smile, lying on my side cradling my stomach. I suspect that sleeping on my stomach will come to an end soon. When I awaken, I roll over to squint at the clock. It's three twenty.

I stretch and yawn. My hands instinctively cradle my stomach; is the lump still there? Yes, it is. I roll slowly out of bed and walk over to my full length mirror, turning sideways and lifting my shirt to see if it's noticeable when I stand up. I twist from side to side, gazing at my reflection with a critical eye. There is the slightest bulge between my hip bones, but not enough to show if I wear loose clothing.

I smile and the reflection in the mirror smiles back. I can keep the secret.

Wandering into the living room rubbing my eyes, I sit on the sofa and tuck my legs under me, being sure to balloon my shirt out.

"Hey, sis. Still taking afternoon naps?" Jeff asks. His grin is less goofy these days.

I nod and smile. He's flipping aimlessly through the channels. "Don't you have homework?"

"Nah," he shrugs, continuing to flip through channels. "Had two tests today, so no homework. Still puky?"

"Yes."

"That sucks." He finally lands on a baseball game and his jaw goes slack. He'll always be goofy.

"When is Rick going to call?" Debbie pokes her head out of the kitchen.

"I don't know. Hopefully soon," I respond.

"Will I get to talk to him this time?" she whines.

"I don't think so, Debbie. I barely get to talk to him when he calls. He often gets cut off before we can finish."

She rolls her eyes. "I know. That's what Mom said, too," she replies glumly, ducking back in the kitchen.

It is another five days before Rick calls. He's got good news: the date of his return. He's even got his flight information already. I can barely contain myself.

"Rick, that's awesome! I can hardly wait. Let me check the calendar…how many days is that?" I turn toward the calendar and start counting to myself, but Rick interrupts.

"It's seventeen days," he crows. "We're in the home stretch!"

"Before I forget, I have something to share with you, Rick. I haven't even shared it with my family. I can *feel* the baby. The baby isn't moving that I can tell, but I'm starting to show. It's really cool! I can't wait for you to see it."

"Really? Already? Wow. How are you feeling? Still getting sick a lot?"

"Well, yeah. But it's not as bad as it was. I still get queasy and don't like certain things, but it's getting better."

"Good. I don't want you to suffer."

"Hey! One more thing I have to talk with you about. We haven't talked about where we are going to live once you get back, before we get into base housing. What do you want to do?" I purposefully keep my mouth shut regarding my own preference.

Rick is quiet for a moment. "Well, did you have something in mind?"

"My parents have said we are welcome to stay with them, or we can get an apartment."

"What do you want to do?" he asks.

"What do *you* want to do, Rick?"

He exhales loudly. "I think we could get an apartment. I will get a housing allowance that will cover the rent easily."

I gulp. That's not the answer I expected. "Okay. If that's what you want. Do you want me to start looking?"

"That would be a good idea. I'm sure your parents have some helpful thoughts about where we could go. Of course, in a safe neighborhood and what we can afford."

"Rick, we don't have any furniture or anything," I remind him.

"Good point. Be sure to look at furnished apartments then. We can start buying furniture slowly to move into our house on base."

"Okay."

"I have to get going. You got my flight information down and everything?"

"Yes."

"Good! I'll call you when I get to Japan. Tell your parents it will be collect, but I'll pay them back when I get home. I love you. Be good to yourself and hug your belly for me." I can hear the smile in his voice.

"I love you, too." We say our goodbyes and end the conversation without being cut off. Once I replace the phone in the cradle, I stand there, dumbfounded. Rick actually wants to get an apartment for a few months?

"Everything okay?" Dad asks.

"Yeah. Everything is great! He'll be home in seventeen days." I thrust the piece of paper in his direction and he grins broadly, taking it from me.

"Louise! Rick will be home in seventeen days!" he yells down the hallway.

I am excited to be counting days rather than months. If Rick wants to get an apartment, that's fine. He'll be *here* with me. That's what matters. I would live in a one room shack if I had to, just to be with him.

When I tell my parents that Rick would prefer to get an apartment, they're thrilled for us. My mother relieves my concern about not having anything to set up an apartment.

"I have been setting things aside for some time for you to set up housekeeping. We've got your basics covered. Those are things you would need when you moved into base housing anyway." She's collected towels, dishes, and other items plus we'll actually be able to use our wedding gifts, too.

"You're starting your own family," Mom adds, smiling gently. "It's pretty exciting."

I couldn't agree more.

"Would you like to see what I've saved?"

I glance from one parent to the other before nodding. Mom leads me to the storage room by the back porch, where she begins to pull out box after box. All told, there are seven boxes. That doesn't include all the boxes of items from our wedding.

"How long have you been saving up?" I ask, incredulous.

"Oh," Mom starts, pulling open the top flaps of one of the boxes. "For a number of years, actually. Just little things here and there." She holds up a dinner plate for me to examine. "I've got a number of boxes started for Jeff and Debbie, too. Not as much, of course, because you're the oldest, so we expected you to move out first."

Between our wedding gifts and what Mom has managed to squirrel away, everything we need – including pots, pans, dishes, towels, and even a toilet brush, is covered.

"Thanks, Mom," I say quietly, grabbing her in a hug. "This is really awesome."

She hugs me tightly. "You're welcome. Now, let's put it away and start looking for an apartment! Rick will be home before you know it."

Our search for apartments yields quite a few choices, some not so nice, but others in neighborhoods that my parents and I both approve of. The rental rates are in line with what Rick told me we would be able to afford, taking into account utilities, a phone, and renter's insurance. The furnished ones aren't as bad as I thought they would be. I can even bring my own bed, which is something I was concerned about. I don't want to sleep in a used bed.

Within a week and a half, we have it narrowed down to three choices. Unable to get Rick's input, my parents and I discuss the options and decide on one that is close to both my parents and the base. The model we saw is large enough for the two of us, clean, has a washer and dryer in the apartment, and a nice pool. The weather has turned hot, and it will be nice to have the pool, especially while I'm pregnant. I'm thrilled I won't have to say goodbye to Rick anymore.

My parents come with me to sign the rental agreement. My father peruses the document carefully and questions the landlord occasionally, who is gracious and patient.

"Please don't worry, Mr. Scott. I understand your concerns, but we are a very safe complex and there are a number of military folks that live here. Mrs. Johnson and her husband will really like it."

"But you do understand that they're on the waiting list for base housing. How is that going to play out with this being a one year agreement?" Dad presses.

"May I?" The landlord retrieves the document from my father's hands. He flips through a few pages and points to a specific paragraph. "Right here is the military clause. We go through this all the time; it's not a big deal."

Dad squints as he reads the paragraph, his lips moving silently. Once he's done, he taps the document twice and gives a satisfied nod. "Very good. Heather, looks like you're in good shape."

I sign the agreement, pay the deposit, and the landlord hands the keys over to me. "You can move in any time you like."

Just like that, I – we – have our own apartment. I work to control the trembling in my hands. This is a huge step.

"Let's go look at it," Mom grins as we leave the office.

Climbing the steps to the apartment, I turn and scan the view. There are a few palm trees in the courtyard and the pool is within easy walking distance in this relatively small complex. Inserting the key, I turn it and open the door. The living room is spacious enough with a light mauve colored carpet. The furnishings are simple; the living room has a sofa and love seat separated by a small end table. There's also a coffee table in the center. There is a table to place a television on against the wall. Once the door is closed, I can see the round dining room table with four simple chairs adjacent to the galley style kitchen. The washer and dryer are tucked into a closet in the hallway that also has a door to the bathroom and another to the surprisingly large bedroom. There is a space where my bed will go plus two dressers and two end tables.

"There's plenty of room here for your queen-sized bed as well as a crib, if it comes down to it," Dad says, walking slowly around the room, eyeing it. Mom mumbles her agreement.

"I hope it doesn't come to that. I would rather be moved into housing before the baby comes," I reply, patting my stomach.

"Well, we can go ahead and start moving stuff in," Mom offers.

"I want to wait to move in until Rick is home. We can make our first night here our first night together."

"Sure. But we can start bringing all of the dishes and things and get it all set up. Your bed will be moved last, of course."

"That's a good idea."

Mom and Dad discuss some logistics of the move while I am lost in thought, looking around the expanse of the apartment. I have never lived apart from my family before. I know when we first dropped Rick off at the airport last year, I was bummed that I still had to live with my parents, but it has been a lot easier. Now, I get to finally live with my husband. But I'll also have to cook every day and clean a whole apartment. I should have spent more time in the kitchen with Mom, like I planned. Poor Rick; he has no idea what he's in for.

In the final countdown to Rick's homecoming, my family and I split our time between the apartment and home bringing in boxes and other items. Mom helps me set things up in a way that makes the most sense for ease of use. I had never given much thought to the placement of pots, pans, and plates before.

"You'll want to put your plates in this cupboard because it's next to the stove where you'll be cooking," she instructs as she stacks the plates and bowls in the cupboard indicated.

"Mom, I can't cook."

Mom chuckles. "I know, but you'll be all right. You'll learn."

"I wish I had learned with you."

"Me, too, but you had other things on your mind."

Getting things unpacked and settled into the apartment helps time to pass quickly.

One week before Rick is scheduled to return, I have my third OB appointment and once again, I see a new doctor. This one chastises me for not gaining weight even though I've stopped losing it. I say as much and am rewarded with a stern look. I recognize a pattern; wait, have your name called, wait, pee into a cup, wait, have your name called, wait, see whatever doctor is available, wait, schedule your next appointment, go home. Mom and I both bring something to read this time. At least I got to hear the heartbeat a little longer than last time. It's strong and steady. I also notice that my pants are getting uncomfortably tight. I may not be able to save my expanding belly to surprise Rick with.

"You are still measuring correctly, despite your lack of weight gain, young lady," the newest doctor scolds me. "I suggest you consider wearing maternity clothing. You're reaching that point, you know."

My mother takes me shopping to get some maternity clothes, but warns me against purchasing too many. "You're only going to wear them for a few months, so don't go crazy."

I settle for purchasing some nice mix and match pieces that will be good for the warm weather. When I step out of the dressing room wearing the first outfit, I hold my arms out to the side and look at my mother. "Well, what do you think?"

Mom's lip trembles and her eyes glisten. "I think you look like a little mommy. Oh, my baby is having a baby!" she cries gleefully, clasping her hands together.

"Mom, please try to control yourself." I glance nervously around; there isn't anyone within ear shot of her embarrassing outburst.

"I'm sorry," she wipes her eyes and grins. "It's just…well, now you're starting to show."

"I know. It freaks me out, too, sometimes," I say, rubbing the bulge of my lower belly. "I can't believe I'm going to be a mom."

"It's exciting!" she exclaims.

After my purchases are made, we head home and I immediately change into a pair of maternity shorts. It's so much easier than leaving the button undone and the zipper halfway open on my own shorts. "Ahhh," I sigh, reveling in the comfort. "Much better."

Jeff and Debbie react much as I thought they would when they see me in maternity clothes for the first time. They're a little uncomfortable.

"Wow, you're really starting to show," Debbie says, staring wide eyed at my belly.

"No kidding. You're going to get *huge*," Jeff adds.

I frown at Jeff, my cheeks pinking. "I am not going to get *huge*." I hope not anyway.

Their reactions got me thinking about Rick's reaction; I hope he doesn't think I'm huge when he sees me. I regard my reflection one morning, cupping my burgeoning belly. It still looks small to me, but it's definitely rounding out. My mind drifts to his reaction when he first found out, and a slow smile spreads across my face. "He'll think I'm beautiful," I whisper to my reflection.

****

May, 1989

Two days before Rick is scheduled to come home, I walk around the apartment one final time before we officially move in. It's decorated simply, but very nicely. It doesn't look like a naked apartment anymore. It's a home; our home. The only glaring absence is the space in the bedroom that my bed will occupy.

"It's perfect; we will move the bed in here in the morning and pick Rick up in the afternoon," Dad says, smiling. "I love it when a plan comes together."

"We need to go grocery shopping for you guys tomorrow, Heather. There's not a cracker to crunch on in this place!" Mom interjects.

"I like it here," Debbie says, running her hand over the sofa before pouncing on it. "Can I come and visit and swim?"

"Debbie, you have to let Heather and Rick have their own space," Dad warns. Debbie droops in disappointment.

"Once school is out, you can come and swim with me while Rick is at work." She perks right up.

"Are there any hot babes around here?" Jeff asks, peering out the window.

"I'm sure I don't know," I respond, glaring at him.

He shrugs, his eyes continuing to scan the view.

The remaining hours go by quickly in the final countdown to picking Rick up at the airport; Mom helps me compile a grocery list and off to the store we go. It would've been nice to save money by shopping at the commissary, but Mom doesn't have an ID to get in and I don't want to shop without her, so we settle for our local grocery store instead.

"Now, this should last you guys at least a week if not longer. You'll have to shop for fresh fruits, vegetables, and milk in between, but everything else will get you through just fine," Mom reports while unloading the bags and filling my cupboards and refrigerator. When we're done, she pulls what appears to be a large number of index cards bound together with metal rings out of a bag and hands it to me. "I made this for you."

Puzzled, I take the item from her. "What is it?"

"My recipes. All your favorites are included, too. I wrote them down and put them together, alphabetized and broken down into categories. See," she retrieves the stack and flips through them. "I labeled them with breakfast, lunch, dinner, side dishes, and desserts."

I gasp, realizing what a treasure this is. "Mom, wow. I don't know what to say," I look up through tears. "Thank you. Thank you so much."

We hug and then sit down at the small dining room table. I flip through the recipes slowly, reading the lists of ingredients and the careful instructions written in my mother's beautiful script handwriting.

"This is amazing," I say in awe. She made sure to be very detailed in the instructions, knowing I would need it.

"I thought it would come in handy. When we made your grocery list, I made sure you bought ingredients for meatloaf, mashed potatoes, macaroni and cheese, and chili to get you started for the first few days. It might even last you a week if you have any leftovers."

Mom's thoughtfulness overwhelms me.

****

That night, lying in bed in my room for the last time, I have a hard time getting to sleep even though I'm exhausted. My mind races, realizing I will never again look up at the same ceiling or hear the same creaking of the house as I do now. I am, in a sense, fully graduating into adulthood. Tomorrow, I will sleep in this bed, but it will be enclosed in four different walls and my husband will be beside me. We won't have limited days together or any other countdown for him to leave.

It's been a long year; an incredible year. When Rick left, we were newlyweds and now we have our own apartment and are well on our way to being parents.

"Wow," I whisper in the darkness. "Onward and upward." Cradling my belly, I close my eyes and finally give in to sleep.

"Heather? Heather, wake up," Moms urgent voice whispers loudly. "Heather, Rick is on the phone. Wake up."

My face puckers at the intrusive light glaring from the hallway. Mom is hovering over me, her billowy nightgown pooled around her. "What?" I say, propping myself up on my elbow.

"Rick is on the phone. He's in Japan. Quick, come before he has to catch his plane," Mom speaks hurriedly, pulling the blanket off of me.

Recognition breaks through the fog in my brain, and I follow my mother quickly into the kitchen, lit only with the light over the stove for illumination. Mom pulls the handset off the wall phone and says, "Okay, Leonard, you can hang up. Rick, here's Heather." She hands the phone to me.

"Rick?" I croak, clearing my throat. "Are you there?"

"Sorry to wake you. I know it's early, but I promised to call from Japan when I got here. I only have a few minutes before I have to board my plane, so I can't talk long."

"Are you still getting here on time?" I ask, my voice stronger now.

"Yes, I'll be there on time. Everything is good to go. I can't wait to see you. How are you doing?"

"I'm fine. The morning sickness is starting to go away and we have an apartment."

"Really? When do we move in?"

"Tonight. I picked up the keys about a week ago."

"You're kidding! That's awesome! I can't wait to see it. Our first home together," he laughs. Loud gibberish interrupts him. "Hey, I gotta go. They're calling final boarding for my flight. I love you, and I'll see you soon!"

"Love you, too, sweetie. Be careful!"

"I will."

We say our goodbyes and hang up. I grin, relishing in the knowledge that this is our last long distance phone call. I won't have to talk to him on the phone anymore because he'll be here. Glancing at the clock on the wall, I notice it's four o'clock. Poor Rick; he's in for a long day. I hope he can sleep on the plane. His flight isn't due until almost seven tonight. When he gave me his flight information a few weeks back, he mentioned that he had to change planes in Honolulu and Los Angeles before arriving here.

Climbing back into bed, I surprise myself by going back to sleep quickly.

When I awaken, it's almost nine thirty. I stretch and grin like a Cheshire cat. Rick will be home today. Happiness bubbles up and overflows inside me. I close my eyes and cradle my stomach.

"Daddy will be home today," I whisper.

A fluttery sensation inside my belly answers me and I gasp aloud, my hands gripping my stomach. Knowing beyond a shadow of doubt what it is, I wait anxiously for a repeat performance. Long moments go by and just as I think that I imagined it, I feel another flutter.

"Whoa," I whisper. "Hi, baby," I talk softly, rubbing the bulge in my belly. "Daddy can't wait to see you." Another flutter answers and I giggle.

This is one of the best days of my life. Others include the day I met Rick, the day we got married, and now this. I feel our baby move for the first time, and he comes home.

"Thank you, God," I whisper, staring at the popcorn ceiling.

When I tell my family about feeling the baby move, they are all excited and want to feel it, too. Jeff is not included in the excitement; he is excited in his own way, but he's still a teenager and wouldn't be caught dead putting his hands on his sister's stomach or anywhere else for that matter.

"I didn't feel it with my hands, I just felt it from the inside," I remind them.

Three faces fall simultaneously. "That's all right," Mom says. "There is plenty of time when the baby gets big enough for us to feel the movement. Just be sure to let us know!"

The day ticks by quickly; first on the To Do list is to transfer my bed to the apartment. Mom has it stripped and the linens in the washing machine before I'm even out of the shower. I walk into the bedroom and find a naked bed; my pillows are even gone.

"Well, there's no time to waste," Dad quips when I inquire about it.

"But I just got out of the shower," I protest.

"Yes, and you weren't planning on going back to bed, were you? Now listen, Jeff's friends are coming over in about an hour and they're going to help us move, so we need to be ready."

Talk about a whirlwind of a Saturday.

While I finish drying my hair and getting dressed, Dad and Jeff disassemble the bed and frame in preparation for transport. I pack up the remaining clothes and other items from my room and stuff them into the luggage my parents bought for me on my sixteenth birthday. Once I've emptied the closets and drawers, I look around at the partially disassembled and mostly vacant room that has been my sanctuary most of my life, and pause to reflect. I really am making The Transition into adulthood. A flutter in my belly draws my hand instinctively to it.

This is a transition indeed.

Thankfully, we have Rick's truck. I couldn't imagine getting all the parts of my bed plus the mattress and box spring into Dad's Subaru or Mom's car or my Honda.

Once we, well *they*, grunt and groan and sweat and finally get my bed loaded in the truck and set up in the bedroom of the apartment, I sit on the sofa with a big yawn like I actually did real work. Fortunately, I'm not as tired as I was even a few weeks ago, but a small nap would be nice.

"You just rest, Heather. I'll make your bed for you once I put this in the fridge," Mom says and disappears first into the kitchen and then down the hallway.

Puzzled, I get up and check what Mom put in the fridge. There's a square glass baking dish covered with foil with a note on top that reads, "Heat in a 350 degree oven for about 20 minutes. Enjoy!" Next to the square dish is a smaller plate, also covered with foil. When I lift up the corner, I see there are two frosted brownies there; one for me and one for Rick. Mom made Rick dinner and brownies for both of us.

I go back to my bedroom where the mattress is just being placed on top of the box spring. Mom's arms are loaded with bedding. I walk up and hug her as best I can. "Thanks, Mom," I reply gratefully.

"You're welcome, sweetie."

I return to the living room and plop on the sofa once more, smiling as I rest my head back.

"I'm going to miss you," Debbie says, sitting down next to me with a mournful expression.

"Me too, Debbie. But I'm not gone; I'm just down the road."

"But I still won't see you as often. I like having you as a big sister."

I squeeze her hand. "I like having you as a little sister."

Mom and Dad buy pizza and soda for everybody to thank them for helping with the move. My apartment is bursting at the seams with people, all just to move one bed. Five of Jeff's friends showed up; I found out later that he had spied a "hot babe" at the complex pool and shared this observation with his friends. We had more than enough volunteers.

My parents, Debbie, and I sit at the little dining room table with our paper plates while Jeff and his friends spill out of the open front door, on the lookout for the reputed hot babes Jeff boasted about.

"Only a few more hours left," Dad says, wiping the grease from his chin. "Getting excited?"

"I can hardly stand it! Plus, look at this place," I sweep my arm in the general direction of the living room, which has been transformed from the first day I saw it. "You guys did a great job helping me decorate and get everything ready. It actually feels like a home now."

"It *is* your home now," Mom says softly. "It's absolutely adorable. Rick will love it."

"I think so," I add. "Thanks again for his dinner. What did you make him?"

"Oh, just some left over roast beef, mashed potatoes, gravy, and green beans. I'm sure he'll be plenty hungry when he gets here and won't want cold pizza for dinner."

"I saw the brownies, too."

Mom smiles before tearing another bite from her pizza slice.

Debbie grins and grabs another slice of pizza. "I wish I lived in a cute apartment like this."

"You will one day," I laugh, happy that the pizza tastes good and my stomach is agreeable. I haven't thrown up in almost a week. Now that I'm in my second trimester, hopefully morning sickness is a thing of the past. Based on the books I've read, the second trimester is supposed to be the best of the three.

Once the pizzas have been devoured and the garbage happily trotted off to the dumpster by Jeff and all of his friends (still in search of hot babes, which I doubt hang out around dumpsters), it's time to go home to drop Jeff and his friends off before we make our way to the airport. Everyone piles into one of the three vehicles for the brief trek home. Well, to my parents' house now. I follow Dad in his Subaru, driving Rick's truck and Mom follows me in her car. Rick and I will pick up my Honda tomorrow and bring it back to the apartment.

Dad leaves strict instructions with Jeff before Mom, Debbie, Dad, and I head to the airport. At my insistence, I drive Rick's truck by myself and follow my father. Jeff stays behind with his friends. Just as we're pulling out of the driveway, Jeff yells for me to stop.

"What?" I ask, frowning as he trots up to my open window.

Jeff hesitates briefly before reaching in and hugging me awkwardly. "Good job, sis. You made it." He releases me, wheels around and trots back toward the house. Just before he reaches the front door, he turns to me with a grin. "Tell Rick I said welcome home!"

I'm stunned into silence. That's the most affection Jeff has given me in years.

Two honks break through the shock. I stretch to look behind me; Dad has his hands up as if to say 'What gives?' I put the truck into reverse and pull out, close on my father's tail pipe.

CHAPTER TWELVE

May, 1989

I'm nervous for Rick to see me. The baby is feeding off of my nervousness; the fluttering movement is constant. The baby is excited to meet daddy, too.

Finally, Rick's sandy blond hair comes into view and I clap and scream with glee. He may have heard me because at that moment Rick's head bobs around those in front of him, shouldering his way through the queue. His eyes rake up and down my form, curiosity in his brown eyes and a smile on his gorgeous face.

I turn to the side and cradle my stomach, obliging him with a full view of what he's searching for.

His eyes bug out and his smile widens. "Hey!" he yells, trotting over to me once he reaches the portal, dropping his bag and placing his hands on my stomach. "Wow, you really are showing, aren't you?" When his gaze returns to my face, his eyes are glistening. "You do look…thinner, though. I thought I told you to plump up."

Ignoring his comment, I grab him and pull myself to him hard. He pulls back ever so slightly, "Whoa. Don't hurt the baby."

"I won't," I whisper and kiss him fiercely. "I'm so glad you're home for good," I breathe.

He rubs my back, inhaling the hair at my ear. "Me, too. It's so good to be home."

"Welcome home, son!" Dad beams, clapping Rick on the back. "You finally made it."

"You're going to *love* your apartment!" Debbie squeals.

"Well hey, squirt! How you been?" Rick rumples Debbie's hair. He turns to me. "I can't wait to see it."

I kiss him once more and nod. "I think you're really going to like it."

"It's a real nice one," Mom adds, smiling at Rick. "It's furnished and has a nice pool. It's in a good neighborhood and there are a lot of military folks there."

"Hello again, Mrs. Scott – I mean Louise," Rick amends. "I'm glad to hear that."

I smile, lacing my fingers in his. "We are moving in together tonight. I wanted to wait for you."

His eyebrows rise. "You haven't stayed there at all?"

"Nope. Our first night together will be my first night in the apartment."

"Yes, we moved her bed over this afternoon," Mom says.

"Let's get your luggage and hit the road," Dad announces.

"Are you hungry, Rick?" Mom's brows furrow.

"Yes, ma'am. As a matter of fact, I am starving."

"Good. I left your dinner in the fridge." She turns to me. "You be sure to heat up the oven as soon as you get home so it's nice and hot."

"I know, Mom. I will."

Rick turns to me, puzzled. "Are we going to their house or are they coming to ours?"

I smile and shake my head. "No, they're going home and so are we. To our home."

He blinks a few times before his smile broadens. "You mean I get you all to myself just like that?"

A thrill runs through me and I grin, anticipating our reunion. "Yes, sir."

Once we pick up Rick's luggage at baggage claim and get to our vehicles parked side by side in the parking lot, Dad takes the lead after Rick's luggage is loaded in his truck for our journey home. "Well, son, take good care of her. We're so glad you're home," his voice chokes and he gives Rick a manly hug followed by two good slaps on the back.

"When are you guys coming over?" Debbie whines.

"Deborah, we talked about this," Mom replies sternly.

Rick grabs Debbie in a bear hug and lifts her off the ground. "We'll be over real soon, squirt. I need a rematch at Connect Four." When he places her back on the ground, she giggles.

"Thank you both for taking such good care of her while I was gone. I'm forever grateful. I'm thankful you're part of my family," Rick extends his hand out to shake my father's hand and my mother reaches in for a hug, whispering something in his ear that I can't hear. Rick grins. He nods and replies, "Sure thing, ma'am."

Mom, Dad, and Debbie all hug me, too. Finally, Dad pipes up, "Let's hit the road, girls. You two drive carefully and…we'll talk to you real soon." I would swear I saw my father's chin quiver, but he turned his head and ducked in the car so fast I couldn't be sure.

Mom and Debbie follow suit and Rick helps me climb into his truck, even though I don't really need it.

When we arrive at our apartment, Rick insists on taking two trips to bring his luggage up. He refuses to allow me to carry anything other than my purse. When we get to the door and I place the key in the lock, he drops his bags and places his hand over mine, "Wait."

Before I can mount a protest, he sweeps me off my feet, deftly opens the door, and carries me across the threshold, grinning broadly.

"Welcome to our new home!" he says, although he's the one who's never seen it before. Ever so carefully, he places me on my feet again and his eyes sweep the apartment from the living room to the dining area to the kitchen and down the short hallway. "Wow. It's awesome," he says, turning to me. "And it's all ours." He grabs my face in his hands and kisses me so passionately that I swoon.

He quickly retrieves his bags, easily finding his way to our bedroom – there aren't many doors to choose from – and plops them down in the corner.

I remember my mother's instructions and turn the oven on, removing the glass dish from the fridge.

"I'm going to get my other bags and I'll be right back," he ducks his head and disappears, reappearing in record time with his remaining luggage which he places in the corner of the living room. If he put any more luggage in the bedroom, we would have to crawl over it to get to the bed.

"What's for dinner?" he asks, patting his stomach. "I'm really starving."

I show him the dish and he gulps heavily in anticipation. I hope one day he'll do that for food I make. I am thankful for the recipes Mom gave me.

"She also made dessert," I tell him happily, showing him the smaller plate. His eyes widen when he notices the fridge is stocked.

"You guys went grocery shopping already? Did you go to the commissary?" he asks incredulously, his eyes roaming the shelves laden with food.

"No. Mom wanted to go with me, but she can't get into the commissary."

"Oh, that's right. Well, you can go to the commissary from now on."

While his dinner heats up, I take his hand and guide him around our apartment; it only takes a few steps, but I am eager to show him everything, including the bathroom. He smiles when he sees the matching pink rug, seat cover, and towels.

"Well, as long as the whole apartment isn't done in pink and flowers, I guess I can live with a pink bathroom." He inhales deeply, sighing. "I smell dinner."

Rick eats his dinner heartily, not leaving even a swipe of gravy. When it's empty, he sits back in his chair with a satisfied grin.

"Want dessert?" I ask.

His eyes rake lazily over me. "You or the brownie?"

"Both, but the brownie first," I smile and rise to retrieve the brownies. Rick pulls me into his lap to nuzzle my neck. I sigh in pleasure. "Oh, I'm so happy you're home, sweetie. It's been a long year."

He hugs me tightly before resting his hand gently on my belly. "Yes, it has. But we made it. I'm home."

"We're both home," I reply, kissing him. I'll never tire of kissing Rick.

The brownies are delicious; I make a mental note to see if that recipe is in the collection. If not, I'll have to get it.

Much later, Rick and I are lying in bed with our legs tangled together, both happy and satisfied, staring up at the ceiling.

Rick gently disentangles our legs, lies on his side, and places his warm hand over the bulge in my belly, rubbing gently back and forth. "This is amazing," he murmurs.

I turn to regard his face, barely visible in the golden glow cast through the doorway from the light we forgot to turn off in the living room. His eyes follow the path his hand takes. He looks like he's glowing, but it could just be the light from the doorway. I prefer to think it's the former. "Yes, it is," I reply, placing my hand over his.

"I mean, I can actually *feel* the baby already," he murmurs in awe. "Your stomach used to be flat and now it's…not. Wow." He turns his gaze to me. "Is the baby moving?"

I pause and slowly shake my head. "Not right now."

He bends down so that his lips almost touch my belly. "Okay, baby," he coaxes gently. "Daddy's home. I want to feel you move. Come on now. Say hello."

I laugh, which makes my stomach jump.

"No fair," Rick scowls mockingly at me. "Hold still." He turns his attention back to my belly and starts talking to it again. I can't help myself; I crack up.

We spend the better part of the late night talking, laughing, and loving each other. Eventually, the living room light is turned off and we go to sleep.

When I wake the following morning, not only is my hand on my bulging belly, but Rick's hand is there, too, covering mine. I look at his face and he's sound asleep. I find it remarkable that even when he's unconscious, he's present.

Not wanting to wake him, I carefully remove his hand and slip out of bed. After using the restroom, I plod into the kitchen to brew coffee while I cook some eggs; I'm really *hungry* this morning. I open the blinds near the dining room table just a little so that I can peer out into the world on the first morning in our new apartment. I square my shoulders, reveling in the grown up feeling.

When I scrape the last of the eggs from my plate, Rick stumbles into the living room, scratching at the scruffiness on his chin. "Morning," he mumbles, yawns, and plops into a chair next to me.

"Hi, sweetie," I lean in to give him a kiss. "Hungry?"

"Sure," he replies, rubbing his face. "Sleep okay?"

"Very well," I add, kissing him again before heading into the kitchen. "I've got coffee on. Would you like a cup?"

"Please."

"How do you like it?" I ask, dismayed. "I don't remember."

He grins. "It's okay. Two sugars and a splash of cream, please."

I pour two mugs and prepare them both. I hand Rick his mug.

He smiles, inhaling the rich aroma before sipping carefully. "Ahhh. Perfect. Thanks."

Once his eggs are cooked – it's one thing I don't need a recipe for – I place the plate in front of him, and he eats just as heartily as the night before.

"Didn't they feed you over there?" I ask, watching him clear his plate in record time.

"Sure, but there's nothing like good old home cooked food."

The compliment warms me as much as the coffee.

"What do you want to do today?" Rick asks, swallowing his last bite.

"Stare at you. I am so glad you don't have to go away," I respond, propping my chin in my hand and gazing at him. Even with tousled hair and a scruffy chin, he's handsome.

"Well, that's true, but I do have to go to work in a week, though," he replies, taking his plate to the sink and rinsing it.

My mouth falls open. "A week? You only get one week's worth of leave?"

"Yes," he sighs. "But I will still be home every day after work. Better than not seeing you for months at a time. Now, I'll ask again – what do you want to do today?" He walks over and brings me to a standing position, wrapping me in an embrace and nuzzling my neck.

We spend most of the day enjoying each other's company and unpacking his things. It feels good to see his luggage and duffel bag slowly deflate and eventually be folded and stuffed into the bottom of our closet.

The afternoon is spent doing some laundry and lazing around the pool, which isn't too crowded for a weekend. There are only six other people there, one of which is a toddler with her mother.

"Rick," I ask, watching the mother and toddler interact while Rick and I lounge of the steps of the pool. "What do you think our child will look like?"

"Hm? I don't know, but he'll be handsome or she'll be awfully pretty, especially if she takes after you." He kisses the tip of my nose, leaving a drop of water dangling there. I shake it off, laughing. "When will we be able to find out if we're having a boy or a girl?"

"I was told I'll have an ultrasound at the next appointment," I reply, my eyes following the chubby toddler's antics.

"Really? When is it?" he asks excitedly.

"It's in a couple weeks. You'll be able to come for that, won't you?"

"I'm sure I can. When I left last year, the shop was pretty laid back. I'm not worried about it," he says splashing water on his arms. "I can't believe how fast it's going by, you know? I mean, it feels like I just found out you're pregnant and now we'll know if it's a boy or a girl."

My hands rub my bulging belly. "Tell me about it. It's crazy."

"Crazy? No, I think it's amazing."

"Rick, tell me how you really feel about this. Is it happening too fast for you?"

"No," he answers quickly. "I mean, we had planned on waiting a little longer, but apparently God has another plan. So here we are. Besides," he pulls me close and kisses me fiercely. "You're one hot mama."

I giggle and push back a little, glancing around. I've always been uncomfortable with public affection. "You're one hot daddy, too."

Eventually, we make our way back to the apartment where we take a nice, long shower together before dinner. The bathroom is pretty steamy before we're done.

"Rick, would you go check the mail?" I cinch my robe and hand him the mailbox key. I have to get him out of the apartment for five minutes.

"Sure," he replies, quickly putting on a pair of shorts and a T-shirt. "Be back in a jiffy." He ducks out of the apartment. I watch his head bob down the stairs and disappear. As soon as he's out of sight, I bolt for the linen closet in the hallway and pull out the surprise. It's a nice crisp, white linen tablecloth with two white linen napkins. There are two crystal candlestick holders rolled carefully up inside. Removing the candlestick holders and placing them aside, I hurriedly shake out the tablecloth and smooth it over the dining room table. I quickly place silverware and the two crystal goblets we used to toast at our wedding at each place setting. Next, I pull the bottle of sparkling grape juice out of the back of the fridge and place that in the center of the table, followed by the candlestick holders in which I insert two long tapered white candles, quickly lighting them both. I step back to admire my work; it's not as fancy as the suite we had at the hotel, but it will have to do.

I finish just in time for him to return. I whip around and stand to the side of the table, grinning as he makes his entry. He is empty-handed, of course; I didn't expect any mail.

"What's this?" he asks, taking in the table setting.

"It's our first official dinner together in our first official apartment. I wanted it to remind us of our honeymoon suite."

He grins, strides over and embraces me. "It's beautiful. Very thoughtful. What's for dinner?"

"Well," I grimace. "The actual food won't be fancy, I'm afraid."

Dinner is simple; I have to get used to planning meals. I forgot that meat needs to be thawed before it can be cooked. We settle for hot dogs and potato chips washed down with the sparkling grape juice in crystal goblets flickering in the candlelight.

After we're done, Rick places his napkin on the plate and smiles. "That was the best hot dog and chip dinner I ever had."

"I really am sorry. I will plan better from now on."

He waves me off. "I don't care, really. I appreciate that you went to all this trouble. It was very special. Thank you."

While we clear the table, I feel the fluttering in my stomach. "Quick, I just felt the baby move!" I grab his hand and place it over the spot where I felt the movement. Rick waits, his head cocked in concentration. Long moments go by.

"Do you still feel it?" he finally whispers.

I snort a laugh. "You don't have to whisper, Rick. Not right…" A flutter bubbles in me. "There!" I press his hand harder to the spot. Another flutter and Rick gasps, his eyes wide.

"My God," he breathes. "I felt it." Another flutter and he gasps again, anchoring his hand firmly to my belly. Slowly, a grin blossoms on his face.

"Cool, huh?" I ask. His eyes are riveted to my stomach.

He nods slowly and drops to his knees in front of me. "Wow. We're going to be parents," he murmurs, his eyes shining. "Wow."

****

The rest of the days he is on leave are spent either at my parents house, at the pool, or just hanging out around the apartment, enjoying each other.

The following Monday after lunch, I concentrate on what Rick is saying while we drive to the base. He's talking about processing into his squadron.

"Now, you'll meet the First Sergeant. He's a nice guy; I met him this morning. He's new to the squadron."

"Okay. Why do I have to meet him?"

"It's good to know some people. He's sort of the spokesperson for the enlisted people in the squadron, and talks directly to our commanding officer."

"Oh."

Once we are waved onto the base by the front gate guard, Rick takes an endless number of turns before finally arriving at a building that looks like most other buildings on the base; they're all either tan or beige. I suppose it doesn't matter, unless I plan to find this particular tan or beige building again. We walk into a spacious office divided into cubicles with real offices on the perimeter.

"Hello, I'm Airman Johnson here to see the First Sergeant," Rick smiles at the receptionist dressed in a crisp blue uniform. She has a few more stripes than Rick does on her sleeve, but not much.

"Yes, I'll let him know you're here," she smiles and ducks her head into one of the perimeter offices. When she emerges, a tall gentleman, also dressed in a crisp blue uniform but with quite a few more stripes than either Rick or the young lady have, accompanies her. He approaches us both and, smiling broadly, offers his hand first to Rick and then to me when Rick introduces me.

"Hello again, Airman Johnson." He turns to me. "This is the lovely wife you told me about. I'm Sergeant Buttini." He pronounces his name *beyou-tee-nee*. He pumps my hand and gestures for us to follow him into his office, where he politely pulls out a chair for me. I successfully stifle a giggle when I read the spelling of his name on the name plate positioned front and center on his desk. I am so glad he said it first, or I would have pronounced it phonetically and most likely would've gotten Rick in trouble on his first day.

"Thank you," I reply, smiling sweetly, as I take the offered chair. Rick sits in the chair next to me.

"So, I hear you're expecting your first child? What a transition, huh?" Sergeant Buttini jokes.

"Yes, sir. It's wonderful. She's due in October, and we're hoping to be in housing before then," Rick replies.

"Please don't call me sir. I work for a living." Sergeant Buttini proceeds to laugh heartily at his own joke.

"That's a good one," Rick laughs along with him at the ridiculous joke. I follow Rick's lead and cough out a laugh, even though it's not funny.

"I assume you're already on the wait list for housing, then?" Sergeant Buttini asks, switching from jovial to serious faster than anyone I've ever seen. Rick follows suit.

"Yes, my wife put us on the list about two months ago," he looks to me for reassurance and I nod.

"Good, that's good," the sergeant replies. He then launches into a recitation of how the Air Force is a family and we're all part of a great team, etc. It sounds like he's delivering lines in a play that he's been a part of for years. I smile and nod occasionally.

When he's finished delivering his lines, he asks if we have any questions. I shake my head while Rick answers for the both of us, thanking him profusely for taking time to meet with us. We rise, shake his hand once more, and leave.

I concentrate on where Rick turns as he drives, trying to remember how to find this place again, should I ever need to. I need to become more independent on base. While we were dating, I didn't spend much time on base with him and didn't venture over here while he was gone. Since we'll be living on base soon, that has to change.

More adjustments.

****

Rick's first official day on the job is two days later. In the meantime, he is busy driving all over the base for various appointments with offices that have names like finance and accounting and support services. He's required to wear his uniform for all of it. I don't accompany him on these appointments – Rick encourages me to rest with my feet up.

"I'm sure you'll wish you could once the baby comes," he reminds me.

Finally, when his first official day on the job arrives, he's excited. I am excited for him, so I wake up early to fix a hearty breakfast and spend some time with him before seeing him off.

Glancing at his watch after his second cup of coffee, he jumps up and pecks me on the cheek. "I gotta go. I don't want to be late for my first day!"

I follow him to the door and squeeze him one more time before he trots down the stairs with a smile and a wave.

Contrary to his advice, I don't spend the day sitting with my feet up. I scrub the apartment from top to bottom. It's not dirty, but I don't want it to get that way. I'm done by one o'clock and the whole place smells of cleanser and pine sol. That translates to *clean* in my book. I am munching on a lunch of a sandwich and some pretzel sticks when the phone rings.

"Hello?" I answer.

"Hey! How're you and the baby doing?" Rick answers.

I smile; there's no crackle on the line. Not anymore. "We're fine. I'm just having lunch. How is your day going?"

"Fine, fine. Listen," he clears his throat. "I just wanted to let you know that my regular schedule starting this weekend will be evening shift, and my days off are Thursdays and Fridays."

"Oh? So are you off this week on Thursday and Friday or...?"

"Uh," he clears his throat again. "No. My new shift doesn't start until Sunday, so I will have Saturday off, but then I have to come in at three on Sunday afternoon."

"Okay." I hadn't given any thought to the possibility of him working anything but normal hours; Monday through Friday and home by five, just like Dad.

"I just wanted to give you a heads up. All right?"

"Okay."

"Hey, I gotta go, but I'll be home by five at the latest. Love you."

"Love you, too." *Click.*

That means no dinners together each night and no evening activities, either. Well, I'll adjust. We can do things together in the morning instead of the evening. It will work out. At least he's home.

I call my mother after lunch.

"Can I have that brownie recipe? I didn't see it in the collection and we loved them."

"Of course," she laughs. "Do you want to write it down or have me write it on an index card for you to add to your collection?"

"I'll get it from you when we come over this weekend."

"Not a problem. What time will you guys be here on Saturday?"

"About one-ish."

"Good. We'll be barbecuing steaks and chicken."

"Sounds yummy! Can I bring something?"

"No, just come."

"Mom, I can bring something."

"Bring a bag of chips then, if you must," she laughs.

I roll my eyes. "All right. I'll bring chips this time. Next time, you have to let me make something."

****

The barbecue is wonderful, of course. Mom's food is spectacular and Dad hasn't lost his touch at the grill. They even sprang for filet mignon instead of the usual sirloin; Dad said it was in celebration of Rick's return and why shouldn't he splurge a little?

Rick ate two steaks and countless chicken legs plus heaps of baked beans, potato salad, and every other dish Mom made. Jeff kept pace with Rick and also finished off the chips I brought.

Debbie reminded Rick of their face off with Connect Four; she had it set up on a card table under the awning of the back patio in a jiffy once he finished eating. Now, they are staring pointedly at the board, both measuring their moves before they make them, like grandmasters in chess. My mother and I sit in wicker chairs in the back yard, watching. Mom and I enjoy the sun and warmth. I have always enjoyed the Texas heat with the exception of the most intense summer heat. I turn my face up toward the late afternoon sun, close my eyes, and breathe in deeply.

"How do you all like the apartment?" Mom asks.

"I love it," I reply, slowly blowing my breath out. "I am finally a real grown-up."

"Yes, you are," Mom chuckles. "How are you feeling?"

"Great," I reply, rubbing my protruding stomach lovingly. "I feel absolutely wonderful. I'm glad the morning sickness is done."

"When's your next appointment?"

"Next week. Rick said he should be able to come with me. I hope so – it's the ultrasound, and we should find out if it's a boy or girl."

"That's nice. If Rick can't make it, you can always give me a call."

I squint at my mother. "You mean you're not coming with?"

"Heavens, no. Rick needs to go to the appointments with you now, Heather. I'm just the back up." She grins. "I know you'll call and let me know what the doctor says."

"Are you sure you don't want to come?"

Mom reaches across and pats my knee. "No. This is your time with Rick." She allows her head to fall back and rest on the wicker and I follow suit. We both close our eyes and sit in companionable silence for the remainder of the Connect Four tournament.

****

Sunday afternoon arrives. While Rick changes into his uniform for work, I pack food for him to eat for dinner. We have decided to make dinner at lunch and so I pack lunch for his dinner: sandwiches, fruit, and chips. Cooking a hot meal in the middle of the day means I have to use even more forethought with meals. I have to thaw meat every night before I go to bed in order to cook it at noon.

"I'm ready," Rick says, striding into the living room, uniform freshly pressed and his face clean shaven.

"You look handsome, as always," I reply, enveloping myself in his embrace. "I made your dinner."

"Thanks." He kisses me. "Here's my work number." He points to the piece of paper stuck to the refrigerator with a magnet in the shape of a muffin. "Call me if you need to, but not just because you want to."

My face falls. "Why can't I just call you?"

"They won't like that, even if I would love to hear your voice. I'm on duty which usually means I am on the flight line anyway. I'll call if I can. Of course, if you need me, don't hesitate." He glances at my stomach. "Be sure to ask for Airman Johnson, too, not Rick."

"Oh. Okay."

Once he leaves, I glance around the apartment, unsure of what to do with myself. The apartment is still clean and there's no laundry. An idea makes me grin.

I dial my parent's home.

"Hello?" Mom's voice answers after the third ring.

"Mom? What are you guys up to?" I ask.

"Nothing much, why?"

"Why don't you all come over and swim? Rick just left for work and I'm bored already."

"Oh, that would be lovely! Hang on." Her voice becomes garbled as she cups her hand around the mouthpiece. Moments later Debbie's excited squeal is heard loud and clear, however. "We would love to, sweetie. We'll be there soon."

I've changed into my swimsuit and gathered towels when they arrive.

Dad declined to come saying that his white legs would scare off every resident in a half mile radius. Dad doesn't do shorts, even for the hot Texas summers. Debbie brought her goggles – she has always liked to dive to the bottom. She used to pretend she was a mermaid and would see how long she could stay under water. Impressively, she surpassed a whole minute once.

I'm surprised to see Debbie blossoming into a young lady when she removes her wrap and I see her in her one-piece bathing suit. It's obvious her body has begun to transform. Remarking about it to Mom, she nods in agreement and looks at me significantly.

"Tell me about it," she says. "She's only twelve."

We spend the afternoon splashing in and lounging at the pool, which is more populated this time. Jeff straightens up and puffs his arms out when he notices what appears to be a small group of teenage girls. They are clustered together in a giggly mass, having taken over one corner table and chairs. They notice Jeff when he walks in; their giggles increase in intensity. They continue to cast glances in his direction, whispering things to each other behind cupped hands. I smile and shake my head.

We take up residence in the opposite corner at one of the few empty tables left. Jeff quickly leaves our little group to show off his aquatic skills in hopes of impressing the cluster of teens.

"Do you think he'll have the nerve to talk to them?" I ask my mother, nodding toward the group.

Mom glances at the girls before turning her gaze back to Jeff. "He might. He's gotten pretty bold lately." She chuckles. Jeff executes a perfectly imperfect front flip into the deep end. The teens intermittently sigh and giggle. Jeff emerges, shakes water from his hair, and grins at them.

"They're actually impressed with that," I laugh.

"Oh, Heather. Leave the boy alone," Mom chides, suppressing a smile.

"Mom! Throw in the quarter!" Debbie yells, her head bobbing on the water.

"Oh! Here you go!" Mom tosses the quarter into the deep end. Debbie positions her goggles on her face and dips underwater. Her rear end makes a brief appearance before she disappears completely. She emerges shortly, holding the quarter up triumphantly. "Good job!"

We spend the entire afternoon into the early evening at the pool. We are all a little pink for the experience. It's good Vitamin D, my father would say. Jeff finally speaks to the girls – they are sufficiently impressed with his aquatic antics. Debbie finds another girl to play with; they take turns diving for the quarter or playing Marco Polo.

As we gather ourselves to head back to my apartment, Jeff declines to come. "I'll be there later." He waves dismissively at us, turning his attention back to the gaggle of girls, who are all eager for his attention.

Who knew my brother was attractive or charming?

"Jeff, come back before the sun goes down," Mom reminds him.

He winces and nods, trying to ignore us. We are his family, after all – something to be shunned when there are teen girls to impress.

Debbie's face and shoulders are more red than pink. She and Jeff spent the most time in the pool.

"Oh, boy," Mom laments, squinting at Debbie's face. "I'm glad I brought the Noxzema."

Once we've all showered, Mom applies Noxzema to the worst sunburns on Debbie's face, shoulders, and back. I boil hot dogs and serve them with canned baked beans.

"I'm sorry they're not your recipe, Mom," I apologize.

"It's all right. These are good, too. I'm starved!" Mom says, taking a large bite of her hot dog.

"Me, too," Debbie chimes in, her mouth already full of hot dog.

Jeff shows up an hour later – enviably more brown than red. He has always tanned quickly whereas the rest of us burn and peel first, slowly and painfully developing our tans.

"Well, look who decided to show up! Hungry?" I ask.

"Duh. Does paint dry?" he jokes. He snatches a plate and fills five buns with hot dogs. His first bite is one half of a hot dog.

"Slow down, Jeff. You'll choke," Mom chides him, smiling.

He nods, but downs the other half in one bite anyway.

Rick may not be home most evenings, but I love having my family to spend time with.

****

Rick is able to accompany me to my OB appointment without taking time off from work; an unexpected benefit to the shift. He will be able to make all of my appointments. I am thrilled. Maybe evening shift is a good thing, after all.

I'm not surprised to see a new and unfamiliar doctor once again. Hopefully, at some point I will get the same one twice out of sheer luck. This particular doctor has a good bedside manner and talks with Rick for a few moments about his experience in Korea; he had spent a year there, as well.

"The worst part was being apart from her," Rick glances at me, squeezing my hand.

"I hear ya," the doctor replies, glancing over my sheet. "My wife and I had three little ones at home when I left."

"That must have been awful!" I exclaim.

"Yeah," he shrugs. "But whatya gonna do? Now, young lady, everything seems to be normal...urine, blood pressure. I'm glad to see that you're gaining weight finally. You took awhile doing that." He grins at me. "Go ahead and lie back and we'll check you out."

During the exam, Rick clears his throat a few times and I notice his cheeks get redder and redder until the exam is over. The doctor either doesn't notice or chooses to ignore it.

"The baby appears to be growing normally based on the measurements. All right, now the moment you've been waiting for," he grunts and sits down on a stool, pulling a large machine over. He addresses the ever present silent assistant, "Hit the lights, please."

As the room grows dark, he lifts the sheet to expose my bulging midsection, noisily squirts a clear gel onto it and places what looks like a joystick attached to a thick grey cord into the goop, spreading it around. Shadows and shapes appear and recede on the screen.

"What is all of that?" Rick asks, peering intently at the screen. We both wait with breath held in anticipation, eyes glued to the screen. I can't make sense of any of it.

"Well," the doctor replies, peering at the screen. "Here's the wall of the uterus," he points to a defined line of light gray and darkness. "All of the darkness in the middle is the amniotic fluid, and here," he places the wand over a specific point and rests it there. "is your baby."

The shape that we see moves jerkily at times within the mass of darkness encircling it; tiny definable limbs with visible bones move around. A bulbous little head bobs along with the limbs.

"Is that the face?" Rick asks in wonder, pointing. Suddenly the mouth opens and shuts.

"Yes," the doctor replies. "That's the face." He goes on to describe and outline other parts of the baby, making tiny lines appear and disappear with various clicks on the machine.

"What are you doing now?" I ask, unable to take my eyes off of this tiny little person.

"I'm taking specific measurements of the baby to make sure the growth is in line with where you are in your pregnancy, and that everything is growing the way it should." He continues to make the tiny lines appear and disappear all over the baby's body, clicking away. "Would you like to know the gender?"

"Yes!" We answer in unison.

"Okay," he chuckles. "I guess there's no conflict there. Let's see if the little peanut will show us."

I squeeze Rick's hand excitedly. He grins, keeping his eyes glued to the screen.

The baby and the wand play a game of hide-and-go-seek; the baby jerks and moves in and out of view with the doctor and his wand in pursuit.

"Hold still you little bugger," the doctor chides, chuckling. Rick chuckles, too. "Aha! Here it is." He points to the screen.

"Here *what* is? I don't see anything!" I blurt.

"Exactly," the doctor grins, winking at me.

Rick gasps, his mouth forming an "O". "It's a girl!" he exclaims, pointing at the screen. "Right? Is that what you mean?"

The doctor nods, still grinning.

It's a girl.

Rick hugs me awkwardly while the doctor wipes the goop from my stomach and the machine spits out black and white photos of our baby girl to take with us.

"Congratulations to both of you. She looks to be growing normally," the doctor smiles cheerily. I like him and wish I could see him again. "Do you have any questions?"

Rick clears his throat and jumps right in, his cheeks reddening slightly. "Well, I do have one question." He scratches his head and blows his breath out. "Is it okay to have sex during pregnancy?"

The doctor doesn't even flinch. "Absolutely. When the pregnancy is progressing normally without complications, it's perfectly fine as long as you're both comfortable."

Rick blinks. "Really? I mean," he shifts in his seat. "She won't be...well, born with a hole in her head or anything?"

I snicker before I can help myself.

Once again, the doctor is unflappable. "No, that's not possible. She'll be just fine."

Rick's shoulders relax and he smiles at the doctor. "Thanks, doc."

"Do you have any questions?" the doctor addresses me.

"Yes. Can we see you every time?"

It is a long shot, but I ask anyway.

"I appreciate the compliment, but that's not how it works, unfortunately. The military system isn't set up that way, for now. Hopefully, someday it will change."

When I approach the front desk to make my next appointment, I beg the young man to give me the same doctor for the next appointment, but to no avail.

"Really? Why can't she see the same doctor?" Rick persists.

"It's like I already explained," the young man sighs. "There's nothing I can do about it. You have to see whoever is on duty on the day you come in."

CHAPTER THIRTEEN

September, 1989

"I'm really sorry you're so uncomfortable," Rick says sympathetically, rubbing my aching feet.

It's ridiculous – how can my feet, legs, and back ache so much? I don't *do* anything. I couldn't imagine having a job and going to work while feeling like this. I can only manage short bursts of activity – making the bed and keeping up with the laundry are now defined as short bursts of activity. I am one month away from my due date. It can't come soon enough. Not only did I finally start gaining weight, I have exceeded expectations by gaining forty-five pounds.

"I hope she comes early. I mean," I complain, hoisting myself up on the sofa with a grunt. "One month early is no big deal, right? I can't do this for four more weeks, Rick."

Rick sighs, continuing to rub my feet. "I think there's a reason they call it full term."

I puff out my breath. "Thanks for rubbing my feet."

He smiles. "You're welcome. Anything I can do to help." He flicks a glance at his watch. "Sorry, but time's up. I gotta go to work."

"I know, I know," I sigh, rearranging my large rear end again.

Rick pats my foot twice before pecking my cheek and retrieving his dinner. "Want me to get anything for you before I go?"

I shake my head. "No, I'll be fine. Have a good night, sweetie."

When he leaves for work, I spend a good ten minutes contemplating how badly I actually need to pee. The baby kicks, making the need to get to the bathroom very urgent.

"Boy, if I had known being pregnant could be this miserable..." I mutter, leaving the thought unfinished while washing my hands.

The phone rings and I waddle as quickly as I can to snatch it.

"Hello?" I answer.

"Hello. May I speak with Airman Johnson, please?" The clipped accent and business-like tone of the woman is unmistakable.

"I'm sorry, he's at work. Can I help you?"

"Is this Mrs. Johnson?"

"Yes." I press my hand into the small of my back and sigh.

"This is Mrs. Hokaido from the housing office. I am calling to let you know that a house has become available on base for you."

"Oh!" I blink in surprise. "Good. Uh...when do we move in?"

"The house will be available for occupancy in two weeks."

"Oh, gosh. Our baby is due in four weeks. Can we wait for just a few months?" I cannot imagine moving *now*.

"No. You either have to accept the house when it's ready or we'll put you at the bottom of the list again."

"What? Really? We can't wait at *all?*"

"No, I'm afraid not."

"Fine. We'll take it." The baby kicks and I wince, rubbing the spot – the kicks are stronger the bigger she gets.

"All right. Please have Airman Johnson come into the housing office by close of business on Friday."

"I will. Thanks. Anything else?"

"No. Do you have any questions?"

I have a million, but none she can answer. "Nope."

I make the rare phone call to Rick at work.

"Really? In two weeks? Wow, that's going to be hard," he replies when I relay the information to him. "I'll stop by the housing office tomorrow morning to get it done. Did they give you an address?"

"I just assumed we would be blindfolded and left at the door," I remark sarcastically, rubbing my lower back again. "Can I come with?"

"Of course, if you feel up to it," he replies, ignoring my sarcasm.

****

"Here's your address," Mrs. Hokaido says in her clipped accent. "Please sign here, here, and here." She points to three different sheets of paper. She explains the paperwork to Rick while I tune her out. My body demands my attention. Walking down the stairs from our apartment and everywhere else has made me wish for a magic carpet or an electric wheelchair.

"You all right?" Rick asks, placing his hand on the small of my back.

I nod. "Are we almost done?"

Rick looks to Mrs. Hokaido who nods. "All done here. You can pick up your keys on October third. Congratulations on both fronts! Don't worry, you'll make it." She smiles at me.

"Thanks." I return the smile. Turning to Rick, I say, "Boy that's awfully close to my due date."

"I know. It's going to be okay – your family will help us unpack."

Rick walks slowly next to me as I waddle to the truck where he helps hoist me into my seat. I always appreciated his gentlemanly offers to help me, but now I really need it and am deeply grateful.

"Do you want to drive by the house to see what it looks like from the outside?" Rick asks, instantly perking up my mood.

"Can we do that?"

"Yes," he chuckles. "We can't go inside, but we can at least check out the neighborhood."

"Cool! Let's go!" I reply excitedly. "Do you know how to get there?"

"She gave me a map." Rick pulls out one of the sheets from the stack he was given and hands it to me. A route has been highlighted in yellow with one half of one square circled where the yellow line ends.

"Is it a duplex?" I ask.

"Yes."

"I thought it was going to be a house. That's okay. It will still be our home."

Rick follows the directions on the map and I'm thoroughly confused by the time he pulls over and stops; all the houses are one of three colors – primary blue, green, or red - and identically built. How will I ever find my way home?

"There it is, Heather! Our new home," he smiles, pointing.

I eagerly take a look. It's primary green. At least I have one thing to identify it.

"Which one is it? The left or the right?" I ask.

Rick consults the sheet before stating, "The left one. I'm glad – it has a bigger yard. The one on the right is practically hidden behind the carport."

The carport he refers to does hide most of the right side of the duplex and parks four cars side by side.

"Why are there spaces for four cars here?" I ask.

Rick's eyes sweep the area. "I think two of the spots belong to that duplex right there." He points to the duplex just to the right of ours.

"Oh. That makes sense."

"Well, what do you think?" he asks, squeezing my hand.

"I like it," I reply. "It's going to be really nice."

Rick beams. "I like it, too. Look," he points to the tiny front porch, if it can be considered a porch; it's more of a stoop. "There's a nice area where you can garden if you want. Lots of space to play for Elizabeth." We decided to name our firstborn after my and Rick's mother. His mother's given name is Elizabeth, even though she prefers to be called Lovey. My mother wasn't the least bit offended that her name came second. In fact, she said it wouldn't sound right otherwise. After all, she had asked, who has ever heard of a child named Louise Elizabeth?"

"That's true." Peering at the front window, it looks to be empty. "Rick, I think it's already vacated. Can we at least go look in the window?"

Rick squints at the structure. "I think you're right. Let me go check real quick – it would be creepy if someone is still living there and suddenly they see a stranger peeking in their window." He exits the truck and walks cautiously toward the door. Halfway through the yard, he glances back and motions for me to follow. "The house is empty," he calls out as I heave myself out of the truck.

We not only look through the front window, but check out every window we can get to which is all of them. The living room is spacious; it's got parquet wood floors that gleam and there's a closet right next to the front door. What appears to be a dining room area is continuous with the living room. The kitchen is off the dining area and is separated by a sliding door. The backyard, which is also rather large, is not fenced in, so we peek through the kitchen window. It isn't fancy, but it is larger than the kitchen in our apartment. The concrete patio in the backyard is three times the size of the front porch and completely covered and therefore shaded. I am pleasantly surprised to find a separate dining area attached to the kitchen with sliding glass doors out to the back patio.

"Wow, Rick! Check it out."

"That's pretty cool!" he exclaims. "But, I'm most excited about this back patio. It's huge! I can't wait to grill. It also faces the west; we'll see some incredible sunsets."

"That's true," I echo his excitement; the more I see, the more I like.

The master bedroom is the next one we see; it's just to the left of the sliding glass door. It has to be the master because there are two closets. The parquet wood floors continue throughout the entire house. The bedrooms butt up against the other half of the duplex, so we walk back around to see inside the second bedroom. It's the same square footage as the master, but only has one closet. We are unable to see the bathroom; the window has opaque privacy glass.

"What do you think?" Rick asks, helping me into the truck.

"I like it. It's better than I thought it would be."

****

Fortunately, the military pays for a moving company to pack up our apartment and deliver everything to our new house all in the same day. Even though the timing is lousy, I am thankful to be moving into a larger place. We've only been in the apartment for a few months, but we've outgrown it with all of the baby stuff we've collected.

My family and some former co-workers from Payless and the pet shop threw me a baby shower one week after we saw our new house for the first time. Tina was there, as well. She couldn't get over how large I had become.

Her crazy red hair was just as crazy as ever. There was no attempt to make the shower a surprise; my mother needed to be able to contact my former co-workers, and I had their numbers. There is very little left to buy with the exception of diapers and toiletries. My parents sprang for the crib – bedding included – and my friends sprang for a car seat and stroller. Rick's parents sent us a high chair and a changing table. They're currently touring in Israel. The remaining presents I received provided an adequate wardrobe for our little girl to get started.

Mom donated numerous boxes filled with hooded towels, burping cloths, and various items she had saved.

"I can't believe it. It feels like just yesterday I was using all of this for your baby sister and now…now you're going to use it for my first grandbaby," Mom whispers, dabbing at her eyes.

"Mom, it's okay. Don't cry." I put my arm around her while she stoops over the box, clutching one of the hooded towels.

"I can't help it," she blows out her breath. "It all goes by so fast."

"I'm sure it does."

Mom levels her gaze at me. "You'll find out soon enough. Time flies faster than you can ever imagine." Suddenly, she clutches my arm fiercely. "Promise me, you'll savor every moment, Heather. Promise!"

Her intensity catches me off guard. "Yes, Mom. I will."

An emotion flashes across her features briefly before disappearing. It looks like panic.

"Mom, are you all right?" I ask uneasily.

Mom cups my face, her eyes searching mine. "I'm fine."

****

October 4, 1989

Moving day is a whirlwind. Thankfully, Rick has the day off. The packers arrive promptly at eight that morning.

Four packers spread through our small apartment, each claiming a room, and before I know it, the entire space is filled with packing paper, boxes, and the sound of ripping tape. Rick reminds them that the large furniture is to remain with the apartment, with the exception of our bed. Overwhelmed, I call my mother and tell her I'm coming over.

"I think that would be best," Rick remarks, enveloping me in an embrace as one of the movers whisks past us with a full, taped up box. "Go on and put your feet up. I'll call when we're all done here." He turns to the mover busily wrapping dishes in the kitchen. "How long do you think this will take?"

"Not long. Probably about three hours, tops," the mover replies.

My eyebrows rise. "Really? Only three hours?"

"Yup," the mover replies, snatching another plate from the cupboard

HELLO AND GOODBYE

and furiously wrapping it. The speed at which they're moving is mind boggling.

Rick calls my parents' house just before noon to let me know the truck just pulled away and he's going to meet them at the new house on base.

"Ready?" I ask my mother, rubbing my back. It's been aching today.

"Yes, but I think you should stay here and rest, Heather," Mom replies. "We can get it all unpacked for you so you can just go from this sofa to your own sofa."

Rick and I had purchased, to my chagrin, used furniture for our new home. We can't afford new, but at least I know the people we bought it from. They're friends of my parents who had decided to redecorate, purchasing new furniture for themselves. They gave us a price we couldn't refuse. It isn't the most beautiful furniture, but at least it's not plaid. We now own a blue sofa, a matching loveseat, a coffee table, and a glass and brass dining table with four chairs.

"All right," I sigh, letting my body decide. I would like to put things where I want them to be, but I can always rearrange it later if necessary. "Call me when it's time to come."

"Will do!" she replies. "We'll lock the door on our way out."

My parents, Jeff, and Debbie all file out of the house and I'm left alone in blissful silence. The only sound is the familiar, comforting ticking of the grandfather clock. I reposition myself into the least uncomfortable position on the sofa and settle in for what I hope will be a good nap, with the help of as many pillows as I can gather.

Unfortunately, my nap is interrupted by three trips to the bathroom and more than twice that amount in repositioning; my back aches horribly, warring with the constant ache in my hips. I feel like I've been horseback riding. My rest is fitful, at best.

Finally, at three thirty I give up and make myself a sandwich. Sitting up makes my back ache even more.

"You've got to be kidding me," I mutter, arching and rubbing the small of my back.

Maybe walking will help. I grunt to a standing position and start waddling around the kitchen in circles. This makes the aching in my hips worse, increasing my frustration.

When the phone rings at five o'clock, I answer breathlessly. "Hello?"

"Hi, honey bun. We're all done with the big stuff. We've got the furniture arranged and the bed put together and set up. Your mom worked hard putting the kitchen together. You can come home any time."

"I'll be right there," I wince; the baby just did a huge somersault.

"See you soon! Drive carefully."

"I will." I hang up and take some slow, deep breaths. That really hurt.

I have a hard time driving; the aching of sitting in one position is almost more than I can bear. There is no distinction between the pain in my hips and the pain in my back now. By the time I get to the house, I have to do my breathing exercises just to get out of the car. My hips feel like they're coming apart at the seam. The aching has wrapped around to the front. She must be doing the breast stroke in there.

Waddling very slowly to the front door holding my belly, I open the door and enter. The first thing I notice is the smell of chicken. My eyes sweep the bright room; just as Rick said, the furniture is all set up and it looks perfect. I focus on making my way to the sofa to sit down and put my feet up. That will help.

Rick's head pops around the corner from the kitchen, grinning. As soon as he sees me, his eyebrows descend into one and his grin disappears.

"Are you all right?" he asks worriedly, walking quickly over to me. "You're panting and your face is red."

"What?" I ask, tuning in to my own breathing; he's right – I am panting. "My back hurts. My hips hurt." I wince and clutch my stomach. "She is moving all over the place."

"Leonard! Louise! Please come and look at Heather!" Rick yells. A little too loudly, I think.

Mom's face pops out of the kitchen, followed rapidly by the rest of my family. Mom takes one look at me and quickly comes to my side.

"Please," I pant. "I need to," wince, "sit down." Rick and my father each put an arm under mine on either side, guiding me to the sofa. I sit down with a huff, grimacing.

Mom places her hands gingerly on my stomach.

My back throbs and I arch, placing my hand behind me to rub the spot.

"It's just my back," I pant.

"Heather?" Mom asks, her expression serious. "How long has your back been hurting like this?"

A pain shoots down both legs and I breathe through it.

"Stupid hips," I mutter through gritted teeth.

"What?" Rick asks.

"My hips hurt, too!" I bark as another spasm wraps around from my back to my belly button and down my legs. I gasp. That one *really* hurt.

"Her stomach is hard as a rock," Mom says. "She's in labor."

"What? *Now?* But she's not due for another week and a half!" Rick cries, looking panicky.

"No way!" Jeff hoots. "Man, that's awesome. I am going to be an uncle!"

"Well, I'm going to be an *aunt*," Debbie responds, not to be out done by her brother. "And that's way more important."

Another spasm rips through me and I cry out. That one really, *really* hurt.

"I have to go to the bathroom!" I yell, trying to right myself.

"Heather, I don't think…"

"Rick, I have to *go*!!" I scream.

Rick jerks back.

"Don't take it personally, son," Dad chimes in. "You should've heard some of the names Louise called me when she was in labor."

Mom tsks. "Leonard, not now." She takes charge. "Heather, I'll help you to the bathroom. Rick, call the hospital and then go pack her bag. Just the essentials for now. Leonard, get the car started – put a towel down on the seat for her and recline it back. Jeff and Debbie, you two stay here. We'll call you when we know what's going on. Be sure to turn that oven off when the timer goes off and eat your dinner. Save some for us."

Debbie and Jeff mount a protest, but Mom cuts them off with one look while I'm helped off the sofa.

Just as I sit on the toilet, a gush rushes out of me. I haven't peed that much in a long time.

"Did your water just break?" Mom asks, her voice high. "Let me have a look." She peers into the toilet and gasps. "Dear God, we have to go *now*." She reaches under the sink, snatches a pad and helps me arrange it in my underwear and get myself together. Just before she flushes I glance in the toilet and notice the water is bloody.

"Mom! Mom! I'm *bleeding!* Why…" A severe spasm rips through me and I feel like I'm splitting in two. I grip the sink, breathing hard. "Mom! God!!"

"Rick! We have to go now! Her water just broke!" Mom yells, wrapping her arm around my waist.

Rick appears in record time, running up and taking my other side. The spasms are coming hard and fast now. I'm not really aware of my surroundings; the pain demands all my attention.

Somehow, I make it to the car. Sitting down is the worst torture I can imagine. Every spasm makes me scream.

I am going to split wide open. I know it.

I don't wanna die I don't wanna die I don't wanna die…

"You're not going to die, Heather. You're just having a baby. It's a natural process," Mom's soothing voice breaks through my concentration. I didn't realize I was talking out loud.

I stare wide-eyed at her, trying to focus, but not really seeing her. Suddenly, the car door opens, warm air rushes in. There are a lot of unfamiliar faces and people trying to pull me out of the car and into a wheelchair.

The wheelchair is more comfortable than the car, but not by much. I grip the arm rest and hoist myself up as best I can, trying to alleviate the pressure. There's an uncomfortable lump down there. Through the pain, realization dawns – the lump is her head.

"Oh, God," I grunt. "She's coming! Rick!!" I whip my head around, searching for him.

He appears in view, his head bobbing up and down. He's running. We're all running. "I'm right here. Hang in there!"

"Don't push! Just breathe! Don't push!" a strange voice commands me. "Put your chin up and breathe through it!"

I try to follow the direction, but it's excruciating. I stare at the ceiling tiles and lights whizzing past, trying to count them as a distraction. Suddenly, the ceiling tiles stop moving and arms are all over me, lifting me from the wheelchair and onto a flat surface – I don't know if it's a bed or a gurney and I don't care.

I'm being torn in two.

Cool air hits my legs as my clothing is removed. Spasms of pain everywhere.

Strange voices saying strange things.

"Honey bun, honey bun, it's all right," Rick's face is right in front of mine, his familiar voice breaking through. He jerks his head, glancing down below before whipping back to stare into my eyes. "It's all right. They're going to check you."

Spasms. Pain.

An urge to push. I can't fight it.

My body curls. I scream as the pain burns and radiates all over me.

"She's complete and crowning," a vaguely familiar and calm voice floats into my consciousness.

I am not complete! I want to say; I'm going to be two halves very soon!

"Push, honey bun! Push!" Rick's voice.

I couldn't do anything else if I wanted to.

I don't know why, but I count each push and store it in the deepest recesses of my mind. I push twenty times before I feel an incredible emptying sensation. The pain departs with the baby.

I fall back, exhausted, heaving.

Almost immediately, I hear the high pitched, strong wail of my daughter. Relief floods my heart and mind; we're both alive! We survived!

"She's got a pair of lungs on her!" Another strange voice chuckles.

Thank God.

"Oh! Look at her, Heather! Look at her! She's beautiful!" Rick sobs. I open my eyes and see my husband's glistening eyes and wet cheeks. He kisses me firmly on the mouth. "You did great, honey bun! She's just beautiful!"

I look around at my surroundings, finally. I am indeed on a gurney in a large room. There is equipment and people everywhere. They're all dressed in identical green hospital scrubs with their faces covered in surgical masks.

"Where are we?" I ask, confused.

"We're in the delivery room," Rick answers me immediately. "We almost didn't make it!"

"Thank God," I sigh.

"Indeed," Rick answers, kissing me again.

"Where is she? Is she all right?" I ask, anxious to meet my daughter and see her face for the first time.

"They're cleaning her up and checking her right now," Rick says, glancing at a cluster of green-clad people in a far corner.

"Can momma meet baby yet?" The familiar, calm voice makes a second appearance. I glance down at the source. The man meets my gaze, winking at me before returning to his work; he is the doctor that delivered Elizabeth. I squint, trying to recall why he sounds familiar.

Suddenly, it dawns on me and I grin, looking at Rick.

"I remember him! He's that one doctor we had when you had the sex question!" I blurt. A ripple of stifled laughter floats around the room.

"I told you she wouldn't have a hole in her head," the doctor says. The laughter is a little louder this time.

Rick's cheeks pink before he laughs, too.

"So, can momma see baby yet? She's earned the right," the calm doctor repeats.

"Absolutely! But all little ladies want to look good when they make their debut, so we got her all fancied up for you." A beaming nurse approaches with a swaddled bundle in her arms. She carefully turns the bundle toward me, placing her face to face with me on my chest. The tiny head is covered in a knitted pink cap that has a pink satin bow on it. Her eyes are wide open, blinking at her surroundings. The curl of her tiny nose is perfect, as is the rose bud shape of her little mouth.

I drink in every feature of her face. Her mouth opens in a small "o" when I stroke her cheek.

"Rick, feel her cheek! It's like velvet," I say in wonder. "I've never felt anything so soft."

He slowly reaches his hand in and strokes her soft, plump little cheek.

"Hi, Elizabeth. It's nice to meet you," I whisper, carefully pulling her to me. I kiss her cheek gently and smell her new baby smell. It faintly reminds me of cocoa powder and I say so. Another ripple of laughter floats around the room.

"Well, that's something I've never heard before," the doctor says, chuckling. "We're almost done here. We'll sit you up and get you into recovery." He glances up at me. "Nice work, young lady. You did a good job."

I reluctantly take my eyes off my daughter briefly to smile at him. "Thank you."

"Thank you so much, doctor," Rick beams. "What's your name again?

It's been forever since we've seen you."

"I'm Doctor Payne, and we are done here. Let's sit you up so you can get a better view of her." He pushes his stool back, de-gloving as the nurse situates me, arranging the linens and repositioning the gurney to a sitting position.

"It's nice to see you again, Doctor Payne. I'm glad you were here," I say gratefully.

"Oh, it would all be fine whether I'm here or not. You're quite the trooper. Let's have a look at the little lady," Dr. Payne peers over me. "Oh, she's a beauty, all right. Good job, you two." He shakes Rick's hand and winks at me again.

"Thank you, sir. Thank you very much," Rick replies, pumping the doctor's hand. "For everything."

"Pshaw! I was just there to catch her. She did all the work." Dr. Payne nods at me.

When we get to the recovery room, Mom and Dad are there to meet us. They rush to my side as soon as the bed has been parked in the stall. The nurses work silently, trying to be as unobtrusive as possible. One nurse whips the curtain closed around us, cocooning us from the other recovering mothers and their families. From what I can tell, it's been a busy day of deliveries; there are at least five other women here.

"Let me see her!" Mom cries, literally, tears and all. She carefully gathers Elizabeth into her arms like she's holding a priceless porcelain vase. Her mouth falls open as her eyes scan the baby's face over and over again. She is enraptured. "My God, she's beautiful. Just beautiful," she whispers reverently. She carefully leans in to kiss her forehead.

"My turn," Dad says. They pass her carefully between them. His expression is a mirror of my mother's; they are going to spoil her rotten, as any good grandparent should.

"Rick, you need to call your parents. Did you call Jeff and Debbie yet?" I ask my mother.

"Oh! Leonard, go call them and let them know," Mom says, keeping her eyes riveted on the baby and cooing.

"I think my parents are asleep right now," Rick says, glancing at his watch. "I'll call them in about eight hours or so."

"Sure. Send me off so you can get her all to yourself," Dad jokes. "I'll get my turn." He quickly ducks out to call my siblings.

"What about us?" I ask my mother. "We're only her parents, you know."

Mom looks at me, dismayed. "I'm sorry, sweetie. You're right. Rick, would you like to hold your daughter?"

Rick nods eagerly, taking Elizabeth gingerly from Mom's arms, which look like they ache from the emptiness. Rick takes a seat in the chair next to my bed. He slowly pulls the cap off her head to reveal fine wisps of dark hair.

"Heather! She has your dark hair and blue eyes!" Rick exclaims, delighted.

"I wouldn't make that call just yet," the nurse at my side replies. "All babies are born with blue eyes and often have darker hair at birth, too."

"Really?" I ask. "It may change?"

"Yes," she nods, pushing buttons on a machine. "It can take weeks or even months for the true colors to come out."

"Well, whatever colors she sticks with, she's going to be beautiful," Mom declares.

"I see that you've chosen to breastfeed. Let's see if we can't get her latched on," the nurse says.

After a few awkward false starts, Elizabeth latches on and begins eagerly sucking. A deep sense of satisfaction at this first measure of motherly success settles over me.

Dad returns quickly to report that Jeff and Debbie are eager to meet the newest family member. He blinks rapidly, stumbling in his report, when he notices the baby attached to my uncovered breast. It's an awkward moment for us both that is quickly remedied when Rick pulls a sheet up around me.

"Sorry, Dad," I mutter sheepishly.

"It's okay, pumpkin. Just caught me off guard is all."

A few hours later, I'm moved to my room for the remainder of my stay, which will be for three days. That's the hospital policy for all new mothers and anyone who has a C-section.

To say that I become sleep-deprived would be a gross understatement. The visiting hours of nine in the morning to eight at night are strictly enforced. This is also a mother/baby unit, so there is no nursery. I have to wheel her bassinet into the bathroom if I want to use it when my family is not present.

Too bad it's not a mother/father/baby unit – Elizabeth is fretful the entire time. I am lucky to get eight hours of broken sleep in those three days.

My family tries to help me rest during the time they're allowed to be with me, but there's so much activity by the medical staff and my room mate that sleep isn't an option, no matter how desperately I need it.

By the third night, my eyes fill with tears watching my family and Rick reluctantly go home at eight o'clock sharp. I know I won't have any help until nine o'clock the next morning. The nurses, although they answer the call light, make the briefest appearance when they must and leave as quickly as possible.

"Tomorrow. We can go home tomorrow," I murmur to my daughter, kissing her forehead. I position myself on the side, trying to latch her on in hopes that she'll be comforted long enough to allow me some rest. Rick and I had to attend new parenting classes today with all the other new moms – I don't even remember what was said. I'm so exhausted; it was all I could do to stay upright in the chair. At least we got a free diaper bag and some simple supplies to take home. I would gladly trade them in for a few uninterrupted hours of sleep.

"Mrs. Johnson," a whispered voice interrupts my slumber. "Mrs. Johnson, you have to put the baby in her bassinet."

I squint reluctantly up at the intrusive face attached to the voice. "What?" My eyes are having a hard time staying open.

"Mrs. Johnson, you cannot sleep with the baby in the bed with you. You have to put her in her bassinet."

"Please, God, just let me *sleep*," I sigh. Reluctantly, I force myself up to a sitting position, feeling dizzy and beyond exhausted. "Fine." I shake my head and rub my eyes, hoping to alleviate some of the dizziness. I scoop Elizabeth's sleeping form very slowly and carefully up and place her just as slowly and gently into the bassinet at my bedside.

Without another word, the nurse turns on her heel and walks out.

I lay back on the bed and just as slumber is about to envelope me, Elizabeth stirs and begins to whimper. Hoping against hope that she'll go back to sleep, I don't move a muscle, silently begging.

Soon enough, however, her whimpers turn to wails and I start to cry, too, gathering her back up in my weary arms. I have never felt so lonely or abandoned in my life.

CHAPTER FOURTEEN

October, 1989

It's discharge day an I am ecstatic. Labor was excruciating, but at least it was relatively quick compared to the dragged out hell of the mother/baby experience. Rick is angry and tells the head nurse so.

Mom's concern is clear in the furrows of her brow. "You look as pale as death, Heather. The shadows under your eyes look like bruises. We'll get you home and take good care of you. I can't believe this place – whoever heard of a hospital with no nursery? It's ridiculous!"

Breathing in the fresh air when the hospital doors open revives my spirit; I never want to darken the halls of this hospital again.

Rick drives very carefully, taking turns slowly and avoiding bumps at all cost. I sit in the back seat with Elizabeth strapped securely in her car seat while Mom sits in the front. When Rick parks very slowly in our slot of the carport, he turns to me. "Stay put. I'll come help you out."

He rushes around to help me out of the car before reaching in to release the car seat from its base. Dad, Jeff, and Debbie come jogging out of the house to gather the rest of the things.

Rick holds the precious cargo of our daughter in her seat in the crook of one elbow, while he keeps his other arm around my waist.

"Rick, I'm fine, really," I chide him. He ignores my protest. At least he let me carry the beautiful flowers his parents sent. The heady scent of red and yellow roses fill my nostrils.

"Just put everything over there," Dad directs Debbie and Mom when I enter. "Let's show her the nursery."

I look at Rick, puzzled. "What do you mean? What's up with the nursery?"

Rick kisses the tip of my nose, releases his hold on me and carefully sets the car seat on the floor, retrieving Elizabeth's sleeping form gently from the nest of her seat. "We wanted to decorate the nursery before you came home."

"Yes, now you can actually just get some *real* rest, sweetie," Mom replies, her tone clipped. "I cannot believe that hospital."

"You look awful, even for just having a baby," Jeff quips. I shoot a glance at him, but his expression is void of sarcasm. He looks genuinely concerned.

"Let's show them the new room," Rick speaks quietly, gently patting Elizabeth's tiny, sleeping back.

We file down the small hallway with Rick and Elizabeth leading the way. The door is closed and Rick turns to me, whispering, "Voila!" and opens the door with as much of a flourish as he can muster.

The door opens to a room that has been beautifully, but simply, decorated. I recognize the crib and the changing table, but the addition of a nice reclining rocking chair with a matching foot rest make me smile. A small table sits next to it. There is an adorable pink floral border trimming the room where the wall meets the ceiling. The same pink color is found in the cushions on the rocking chair, foot rest, and diaper pail. There's even a pink rug in the shape of a daisy on the floor.

"Look, we even hung up her clothes and things in the closet," Debbie chirps, sliding the closet door open. "Aren't the hangers adorable? They're so small!"

"Shhhh," Dad whispers. "Don't wake her up."

"You don't have to whisper, Leonard," Mom chuckles. "She'll have to get used to the noise of a house anyway."

"Still," Dad says, his face softening in adoration as he stares at his first grandchild. "She's my grandbaby."

"It all looks amazing," I say, running my hands over the fabric on the rocking chair. "This is really nice."

"Try it out!" Mom encourages. "It was Rick's mother's idea and we sort of picked it out together over the phone."

I sit gingerly on the rocker; I'm still sore. It fits like it was made for me. I place my legs on the foot rest and rock gently back and forth; the foot rest moves with me. "I could so get used to this." I close my eyes and open them quickly; if I close them for too long, they may not re-open.

"Is it comfortable?" Rick asks.

"Very," I murmur, continuing to rock back and forth.

"Are you hungry, sweetie?" Mom asks. "I could make you a sandwich or something."

"Actually, I am. I'm thirsty, too."

"I bet you are. When you're breastfeeding, you'll get very thirsty. Come and lie down on the sofa. I'll make your sandwich."

"Can I hold her?" Debbie asks.

"Of course, squirt. Let's go sit on the sofa," Rick replies.

Mom disappears into the kitchen while we all settle into the living room, which fills up with everyone there. Dad and Jeff make short work of putting all the bundles we brought home from the hospital into their proper places in the house. I see a pile consisting of blankets and two pillows neatly folded in the corner of the living room.

"Rick," I ask, pointing at the pile. "What are those for?"

"That's for your mother. She's offered to stay with us for a few days to help us get settled in. Isn't that nice?"

Mom comes around the corner carrying a plate with a thick sandwich and some grapes in one hand and a full glass of water in the other. She places it on the coffee table in front of me.

"Yes, I am going to stay and help out. You especially," she nods toward me. "need to get some rest, young lady. When you're done eating, go in the bedroom and close the door. If Elizabeth needs to be fed, we'll bring her in to you, but otherwise get some sleep."

"Thank you," I say gratefully, taking a huge bite out of the sandwich. I'm ravenous. I devour everything on my plate and empty the glass.

Rick decides to lie down with me for a nap, too.

Dad waves us off. "You both need some rest. Don't worry – we'll take good care of Elizabeth."

I am so very grateful to be in my own bed with no nurses, no room mates, and no worries.

Rick nestles me close to him and with a sigh of contentment, I close my eyes. Slumber overtakes me instantly.

"Sweetie? Sweetie?" Mom's gentle whisper in my ear. "Baby girl is hungry."

"Huh? Oh, okay," I whisper, my voice thick. I lift my shirt and position myself to latch her on while Mom presses her to me, tucking the blanket around us both. "I'll be back in about twenty minutes to get her. Sleep good." She kisses my forehead.

I smile and close my eyes as Elizabeth begins to nurse hungrily.

"I think I'll get up now," Rick kisses my ear.

"Are you done sleeping?" I whisper.

"Yeah. You sleep as much as you need to." He carefully rises, comes around and kisses me first before kissing Elizabeth's tiny velvet head very sweetly. "I love my girls."

"Love you, too."

I didn't even realize I had fallen back asleep until my mother's soft hand smooths my hair. "Is she done?" she asks, softly.

"Huh? I don't know." I squint down to see that she's fallen off the breast and her tiny mouth is lolled open with just a drop of milk pooled at the corner of her mouth. "I think so. Has it been twenty minutes already?"

Mom laughs quietly. "Actually, it's been about forty. I checked on you earlier – she was nursing away and you were sound asleep."

"Wow," I yawn. "I didn't realize I could do that."

"Well, now you can if you want. Here, I'll take her." Mom slowly pulls the blanket off and carefully removes Elizabeth's sleeping form. Her tiny face screws up and her body stiffens. Mom starts cooing and patting her bottom which sends her off to slumber quickly. "Sleep good, sweetie." Mom retreats, still cooing and gently closes the door.

When I open my eyes again, I feel refreshed enough to get up. I stretch and yawn. Glancing at the clock, I note four hours have passed.

I'm hungry and thirsty again.

Rising slowly, I put on my robe, make a side trip to the bathroom, and join the quiet and happy voices I hear in the living room. The smell of pasta and tomatoes greet my nostrils and my mouth waters.

"There she is!" Dad beams at me.

"Hey, honey bun. Feel better?" Rick asks.

"You can sleep some more if you'd like," Mom adds.

I shake my head. "No, I'm fine. I feel much better. I'm hungry again."

"Perfect timing. I just made dinner and Elizabeth should be getting hungry again soon, too," Mom remarks, wiping her hands on a dish towel.

On cue, Elizabeth starts to whimper and fuss.

I settle myself on the sofa and reach my arms out to her. "Here, let me have her. I'll eat when she's done," I sigh.

"That won't be necessary," Mom answers, placing her hands on her hips. "You all go ahead and get your plates. Heather, I'll set you up so you can eat while the baby does."

"How are you going to do that?" I ask, bewildered, while I quickly latch Elizabeth on under the receiving blanket. Jeff and Dad wouldn't appreciate getting a glimpse of this, I'm sure. As a matter of fact, they're the first to rise at the command to get their plates.

"You'll see," Mom says, disappearing into the kitchen.

My stomach growls and I gulp; it really does smell heavenly.

"I'll eat in here with you. There won't be room at the table anyway." Rick grins.

"Rick?" Mom appears in record time with my food and a large glass of water. My dinner is served in a large, shallow bowl and has been cut up into bite sized pieces with the exception of the two thick slices of garlic bread, which have been left whole and nestled on the rim. "Would you like me to make your plate for you?"

"No, ma'am. I'll take care of that, thank you. I'm going to eat out here with Heather." He rises and gathers his dinner, joining me on the sofa.

I eat easily, albeit awkwardly, while Elizabeth nurses.

"Your mother is awesome, you know that? Your whole family is," Rick says, scraping his plate clean with his fork.

"I know. Believe me, I know."

****

My mother stays with us for five glorious days. She is an angel sent from heaven; Rick and I are overwhelmed with new parenting. We could not have made it without her. Dad, Jeff, and Debbie spend as much time with us as they can between work and school. Debbie is as enchanted with Elizabeth as everyone else. I only get to hold her when I nurse. She is never in want for arms.

The first time Rick changes her diaper, he looks as unsure and awkward as a teenager about to deliver a first kiss. It takes a few tries for him to get the diaper on straight. There is too much overlap on one side or the other. It doesn't help that he tries to change her when she is hungry – her protests grow louder and her flails more urgent until Mom takes over just to complete the task, reassuring Rick the whole time that he will get the hang of it.

Rick's worried expression follows Elizabeth from the changing table to my mother's arms to me, waiting in the rocking chair.

Once I successfully stifle Elizabeth's cries by latching her on, I reach for Rick's hand.

"Don't worry, sweetie," I squeeze his hand reassuringly. "You can change all her diapers from now on until you get it right."

"Gee, thanks," he chuckles and his face relaxes.

"You're going to be a pro," Mom reassures Rick. "Heather, would you like a glass of water?"

"Mm hmm," I reply, stroking Elizabeth's cheek as her jaw works furiously.

Once my mother leaves the room, Rick kneels down next to me, gently patting Elizabeth's cleanly swaddled bottom.

"I don't know how to do this," he says, worry creeping back onto his face.

"What do you mean?"

"I don't know. I just don't know how to do any of this. She's so small."

"We'll figure it out." I lean forward and he kisses me. "I am sure every new parent goes through this. We'll get it and you'll be a good daddy."

"Yes, you will," Mom says, placing the glass of water on the table next to me.

"Thanks." I pick up the glass, draining half of it.

Mom smiles. "I'll get the dishes done and dinner started." She pats Rick on the shoulder and leaves the room, quietly closing the door behind her.

After dinner that night, Mom announces she is going home. My heart sinks.

"What? Why? Can't you stay a few more days?" I ask, feeling desperate.

"Heather, you're fine. You know everything you need to know and I'm just a phone call away."

"Louise, are you sure? I mean, you feel welcome here, right?" Rick asks.

"Of course I do. You guys couldn't be sweeter. It's time to go home. You're both doing wonderfully and I miss my own bed."

I bite my lower lip. How will I manage without her? She lives close, but I will still be here by myself when Rick goes back to work in a week. Elizabeth is so small and new. Dread fills my chest. What if we really can't do this? What if we're the first parents in the history of parenting that really, actually, cannot be parents?

"Can't you stay just a little bit longer, Mom? Please?" I beg.

Tears spring in Mom's eyes. "You are a fine mother, and Rick, you are a fine father. You both know what to do and how to do it. I need to get out of the way and let you do it. Every new parent is scared to death – that's part of the job description, didn't you know?" She chuckles.

"Thank you, Louise. You've been so helpful. We'd have been lost without you," Rick says, sincerely appreciative.

She drops her bag at the front door while Dad sways back and forth making baby sounds and faces at Elizabeth who is scowling in concentration at his antics. He arrived to take Mom home.

"Heather, it's time for you two to take over. You're well rested now. I have your fridge and freezer packed and ready to go with food to hold you over for another week or so. You'll be *fine*." Her confidence bolsters me, slightly.

Watching them drive off, I feel a sense of panic welling. "Rick," I whisper, my hand wrapping around my throat. "We're on our own."

"Yes," he kisses my neck. "We are."

I turn to face him. "Can we do this?"

Rick encircles me with his free arm; Elizabeth is nestled in the other. "We have to. She's not going anywhere."

"Oh, boy," I take a deep breath and blow it out. "Here we go."

Rick and I slowly develop a rhythm. At night, Rick changes her diapers before bringing her to me to nurse, and during the day, we take turns doing household chores and taking care of Elizabeth. I am able to get plenty of rest while I nurse.

When Rick's leave is up and he has to go back to work, fresh panic sets in. My first instinct is to call my mother and plead with her to come back and stay with us, but I resist.

I have to do this.

Rick emerges from the bedroom, dressed in his uniform and cleanly shaven once again; he had allowed his face to get scruffy while on leave. "You'll be just fine," he assures me. He bends down, cradles Elizabeth's sleeping head and kisses her lovingly. "I am going to miss my girls."

"Say bye to daddy," I lift her tiny hand and wave it toward Rick. He kisses the small fist.

"Be good for mommy, sweet pea. I love you," Rick says, reaching down for a quick kiss before he leaves.

His truck disappears down the street, and I swallow hard. This is my first time since being in the hospital that I've been completely alone with Elizabeth.

I look down at her sleeping face; her rose bud mouth is puckered, making sucking motions. Her eyes move back and forth under her delicate shell pink eyelids. Suddenly, she sighs contentedly and a little smile forms on her mouth.

"We'll be fine, won't we?" I whisper, kissing her microscopic button nose. "We have to be."

CHAPTER FIFTEEN

July, 1990

Elizabeth crawls lopsidedly toward me, grinning her four tooth grin.

"Come on! You can make it!" I encourage her, clapping my hands.

At nine months, she has just begun to crawl. At first, she couldn't coordinate her arms and legs to accomplish forward movement. She looked like she was plucking at the floor. She would have her eyes focused on her target, but couldn't make it happen. There were times she moved backwards which resulted in wails of frustration.

Now, she is actually moving forward. Her arms and legs move awkwardly in their plucking action, inching forward. It takes three full minutes, but she determinedly moves slowly forward until she reaches my legs.

She throws her head back, grinning from ear to ear, rocking back and forth on her hands and knees in celebration.

"Yay! Good job, sweet pea!" I scoop her up, swinging her around in the way that always results in peals of laughter. Her blue eyes sparkle in delight while her sandy blond curls whip around her head. "Let's call Daddy and tell him what his big girl is doing today."

He's thrilled. "That's wonderful! Give her big kisses from Daddy."

We have settled in nicely to the routine of family life. Rick remains on evening shift. Elizabeth has him wrapped around her little finger. He lights up when he walks in the door and sees the still mostly toothless grin on her face.

The first summer of this new decade finds me content. I have met our neighbors and developed a special friendship with one in particular – Angeline Baker. She and her family live in the duplex next to, but not attached to, ours. Her husband's name is Chris, and she has two rambunctious boys – Edward and Ronnie. They're a year apart at four and three. Her hands are very full. I couldn't imagine. Rick and I didn't plan on having Elizabeth so soon, but having two kids that close together? No, thank you.

Angeline has helped me so much in the last several months, not just with parenting but also with navigating my way through the learning curve of living in military housing.

First of all, I didn't know there would be monthly inspections.

I had put foil up in the window of Elizabeth's room to keep it dark and cool for her naps. One day, a white truck was slowly trolling through the neighborhood. That afternoon, I went out to check the mail and saw a sheet of yellow paper taped to the screen door. It was from the housing office informing us of our first violation and demanding we remove all "unauthorized window coverings, to include aluminum foil." They didn't even knock on my door to give it to me. Cowards.

Four months after we moved in, the dishwasher made a strange noise whenever I used it and the dishes weren't getting clean. When I called the housing office, the man that answered the phone told me, "I'm sorry, but there's nobody available to look at your dishwasher right now. We are working on commander's houses at the moment and we'll get to you when we can." He wouldn't even give me an approximate time that we would have to wait.

Five months later, I am still washing dishes by hand. Rick asked me not to rock the boat, so I am trying very hard to keep it steady. Even with the soon-to-be rank of Staff Sergeant, I'm reminded that he doesn't hold any real rank every time I hand wash dishes.

I call the housing office to ask how much longer it will be before the dishwasher is repaired.

"What's your address?" the voice on the other end asks. I provide the information and wait while I hear the shuffling of papers. "I'm sorry, we don't have a work order for that."

"What?! You've got to be kidding me! I called you people *five months* ago."

"I'm sorry, but there's no record of it here. Let's get that taken care of."

I close my eyes and grind my teeth, trying to remember to be nice.

God, help me.

I relay the information once again, speaking very slowly and deliberately. "How long before this will be taken care of?"

"Welp," the voice sighs. "Should only be a couple of weeks."

I share my frustrations with Angeline thirty minutes later while we sit on the porch swing in her back yard, enjoying the summer heat. Elizabeth has fallen asleep and I pat her back while she drools on my shoulder.

Angeline has an amazing green thumb; her back yard looks like a tropical oasis. There are well thought out bursts of color in full bloom all over her yard; she rattles off the names of the plants effortlessly like anyone else would the alphabet. Personally, I can't tell a petunia from pansy. But I enjoy them, whatever they are.

"Ronnie! Take that out of your mouth!" she yells. Ronnie drops the stick and scampers after his big brother, who is climbing on the large toy fort they have set up. Angeline clucks her tongue. "That boy puts everything in his mouth. Who knows what he'll catch. Do you know he ate a fly yesterday?"

"What?" I ask, wrinkling my nose in disgust. "How did he do *that?*"

"He just plucked it off the screen and stuck it in his mouth." She shivers. "I gagged. Couldn't help myself. I swept his mouth with my finger, but he had swallowed it already."

"Ew! Is he okay?" That is the grossest thing I have ever heard.

"The jury is still out on that one. How okay is a child that eats a fly?"

I have to change the subject. "So I called the housing office today about my dishwasher."

"What did they say?"

"They have no work order. It's like I never called in the first place."

"Naturally," Angeline says, shaking her head. "I deal with them as little as possible."

"Well, hopefully this time they will keep track of it. The guy said they should be able to come in a couple of weeks. We'll see."

Angeline turns to me. "I have some news," she blurts, sucking in her lips until they disappear.

"Good or bad?"

"It depends on how you look at it, I suppose," she ponders, staring at her hands. "I haven't decided yet which it is."

Puzzled, I press her for more information. "Out with it. What is it?"

She takes a large breath, holding it.

"*What?*" I demand.

She blows her breath out hard. "I'm pregnant."

My mouth falls open and I blink rapidly. "What? Wow! That's….wow. Congratulations!" I grab her in an awkward, one-armed hug. "How do you feel? How far along are you?"

"Well," she sighs, glancing at her boys that are now wrestling each other on the ground. "To be honest, I'm terrified. These boys keep me busy enough, and I don't know how we'll handle one more. But, here we are. I am only a few months along, and I am tired. No morning sickness or anything."

I see terror in her eyes.

"Oh, Angeline," I squeeze her hand before repositioning Elizabeth. She stirs and yawns, squirming in my arms. She stretches and wiggles until she is facing front. While she squints at her surroundings, I grab Angeline's hand once more. "It's going to be all right. I promise. Maybe you'll have a little girl this time."

"Maybe," she says, watching her boys wrestle. Her gaze turns to Elizabeth, and she smiles. "It would be wonderful to have a sweet little girl like Elizabeth."

Elizabeth yawns widely and rubs her eyes, settling back with a sigh. Her squinty gaze watches the boys rolling around on the grass.

"Mommy! I'm hungry!" Edward cries, sitting on his brother's back.

"See what I mean?" Angeline mutters. "Well, get off your brother's back, and I'll get you something to eat."

Edward leaps off his brother and scampers toward the house with Ronnie in tow.

"I'll be right back. Do you want anything?" she asks.

"Do you have iced tea?"

"You know I always have iced tea." She grins and disappears into the house, returning quickly. She sets two paper plates with apple slices and a dollop of peanut butter onto the little plastic picnic table next to the swing. The boys follow her outside, each carefully carrying a plastic cup of water. Once they sit down, they start noisily dipping and crunching. She disappears and returns with two glasses of iced tea plus a teething biscuit for Elizabeth.

"Say thank you," I tell Elizabeth when Angeline hands her the biscuit. Elizabeth doesn't respond, of course, but it's never too early to teach manners. She pops it in her mouth and starts sucking. "Thank you," I say to Angeline when she hands me the glass. Her sweet tea (is there any other kind?) is the best in Texas. She swears she doesn't do anything special, but I have tried to make her tea and it never quite turns out the same. I even watched her make it more than once and I can't figure out why it's better. It just is.

"Does Chris know yet?" I ask, sipping the ice cold amber brew.

She shakes her head, keeping her voice low. "Not yet. I found out two days ago and haven't gotten the nerve to tell him. You're the first person I've told other than my mother. I'll probably tell him tonight. I'm worried because he's only a Staff Sergeant, and we barely make ends meet as it is."

"Don't worry about it. Let me know how it goes. I have to get this girl inside and feed her." Elizabeth has finished her teething biscuit and is rubbing her gummy hands all over her face and hair, getting agitated.

I rise and give Angeline a hug and thank her for the tea. She promises to call and let me know how the conversation goes.

While I feed Elizabeth some green beans, I slowly eat my dinner – heated up chicken and dumplings from yesterday. It has become one of Rick's favorite meals, so I make it often. I am confident enough to venture beyond my mother's recipes; this recipe is hers, but I altered it by adding carrots and broccoli. We love vegetables.

I cool off one dumpling, and place it on the tray for Elizabeth to play with and taste. The jar of green beans was quickly devoured and now she can enjoy the dumpling with her hunger abated. At first, she stares at it like it's the most fascinating thing in the world. Her fists curl and uncurl, and her legs kick. Finally, she goes in for the kill; her flat chubby hand smashes into the dumpling, squishing it between her fingers. Finally, she brings her fist to her mouth where she licks and sucks on it.

"Silly girl," I chuckle, taking another bite of my own dinner.

Once she devours most of the dumpling, she promptly deposits the rest in her ears and hair. This is why I give her baths in the evening; she enjoys making a real mess at meal times and saves the worst for dinner. Since it's just she and I in the evenings, I keep things low key and calm. Her bedtime routine is the same every night; dinner, bath, play time in her play pen while I do the dishes in full view, night nursing in her rocking chair, and bed. Works like a charm; she sleeps through the night, and we never have issues. The only time our routine is altered is if she's sick or teething. Fortunately, she rarely gets sick and the teething lasts just a day or two.

I have just settled in to watch a little television at eight thirty when the phone rings.

"Hello?" I answer, expecting to hear Rick's voice. It's Angeline.

"Hi, Heather, it's me," she says, her voice a little shaky.

"Is everything all right? How did Chris take the news?" I ask anxiously.

"Well, he took it all right, I guess. But he found out today that he didn't make Tech Sergeant, so we're going to be really tight, especially with a new baby."

Chris had tested to make the next rank. I forgot the results came in today. We are anxiously waiting for Rick to pin on Staff Sergeant. The bump in his pay isn't much, but it will help.

"I'm so sorry," I reply, not sure what to say.

"Me, too. I have a bad feeling, Heather. This isn't a good time for us to be pregnant."

My brows knit together. "What do you mean?"

"I don't know. My mother is like that, too. She just gets these weird feelings sometimes and that's how I feel right now. It's just a….a bad feeling, is all."

"Do you think there's something wrong with your baby? Is that what you mean?"

"I don't think so. I don't know. I can't explain it. It probably sounds crazy to you."

"No, not crazy, just odd. Is it because of the finances or something else?"

"I think it's something else. I don't know. Listen, I just wanted to let you know that Chris knows now, and we'll be all right."

Angeline doesn't bring it up again. The end of July rolls around and life is good. She has calmed down and even had her first OB appointment, where she received a clean bill of health. Aside from being tired, which she combats with coffee, she isn't the least bit nauseated.

"I'm so jealous," I retort when she tells me she has no food aversions. "I could barely keep anything down the first half of my pregnancy."

"I felt so bad about that, being half a world away," Rick joins the conversation, swooping Elizabeth around on her belly like an airplane on his forearms. Elizabeth's laughter fills the air.

"I'm just glad you're home now for good," I reply, watching Rick swoop Elizabeth up and down.

"I don't know what I would do if Chris were to ever have to do a remote tour," Angeline says, shaking her head. "I don't think I could make it. Especially now."

"Well, I don't think you'll have to worry about that any time soon. Surely they wouldn't give him orders for a remote while you guys have small kids at home, would they?" I ask.

"I hope not," she replies, laughing as Elizabeth screams happily.

"Do me! Do me!" Ronnie cries, lifting his hands up to Rick.

"Okay, buddy, but you're a big boy, so you can't fly as high," Rick laughs, handing Elizabeth over to me.

He picks Ronnie up and starts swinging him around by holding him under his armpits. Soon the air is filled with Ronnie's laughter. Elizabeth laughs and claps her hands together, delighted to watch her friend. She's an unselfish child. She doesn't mind when someone takes her toys, or doesn't play with her. Her crawling is now flawless, and she prefers to be mobile. She squirms in my lap. She grunts and coughs, trying to pull my hands away from her chest.

"All right," I say. "Go ahead and crawl around in the grass if you want. Rick, watch out for Elizabeth. She's on the ground." I place her on all fours, and she freezes, looking down at her hands. She starts to clutch and unclutch the grass, unsure what to make of it.

Rick doesn't have to leave for work for another few hours, so we're enjoying another beautiful summer day outside. Angeline's husband works twelve-hour day shifts, so he's still at work. The trade off is that he only works three days in a row before having two days off. His days off change every week whereas Rick works eight-hour shifts for five days with two days off.

"Hey, let's have a barbecue this weekend," Rick says breathlessly, landing Ronnie safely on the ground. Ronnie immediately puts his arms up for more. "Oh, buddy. I'm sorry, but these propellers have to take a rest."

He joins me on the swing to catch his breath, putting his arm around me lazily.

"Leave Mr. Rick alone, Ronnie, and go play with your brother," Angeline admonishes.

Elizabeth plops down on her bottom, content to explore the wonders of grass with her senses rather than crawl around in it. She pets it like a cat, fascinated.

"Doesn't Chris have this Friday off?" Rick asks.

Her eyes don't leave her boys. "No. He has next Friday off. That's the third of August, right? Edward, let your brother play with you!"

"I think so," Rick answers her question. "So, let's barbecue then. Burgers and dogs? We can have your family over, too," Rick adds, his breath coming more evenly now.

"It sounds like fun," Angeline says, grinning.

Dad and Rick coordinate the grilled meats among themselves while Mom, Angeline, and I split up the side dishes.

Angeline and I go commissary shopping together on Wednesday, the first of August so we can spend Thursday cooking the side dishes. I am excited to make my own potato salad as well as the pasta salad. I can get them done during Elizabeth's afternoon nap.

I stay up late Wednesday night, waiting for Rick to come home.

"Hey there," Rick says, walking in the door close to midnight. "What are you doing up?" He drops his hat on the sofa and gives me a kiss.

"I just wanted to wait up for you. I like to do it every once in awhile."

"That's nice. Are you all right?"

"I'm fine. I'm just excited about Friday's barbecue. I'm actually going to make my own recipes for it. I hope they'll turn out good."

"They will. You're quite the cook in your own right, you know."

When we go to bed that night, I am deeply satisfied with life. Everything feels right; Rick is home, our child is healthy, and I like married life.

Maybe this military thing is going to work out after all.

****

August 2, 1990

The following morning, after changing Elizabeth and nursing her, I pour myself a cup of coffee and turn on the news, mainly to check the weather for the barbecue this weekend.

The first image that fills the screen is of tanks rolling across a desert landscape. Did I put it on the right channel? I did. This is a CNN news feed, but it's on the local channel. Is our cable messed up?

Confused, I turn up the volume. The news anchor is talking about someone named Saddam Hussein and a country named Kuwait. It sounds like a fruit; I have never heard of it. What does this have to do with anything? Why is it on my local news channel?

A prickly feeling creeps up my spine and goose bumps cover my arms. Frozen, I stare at the screen. The news anchor is talking about an invasion from Iraq into this tiny fruit country. As he continues to talk, he mentions something about President Bush making a statement soon.

I gasp; something hot splashes on my arm and I jerk. I've spilled my coffee. I'm shaking. I put the cup on the coffee table and hurry to grab some paper towels.

Just as I dump the soiled paper towels into the garbage, the phone rings. Hoping to keep it from waking Rick up, I answer it quickly. With half my attention on the television, I hear an unfamiliar voice on the other end.

"I'm sorry, who is this?" I ask the unknown caller.

"This is Sergeant Whitaker. May I speak with Airman Johnson?"

"Uh, he's sleeping right now. Can I take a message?"

"No, I need to speak to him, please."

I shake harder. "Okay. Hang on." The phone rattles onto the side table. My breathing increases. I hurry down the hall and open the bedroom door. Rick is snoring softly, sprawled across the bed with one leg hanging out from under the sheets.

"Rick? Rick, you have a phone call," I whisper, shaking his arm urgently.

"Hmmph?" he grunts.

"Rick, you have a phone call. You need to wake up."

"Wha..huh?"

"Rick, get *up*." The ball in the pit of my stomach is made of lead. This is bad. This is very bad.

His eyes blink open. "I have a phone call?" he asks, confusion on his face.

"Yes. Please, get up now."

His brow furrows. "Is everything all right?"

"I don't know."

He sits up quickly, rubs his face, and rises with a deep sigh. He shuffles down the hallway and picks up the phone.

"Hello?" he yawns and pauses. "Yes, this is Airman Johnson." He clears his throat, rubbing his eyes. Suddenly, he stiffens and is instantly wide awake. "What's going on? What happened?" More silence. "No, I just woke up." Pause. "All right." He turns his attention to the television. "Oh. When do I have to report?"

My knees buckle and I drop onto the sofa. My full attention returns to the television while Rick finishes his conversation. I know deep in my bones that what I'm seeing on the television is directly related to whatever Rick is hearing on the phone.

I'm scared. No, I'm terrified.

PART TWO: DEPLOYMENTS

1991 – 1996

CHAPTER SIXTEEN

March, 1991

Angeline and I sustain ourselves by keeping busy. Rick reported to work immediately and lost his days off. He prepared for deployment and left one week after he got that fateful phone call. Chris left three days after Rick. We never did have that barbecue.

I watched in horror as our lives skewed painfully off the comfortable path we had been on. There were additions to my vocabulary – Saddam Hussein, Norman Schwartzkopf, Kuwait, Iraq, scud missiles, Persian Gulf, Kurds, Sunni, Shi'ite. Strange, foreign words, names, things, and places. They're intricately woven into our psyche and destiny now.

Our husbands have been gone for seven months. Seven very long months. I thought Rick being in Korea was bad; that was a cake walk compared to this.

At least in Korea, he was safe.

Every time I watched the news and saw the explosions and ghastly green lights whipping around in the desert night skies on the other side of the world, my heart would hammer and my mouth would go dry. I knew Rick was there, somewhere. He was near all of that. When he left, he couldn't tell me where he was going, what he would be doing, or how long he would be gone.

On the news, I saw images of men and women in uniforms that looked exactly like Rick's donning gas masks and gear to protect themselves from the chemical weapons we were sure Saddam Hussein was using. After all, he had used them on his own people. I saw the pictures of women and children - all dead, frozen with their mouths open in a forever silenced scream. I remember the hollow eyes on one particular dead baby still held in its mother's arms. That image is seared into my mind.

I have nightmares.

We declared victory in February, but the troops are not home. The name of the war changed from Operation Desert Shield to Operation Desert Storm. All I know is I am terrified every day that I will get a call or even worse, a visit, from someone telling me the unthinkable.

One afternoon, I saw a dark navy blue car pull up to the house across the street and down a few houses from mine. Two officers got out and approached the door. Ice water rolled down my spine; I knew why they were there. My eyes remained riveted to them as they knocked. After a few moments, an arm pushed the screen door open and allowed the uniformed visitors to enter.

I held my breath, imagining what was transpiring inside that home, feeling a deep twinge of guilt for being thankful and relieved they didn't stop in front of mine.

I didn't realize how hard I was squeezing Elizabeth until she whimpered, "Mommy, out!" She wriggled against my vice grip, which I immediately loosened, allowing her to push herself away from me toward her toys.

My eyes remained on that door.

A blood curdling scream echoed through the neighborhood and into my open windows.

It came from that house.

"God, no…" I gasped, struggling to breathe. This wasn't supposed to be happening.

I don't know when those men left. I couldn't watch anymore. The lady and her children left a week later. Moving trucks came one day and cleared the house out afterward.

Our neighborhood is shrouded in yellow ribbons. Angeline and I, along with a number of other wives left behind spent an entire weekend tying them around every tree and taping them onto every mailbox we could. Everyone is eager to help and show support.

My education in military life continues.

Financially, we are all suffering in some way. Some families have had to go on food stamps to survive. Military pay is based on the one who wears the uniform, so when their situation changes, their pay changes. The military pay is broken down into several parts; there's the base pay based on rank, then there are the allowances – basic allowance for subsistence (food) and basic allowance for quarters (housing). When the family member in uniform deploys, the food allowance disappears because they are being fed on site.

Most families in the lower enlisted ranks cannot absorb that loss of pay, so many are forced to apply for food stamps. I had to tighten our belt at first, in spite of Rick's recent increase in pay from putting on Staff Sergeant. When Rick's parents found out (through Rick), they began sending us money every month over my protests. It is helpful, but I feel guilty. They wire the money to our account every month without hesitation. Rick told me to just be thankful because they are not only willing, but able to do so. I thank them profusely when I talk to them each month.

Angeline isn't as lucky – she is one of the families that need food stamps. She's also on WIC because of her boys and her pregnancy, which is coming to an end without Chris.

My parents are baffled.

"How in the name of all that is holy is this right?" Dad fumes. "My God – these boys are over there fighting for freedom and to protect us from these savages, and their families have to get food stamps to eat? That is a crime!" He pounds his fist on the table. Dad promptly starts writing letters to his Congressman, encouraging me to do the same.

I have not heard from anyone in Rick's squadron since his deployment other than a cursory message left on my answering machine a week after he deployed. It was from the First Sergeant informing me that if I need anything, please call. He left a phone number that I scribbled down somewhere. I am so very grateful for Angeline and my family. I don't know what I would do without them.

During Rick's absence, I am still required to maintain the outer appearance of our home for the ongoing monthly housing inspections. My father and brother have taken to mowing not only my lawn, but Angeline's, too. As much as she loves yard work, she just can't do it now.

One morning after mowing the lawns, red-faced and sweaty, Dad walks in the door. He mops his brow and drains an entire glass of water. "I thought the military took care of its own! Why aren't they out here taking care of this for you gals?"

"I don't know, Dad," I sigh. "Maybe there's nobody left because they're all deployed."

Dad mutters under his breath, refilling his glass in the kitchen. He rants a lot these days.

"Guppa! Guppa!" Elizabeth toddles into the kitchen, thrusting her chubby arms up toward my father, wanting him to pick her up. At seventeen months, Guppa is the closest she has gotten to saying Grandpa. I haven't heard her say Dadda yet. Rick left long before she said her first words. I try to keep her acquainted by showing her pictures of him, which I leave at her eye level on the refrigerator. I also put the phone up to her ear when he calls, but she usually just stares at the phone, not really understanding what it's all about.

"Hey there, short stuff!" Dad says, bending to lift her up with a grunt. "How's Guppa's favorite little girl?"

Elizabeth grins and pats Dad's face. He nibbles her little hands and she squeals in delight.

"Hey! Is anyone home?" a friendly voice calls from my front door. It's Nicole Hamilton; she moved into the house across the street that was vacated by the family of the fallen airman. I met her by chance one day at the commissary. I literally ran into her cart coming around the corner. Amid my multiple apologies, we realized that we lived on the same street. The fact that she has twin girls, Hailey and Bailey, who are the same age as Elizabeth gave us an instant bond. I don't know how she handles two when I scramble to keep up with one.

Now, I hurry to the door to let her in. "Hey there, yourself!" I smile.

"What's up? I see your dad finished the lawns once again, the poor man. I think it should be considered elder abuse."

Dad waves her off. "Please. I'm not elderly yet." He grins and puts Elizabeth down.

"I'm thankful my husband is still here," Nicole comments, but quickly backtracks. "I'm sorry, that sounded insensitive."

"It's okay," I reply.

"It would be nice for Angeline if Chris could come home before the baby is born," Nicole laments.

"I agree. We'll keep praying," I sigh. I have been attending chapel services on base for a number of months now with Nicole. Angeline even comes most Sundays, when she can get her kids together in time. It's a struggle. I find the services comforting. To be surrounded by other people who are going through what we're going through helps, if only in some small way. Every week we pray for our deployed loved ones; there's a running list of names posted in the vestibule for the attendees to see. Whenever one returns home, their name is highlighted in yellow. There have been a few names highlighted each week. But the list is very long.

"Most definitely. I wanted to see if you'd like to come to the park with me and the girls for a picnic. It's gorgeous outside."

"Sure. I'll pack our lunches. When did you want to go?"

"Well," she consults her watch. "It's almost eleven now. How about in an hour or so? I'll stop by and ask Angeline, too. I gotta run – I left the girls playing in the living room, but I can't be gone too long."

"I'll check with Angeline. You go on home."

"Thanks. See you in a bit!" She waves and ducks out the front door, trotting across the lawn.

I turn to my father. "Dad, I'm going over to Angeline's for a second. You'll be okay?"

"Of course," he grins at Elizabeth.

When I knock on Angeline's door, bedlam breaks out behind it. Her boys are yelling and making all kinds of racket. I hear Angeline's sharp voice rise above them both.

She opens the door, red-faced and scowling. When she sees me, her expression instantly brightens.

"Oh, hey, Heather," she wipes her hand across her brow. "Come on in. What's up? Don't step on those," she warns, pointing to a pile of blocks near the door.

I deftly side step the toys and enter the melee that is her living room. Ronnie is bouncing up and down on the sofa while Edward spins in circles, a toy plane grasped tightly in each hand. Apparently, the planes are engaged in aerial combat.

"Sorry about the mess." Angeline sweeps her hand in front of her apologetically before snapping her fingers at the boys. "Will you two sit *down!*"

The boys stop for a split second before continuing their antics.

Angeline shakes her head, rubbing her enormous midsection. "What's up?"

"Nicole just stopped by. She wants to know if we would like to go to the park and have a picnic for lunch and let the kids play." I side step another toy on the floor. Perhaps it's best if I just stand still.

"I think that would be perfect. These two are bouncing off the walls. I'll tell you something, I cannot wait until Edward starts kindergarten in the fall." She presses her hands into the small of her back, grimacing.

"Are you all right? How's the baby?"

"I'm fine. She's just really crowded in there and my back hurts all the time. I feel like I'm about to explode," she groans. "Three and a half weeks left. I hope Chris will be home in time."

Angeline was over the moon to find out they were having a little girl. She said that now she has her little girl, she's done having babies.

"I hope they'll both be home soon. Do you want me to pack lunches for all of us? I don't mind, really."

"Oh, Heather. You don't have to go to the trouble…" she protests weakly.

"I'll take care of it. You bring a bag of chips. Sound good?"

"Yes, thank you. What time?" she asks, flicking a glance at the clock on her wall that is sitting slightly askew.

"Nicole said around noon. Will that work?"

"I should be able to corral the boys by then." She rubs her stomach. "This girl is really active today – kicking me all over the place!"

"Will you be all right to walk to the park?" She waddles a lot lately.

Angeline shakes her head vehemently. "Trust me; I need to get out of this house. Besides, the park isn't far."

"All right. But if it's too much, we can take the car instead."

"To go five blocks? Are you kidding? That'll be the day," she chuckles.

I go home to make the lunches, packing sandwiches, fruit, and water.

"Dad? Do you want to go to the park with us?" I ask, arranging the lunch in the insulated cloth cooler.

"No, thanks," Dad says, groaning to a standing position. "I think I'll head home and take a shower." He turns toward Elizabeth and wrinkles his nose. "I stink."

"Tinky! Tinky!" Elizabeth giggles. She adores him.

Just before noon, I spy Nicole pushing her double stroller across the street toward my house. I gather the cooler, place it in the bottom basket of my stroller that I keep parked on our tiny porch and strap Elizabeth into her seat.

"Hey!" Nicole waves at me when she is close enough not to shout. "Is Angeline coming, too?"

"Yes, let's head over and see if she needs any help."

We push our strollers over and park them in Angeline's driveway while Nicole knocks on the door. Angeline emerges shortly holding one of Edward's hands while his other hand clutches a grocery bag containing the chips. She's working to get a reluctant Ronnie into his stroller. He's almost too big for it, but I know it helps Angeline to have him in a more controlled mode of transport. He's liable to take off running, and in her current condition, she wouldn't be able to stop him.

"Ronnie, get in the stroller. I'll let you have your dinosaur once you're strapped in," Angeline encourages him. "Look at all your friends. They're in their strollers." Ronnie's face puckers as he looks around. Finally, he relents and allows his mother to strap him in. When she hands him his favorite toy, he relaxes.

Angeline rises with a groan. "Whew! Edward, do you want to carry the bag or put it down here?" She gestures to the bottom basket of her stroller.

"I'll carry it," he replies confidently. Once we finally begin our walk toward the park, however, it isn't far before Edward changes his mind and drops the grocery bag containing the chips into the bottom of the stroller. Apparently, it interferes with his ability to jump over sidewalk cracks and run circles around every tree we pass.

Once we get to the park and claim a picnic table, we feed the kids. While they busily munch on their lunch, we sit back and leisurely enjoy ours.

"So," Nicole starts, taking a bite of her sandwich. "Have you guys heard anything about when your husbands will be home? It should be soon. There are waves of people coming home all the time on the news."

"Chris said he thinks it might be soon. I really hope it's before Leila gets here." She pats her stomach. "I can't do this by myself."

"Rick still has no idea when he'll be home. Are your parents coming for the birth?" I ask, popping a grape into my mouth.

"No," she sighs. "They can't afford it. My family has no money. I talked to my mom a couple days ago and she was crying about it."

"Oh, that's terrible!" I place my hand on her arm. "I'm so sorry,

Angeline."

"Mommy, I'm done," Ronnie announces, squirming out of his seat.

"Hang on, buddy. You have to wait for your friends, too," Angeline warns him.

Ronnie throws his head back and moans.

"They're almost done, sweetie," Nicole smiles sweetly at him. "I have a special treat for all of you if you behave yourselves and play nicely today. But you have to wait until the end." She holds up her finger, looking each of them in the eye.

They all straighten up and her twins clap their hands together in glee.

"What is it?" Edward asks, eyes round in anticipation.

Nicole shakes her head, smiling. "You'll have to wait until the end, and you have to behave yourselves first."

When they're done, the kids half run, half toddle toward the play structure to play in the heat of the afternoon sun. The three of us settle back and watch them. Elizabeth, Hailey, and Bailey happily settle into the sand box where they re-plant weeds they pluck from around the box into the sand. Edward and Ronnie chase each other in a game of tag.

Angeline cups her hands around her mouth and yells, "Edward and Ronnie! Don't run so fast near the girls! Go do that in the field!" She waves them off to the side of the structure. The boys' faces turn toward where she gesture and run in that direction. She shakes her head. "Those boys…"

"They're fine. They're just energetic, and that's a good thing," Nicole says.

"Yeah, I know. I love them, but they wear me out."

"You know, we're here for you and my family loves you to pieces," I remark. "If Chris isn't home in time, you'll still be taken care of."

Angeline turns her gaze on me, her eyes misty. "Thank you." She looks at Nicole. "Both of you. I don't know what I would do without you. This really stinks."

"Tell me about it," I snort.

"I don't know why Stan didn't get deployed, but I guess they don't send everybody," Nicole adds guiltily.

"Don't feel bad. We're happy for you," I reassure her.

"Yes, we are," Angeline pipes in.

The kids play happily for over an hour until the heat of the day gets to be too much.

We pack them up in their strollers for the walk home. Nicole pulls a bag out from the basket under her stroller and says excitedly, "You've all been little angels today. We had so much fun. Who's ready for their treat?"

A chorus of hands and shouts of "Me! Me! Me!" fills the air.

Nicole unwraps the treats, which are chocolate chip cookies. She passes them out one by one after each child says "please" and "thank you."

They happily eat their cookies and chatter quietly amongst themselves while we make our way home. By the time we get home, however, everyone has fallen asleep with the exception of Edward, who walked. He looks like he'll collapse when he gets in the door. His feet drag, and he has no interest in running circles around trees anymore. He is content to hold on to the stroller ferrying his brother and walk beside us.

The walk home takes longer – Angeline walks very slowly, waddling from side to side.

"Are you sure you're all right?" Nicole asks, casting a worried glance at our friend.

Angeline waves her off. "Yeah, my back hurts. I need to sit in my recliner."

"I don't know, Angeline. That's how my labor was, too. All back pain." I look at her knowingly.

"This isn't my first round in this rodeo. Trust me. I'll know when I'm in labor."

"Still, I will have my phone near me all the time."

"Me, too," Nicole pipes in. "All you have to do is call."

"Don't worry. I plan to!" She laughs.

By the time we reach her driveway, she is barely moving. "Okay, girls. I've had enough. I'll see you later. Thanks for the fun!"

I bend down and unbuckle Ronnie, pulling him out of his stroller and lay his head against my shoulder. Beyond a quick sigh, he doesn't stir. "Where do you want me to put him?"

"Just lay him on the couch, and thanks," Angeline remarks, waddling up her driveway with her hands pressed into her back. She addresses Edward. "Go on and lay down, too, sweetie. I think maybe we'll all take a nap."

I follow her inside and carefully lay Ronnie's sleeping form on the sofa. He immediately turns on his side, curling into a ball. Edward flops on the other end of the sofa, taking a similar position.

With a grunt, Angeline dumps herself into her recliner, quickly pulling on the lever to deploy the foot rest. "Ah," she sighs, closing her eyes briefly. "Much better. Thanks again, Heather. I really appreciate it."

"No problem. I'll catch you later! Call if you need me." I smile and close the door. Nicole brought Angeline's stroller up to the porch and parked it on the side.

"That was a lot of fun. Good idea, Nicole," I remark as we walk the short distance to my house.

"I thought we all needed to get out and have some fun." She grins. "It worked wonders on the kids. They'll take a good nap and sleep well tonight, too." Her twins have their heads lolled back and mouths wide open in their stroller. Elizabeth is in a similar position.

"I'm glad. I've got some housework to catch up on. I'll see you later.

Tell Stan I said hi." She smiles and waves. I turn to go up my own driveway while Nicole crosses the street.

Once I place Elizabeth's sleeping form in her crib and unpack the remains of the picnic lunch, I sit down to write Rick a letter, telling him all about our day. I include how much we hope he and Chris will be home soon, especially with Angeline in her condition and the baby almost here.

Next, I pen a letter to his parents. They were vacationing in Spain last month when they called. I dutifully send them pictures of Elizabeth and keep them updated about her. They hear from Rick about as much as I do. I am sure to thank them for their monthly generosity, as well.

Unfortunately, I only get to talk to Rick about once a month, if I'm lucky. This is war, and we are at the mercy of those in charge of running it. So I pour my heart out in letters to him. There are times when I get a lot of letters in a week and sometimes only one, or none for a few weeks. It just depends on when he can take the time to write.

My thoughts linger on Angeline; how on earth is she going to handle a new baby with her two lively boys? I shudder, remembering my own exhaustive induction into parenthood with just one baby, my husband and family surrounding me to help. Nicole, my family, and I will certainly do everything we can.

Angeline's need for our help comes in the middle of the night four days later. The insistent blaring of my bedside phone wakes me from deep slumber a little after midnight.

"Hello?" I answer groggily, propping myself up on my elbow.

Panting answers me, followed by a low moan.

I bolt upright, instantly awake. "Angeline? Is that you?"

"Yes, I need to get to the hospital *now!*"

"Omigod! Omigod!" I jump up and pace a small pathway in front of my bed. "Okay. I'm going to call Nicole and have her come watch our kids, and I'll call my parents, too. I'll be right there!"

"Hurry!" The phone goes dead.

I quickly dial Nicole's phone, and then my parents. Nicole arrives at my doorstep within minutes, bleary-eyed and wearing a robe and slippers over her pajamas. I barely had time to pull on a pair of sweat pants and T-shirt when she rang my doorbell.

"Is she sure?" Nicole asks, her brow furrowed with worry.

"I think she's very sure – you should've heard her on the phone," I reply, quickly tying my shoes. "I'm going to take Elizabeth to Angeline's house. There's no need to wake up her two boys. Just let her sleep on the sofa. I'll call when I have news. My parents are on their way."

"Sounds good. I'll go see if she needs help with anything." Nicole ducks back out the door and scurries into the darkness.

I quickly retrieve Elizabeth's warm, limp body from her crib, cover her with her blanket and hurry across the lawn. When I arrive at Angeline's wide open door, the living room is lit softly by the light of just one lamp. Angeline is pacing quickly back and forth in her living room, her face creased in concentration. Nicole is standing in the middle, looking worried.

"She's ready," Nicole states, her eyes on Angeline's pacing form.

I lay Elizabeth down gently on the sofa. She sighs and curls over on her side. Her eyelids don't even flutter. I tuck her blanket around her and turn my attention to Angeline.

"All right, let's go. Nicole, keep an eye out for my parents." I put my arm around Angeline's waist and guide her to my car. Just before I help her in, I turn to her. "Did your water break yet?"

She nods her head quickly. "Right before I called you."

"Holy moley. Okay, get in." I gently settle her into the seat and click her seatbelt in place.

She pushes her head back, rubs her stomach and starts moaning as I close the door. I hurry to the driver's side and get to the hospital as quickly as I can, Angeline yelling with every contraction.

"I'm hurrying, Angeline," I encourage her. "Just keep breathing."

When we pull into the semi-circle entrance to the emergency room, I slam the car in park and turn to Angeline, "I'll be right back!" I leap out of the car and run in, my eyes sweeping the room for the registration desk. "My friend is outside in heavy labor!"

The medical staff bolts into action; a wheelchair magically appears along with three staff members who jog outside. Angeline has her door open and is leaning halfway out of the car, panting heavily as she grips the door.

In a whirlwind, she is placed in the wheelchair and hurried inside and down the hallway. One staff member stops me from following with her hands up.

"Go ahead and park your car. We'll get her up to Labor and Delivery. She'll be fine. We'll take good care of her. Go!" She sweeps her hand at me.

I nod and return to my car. Once I've parked, I hurry back into the door I originally entered and see the familiar face of the staff member. I approach her. "Can I go up now?"

She smiles. "Of course. Tell her good luck!" she calls after me as I disappear down the hallway. I remember how to get to Labor and Delivery; my own experience being so recent. When I arrive at the reception desk, I quickly ask for Angeline's room number.

"They're still settling her in, I believe. Hang on," the woman informs me. She rises and disappears briefly around the corner. When she returns, she points to her left down the hall. "Yes, she's in room twelve."

"Thank you," I reply, hurrying down the hall. When I enter the room, the curtain is pulled closed around the bed and there's a bright light emanating from behind it.

A male voice addresses Angeline. "It's all right, Mrs. Baker. You're at six centimeters and making great progress." I hear the unmistakable *snap* of a pair of rubber gloves being removed. "Would you like an epidural?"

"Yes!" Angeline yells before moaning and panting heavily.

Suddenly the curtain whips open, startling me.

The voice is now attached to a face. The face smiles at me. "Hello. Are you a friend of Mrs. Baker?" I nod. "Good. I'm Dr. Hunter. I'm going to let the anesthesiologist know she'd like an epidural. He should be in shortly." He nods to the two nurses working quickly at Angeline's bedside before retreating.

Angeline's eyes are squeezed shut and she's turning her head from side to side, intermittently panting and moaning. One nurse has a tourniquet tied to my friend's arm, trying to insert an IV. The other nurse is fidgeting with the machinery that measures the baby's heartbeat and the intensity of contractions. The rapid thumps of the baby's heartbeat suddenly fill the room before the nurse adjusts the volume.

"Got it!" The IV nurse proclaims proudly. With a flick of her finger, she releases the tourniquet and attaches the IV fluids, tapping buttons on the front of the machine.

I find the whole business fascinating now that I'm not the one in labor.

Angeline's eyes have opened and she's breathing easier, but panic rims her eyes. She looks around the room, her gaze finally resting on me. She offers a faint smile.

"That was a hard one," she says breathlessly, licking her lips. "I hope he hurries up with the epidural."

"Me, too. I know it hurts like hell," I smile and pat her hand.

She grips my hand in response. "Thanks for bringing me."

"It's my pleasure."

She grimaces suddenly, clutching my hand fiercely. Her eyes become unfocused and she starts moaning and panting again. My eyes flick to the monitor. The little needle starts to climb as the contraction builds in strength.

"Keep breathing, Mrs. Baker. It's almost to the top now. You're doing fine," the nurse calmly encourages her, eyeing the machine.

"Wow, that's a big one!" I exclaim, watching the needle continue its steady climb. The nurse glances at me and nods.

Angeline squeezes her eyes shut, throws her head back, and starts to yell.

Her grip on my hand is painful, but I don't care. I remember how badly it hurt.

A different man, who I presume is the anesthesiologist, enters the room with a rolling cart and pulls it right up to the bed. He checks the name on Angeline's name band secured around her wrist. She doesn't notice – she is whipping her head back and forth and still yelling.

"That will probably be one of your last contractions, Mrs. Baker. We'll get your epidural going and make you more comfortable," he says over her yelling. I don't know if she hears him.

The nurses work around me and go back into action quickly, setting up for the epidural. The doctor converses with the nurses about the baby's heart rate and vitals while donning his sterile attire.

Angeline's grip on my hand has started to relax. I glance at the machine – the needle has crested and is rapidly descending.

"Oh, God," Angeline pants, sweat beading on her upper lip. "I sure hope so."

"I need you to sit up and dangle your feet over the edge of the bed, Mrs. Baker," the anesthesiologist says. The nurses and I help her to a sitting position and do as he says. The doctor looks at me. "Are you all right to help? You can stand in front of her and let her head rest on your shoulder. I need you to curl your back, Mrs. Baker."

I nod and plant myself in front of Angeline. She leans on my shoulder. "Go ahead and put your arms around me, Angeline. It's okay."

"No! *No!*" she suddenly yells, holding me in a death grip as another contraction takes over. I tense my body and stagger my feet as the needle on the machine begins to climb. Angeline intermittently pants and screams while the needle climbs much higher than before.

When it finally dissipates, she's trembling and sweating. "Hurry, please!" she cries.

"I am, Mrs. Baker," the doctor replies calmly. "I'll be done very shortly." I am sure he's been through this many times.

Angeline suffers through one more contraction before the doctor is able to get her epidural in and the medicine flowing. As soon as he does, he smiles and looks at me. "You did great, Mrs. Baker's friend." He then addresses Angeline. "You should feel relief instantly. If you feel the next contraction at all, it won't be anything like it was."

"I hope so," she replies shakily. "I can't take it anymore." The nurses help settle her back on the bed.

"We are going to check you again, too. I think you've probably made great progress," one of the nurses says. Once she is finished checking her discreetly, she smiles. "Yep. You're at eight. I think you'll be ready to deliver soon. The head is right there. We'll get you to the delivery room." Her eyes flick to the monitor. "And you're having a contraction right now. They're almost on top of each other."

Angeline's head whips to the monitor while her hands go to her belly. "Wow. I can feel a little heaviness and tightening, but the pain is gone. Thank God for epidurals!"

"Indeed," the doctor grins and reaches his hand out, shaking first Angeline's hand and then mine. "Have a safe delivery! I'll be around to make sure you stay comfortable." He ducks out of the room. The second nurse is almost done cleaning up from the epidural placement. The first nurse starts packing Angeline up for her short trip to the delivery room.

"You are welcome to come in the delivery room, but you have to put these on first," the second nurse informs me, thrusting a folded pile of blue disposable clothing at me. "Don't forget to put the hair cover and booties on, too. Is the father here?"

I shake my head, "He's deployed," while quickly donning the clothing as instructed, following as they guide the bed out of the room and down the hall. When we arrive in the delivery room, Dr. Hunter is sitting on a stool in the center surrounded by medical equipment and a soon-to-be occupied bassinet. There are a number of people scattered throughout the room waiting for us. It's overwhelming, so I keep my focus on Angeline, who is breathing heavily.

"Are you in pain?" I ask.

"It hurts a little, but it's not that bad," she reports. "I just feel a lot of pressure."

Once she's in position and told to start pushing, it takes almost two hours for her to deliver her little girl. She looks huge compared to Elizabeth when she was born. Watching the process from the outside is an experience I'll never forget. It is incredible.

"Is she all right?" Angeline's voice is shrill, her cheeks pink and face wet, once the baby emerges but doesn't immediately cry.

"She's perfectly fine. They're checking her out," the doctor replies calmly.

Suddenly a loud wail fills the room, and Angeline and I both relax. I hadn't realized I was holding my breath until I exhaled sharply.

"Thank you, God," Angeline whispers.

"You did so good!" I smile and squeeze her hand. She grins.

"Great job, momma," one nurse adds.

"Thank you," Angeline says breathlessly. "When do I get to hold her?"

"Right now," another nurse appears with the warm pink bundle, tucking her gently into Angeline's outstretched arms.

"How much does she weigh?" Angeline asks, taking in the precious little face.

"She's a bruiser at nine pounds and four ounces. She's twenty-two inches long," the nurse replies.

"Holy smokes, that's a big baby. You're a champion, Angeline!" I cry. I can't imagine.

"Wow." That's all Angeline can say – she's busy drinking in the face of her new little girl. "I have a girl, finally. You were worth it." She leans in and kisses her daughter.

The doctor takes quite awhile sewing her up. When she is settled into the recovery room, I am suddenly overwhelmed by exhaustion. It's almost five-thirty. I hadn't realized how much time had gone by.

"You look terrible," Angeline remarks as I rub my face, yawning widely.

"You should talk! I'm not the one that just delivered a Thanksgiving turkey," I joke.

She laughs. "Yeah. I can't believe how huge she is. My others were only seven pounds and some change. I don't know why all of a sudden I have a big baby. But still," her gaze falls lovingly on her sleeping baby. "She was worth it."

I rise and bend over to stare into her sleeping face. "She totally is. Hi, Leila Marie. That's such a beautiful name, Angeline."

"Thanks. I need to let Chris know," she says quietly, her chin quivering. "He's a daddy again."

"We can get hold of your husband," a nurse that had been hovering in the background suddenly chimes in.

"Really?" I ask.

"Of course. We do it all the time for our patients. A lot of deliveries these days happen without dad around because of deployments. Would you like me to see if I can get him on the phone?"

"Yes!" Angeline replies excitedly.

She nods and disappears. It takes almost thirty minutes, but she finally returns with a phone that she plugs into the wall, getting ready for the connection.

"I'm going to step out and let you guys have your conversation. I think I need a cup of coffee anyway." I pat Angeline's blanketed leg and retreat to find a vending machine. At one point, I walk in front of a bank of windows that are facing east and stop, staring at the most brilliant sunrise I have ever seen. The flashes of pink, orange, red, and even purple painted across the sky bring a tear to my eye in their brilliance. Rick and I haven't been able to see any sunrises or sunsets in quite awhile. I miss our adventures.

"Wow," I whisper.

"It is gorgeous, isn't it?" a male voice intrudes, interrupting my reverie.

I turn to the voice and see that it's Dr. Hunter. He is blowing on a steaming cup of coffee, taking in the view alongside me.

"Yes, it is. Amazing. A new day and a new little person all at once," I reply, returning my gaze to the changing sunrise.

"Yes. I never tire of it. Mrs. Baker did a great job. She's a beautiful baby," he remarks, sipping from his cup.

"You did a great job, too. I'm just sorry her husband couldn't be here."

He raises his eyebrows in question. "Deployed?"

I nod.

"Thought so. There are a lot of us who are gone. I hope he comes home soon. Enjoy your day!" He raises his cup to me and disappears through a set of double doors at the end of the hallway.

I turn back toward the bank of windows; the sunrise is complete and the colors are fading. Unfortunately, I never did ask that nice doctor where I could get a cup of coffee. The weariness is creeping into my bones now that the adrenaline rush has worn off. All I want is my bed. Dismissing the idea of drinking coffee, I return to the recovery room to find Angeline with tears streaming down her face, and a nurse comforting her.

"What's wrong?" I ask, noting that Leila is safely ensconced in her bassinet at Angeline's bedside.

Angeline shakes her head. "I miss Chris. He doesn't know when he'll be home."

The nurse pats her arm. "It's okay, Mrs. Baker. I know how you feel. My husband is deployed, too."

"He is?" I ask. I hadn't thought about that. The nurses are people. They have families.

"Oh, yes. He's been gone about six months. He wasn't in the first wave of deployments, but he finally got his orders. I'm just glad that I'm still here," she says, a tinge of sadness in her voice.

"You're in the military?" I ask, surprised.

She nods. "We have two kids at home, and I can tell you, I do not want to leave them."

My mouth drops open. "They wouldn't do that, would they? Send both parents away?"

"Yes, they would. There are a number of us here that are dual military couples. Quite a few left within days of each other."

"You have got to be kidding!" Angeline wipes at her cheeks, her attention shifted to the nurse. "Do they have children?"

"Yes. They had to deposit them with parents or whoever can take them. It's awful. But we joined the military knowing this was a possibility. We are required to have a plan in place at all times for things like this. If I get deployed, my children will stay with my parents."

"That's terrible," I exclaim.

"I hope and pray it doesn't happen, but my husband and I volunteered to wear the uniform. There is no draft anymore. We made this choice."

"Are you going to stay in and make it a career?" Angeline asks.

The nurse ponders the question. "I don't know. I have one year left on my commitment, and we'll decide when the time comes. I haven't made up my mind. But don't worry, your husband has been gone longer than mine, so I'm sure he'll come back first." She hugs Angeline. "It will all work out."

While driving home from the hospital after seeing Angeline settled into her room, I linger on the nurse's situation. I can't understand how the military can do something like that – send both parents off to fight in a war and leave their children behind. I don't care if it is an all volunteer force.

Some things just shouldn't be.

At the same time, I deeply admire her and her husband for their courage and sacrifice. They don't have to do this, but they choose to. She is there taking care of people like me and Angeline every day. Wow. I hope she doesn't deploy.

I could never leave Elizabeth for months at a time. It's hard enough having Rick gone for so long. She doesn't even know him, has no memory of him. I don't want a fractured family.

Am I strong enough to do this? Am I worthy of this calling?

CHAPTER SEVENTEEN

April, 1991

We took the boys to meet their new baby sister later in the day. They were very careful with her, and excited about the new addition to the family. Edward was barely a year old himself when his brother was born, so he doesn't remember having a new baby in the house.

My parents, Nicole, and I make sure Angeline's house is clean and the boys are taken care of while she is in the hospital. Her refrigerator and freezer are stocked with meals my mother spent considerable time preparing.

When Angeline returns home with Leila, she is exhausted and very glad to be home. We all welcome her with balloons and a banner proclaiming, "It's a girl!" taped across her front window.

"This is amazing!" Angeline proclaims as she steps across the threshold of her home. "My house hasn't been this clean in months." The boys clamber around her heels until she sits down.

"Mommy! Mommy! You gotta come look in the fridge!" Edward exclaims. "Come look!"

"What? Why?" Angeline asks, confused.

"Just come *look!*" Edward whines.

Angeline looks from me to Nicole. We remain silent, wanting to savor the surprise. "All right," she sighs. "Would you hold Leila?" She hands her to me and rises to follow her eager son.

When Angeline sees all the meals and food that have filled her refrigerator, she bursts into tears. "I never thought…"

"We are happy to do it," I reply, cradling Leila's sleeping form.

"The boys are welcome to stay over at our house whenever they want to. You need the rest," Nicole adds, hugging Angeline.

When Nicole and my family gathered to clean her house, my mother was deeply disturbed to see how barren Angeline's refrigerator and cupboards were.

"There isn't enough food to feed a family for more than a day!" Mom had exclaimed in dismay. "Leonard, we are going shopping." She spent the rest of the day and into the night cooking and packaging meals.

Mom had planned to stay with Angeline and help her like she helped me, but she was exhausted from cooking.

"Tell your mother thank you. I'm sorry she isn't feeling well enough to be here," Angeline implores.

"You can thank her the next time you see her."

****

A few weeks later, Angeline hurries over to my house, grinning from ear to ear. I had just put Elizabeth down for her afternoon nap. Without even bothering to knock, Angeline bursts into my house and exclaims, "He's coming home! He's coming home!"

I gasp. "Are you serious? Really? When? Maybe I'll be getting a call soon, too."

She springs up and down on her tiptoes. "He said he should be home in about a week!"

"Angeline, that's wonderful!"

Her face suddenly crumples, and she bursts into tears, covering her face with her hands.

Shocked, I lead her over to the sofa and sit down next to her. "What's wrong?"

She sobs a few more times before answering. "I don't know. I can't seem to get hold of myself. I cry all the time!" She swipes angrily at her face. "It's ridiculous."

"I think it's just new mommy hormones. I felt a little like that after I had Elizabeth."

She turns to me hopefully. "You think so? I didn't feel like this with the boys."

"Well, they say every pregnancy is different."

"Yeah, I guess," she replies, wiping at another tear. "I'm just so happy Chris will be home!" She sobs again.

"It's okay, Angeline," I chuckle. "Go ahead and cry all you want."

She does.

****

May, 1991

Chris arrives exactly five days later to great fanfare. Leila is one and a half months old. There are a lot of troops that came home with him – the news coverage shows large waves of them coming home all over the country on a regular basis. Rick isn't among them yet, and my heart grows heavy.

One Friday afternoon a few weeks later, Rick calls with the exciting news that he will be home in three days.

"Three days?" I scream into the phone. "You'll be here in three days?!"

"That's right! I'm coming home, baby!" he crows into the phone, letting out a whoop.

This is the longest we have ever been separated in one stretch, and it's finally, finally coming to an end. Rick is safe and whole. My friends and family are elated when I tell them.

We all gather with a large number of other families, waiting for the plane that carries our loved ones to land. When it arrives and parks, we hold our collective breath for the faces we've longed for to emerge from the belly of the giant green beast of a plane.

Finally, two by two, they emerge in a line and walk down the ramp and onto the tarmac. The crowd starts cheering loudly. Flags, banners, and balloons wave as more and more troops rapidly emerge from the plane and walk briskly across the tarmac. Bursts of excited noise come from the crowd as loved ones are recognized and reunited.

I wave my banner like everyone else; Elizabeth and I made it last night. Mostly, I made it, but Elizabeth's hand prints are all over it in blue paint. It says, "Welcome home, Daddy!" with his name underneath in bold red, white, and blue letters. Mom, Dad, Jeff, Debbie, Nicole, Stan, Angeline, and Chris with all of our assorted children are clapping, cheering, and yelling excitedly.

I can't find Rick. My eyes sweep the throng anxiously, looking for some clue that would point him out. My gaze rests on one uniformed man, walking very quickly toward us, even though he's weighed down by all kinds of gear, a back pack, and two duffel bags.

Squinting and holding my breath for a moment, recognition dawns. I forget everything and everybody – I scream, drop the banner, and start running for him. "Rick!!!"

When he's twenty feet away, he drops his bags and somehow also drops his back pack. We slam into each other and squeeze so tight, I swear we could literally merge into one being if it were in any way possible.

"Hey, honey bun," his breathless muffled words are lost in my neck. My sobs are muffled in his.

"Rick…"

We stay like that for countless minutes until I hear crying from a familiar voice – it's Elizabeth, and she's bawling loudly. Finally, Rick and I part. I wipe my face before turning back to our own little audience. There are people in similar embraces everywhere. A myriad of reunions occur all around us; laughter, crying, shouts, and a general cacophony of human emotion surrounds us.

I search briefly before settling on my daughter's terrified face. She's staring up at me, looking back and forth between Rick and me.

"Hey there, sweet girl!" Rick bends down to pick her up and she screams, jerks away from him, burying herself in my mother's skirt.

Shock and a twinge of sadness clouds his expression.

"It's all right, sweetie. It's been a long time. She doesn't recognize you yet, but she will soon," I reply.

Rick looks at me, feigning a smile. "I hope so. I really missed her. She's gotten so big and she's walking, too." He smiles down at her – she had peeked out at him, but when he makes eye contact, she buries her face in Mom's skirt once more.

"Welcome home, son!" Dad steps forward and embraces Rick in a bear hug. "You need to stay home now, you hear?"

"Thank you, sir. Once again, thanks for taking such good care of my little family," Rick replies. He goes on to accept hugs and hand shakes from everybody. He spends some time marveling over little Leila, who has grown quite chubby in her short life. She's got beautiful dark little ringlets framing her face. Angeline and Chris are thrilled to have a little girl and are settling in quite nicely together since his return.

"It's so good to see you again, Rick," Mom remarks, hugging Rick around the neck. Elizabeth darts away from Mom and hides behind me when she embraces Rick.

"It's good to see you again, too, Louise," He pulls back and his brow knits together. "Are you working too hard? You look tired."

She waves him off. "Oh, I'm just getting old."

"I can't believe how much all the kids have grown! My goodness, it seems like I've been gone years rather than months! Are these the twins I've heard so much about?" Rick exclaims, introducing himself to Stan and Nicole. He's heard a lot about them through my letters.

Eventually, we all settle into our cars and return to our own homes, my family following us to our house.

Dad insists on helping Rick carry his baggage inside while he tries to cajole Elizabeth to come sit on his lap. After much effort and with the help of her favorite story book, he has to settle for her sitting next to him. She's wary.

"Maybe if you changed out of your uniform, that might help," I suggest.

"Good idea. I'll finish reading the book first and then change," he replies quietly, not wanting to disturb the semi-calm that has fallen over Elizabeth.

"Whew, I am worn *out*," Mom exclaims, closing her eyes and allowing her head to lean back on the sofa.

"You ready to head home?" Dad asks, concerned. "We hope to see you two this weekend. Time for another barbecue."

"Yes, sir," Rick chuckles. "That sounds wonderful."

Once my family has left and it's just us, Rick tries once more to interact with Elizabeth. She won't allow him to do anything but read the book to her. Even when he changes into normal clothing, she still doesn't want anything to do with him.

After dinner and the evening activities are done, Rick helps me bathe her. She continues to look warily at him, only allowing him to hand her toys, but not allowing him to wash her or in any way touch her. Once I put her to bed, closing the door quietly behind me, I return to the living room to find Rick sitting on the edge of the sofa with slumped shoulders, staring at his hands.

There's anguish in his eyes.

I sit next to him. "What's wrong?"

In a rare moment, his eyes glisten. "My own daughter doesn't know me."

My heart hurts and a lump builds in my throat. I rub his buzzed head. "Don't worry, sweetie. She'll get to know you again. When you left, she was still a baby. Now she's a toddler. It won't take very long."

He nods and swallows. "I hope not."

"Come on, sweetie." I grip his hands, pulling him up from the sofa and walking him toward our bedroom. "I want to get to know you again, too."

****

Having Rick home is heaven, but we have challenges that I didn't expect. Rick is afforded two weeks off. In that time, he tries hard to reacquaint himself with Elizabeth. She is very slow to warm up to him, despite his efforts. It hurts. I keep reassuring him that she will come around. She has to.

When we spend the day at my parent's house for the barbecue that weekend, Elizabeth readily goes to everyone's arms and laps, but not Rick's. He tries to mask the pain behind a shrug or a smile, but his eyes are sad.

"How is it going, being home?" Dad asks, popping a chip into his mouth.

"It's wonderful. It was really hot over there. Nothing but sand as far as the eye can see," he replies, taking a swig of his root beer.

"Was it scary?" Debbie asks. Her childish crush has transformed into respect and admiration.

Rick casts a glance my way before responding. "Uh, yeah. There were some scary moments."

My heart squeezes. I am thankful he doesn't elaborate; I don't want to know.

"Did you get to take anybody down?" Jeff asks eagerly.

"Jeffrey..." Mom reprimands him, dropping the hot dog bun she's been picking apart. Her plate remains mostly untouched. Jeff shrugs and looks surprised at her reaction.

"No," Rick chuckles. "That wasn't my job. I work the flight line, not the front line." He deftly turns the conversation to other topics.

Midway through the afternoon, Mom rises and yawns. "It's lovely to see you two. I'm really sorry, but I need to go take a nap."

"Another nap, Mom? You take more naps than Elizabeth," I joke.

"It's just really warm and it wears me out," she replies, patting me on the shoulder as she passes. I watch her disappear into the house before turning to Dad. "Why is she so tired?"

"I don't know, Heather." Concern flashes quickly across his features before he replaces it with a smile. "I'm sure it's just the heat, like she said. She'll be fine."

****

July, 1991

Rick sits on the sofa eating a granola bar. Elizabeth toddles slowly over to him and puts her chubby hands on his knees, her gaze shifting between him and the granola bar.

He looks down and smiles. "Hey there, baby girl," he says softly, not wanting to startle her.

I watch the interaction warily, hoping against hope she'll warm up. He's been home almost two months and there hasn't been much progress in her acceptance of him. I never thought it would take this long.

Elizabeth's face puckers in thought for a moment. Suddenly, she lifts her arms up and says, "Up!"

I press my lips together to keep from gasping. Rick's grin explodes from ear to ear. He slowly, gently reaches down to pick her up and place her on his lap.

"Mine!" she points imperiously at the granola bar as soon as she's settled on his lap.

"You want my granola bar?" he asks, still grinning.

"Mine!" she repeats.

He pinches off a piece and she opens her mouth to receive it. When he places it in her mouth, she rests her head on his chest, munching happily.

He slowly wraps his arms around her and looks at me in amazement. She doesn't protest, but does demand more of the granola bar. My heart bursts in my chest. When the granola bar is all gone, she's content to stay in his lap. He kisses the top of her head and just holds her there.

"Oh, sweet baby girl. I've missed you," he says softly, the smile never leaving his face.

Slowly over the following weeks, Elizabeth warms up to Rick and finally utters the words we've waited to hear.

"Dadda! Read book!" she commands one evening following dinner. I've just cleaned her face and hands and placed her down from her high chair. I am clearing the dishes from the table.

"You want me to read you a book?" he asks excitedly, wiping his mouth with the napkin.

She nods firmly, grasps his hand and pulls him into the living room.

"Dadda read!" she proclaims.

Just before he disappears around the corner, he turns to give me a thumbs up and a big grin. Relived, I know our little family is going to be okay.

Rick's new schedule is easier on us; he's finally granted a day shift position with Mondays and Tuesdays off this time.

We will adjust. We will always adjust. I am realizing that is my job, at least for now. I'm all right with that.

Elizabeth warms more and more to Rick. She calls him Dadda all the time now, and asks for him when he's gone. I explain to her that daddy has to go to work. She puckers her face before proclaiming, "Dadda go to berk." When he comes home, she runs to greet him, smiling and laughing. He scoops her up in his arms and nuzzles her neck or swings her around; anything to make her laugh.

****

One warm morning later that month, I slather Elizabeth up with sunscreen, put on her bathing suit and pull out the kiddie pool, filling it with water from the hose. She instantly climbs in and starts splashing. Before long, Edward and Ronnie come flying out of their back door wearing swimming trunks and carrying bath toys in their hands.

"Come back here!" Angeline hangs out the door and yells at the boys. They reluctantly come to a stop just short of the pool and hang their heads.

"Don't worry – you can come back when your mom says so," I inform them as they slowly trudge back to their own house.

"Sorry!" Angeline yells in my direction.

"No problem! Come join us!" I yell back.

She nods, herds her boys back in the house, waving at me before disappearing. It isn't long before she reappears carrying three-month-old Leila and two bath towels. She is dressed in shorts and a tank top, her hair clipped on top of her head in a knot. The boys run toward the pool. When they get to the edge, they climb in carefully. They're energetic, but very conscientious around Elizabeth and the twins when all the kids play together.

I pull up two plastic chairs for us in the shade a small distance from the pool. We try to avoid the splash zone. Suddenly my house phone rings.

"Watch her?" I ask, gesturing toward Elizabeth.

"Of course," she replies, turning Leila around on her lap to watch her brothers splash.

I jog into the house and answer the phone before it goes to the answering machine.

"Hey, it's Nicole. I see you got the pool out. Mind if we join you?" she asks.

"The more the merrier." That pool is a magnet.

"Great! I'll be over there as soon as I get the girls' bathing suits on."

When she joins us, Hailey and Bailey are decked out in little sparkly bikinis – one pink and one yellow. Nicole takes up residence in the chair I pulled out for her.

She casts a glance at Angeline. "How are things at the Baker house?"

Angeline's cheeks pink and she stares at the top of Leila's head.

"Is everything all right, Angeline?" Nicole asks.

Angeline avoids our gaze. Her cheeks pink even more.

Frowning, I reach out and place my hand on her arm. "Angeline, what's wrong?"

She bites her lip for a moment before looking up. Her eyes are watery. "I'm pregnant," she whispers.

Nicole and I gasp in unison. I'm speechless. Do I congratulate her or not?

"Congratulations, Angeline," Nicole says quietly, beating me to the punch. "Maybe Leila will have a little sister." She attempts a smile.

Angeline hugs Leila's chubby little body close. Leila sucks on her tiny fist, oblivious.

"When did you find out?" I ask.

"Yesterday. I made a doctor's appointment because I'm just so tired lately. More than I was even a month ago. Plus I didn't start my period again." She pauses to sob, only allowing one heave of her shoulders before she gains control of herself. She casts a furtive glance at the children. "My God! What am I going to *do?*" she whispers, her face panicky.

"Were you guys planning this?" I ask stupidly.

She shakes her head, swiping at another tear. "No. It's just that Chris had been gone so long and…" She looks knowingly at us. "I hadn't started back on birth control yet because I was breast feeding. I thought because of that we'd be okay. I guess not."

"Wow," Nicole says.

"I'm throwing up, too. I hate it."

"Are you going to keep breast feeding while you're pregnant? I mean, *can* you?" I ask.

"The doctor said it should be fine, but I have to be sure to take in enough calories."

"Does Chris know yet?" Nicole asks.

"Yes. I told him as soon as the boys were in bed last night."

"What did he say?" I ask.

"He was shocked, just like me. But he said it'll be fine and we'll get through it." She snorts. "It's easy for him to say. He's not the one who has to carry this baby and go through labor again. I haven't gotten over *this* pregnancy yet!" She nods toward Leila.

"No, but he has to provide for all of you, and that's got a weight all its own," Nicole adds. "Will you guys have to move now?"

I hadn't thought about that. Is their house big enough?

Angeline shakes her head. "No, we have a four bedroom already."

"I'm glad! I don't want you to move. Well, at least you have experience having babies close together, Angeline. I mean, Edward and Ronnie were pretty close together, right?" I offer.

She snorts again. "Yeah, I guess. But it was still only two children – now I'll have *four*. Leila will barely be one when this one is born."

"I had two newborns at once," Nicole adds, grinning. "It is possible."

****

Life is full of unexpected surprises. Some pleasant, some not. Some are a combination of both, like Angeline's news.

Rick comes home from work one day, deeply troubled. When I ask him about it over dinner, instead of answering the question, he says he wants us to go for a bike ride. We haven't done that in quite awhile.

"That sounds like fun, doesn't it?" I smile at Elizabeth who grins and claps her hands.

We strap Elizabeth into her seat, click her helmet in place, and don our helmets, too.

"Where to?" I ask him.

"Let's go to the park," he replies, foot on his pedal at the ready.

"Lead the way!"

I follow Rick to the park on base. When we arrive, he comes to a stop at a picnic table and dismounts his bike, resting it on the kick stand.

"Want to go play, baby girl?" Rick addresses Elizabeth while unbuckling her.

I wait patiently for Rick to bring up whatever is bothering him while we stroll over to the swings. Once she is in the baby swing, I can't take it anymore.

"Rick, what's wrong?"

Rick pushes Elizabeth once more before answering me.

"Do you remember my friend, Neil?" he asks. I nod. I remember meeting Neil a few times. He and Rick got along pretty well. We even had Neil and his wife over for dinner once. Nice couple. "We deployed together. We worked together while we were deployed. He's a good man."

"I remember him and his wife. They were nice."

"Well, they're getting a divorce."

I gasp. "What? What happened? They seemed like such nice people!" I exclaim, shocked.

He shifts his feet, uncomfortable. "She's pregnant."

I blink. "Okay. Why is that a bad thing?"

He looks at me. "He was gone for nine months, Heather. She's only four months along." He waits while I put the pieces together.

Oh. My jaw drops. "That's awful! Does he know…*who*…?"

He shakes his head, rubbing his face. "No. She won't say. But they're getting a divorce."

I don't know what to say. I can't believe something like that would happen.

"Heather, I hope you know it would kill me if….anything like that ever happened to us," he says quietly.

My head jerks. "Rick, I would *never* in a million years do something like that." I hold his face in both of my hands. "I am yours and yours alone, just as you are mine."

CHAPTER EIGHTEEN

November, 1991

Life continues. We've put the deployments out of our minds, sure they're firmly in the past. The yellow ribbons have begun to come down and gradually disappear. Angeline's stomach grows once more even as she carries Leila on her hip. She tries to rest as often as she can; Edward entered Kindergarten and Ronnie started preschool in the fall. For a few hours during the afternoon, Angeline has only one child at home and rests when Leila takes her nap. Chris is still on the crazy twelve hour shift schedule and his days off vary from week to week, but he helps out as much as he can. Much to her dismay, Angeline's once proud garden has been stripped down to the bare minimum.

"I never even got out of maternity clothes!" she laments one afternoon after dropping Ronnie off for preschool. She places Leila down on the play mat and scowls down at her burgeoning form. "I feel like I'm even bigger this time around, if that's possible. I may never get my figure back."

"Don't worry. Chris loves you no matter what," I reassure her.

"Tell me about it. That sick man tells me he finds me sexy." She gestures at her body. "How the hell can anybody find this sexy? I'll tell you one thing – I will start birth control before I leave the hospital this time!"

We laugh, discuss our Thanksgiving plans (or lack of), and watch the girls play. Well, they're in the same room anyway. Eight-month-old Leila rolls over and scoots herself around on her belly. Elizabeth is busy playing in her little kitchen. She's cooking up some rubber eggs for her teddy bear.

Eventually, Angeline and Leila both begin to yawn.

"It's time for our nap, little girl," Angeline says, bending down with a grunt to retrieve Leila's chubby body. Leila grins, exposing the few teeth she has and kicks excitedly.

Angeline blows out her breath as she stands and adjusts Leila on her hip. Watching her waddle across the yard somewhat awkwardly, I feel badly. This is a tough situation. In my heart, I know she'll be fine.

A thought occurs to me, and I call my mother. She answers after the fourth ring, sounding tired.

"Hello?" she answers.

"Mom? Are you all right?"

She clears her throat, and her voice finds its strength. "I'm fine, honey. What's up?"

"I just had a thought. You know Angeline is pregnant, and they're having a hard time and all. Well, how would you feel if I invited them over for Thanksgiving dinner? I was just talking to Angeline, and she hasn't got anything planned yet. I promise I'll come and help do most of the cooking. All you have to do is tell me what to do. What do you think?"

There's a brief pause before Mom answers enthusiastically. "That would be awfully sweet of you, Heather. Please do invite them over. We would love to have them!"

"Thanks, Mom. She thinks the world of you guys."

"Well, we think the world of her, too. Let me know what she says."

At first, Angeline is reluctant. "I don't want to intrude on your family for Thanksgiving, Heather," she protests.

"It's not an intrusion, Angeline. It's an invitation."

She caves a lot faster than I thought she would – she must really need a break, especially from preparing a Thanksgiving meal. Once the invitation is accepted, I call my mother and let her know. I will come over on Tuesday before Thanksgiving to begin preparations. Mom always makes everything from scratch, and it takes three days. I am thrilled to help.

The little cookbook my mother gave me has gotten a lot of use. Most of the index cards are spotted with various ingredients that have either been splashed or sputtered out of pans in my efforts to follow the directions. I plan to pay meticulous attention during Thanksgiving and write down the recipes so I don't forget.

****

I arrive at my parent's house on Tuesday and find my mother ready to go.

She ties an apron around her trim waist. "I'll tell you something, I do not enjoy grocery shopping on a weekend, much less the weekend before Thanksgiving."

"Were you able to get everything?"

She nods, handing me an apron. "Yes, thankfully. At least the store was well stocked."

I pull out a pad of paper and pen and place it on the counter before tying on my own apron. Mom's eyebrows shoot up.

"I want to write all of this down so I remember."

She grins and starts pulling out ingredients to make pie crusts. There are pumpkin, apple, cherry, and chocolate pies to make – that's a lot of pie crusts. I meticulously write down every detail and instruction my mother gives me.

"Don't forget the water must be ice cold," she warns me, dripping water slowly into the flour and butter mixture. "Otherwise you won't have a flaky crust because you'll melt the butter. You've got to get a good feel for it, but don't mess with it too much."

The pies take almost five hours to make – we take breaks for lunch and to care for Elizabeth, who is happy playing with a ball of pie crust dough at the kitchen table when she's not watching Barney on television. She loves coming to Grandma's house.

When the pies are all assembled, Mom plops down with a groan in a chair next to Elizabeth, unsuccessfully trying to stifle a yawn.

"Nap time again?"

Mom smiles wearily and nods. "Of course. I'm sure little Elizabeth here could use one, too." She reaches over to lovingly smooth Elizabeth's hair.

"Same time tomorrow?" I ask.

"Absolutely! We'll both be able to enjoy Thanksgiving with all the work done. Thank you, sweetie. Your help has been greatly appreciated." She rises slowly and gives me a fierce hug. "I love you."

"Love you, too, Mom," I hug her back just as fiercely.

A few minutes after being on the road, I flick a glance at Elizabeth in the rear view mirror and smile. She is fast asleep, head lolled back and mouth wide open. I really enjoy spending this time with my mother as an adult. Our relationship is maturing, growing into more of a deep friendship than parent-child relationship. My heart swells thinking about how much my mother means to me. I could not be where I am without her or the rest of my family. I hope that Elizabeth and I will have the same thing when she grows up. I have a great example to follow.

****

"Ready to go?" Rick asks me on Thanksgiving morning. He is dressed in a crisp white shirt and nice slacks.

"Almost," I reply, concentrating on buttoning up Elizabeth's new dress that Rick's parents sent. We had family pictures taken this past week with her in her new dress, and will be sure to send them copies when they arrive. She's fidgety this morning, probably sensing today is an important day. At two, it's the first Thanksgiving she remembers. Once the last button is secure, I tie her red sash into a big bow in the back. "There! All done!" I turn her around to face me and hold my hands up, smiling.

"All done!" she mimics, raising her hands and grinning, too.

"Don't you look pretty, baby girl!" Rick exclaims, scooping her up into his arms and kissing her cheeks.

"Petty! Petty!" she giggles.

"I'll call and see if Angeline is ready." She picks up after the third ring.

"Hurry up!" she yells away from the phone before answering me. "Hello?"

"Hey, it's me. You guys about ready?" I ask.

"Almost," she sighs. "If I can get the boys to focus enough to get their shoes on, we'll be over in about five minutes."

"Don't feel like you're in a rush. We aren't going to eat for at least another hour."

"Okay, good. I'll see you in a few," she replies.

Just before we hang up, I hear her yelling once more. I shake my head, smiling.

"What?" Rick asks.

"She has her hands full," I chuckle.

"It's too bad Stan and Nicole couldn't join us," Rick says.

"Oh, they're having a wonderful time. They flew to California to be with his family. They don't get to see the twins very often."

"That's true. But still…" his voice trails off.

"I'm sorry we can't see your parents this year. Did you enjoy talking to them this morning?" I ask.

He brightens. "Yes. They're doing well. They're on their way to hike the Andes this month. It's summer down there, you know."

When Angeline knocks on the door almost ten minutes later, she looks beautiful but breathless. She's wearing a gorgeous burgundy sweater with silver thread woven into the fabric and her hair is curled and pulled into a hasty up-do. Her cheeks are pink with exertion.

"Chris has the kids all strapped in and ready to go. We will just follow you," she says hurriedly, already backing away as she talks.

"Sounds good," I reply. She nods and turns toward her waiting family, moving as quickly as she can in her condition.

When we arrive at my parents, there is a flurry of activity as Angeline's boys and Elizabeth spill into the living room. Jeff takes over for the boys, ushering them into his room, informing them he has his old toys ready to go. Although now a high school graduate, he has decided not to go straight to college. He's working full time instead while he weighs his options.

Elizabeth makes herself at home, naturally. Leila is placed on the floor where she eyes Elizabeth, sizing up her reaction to this unfamiliar environment. When Chris comes through the door carrying Leila's diaper bag and another small bag, Angeline immediately pulls out some of Leila's favorite toys from the smaller bag and places them in a semi-circle around her. Once she's busily playing, Angeline turns her attention to Mom and Dad.

"Thank you guys so much for having us over. We are really looking forward to this," she gushes, hugging my parents in turn.

"The pleasure is ours. You're always welcome in our home," Dad replies and Mom smiles, echoing his comments.

"It smells like heaven in here!" Chris exclaims, inhaling deeply.

Mom grins proudly. "It should. We cooked for days."

"When do we eat?" Rick asks, rubbing his hands together. He skipped breakfast and lunch for this.

I elbow him in the ribs. "Sweetie, don't be rude."

"Nonsense," Mom says. "I have some finger foods laid out that should hold you over, but don't fill up. We will eat around one thirty."

We drift into the dining room where Mom has her appetizers laid out on the side table along with some plates and napkins. We each fill a small plate, and head back into the living room. Angeline starts to position herself to watch Leila, but Chris interrupts her.

"You just go sit down and put your feet up, hon," he says. "I'll watch Leila." He proceeds to sit on the floor next to Leila, intermittently playing with her while shoving stuffed mushrooms in his mouth.

Angeline smiles gratefully and takes a seat in the recliner in the corner, literally putting her feet up. "That feels good," she sighs, smiling.

When Rick and I sit down together, Debbie settles onto the love seat across from us. Every time I see her, she's maturing more and more. There are very few traces of little girl left. At thirteen, she is transforming into a beautiful young lady.

"You look beautiful, Debbie," I remark, smiling at her. "I love that color blue on you – it sets off your eyes."

She grins and blushes. "Thanks."

"Don't you think she's becoming a lovely young woman, Rick?" I ask, squeezing his hand.

"Yes, she is. Just like her big sister. But you'll always be a little squirt to me!"

She chuckles before dropping onto the floor to play with Elizabeth. She has taken to her auntie duties whole heartedly – she adores her niece. Elizabeth calls her "Eddie", but Debbie doesn't mind.

The conversation flows well. Jeff and the boys emerge from his room within a few minutes asking about food. Mom smiles and tells Jeff to watch the boys to make sure they save room for dinner. For a nineteen-year-old young man, Jeff is incredibly patient and attentive to Edward and Ronnie.

"Are you kidding? They're great kids!" Jeff exclaims when Angeline remarks about it.

When Jeff and the boys disappear once again down the hallway with their plates, I quietly remark, "I think it gives Jeff an excuse to play with his those toys again."

"I think you're right," Mom answers. "He keeps them for a reason, you know. Heather, would you help me in the kitchen? It's almost time to eat."

I rise immediately to follow her. Angeline slowly grunts herself from a reclining to a sitting position to follow before Mom stops her.

"No, honey," Mom says. "You just stay and rest. We'll take care of it."

"I can help," Angeline protests.

"Absolutely not. Just for this one day, rest and relax."

"Yeah, honey. Just take it easy," Chris adds.

Angeline considers mounting another protest, but decides against it. She sighs and reclines the chair back, cradling her stomach with her hands. "Thank you." There is unmistakable gratitude in her voice.

When Mom and I disappear into the kitchen for the final preparations, Mom whispers to me. "She looks totally exhausted. Is she all right?"

"You should talk, Mom," I chide her, noting the shadows under her own eyes. "She'll be fine, eventually."

Ignoring my comment, Mom continues. "I don't know. She looks wiped out."

"I'm sure she does. She's got her hands full."

"Chris seems like a fine young man. He helps her?" she asks.

"Yes," I nod. "He helps as much as he can."

"Good. Parents have to be a team to make it work. Now, let's get the gravy going."

We finish preparations and call everyone to the table a few minutes after one thirty; my mother is precise with her timing. She had to be – she married Dad.

The dining room table has been extended to its full length and a card table is butted up against the far end to accommodate everyone. Mom pulled out her best linen, which she does for every Thanksgiving and Christmas, as well as her finest china. Angeline is nervous about it because of her boys, but Mom reassures her that they'll be just fine. Still, Angeline and Chris position themselves next to Edward and Ronnie and watch them like a hawk. I, of course, give Elizabeth a plastic plate and utensils to use in her high chair. Leila is content to sit in her car seat, which is nestled onto a dining room chair, and be fed some bits from her mother's plate.

When Dad says grace, he says a heart felt prayer of thanks for every person at the table and asks God's blessings on "these beautiful families here today, together again and safe." I hear Angeline sniff quietly and steel a glance at her. Her chin is trembling and her cheeks are pink. She sits next to me, so I reach over and squeeze her hand under the table. She squeezes my hand back. I close my eyes once again.

When Dad says "amen," we all open our eyes. Angeline quickly dabs at her eyes with her napkin and stuffs it back on her lap. If anyone besides me noticed, nobody mentions it.

"All right," Dad announces, clapping his hands eagerly together. "Everyone help yourselves. Go ahead and take what you would like from whatever is in front of you, and then pass that bowl or plate to your right."

From the lack of conversation for the first ten minutes or so, everyone is just as hungry as I am. Even Ronnie and Edward are quiet, eating with solemnity and gusto.

Chris is the first to break the silence. "This is beyond amazing," he says, preparing another forkful of turkey, cranberry relish, mashed potatoes, and gravy. Echoes of agreement ripple around the table.

"It was a lot of effort and hard work by two fine ladies," Dad responds proudly. He turns to Mom, leaning in to kiss her cheek. "As always, you've made me proud, Louise. Thank you."

She accepts the kiss, smiling. "I couldn't have done it without you, Heather." She raises her glass of iced tea in my direction.

"Hear, hear!" Jeff says, raising his glass while his mouth is still full.

All the glasses rise around the table in a communal toast, clinks filling the air. Mom and I smile at each other.

This is what Thanksgiving is all about – family, friends, gratitude, and love. My heart fills along with my stomach.

It's a perfect day.

After the meal, when we've all – with the exception of Mom, who still picks at her food – stuffed ourselves like the turkey we just consumed, everyone lumbers slowly out of their chairs and into the living room or, in Jeff's case, back to his room. Apparently, the boys have engaged the toys in an epic battle and they're anxious to see how it ends. Angeline takes up residence in the recliner once again with a satisfied smile.

"Would anyone like some coffee or hot apple cider?" Dad asks.

"I would love some cider, thank you," I reply.

"Hot apple cider?" Chris perks up. "I haven't had that since I was a kid. I'll take one."

"Honey?" Dad asks Mom, who has just tucked her feet under her on the corner of the sofa, a look of contentment crossing her features.

"Yes, please," she replies.

"Me, too," Rick quips, falling back onto the sofa with a grunt. He pats his stomach. "I think I can fit at least that much in here still, but just barely."

Dad disappears into the kitchen. When he reappears about fifteen minutes later, he is carrying a tray with steaming mugs. He passes them out to each of us in turn. Each mug has a long cinnamon stick in it – the way it's always served at our house.

A strange sound comes from where Angeline is sitting. When I look over, she has gone slack-jawed and is snoring.

I chuckle. "Is she asleep?"

Chris glances at his wife and nods. "Yeah. Is that okay?" He glances at my parents.

"Of course it is. Don't you dare wake her up." Mom smiles and yawns. "As a matter of fact, I think I'll take a nap, too, when I finish my cider."

She only makes it halfway through her mug before retreating to her bedroom for a nap.

"All right, men," Dad says. "Let's get the table cleared and dishes done. The ladies have done their part and it's time to do ours. Gotta earn your keep!"

I rest my head on the sofa with a satisfied sigh, listening to the sound of male conversation, running water, and dishes clanking together. Leila takes a nap in her car seat next to her mother, and Elizabeth joins the boys in Jeff's room to play. Debbie flips through the channels. Contentment resides.

Once done with the clean-up, the men return to the living room. Rick sits next to me, while Chris sits on the floor next to Angeline.

"There's plenty of room to sit, son," Dad tells him.

Chris waves him off. "I like sitting on the floor, actually."

"Mind if I turn the game on?" Dad asks.

Chris and Rick both perk up immediately. "Please do," Chris replies.

"I thought you'd never ask," Rick grins.

Before long, all three men are completely enthralled in the football game. I am content to just sit and sip my room temperature cider.

"Heather," Debbie whispers to me. When I look at her, she grins and motions for me to come with her. "I want to show you something."

I kiss Rick on the cheek and rise to follow Debbie into her room. She quickly closes the door behind her and turns, excitement bubbling out of her.

"What is it?" Her excitement is infectious.

Rather than answer, she pulls a folded piece of paper out of her jewelry box and hands it to me.

"Read it!" she exclaims.

I unfold the paper and read the short note. It's from a young man named Van and he is asking Debbie to the winter dance.

"What did you say?"

"I said *yes*, of course!" she replies, clapping her hands.

"I guess you like this Van guy?"

"He's the cutest guy *ever*!"

"I'm happy for you! That will be so much fun. Have Mom and Dad met him yet?"

She rolls her eyes. "Not really. But they will. I know Dad's rules."

Dad always insisted that any young man must come to the door and meet him first before we are allowed to go anywhere.

"Are you sure Dad is okay with this? You're only fourteen."

"His parents will have to drive us anyway. Hey! I want you to come dress shopping with me and Mom. I need you to help me pick out something really nice."

"I would love to." I look her up and down. "You really are blossoming, aren't you?"

She blushes.

Debbie and I talk about all sorts of things until there's a light knock on the door. I open it to find Rick standing there.

"Want some pie?" he asks, holding up his plate that has the remains of all four pies on it. "My and Elizabeth's favorite is the chocolate." He grins and licks his fork.

"Sounds good. Is there any left?" I ask, laughing while he shovels another bite into his mouth.

"Mmm hmmm," Rick replies, wandering back down the hallway.

Although there are empty tins on the table, there is still plenty of pie left. I settle for slivers of each because I can't decide on just one. Debbie takes pumpkin and cherry for herself.

Dad, Chris, and Rick are riveted to the television while eating their pie. Angeline has awoken and looks a bit groggy. "Did I fall asleep?" she asks hoarsely, clearing her throat.

"Yes," I reply. "Help yourself to some pie. There's chocolate, cherry, pumpkin, and apple."

"Plus whipped cream," Debbie adds, licking her fork.

"Sounds delicious," Angeline says, pushing the foot rest down into the chair and stretching. "How long was I out?"

"About an hour and a half."

Her eyes widen. "What?" She scowls at Chris. "Chris, why did you let me sleep so long?"

He glances at her briefly. "You needed it."

"Don't be too hard on him," Dad remarks. "Taking a nap is a good thing."

Angeline rubs her eyes and yawns.

"Pie is in the kitchen. Get it while the gettin' is good!" Dad grins and holds up his almost empty plate. All three men whoop at a successful play on the screen.

Angeline grunts to a standing position and shuffles into the kitchen.

"Is Mom still asleep?" I ask.

Dad nods, finishing his last piece of pie.

"Want me to go wake her up?" Debbie asks.

"No," Dad replies. "Just let her sleep. She's worked hard these last couple of days. I'll save her some pie." He rises and disappears into the kitchen. I rise and join him, passing Angeline on her way back into the living room.

"Dad," I whisper, sidling up to him as he folds plastic wrap around a plate of pie pieces. "What's wrong with Mom? Why is she so tired all the time?"

"Hm? Oh, that. I think she's anemic or something. She has a doctor's appointment this week and we'll get it taken care of. Maybe add some iron to her diet." He licks his fingers. "Don't worry, Heather. She'll be all right." He pats me on the back and places the plate in the refrigerator.

"I hope so," I murmur.

"Don't worry. Everything is fine."

Just as I turn to leave, Mom appears in the doorway. "What in heaven's name are you two up to?" she asks, hands on her hips.

"Just had some pie. Would you like some?" I ask, smiling.

"Well, somebody made a fine kitchen out of this mess." She looks around at the clean counters.

"The boys and I took care of it. Did you enjoy your nap?" Dad asks.

"Very much." She leans in and they kiss quickly, but affectionately. "I am refreshed. Where's my pie?"

Jeff, Ronnie, and Edward complete their battle scene and enjoy pie at the table, talking about the most epic of battles *ever*.

Eventually, everyone has eaten more than their fill (and some is packed up – Mom insisted we all take leftovers home), and the game is over. We all prepare to go home long after the sun has dipped below the horizon.

Amid all the thank you's and goodbye's, genuine love is exchanged. When Angeline hugs my mother, the familiar pink creeps into her cheeks and their hug lasts a long time. There's a verbal exchange I can't hear. Mom has a way about her that draws people in.

When we arrive home, Angeline and her husband pull into their carport as we pull into ours. I climb out of the truck and release the buckle on Elizabeth's car seat to extract her sleeping form.

"Hey!" Angeline waves and walks toward me.

"I'll get her," Rick reaches in, pulls Elizabeth out and situates her head against his shoulder. He kisses my cheek quickly. "I'll see you inside."

"Hey, yourself." I grin as Angeline finally reaches me. She's out of breath and cradling her swollen midsection.

"I just wanted to let you know how much I enjoyed today. You have a lovely family, and I'm so glad you're my friend." She impulsively reaches in and gives me a tight hug, sobbing on my shoulder. "I'm sorry," she gulps and pulls away, wiping at her eyes. "I'm a wreck."

"Hormones?" I ask, patting her arm.

"Yeah. I mean, this is all overwhelming. The tears are always right there, you know?"

"Would you like to come in and talk? I can send Rick over to your house."

She shakes her head. "No. No, I'm fine. Really. It's my hormones. I just wanted to thank you for today." She smiles, in control of herself once again. "I'll see you soon!" She waves and turns toward her own home.

I watch her go for a moment, wondering if she really is all right. Perhaps the pregnancy hormones are really bad. She did get pregnant right after having Leila – her body never got the chance to normalize after one pregnancy before dealing with the next.

When I enter my front door, Rick is just emerging from the hallway. "I changed Elizabeth and put her to bed. She's exhausted."

"It was a wonderful Thanksgiving. I have a lot to be thankful for." I press myself against him, wrapping my arms around his waist. "You're home and you're safe."

"There's no other place I would rather be, honey bun." He kisses me fervently and looks me in the eyes. "Want to watch a movie?"

I blink and grin. "I would love that." We watch *It's a Wonderful Life* snuggled together on the couch. It's the perfect end to the most perfect day.

****

December, 1991

While loading lunch dishes into the dishwasher one day, the phone rings. Elizabeth is happily "reading" her picture book to her dolly who is propped up on the chair next to her at the table.

I quickly dry my hands and answer, "Hello?"

"Heather, it's Dad."

"Oh hi, Dad! What's up?"

There's a pause and Dad sighs. "Heather, sit down."

I freeze. "Uh, what? Why? What's going on?"

"Honey, just sit down. Everything…everything is going to be all right."

I remain rooted in place, unable to move. My heart starts to race.

"Heather? Are you sitting?" Dad asks when I don't respond.

"Uh," I look frantically around and finally drop into a dining room chair. Elizabeth looks at me, surprised, before returning to her book. "Yes."

Dad sighs again before continuing. "Well, your mother had her doctor's appointment last week, as you know. And, well…"

"What?" I ask, flicking a glance at Elizabeth. She is engrossed in her story-telling.

"There's no way to not say this, so…" He draws a deep breath. "Your mother has cancer."

CHAPTER NINETEEN

December, 1991

The air is sucked out of the room and into my lungs. My mother has cancer.

Cancer kills people. Cancer can kill my mother.

I jerk out of the chair and walk randomly around the kitchen before hurriedly leaving, the dishes forgotten. I walk to the front door, turn around in a circle and walk down the hall to our bedroom, dropping onto the bed.

"What? She has what?" I ask. Maybe, just maybe, I misheard him.

"Your mother has cancer. It's leukemia," Dad states again, drawing a ragged breath.

"How? When? *What?*" I can't form a cohesive thought.

"It's all right, Heather. We'll get through this, and your mother will be fine. She will," he replies firmly.

My hand reaches up and covers my mouth, struggling to stifle a sob.

Cancer kills people. It could kill my mother.

"No!" I yell. "She can't...she can't..." I gasp and start to sob.

"Heather, honey. Calm down. It's going to be all right. It will!" Dad tries to reassure me.

Suddenly my mother's voice fills my ear. "Heather, honey. I'm all right. We'll get through this. I'm all right."

"Mom," I choke out.

"It's all right. I will start treatment next week, and we'll get this taken care of before you know it." She sounds surprisingly calm and sure.

I take a few deep breaths. "Are you sure? Are you sure that's what's wrong? Dad said you were probably just low in iron or something."

"Yes, they're sure. Denying it won't change it. The doctor said my prognosis is good with treatment, so we'll get started quickly. No time to waste!"

"Oh, mom," I start to cry again.

Mom shares some of the medical stuff with me during the conversation, but I don't hear it. All I hear is my mother has cancer, and she's going to start chemotherapy next week.

"...that means I'll probably be in the hospital for Christmas, unfortunately." I catch the last part of her sentence. "This chemo is nasty business, but the leukemia is even nastier."

"But, but..."

She'll be in the hospital this Christmas. Will she even be here for Christmas next year? The room goes blurry.

After I hang up, I sit on the bed, stunned into immobility. My mother is a strong, vital human being. How can cancer invade someone like that? How *dare* it invade her?

She's my *mother*.

Elizabeth's curious face peers around the corner. "Mommy, why you cry?" She approaches me, clutching her dolly.

I press my lips together and take a deep breath. I can't explain this to a two-year-old. I can't even explain it to myself.

"I'm just a little sad right now. I'm all right, sweetie." I reach down and scoop her up in my arms, burying my nose in her hair and inhaling her sweetness.

She presses her dolly against my opposite shoulder. "Dolly make you better," she says matter-of-factly.

I wish it was that simple.

When I tell Rick the news that night after Elizabeth is in bed, he is speechless.

He holds me tightly while I cry all over again.

"Well," he clears his throat. "It's a good thing they'll start treatment right away." He clears his throat again. "She'll be fine, honey bun. She's a strong lady."

I nod, unable to answer. He holds me for a very, very long time.

****

January, 1992

Christmas was almost over the top in a desperate way. None of us talk about the cancer or what next Christmas may be like. If we celebrate enthusiastically this year, maybe, just maybe it will spill over into next year.

It has to.

When I shared the news with Angeline, she burst into tears. She still cries every time I see her. Her emotions have wreaked havoc on her – she is unable to control them most of the time, especially when it comes to my mother. They have developed a special kinship. Angeline is like another sister, and I am grateful.

Children are not allowed to visit my mother while she's in the hospital because of the risk of infection – Mom's immune system is weakened from the chemotherapy, and we can't risk her fighting an infection along with the cancer.

We finally told Elizabeth in the simplest terms what was wrong with Grandma – she has a bad bug in her body, and the doctors are giving her really strong medicine to kill those bad bugs. The medicine is so strong that it can make her feel a little sick, so she has to stay in the hospital while she gets it. Elizabeth accepted it, drawing pictures for her showing Elizabeth taking care of Grandma in bed.

We dutifully deliver Elizabeth's pictures to Mom when we visit the hospital several times a week.

I help my family out as much as I can. Debbie and Jeff are both as shell-shocked as I am. Mom is unable to go dress shopping with Debbie for the winter dance. Debbie wants to skip it all together, but Mom insists she go.

"There's no sense in putting life on hold," Mom says.

Debbie and I pick out a beautiful satin maroon dress. Debbie and Van make a special trip to the hospital before the dance so our mother could see her all dressed up. The nurses take pictures and everything.

****

March, 1992

"I feel like I'm literally going to burst," Angeline breathlessly laments. She is sprawled out in a plastic lawn chair next to my mother and me while our children play hide and seek in Angeline's back yard. "I am so sick of being pregnant!" She groans as she once again shifts position, trying to get comfortable.

Her due date is tomorrow. There's no sign of labor, however. She looks like an engorged tic in her A-frame maternity shirt and black shorts. She is so much more swollen than she was with Leila.

"Well, at least it's almost over, dear," Mom replies encouragingly. She is wearing a surgical mask and artfully arranged, riotously-colored scarf on her head. Her hair was coming out in chunks from the chemo, so she decided to shave it off and save herself from looking like "an alley cat with the mange," according to her. She has met this beast that is cancer head on. I admire her strength, although she remains physically exhausted most of the time. Today is a good day and she wants to take full advantage of it.

"I hope so," Angeline says breathlessly. "I can't stand this anymore. I just want her *out*." They were happy to find out they're having another girl.

"Did the doctor say your blood pressure is still up?" I ask.

She nods and winces, sitting up straighter and rubbing her stomach. "Yes. But I don't have pre-eclampsia. My urine is still clean. Leila! Leila, come back closer to me. Come! Ronnie! Edward! Come closer so your sister doesn't follow you!" Leila grins and slowly, awkwardly toddles toward her mother. She just started walking a few weeks ago. Leila drops onto her bottom when she gets about three feet away, clapping and giggling.

"She's such a happy child," Mom remarks, clapping with Leila.

"I am so glad she's an easy going baby. If she were anything else, they'd have to lock me up, because I would have gone crazy," Angeline says, shifting position.

"Will they induce you if you go past your due date?" I ask.

"I begged the doctor to do something when I went two days ago. He said he would rather let nature take its course." She winces and rubs another spot on her stomach.

"Labor pains?" I ask jokingly.

Angeline snorts. "I wish. No, she is just really active and there's no room."

"Did the doctor estimate how big she's going to be?" I ask.

Angeline nods, wincing again. "He thinks she'll be at least as big as Leila. God, I hope not, but…" She gestures to her immense belly. "I think he may be right."

"I'm so glad your mother is able to make the trip out here this time. What a help she'll be," Mom adds.

"You'll still be able to pick her up tomorrow, right?" Angeline asks me.

I nod. "Yep. I'll pick her up at six o'clock sharp."

Angeline's family doesn't have much money, so her mother saved up to take a Greyhound bus. She plans to stay for three weeks. My mother is unable to do anything this time because of the chemo, and Nicole and I can only pick up the slack so much.

Nicole is now pregnant, as well. She's early in her first trimester and her morning sickness has been awful. She is supposed to be out here with us, but she can't stay away from the bathroom.

As if on cue, Nicole emerges from her house and hurries over.

"Is everything all right?" I ask, noting the dark circles under her eyes and overall paleness as she approaches with an odd expression.

Angeline and Mom both turn in her direction expectantly.

"Stan just called and we got orders to Germany!" she exclaims.

I sit up straight. "What? When?"

"Just now. We are supposed to be there in three months!" She puts her hands on her hips and shrugs. "I don't see how we can do that. I'll still be pregnant."

"Yeah, but," Angeline interjects, shifting with a groan. "You can fly until you're almost eight months along, Nicole."

"Oh no," Nicole takes a deep breath.

"I'm so sorry," I say.

She shakes her head. "Me, too. I mean, I want to go, but just not yet. This is crazy! There's so much to do…"

"Here," I say, rising and pulling another chair out for her. "Sit down."

She shakes her head quickly. "I can't. The girls are inside."

"Bring them out. Are you feeling better?"

She wrinkles her nose. "Not really. I have thrown up three times."

"You've got me beat. The last time I cleaned myself out was yesterday," Mom quips. Humor is one of her weapons.

"Please! You can throw up in my grass, if you want. It will just wash away," Angeline says, waving her hand at her lawn.

I stare at her, flabbergasted. "That sounds gross."

"Thanks, but no thanks," Nicole replies, smiling awkwardly. I think the idea appeals to her about as much as it does to me. "I'll talk to you guys later." She waves and quickly crosses the street.

I lean toward Angeline and speak quietly. "You would really let her throw up on your *lawn?*"

She looks at me, bewildered. "Why not? It's just puke."

****

Rick and I pick up Angeline's mother at the bus station downtown. Although I have never met her, the resemblance is unmistakable – Angeline's mother looks like an older version of her. The poster board sign with her name on it was a waste of time.

"You must be Nancy!" I exclaim as older Angeline ambles over to us, grinning widely.

"Yes, I am! You must be Heather. It's nice to meet you," she replies with a slight Hispanic accent.

"Let me help you with your bags." Rick immediately reaches over and picks up her two enormous suitcases. "We aren't parked very far away."

Once we get Nancy, her bags, Elizabeth, and Elizabeth's stroller packed in the truck, we begin our trek back to the base. Angeline called ahead to have her mother's name placed on the list for the visitor's center at the main gate, so getting her visitor's pass was a piece of cake.

"Oh, these are very nice houses," Nancy breathes, pressing her face against the window of the truck as we meander our way through the housing area.

Perplexed, I look over at Rick who maintains a beatific smile on his face. I have never considered these houses as "very nice," but I suppose it all depends on your frame of reference.

"Such pretty lawns," Nancy continues to gush. "There are some really beautiful bushes and plants, I see."

I turn in my seat. "Angeline has always had a beautiful lawn. She hasn't been able to keep it up this time the way that she normally does. You know, with her pregnancy and all," I comment.

Nancy nods. "I am not surprised. We have a lot of green thumbs in our family. She comes by that talent naturally." She turns her gaze from the window to me and her brow furrows. "How is she doing, really?"

"You mean with her pregnancy?" I ask. Nancy nods. "Oh, she's very uncomfortable and tired. She didn't really have time to recover from her pregnancy with Leila before she got pregnant again, so it's been difficult."

Nancy's face puckers. "I really wish I could have been here for her. But we barely make ends meet, so…" She shrugs and leaves her sentence unfinished.

"I understand," I reply, reaching back and squeezing her hand reassuringly. "It's expensive. I know she's glad you're here now."

"You and your family have been so very good to my daughter. Thank you so much."

"It's our pleasure."

"We're here!" Rick announces. He pulls into Angeline's driveway to drop her mother off. "I'll get your bags, Mrs. Endozo. Go on inside."

I unbuckle Elizabeth and let her follow me inside with Nancy. Angeline's swollen body slowly rises from the couch with many groans. Mother and daughter embrace for a long time. They're still hugging and talking when Rick appears in the doorway with the luggage.

"Where do you want me to put these?" he asks.

Angeline and her mother separate, wiping their cheeks. Nancy's hands are on Angeline's stomach and she's speaking Spanish quietly to the bulge.

"Just put them in Ronnie's room, please. She'll be staying in there," Angeline replies. Rick ducks down the hallway. She addresses her mother. "We moved Ronnie into Edward's room while you're here."

"Oh, that's nice. Thank you, but I would've been content to sleep on the couch. I'm just so glad to be here," she gushes, grabbing Angeline in another hug.

"We'll leave you two alone. Enjoy your visit!" I wave and head toward the door. Rick is waiting at the threshold.

"Oh, you don't have to go!" Nancy exclaims, releasing Angeline. "Stay for a visit."

"Thank you, but we need to get going. It's close to Elizabeth's bed time." I look to Rick.

"Yes, we need to go and let you guys visit. Have a good night," Rick nods to the ladies, and we depart before they can protest. "You go on inside. I'll pull the truck up."

"All right," I reply. "Come on, Elizabeth. Give me your hand." Elizabeth obediently gives me her hand, and we cross the lawn to our own door. When I get in, I notice the answering machine is blinking with a message. I push the play button and Nicole's voice sounds. She sounds a little panicky, so I turn the volume up to hear it better.

"…know what to do! I mean, Stan has to be there in two months, but we aren't going to be there for another month after that. How am I supposed to do…?" The machine cuts her off.

Rick walks in the door and sees my expression. "What's wrong?"

"Nicole left me a frantic message." I pick up the phone and call her.

She answers on the first ring. "Hello?"

"Hey, Nicole. It's me. What's going on? I only got part of your message."

She starts rambling. Apparently, Stan has to be in Germany in one month, before she and the girls will arrive. It has to do with his job. Nicole will be left to get everything arranged for the movers to pack up their household goods, plus she will have to make travel plans for her and the girls.

"I will have to fly half way around the world *alone* with two toddlers while I'm pregnant!" she wails. "I can't do that! I don't even like to fly!"

"Nicole, I'm so sorry. Are you sure you guys can't do anything about it? I mean, they do realize you guys have twin toddlers and you're pregnant, right?"

"Heather, you know as well as I do that it doesn't matter," she says bitterly.

"Well, I can't fly with you, but we will be here to help you. You know that. Anything we can do, we will."

"I know. Thanks."

"Feeling any better today?"

"I was, until I found this out."

I spend the better part of twenty minutes letting her vent her frustrations, often sharing in them, before she has to hang up because she needs to make a trip to the bathroom.

"What was that all about?" Rick asks.

I fill him in, and he just shakes his head. "Wow. That's going to be rough."

****

Angeline's pregnancy continues for another week and a half. Her doctor stubbornly refuses to intervene. I have never seen one person as miserable as I have seen her. She rarely leaves the couch in her living room, and only does so with great effort. Her mother has taken over everything to do with running the household. I have done her grocery shopping because her mother can't shop at the commissary. Nancy enjoys the bustle – Angeline is one of six children.

One afternoon after lunch, I see Nancy lumbering rather quickly across our front lawn, her expression wild. She's breathless when she reaches my door.

"Heather! Heather! Thank God, Angeline's water just broke all over the kitchen floor. We need to go!" It's exactly five days before Leila's first birthday.

"Oh! Did you call Chris?" I ask.

"Angeline is calling him now. She told me to come over here and get you. Do what you have to, and I'll get her ready." Nancy lumbers back toward Angeline's house.

I spread my hands out and look wildly around my living room. "Okay. Okay." I quickly dial Nicole's number. Although she's still very queasy, she tells me to send Angeline's kids over. "I will put in some Barney tapes and keep them occupied. Here we go again."

When I call Rick, he says he'll be on his way as soon as he can, but he has to clear it with his boss first. Once Elizabeth, Angeline, Nancy, and I are settled in my car, I pull out and start the familiar journey to the hospital.

"How bad are they?" I ask, stealing a glance at Angeline's contorted face. Her lips are pressed together, eyes closed, and cheeks beet red.

"My back is killing me," she spits through her teeth.

"It's okay, sweetheart," Nancy coos to Elizabeth. I check Elizabeth's expression in the rear view mirror. She's very still and her eyes are wide and frightened. "She's just going to the hospital to have her baby. It's all right."

Angeline dips her head, grips the dashboard, and emits a low moan. After a few moments, she turns to me half smiling. "I am having déjà vu."

I chuckle. "Let's not do this again, shall we?"

"Agreed." Her face contorts, and she starts breathing heavily again.

When we arrive at the hospital, I let Nancy out with Angeline while I park the car. Once I turn the engine off, I turn to Elizabeth.

"Are you all right?" I ask.

Her expression is the one she has when she's thinking very hard about something. Finally, she turns to me. "Mommy, where does the baby come out? Does she have to throw up?"

"No. She doesn't have to throw up."

Her pucker deepens. "Then how does the baby get out of her stomach?"

I take a deep breath before answering. "Well, sweetie, she...it's complicated. I'll tell you about it some other time, all right?"

She nods, but her face remains puckered.

"Let's go inside and wait for daddy."

I sit in the waiting room with Elizabeth and wait for Rick. It has a corner with a miniature kid-sized table, coloring books with crayons, and a few toys. She and I are almost done coloring a picture of a bouquet of flowers when Rick strides in the room clutching his hat. It has been almost an hour since we arrived.

"How's it going?" he asks, bracing himself so Elizabeth can crash into his legs. "Hey there, sweet girl!" He picks her up.

I tilt my head up and kiss him. "I don't know. I haven't had a chance to check. I thought it best to wait here with her."

"Oh, yeah. Good idea. Why don't you go check? I'll stay here with her."

I nod and exit the waiting room to approach the reception desk. Angeline is in room three this time. As I approach, I hear her yelling.

I peer into the room and see Angeline writhing on the bed, her face screwed into a mask of pain. Chris is at her side, holding her hand and trying to offer encouragement. His face is anguished. Nancy is in a recliner in the corner, eyes squeezed shut and clutching a rosary, praying.

I sidle up to the bed and address Chris. "How's it going?"

He shakes his head. "She's really hurting."

"Aren't they going to give her an epidural?"

Angeline throws her head back and yells loudly before panting and thrashing once more. Her free hand reaches behind her, pressing on her back.

Chris gasps, grimacing. "Yes, they're supposed to put one in soon. The nurse said the anesthesiologist will be in as soon as he can, but they're really busy."

"How far along is she?"

"I'm only at five," Angeline answers, her voice shaky. "God, this hurts worse than last time."

"Your back?" I ask.

She nods, licking her lips. "I don't know why. This is…God…" She starts to pant but quickly breaks down into a high pitched scream. I watch the monitor as the needle climbs.

Nancy starts praying fervently out loud in Spanish.

"Where the hell is that *doctor?*" Chris scowls at the open door.

"I'll go check," I offer, eager to leave the room.

When I approach the desk and inquire about her epidural, the nurse checks a clipboard before answering. "Yes, there are two more ahead of her. I promise the doctor is working as quickly as he can," she replies sympathetically.

"I understand, but can't you give her *something* to help while she waits? She's having really bad back labor. I'm sure you can hear her screaming."

The nurse looks at me with a condescending expression. "I can hear them *all* screaming. But I'll get her nurse and see if she can give her something to hold her over."

"Thank you."

I duck my head back into the waiting room and update Rick in code, wary of how much Elizabeth hears.

He sucks his breath in. "That's awful. All right, I'm going to take Elizabeth home. Don't stay too long. Chris and her mother are here."

"Yeah, I know. If it's anything like Leila's birth, it shouldn't take long.

I'll call you later, though."

"Sounds good." He hugs me quickly. "All right, sweet girl, let's go home!"

Once they're gone, I return to Angeline's room to find her lying on her side, still moaning and squeezing Chris's hand. "Did she get her epidural?"

"No," Angeline answers. "The nurse gave me something, though. It took the edge off, but…" She starts to breathe deeply and moan. The needle on the monitor is climbing again. This time, the moaning doesn't turn into screaming. "*Please* hurry *up!*" she says through gritted teeth.

"How's that working for you?" A cheery blond nurse pops into the room.

"It helped, but I want my epidural," Angeline answers, impatient and breathless.

"The doctor is doing one other patient right now, and then you're next. Just hang in there. Let's go ahead and check your progress. Your contractions are nice and strong and close together, so I'm sure you're moving along."

Angeline moans as she gets into position; being on her back is very uncomfortable.

The nurse checks her and frowns. "Huh," she says.

"What's wrong?" Chris asks worriedly. Nancy sits up straight, listening.

"Well," the nurse starts, adjusting her position. Whatever she did makes Angeline moan louder and tense up. "It feels like the baby is face up."

"Is that good?" Chris asks.

The nurse frowns. "It's always best if the baby's head is the first thing we feel, but it could be why she's having such bad back labor." She completes her exam and snaps the gloves off. "I'll let the doctor know. They're both going to be fine, Sergeant Baker. I'll be right back."

Angeline immediately turns onto her side, moaning and panting. The needle climbs.

"Is she making progress?" I ask.

Chris shakes his head. "She didn't say." Angeline starts yelling again. "I hope that doctor hurries up."

The doctor appears at that moment, two nurses in tow. "I'm here!" He is pulling a familiar blue cart with him and immediately starts to gown up.

"I'm going to step out," I say. "If you're okay to stay here, Chris."

Chris is very pale.

"I think you should get some air, Sergeant Baker. Follow her," one authoritative nurse instructs him. Her tone leaves no room for protest. Chris woodenly follows me out of the room, leaning against the wall just outside. He covers his face with his hands.

"Are you okay? Do you want to sit down?" I ask.

He sucks in his breath as Angeline's scream spills into the hallway. He drops his hands and stares at me, anguished. "I just can't…this is intense."

"Weren't you there when Edward or Ronnie were born?"

He shakes his head. "No, I wasn't. Angeline didn't want me in the room when she was in labor with Edward, and I was TDY in school when Ronnie was born."

"Oh. I didn't know."

"Yeah," he murmurs, his eyes darting down the hallway. "I didn't know, either."

"She'll be much better when she gets the epidural, believe me."

He smiles weakly.

A nurse walks up and thrusts a cup of water into his hands. "You need to take a quick break and get back in the game, okay?" she says.

He takes the cup and nods mutely.

When Chris has collected himself, the doctor emerges from the room with a smile. "She should be comfortable now. You can go back in."

"What about the baby being face up? How far along is she now?" I ask before he can disappear.

"Oh, well, that will make for a longer labor, and certainly accounts for why she's having so much back pain. Often, the baby will turn into the proper position on its own as the labor progresses, but we will monitor her closely."

"Thank you, doctor," Chris replies, shaking the doctor's hand.

The doctor smiles and speeds down the hallway to his next epidural, I presume.

"Ready?" I ask. Chris squares his shoulders and strides into the room with me following quickly behind.

Nancy is at Angeline's bedside, pressing a cool cloth onto Angeline's forehead. "It's okay, *querida*, you'll be just fine," she says soothingly.

Angeline closes her eyes, taking deep breaths. She's more in control.

"Is it better, honey?" Chris asks, taking her free hand between both of his.

She glances at him and manages a half smile. "Yes, much better." She grips his hand harder, and her brow furrows. She starts to breathe in and out very deeply. The needle on the monitor is climbing once more.

"They're coming awfully close together," I note, looking at the nurse fussing with the IV machine.

"Mmm," she answers, clicking away at the machine. Once she's satisfied with her task, she turns to me and smiles. "She's at six now. Progress is slow, but it is still progress."

"*Bueno*. That is good," Nancy murmurs, carefully turning the washcloth on Angeline's forehead over, pressing it in place once more. "The baby will come when she is ready."

At five o'clock, I encourage Chris and Nancy to go to the cafeteria and get some food. "I promise, she's not going to deliver before you get back. I'll stay until you return, and then I need to go home." I remain at Angeline's bedside until almost six. She's only progressed to six and a half centimeters. My stomach growls loudly.

"Go home," Angeline encourages me. Her epidural is effective. She barely notices the contractions now. "I'll be fine. Thanks again." She squeezes my hand. I give her an awkward hug.

"All right. Be sure to have Chris call me when the baby comes, okay? I don't care how late it is."

She smiles wearily. "I will. Don't worry. Go home to your family."

Driving home, I mull over not only her situation, but Nicole's situation, as well. This is not an easy journey for us as military wives. It's hard, unfair, and down right hell at times. We have each other. To endure this and come out standing is amazing.

We are strong. We have to be.

My thoughts turn to my mother. I am thankful to have my family close by.

Mom has responded well to her treatment – the doctors are optimistic she'll be in remission, possibly even cured very soon. They can't really call her cured, however, until she's been cancer free for five years, so the clock will be ticking for a very long time. But it is hope, and we'll take it.

****

I awaken the next morning to the alarm going off at six o'clock. I hit the snooze button, blink and orient myself. What day is it? Something happened last night… Angeline's labor.

"Oh!" I bolt upright.

Rick grunts and turns his head in my direction. "You okay?" His speech is slurred.

"It's Angeline. Chris never called," I whisper.

Rick sighs. "I'm sure everything worked out. She probably didn't want to wake you up."

"I told her to call, no matter what time it was." I swing my legs down and hurry into the living room to check for a message. There are none.

I call the number to the hospital as Rick shuffles into the living room, yawning and scratching his stomach. To my astonishment, Angeline is still in labor.

"Would you put me through to her room, please?" I ask. While I wait to be connected, I turn to Rick and fill him in. His eyes widen and he shakes his head.

"I'll go make coffee," he says, disappearing into the kitchen.

"Hello?" Chris's voice answers wearily.

"Chris? It's Heather. What's going on?"

"Well," he sighs. "She's almost complete. The baby's in the right position as of an hour ago. They were considering doing a c-section, but she's a go for a natural delivery at this point."

"Wow," I breathe. "I'm so sorry. How are you and Nancy holding up?"

"Nancy and I doze off and on when we can. The epidural has helped Angeline to doze a little, too. But we're all pretty tired."

"Are the boys and Leila still at Nicole's?"

"Uh, yeah. Nicole called at about ten o'clock last night to check on us and said they could stay the night there."

"Wow. Okay. Keep me posted. Can I do anything?"

"I don't know," he sighs wearily again. "I just hope the baby comes soon. Angeline is exhausted, and so are we."

"Well, call me if there's anything we can do. Hopefully you'll call soon letting us know the baby is here. Don't worry about the kids, I'll call Nicole in a little while and see if I can bring them over here and give her a break."

"Yeah, thanks, Heather. Hey, I gotta go."

"No problem. Call when you can."

After hanging up, I plop down on the sofa.

Rick shuffles over carrying two steaming mugs and hands one to me. "She's still in labor, huh?"

I inhale the aroma and take a small sip. "Chris said she is almost complete."

Rick sits down next to me, sipping from his own mug. "It won't be long now."

It isn't long before Elizabeth toddles into the living room, her hair wild. She is dragging her Pooh Bear blanket behind her. Yawning widely, she thrusts her arms up for Rick to pick her up. She settles into his chest, fingering her blanket.

Eventually, Rick has to get ready for work. I make breakfast, which Rick eats hastily.

Once breakfast is done, Rick is off to work and Elizabeth and I are dressed, I call Nicole and fill her in.

"What? She hasn't had that baby yet?" she asks incredulously.

"I know, right? Crazy, but she's still at it. How was your night?"

"It was easy. The boys crashed on the sofa, and Leila slept beautifully in the portable crib in the girls' room."

"How are you feeling?"

"Oh, you know, just really tired. I'm not that nauseated today. So far, anyway. The kids are playing in the living room. I just got Leila cleaned up from breakfast. She's got a good appetite!"

"I'll be over in about ten minutes, all right?"

"Sure."

I keep the kids occupied throughout the morning, anxiety building as lunch approaches and the phone remains silent. I call Nicole – she hasn't heard anything. I consider calling the hospital again, but don't. The phone will ring when there is something to say.

Finally, at two o'clock, the phone rings. Chris's weary and shaky voice informs me that their newest daughter, Sophia Rose, is finally here.

"Oh, I'm so glad! How did it go? Is everything all right?"

"Well," he starts, taking a deep breath. "Everything is fine, I guess. They're still sewing Angeline up. The doctor said she got a fourth degree laceration, which I guess is the worst? I don't know. That's what they said. She pushed *forever*. They had given up, and were talking about doing a c-section, but suddenly she just screamed, almost sat up and Sophia practically fell out. It's crazy! She weighs ten pounds, eight ounces."

"Oh, wow. That's...wow. Are Angeline and the baby all right?"

He takes another deep breath, blowing it out loudly. "Um...yeah. Like I said, they're still sewing her up, it's been about forty-five minutes, and there are two doctors working on her. Sophia is fine – she's got some lungs on her. Her head looks like an hour glass." He chuckles. "I've never seen anything like it."

"Chris, are you all right?" I ask.

"Uh...yeah. Yeah. It's just...crazy, is all."

"How's Nancy?"

"She's good. We are all tired, but she's still in there with Angeline. I had to step out to...call. So..."

"Chris, are you *really* okay? It's all right not to be okay, you know."

There's silence on the other end for a long moment. When he answers, his voice is shaking. He sounds like he's crying. "I will be fine. I'm just overwhelmed."

"Hey, do you want me to come pick you and Nancy up? We can go get your car when Rick gets off work."

He clears his throat. "No, no. I'll be all right. I will get myself together before we leave, which won't be any time soon, I don't think."

"Well, if you change your mind, call. Otherwise, we'll stop by when Rick gets off work."

"I will. Hey, thanks, Heather. From both of us," he says sincerely.

I call Nicole and tell her the news. She's floored by Sophia's birth weight.

"That's crazy! I can't imagine it," she says. "The doctor says I should be all right to have a natural birth with this baby, even though I had a c-section with the twins. I hope my labor isn't that bad."

"Me, either. Hey – do you want to come to the hospital with me when Rick and Stan get off work? We can leave the kids with them."

"That would be perfect."

When Nicole and I arrive at the hospital after eating a hasty dinner, we stop at the gift shop and pick up a nice bouquet of flowers and a card.

When we inquire at the reception desk, they inform us Angeline is still in recovery. We aren't allowed to take the flowers there, so we are forced to leave them at the desk until she is in her room.

While walking down the hallway toward recovery, Nicole whispers, "She's still in *recovery?* Wow."

I shrug, unsure what to say.

When we enter the recovery unit and are pointed in the direction of the bay where our friend is, we approach hesitantly. When we peek around the curtain, Angeline looks up and smiles.

"Hey, you two! Come meet Sophia," she says wearily, tucking the blanket away from the baby's face for a better view.

I prefer to search Angeline's face to gauge how she's doing first. She is very pale, and there are dark shadows under her eyes. I glance at the machinery hooked up to her and see quite a few IV bags along with some other things I don't recognize. One IV bag looks like it has the remains of blood in it. Did she get a transfusion?

"She's huge, Angeline! And she's beautiful," Nicole bends over the baby, smiling at her chubby little face.

Chris sits next to Angeline, leaning over the side rail with his hand on Angeline's shoulder. Nancy is in a chair next to Chris, looking ten years older than she did yesterday. Her gaze rests on her newest granddaughter.

"How are you doing, Angeline?" I ask.

She drags her gaze up to my face, smiling wearily. "Honestly, I feel like I've been through hell and back. Apparently, I lost enough blood for them to give me two units." She gestures with her chin at the empty blood bag. "I don't remember most of it, though. After Sophia was born, I don't remember much of anything."

"It was a difficult birth," Nancy informs me solemnly. "But God is good, and they're both fine now."

"How much longer before you go to your regular room?" I ask.

"I don't know," Angeline says.

"They said they're going to keep her here for about another hour or so and then, if she stays stable, they'll take her to her room," Chris replies wearily. "It was really touchy there for a bit."

"What happened?" Nicole asks quietly.

Chris goes on to inform us that after he returned from talking to me, Angeline had passed out because her blood pressure dropped suddenly, and they gave her lots of IV fluids plus the blood. Sophia was so large that the doctors took almost two and a half hours sewing her up.

"I don't think there should be any more babies," Nancy pronounces firmly.

"Agreed," Chris says quietly.

"You get no argument from me," Angeline chuckles. She turns her gaze to Sophia and gently strokes her cheek. "We are complete now."

Nicole and I are able to stay long enough to see Angeline settled into a private room – the doctor insisted she get one. Angeline is helped to a standing position by a nurse who encourages her to at least walk a few steps around the room.

"Trust me, you'll heal faster if you don't stay still all the time," the nurse informs her.

Angeline is very slow to get up, and winces when she stands upright. She quips that her walk is that of a ninety-year-old arthritic person.

"Well, what do you expect?" I ask jokingly, attempting to lighten the mood. "You just delivered another turkey!"

Angeline smiles at me, continuing her stooped, slow walk around the bed. Chris's expression remains grave as he holds little Sophia.

When Angeline is settled as comfortably into her bed as possible, Nicole and I present her with our flowers and card.

"They're gorgeous. Thank you," she says, smelling the flowers. She props the card against the vase after she reads it out loud.

We offer once again to take Chris and Nancy home, but they both decline.

"Nancy, why don't you go home? I'm sure Leila and the boys would like to see you, and hear about their new sister," Chris pipes up.

Nancy finally agrees to go after Angeline insists, as well. We stay and visit for another few minutes before leaving the new parents alone for the first time. Nancy is contemplative on the way home, not wanting to engage in anything beyond polite conversation.

When we arrive home, all three kids run up and hug Nancy's legs. She sits down and tells them all about their baby sister. They're very excited to meet her, but disappointed to find out they won't be able to until tomorrow. Stan and Rick tell her the kids have been fed and they even saved a plate for her. It's a simple meal – tuna sandwiches and pretzel sticks, but Nancy accepts it gratefully.

"The hospital food isn't bad, but I am tired of it," she says.

"I bet you're just plain tired," Rick replies.

She looks at him and her shoulders slump. "More than words can say. But God is good."

I help her the rest of the evening with the kids' baths and such. Chris finally comes home around seven o'clock. He is only home long enough to eat and shower before he leaves again, informing us that he convinced the doctor to write an order allowing him to stay the night with Angeline.

"She needs rest badly, and there's no nursery. I want to let her get some sleep," he says, hoisting an overnight bag onto his shoulder.

"That's nice of the doctor to do that. I wish I could have had that with Rick when Elizabeth was born."

"You're such a good father," Nancy says, hugging Chris. "Take care of my baby. I'll take care of yours."

He ducks his head sheepishly. "Thanks. I will."

Everyone that night sleeps like the dead after the events of this day. I hope that's the case for Angeline, Chris, and Sophia, as well. Nobody could've imagined the birth would have gone like it did, but again – life is nothing, if not unpredictable.

And fragile.

CHAPTER TWENTY

May, 1992

"I don't know how I'm going to cope," Nicole says, patting the bulge of her stomach. She's entered her second trimester and only started wearing maternity clothes a week ago. Her husband, Stan, is flying to Germany tomorrow. She and the twins will join him next month.

"It'll be fine. In the grand scheme of things, it's only one month of your life. You'll get through this like we military wives get through everything," I encourage her.

"At least you have us," Angeline says, shifting Sophia on her lap. Sophia is the chubbiest two-month-old I have ever seen, and always smiles. Her fat rolls have fat rolls. Angeline has almost recovered from Sophia's birth. She still sits carefully on well-padded chairs only. It didn't take any urging beyond her doctor bringing up the topic to have her tubes tied. As a secondary precaution, Chris had a vasectomy.

She was further warned by the doctor to take it easy and not work to lose the baby weight until Sophia was at least six-months-old. The difficulty of her birth requires extra healing time.

On this very warm day in early May, we are sitting outside watching the kids run around in the sprinkler on my lawn. They have completely outgrown the kiddie pool. Leila does her best to keep up with her brothers and although she wants to run, it's an awkward toddler sort of lurch. Elizabeth is helpful and attentive to her little friend, holding her hand while they jump together over the oscillating sprinkler.

"But there's *so much* to do. I mean, I have to coordinate the movers, get our medical stuff taken care of, have my next OB appointment, clean our house for final inspection…" She ticks the list off on her fingers.

I smile. "We'll get it all done, and get you on your way."

Nicole looks at us, her chin quivering. "How am I ever going to leave you two? You're my best friends."

"I don't want to think about it," Angeline says, kissing Sophia's fuzzy head. "I feel the same way about you guys."

"Me, too," I reply, clearing my throat. "Let's change the subject."

"How's your mom doing?" Nicole asks.

I didn't mean that subject, but all right. "The treatments seem to be working. The doctors are optimistic about her long term prognosis."

"I'm so glad," Nicole replies. "Your mother is such a doll."

Angeline nods. "How much longer does she have to stay in the hospital this time?"

"Well," I start, not sure how much I can say with a steady voice. "She's…I don't really know. The side effects of the chemo are really bad this round. She's got sores all through her mouth and can't keep anything down. She's lost so much weight." I clear my throat.

Nicole dabs at her eyes. "She'll be fine, Heather. Just wait and see. She'll be just fine."

"She has to be," I reply quietly, my voice quivering.

"My mother lights a candle and prays for her every day. She loves her," Angeline adds, patting my leg.

I smile and nod, words failing me. The last two rounds of chemo have been very difficult. Mom has spent more time in the hospital than out of it because of the side effects. Somehow, she continues to be positive and even make jokes about the whole thing, but there are days when I can't visit for long, watching her suffer. She's always been trim, but now she's a mere wisp of herself. Every bone in her body is sharply defined. Her frailty is frightening.

Dad, Jeff, and Debbie are dealing with it as best they can. Dad would never leave her side if he didn't have to. I divide my time between my home, my parents' house, and the hospital.

"She should be out and doing at least a little better by prom, shouldn't she?" Angeline asks, adjusting Sophia on her lap.

Even though Debbie is only a sophomore, she has been asked to go to the prom by a junior. Prom is in a few weeks, and Mom is hopeful to be out of the hospital for it.

"I certainly hope so. Her last round of chemo was yesterday, so today is a bad day."

"Is this the very last one, or does she have to go back again?" Nicole asks, her eyes tracking her twins, who are happily skipping around the sprinkler.

"Hopefully this is the last one. We have to wait and see if it wiped out the cancer cells. The doctor thinks this will do it. Then she enters the maintenance phase which could last a couple of years."

"Wow."

I draw a deep breath. "Yeah. Wow is right." I clear my throat again, sucking my lips in.

"So, what are you doing for your anniversary, Heather? It's next week." Angeline abruptly changes the subject for which I am grateful.

"I am planning to make grilled steaks and shrimp, my mother's cheesy mashed potatoes, asparagus, and a chocolate mousse for dessert," I proclaim proudly.

"Whoa!" Nicole exclaims. "That's pretty ambitious! Don't you want to go out to eat instead? Especially for your anniversary, I would think you would want to leave the work to someone else."

"No, we really can't afford it and besides, it's sort of a tradition of ours. I set up the white linen tablecloth and put out the nice china."

"Oh, I remember you telling me about that," Angeline breathes. "That was awesome."

I grin. "Yes, it was."

****

That Friday, our anniversary, is a blur. Mom is released from the hospital in the morning. There is a lot of bustling going on to settle her in at home. I am hesitant to leave Elizabeth at the house, as scheduled.

"Don't you need your rest, Mom?" I ask worriedly.

"Oh, for heaven's sake!" she exclaims. "It's your anniversary. Quite the contrary, Elizabeth lifts my spirits. I want to put the hospital behind me, and have a tea party with my granddaughter." She smiles widely at Elizabeth, who grins just as widely back. "Besides, your father is here to help, too."

Mom insists I take her good crystal goblets to serve my chocolate mousse in before I leave. "We'll see you two tomorrow."

Later, while marinating the shrimp and seasoning the steaks, I check on the mousse-filled crystal goblets in the refrigerator. I will top them with raspberries and whipped cream. Mom is right – the mousse looks gorgeous.

Glancing at the clock, I hurry and set the table before Rick comes home. He should be home in less than thirty minutes. I pull the freshly ironed linen tablecloth and napkins out, and set the table with the china, some candles, and silverware. I step back to admire my simple handiwork. Nodding in satisfaction, I make my way out to the back porch to light the grill and get the coals ready.

Just as the flames have begun to die down, and the coals are turning white, Rick pokes his head through the sliding glass door with a dozen red roses clasped in his hand, and a grin on his face.

"Hey, honey bun! Happy anniversary!" He presses the roses into my hand and kisses me. "The table looks great! What are we having?"

I inhale the heavenly scent of the roses before answering. "Grilled steak, shrimp, cheesy mashed potatoes, and asparagus."

"Wow!" he exclaims, rubbing his hands together. "I can't wait. Want me to grill?"

"Nope. You go change out of your uniform. I'll take care of it." I not only have a knack for grilling, but I love it. There's something about the smell of food cooking on the grill that makes me very happy. Maybe there's a small bit of pyromania in my personality. Rick is a great griller, too, but tonight it's my turn.

Minutes later, Rick emerges wearing my favorite red dress shirt that make his eyes look like pools of melted dark chocolate. When he approaches, I catch a whiff of his cologne and smile.

"You look and smell delicious," I murmur, wrapping my arms around his waist, pulling him in for a kiss.

"Would you like to go change while I finish up with the grill?"

I blink, feigning offense. "What? You don't like my T-shirt and shorts?"

"You look great in anything and nothing, but I know you want to dress up, so scoot along," he says, patting my back side.

I change into a blue dress – Rick's favorite – put on my diamond earrings, and spray a little cologne on my wrists. When I emerge, Rick has already placed the food on the table, and lit the candles. The roses are stunning in a vase against the white linen cloth, and he is standing behind my chair, holding it out for me.

"Madam, dinner is served," he states formally, bowing.

We enjoy our meal immensely and leisurely. Rick smiles when I present him with the chocolate mousse; we actually feed each other. It is just like being in an old romantic movie, and we are the stars.

"Here's to four years plus fifty more," Rick raises his glass in toast when we've finished our dessert. "I love you, Heather."

I raise my glass and gaze into the beautiful pools of chocolate that are his eyes. "Here's to fifty more years, and I love you, too."

****

"What do you think about visiting the base chapel for services tomorrow?" Rick asks the next morning as we lie lazily in each other's arms, savoring the fact that we don't have to get up until we want to. Rick is on leave today.

I blink, surprised. "What brought that up?"

He shrugs. "One of the guys at work talks about it. He and his family go there and like it. I think we should give it a try. Elizabeth needs to be brought up with some sort of faith, don't you think?"

"Sure. I guess so. I've never really thought about it. I went to the chapel for services while you were deployed. It was comforting to be around a lot of other spouses going through the same thing." I roll onto my side, propping my head up in my hand. "Have you given this a lot of thought?"

He is contemplative for a moment. "Well, not a lot. But since we had Elizabeth, I want her to be grounded somehow. Your mother's diagnosis and seeing how religious Angeline's mother is… I guess it all just got me thinking."

"Did you go to church much when you were growing up?"

"Not really. I mean, we went to services for Christmas and Easter, but not much else."

"Do the services still start at eleven?"

"That's what my co-worker said."

"Sure. Why not?"

He grins and kisses me. "Good. We'll see what it's all about."

Now that the matter is settled, we enjoy the rest of our lazy morning together. Rick whips up delicious cheese omelets and bacon for breakfast. I brew coffee and enjoy the warmth of the sun filtering in through the windows facing our backyard. It looks like it will be another gorgeous day.

"What time is Stan supposed to leave today?" Rick asks as he expertly flips an omelet over in the pan.

"He has to be at the airport at two," I reply, pouring coffee into our mugs. The steam curls upward into the stream of sunlight bathing the counter.

"How's Nicole holding up?" he asks as he slides the omelet onto a plate before pouring more eggs into the pan for the second omelet.

"She's hanging in there. I can't believe Stan couldn't make alternate arrangements for this." I can't keep the edge of bitterness out of my voice.

Rick sighs and sprinkles cheese onto the partially cooked eggs before responding. "Honey bun, it's not just the military these things happen to. It happens because it's part of life, uniform or no uniform."

I nod and place bacon on each plate as he slides the second omelet onto a plate. "I know."

Neither of us talks as we sit down to eat. The roses are just starting to fully bloom in their vase. Bathed in the morning sunlight, they look like velvet.

"Heather, let's talk about this," Rick says gently, wrapping the gooey string of cheese around his fork of eggs before stuffing it in his mouth. "You've told me you support my decision to make this a career. Do you still stand by that? Even after what we've been through? You know I have to decide soon about re-enlisting. I will have eight years in at the end of this year. If I re-enlist for four more years, that will put me over the ten year mark. More than half way toward retirement."

I sigh and place my fork on the plate, leaving the food untouched. "I remember what I said."

He sips his coffee deliberately. "I still want to make this a career, and I want to tell you why it's also a good life."

I stare down at my plate. "I am listening."

"Heather," he says, reaching across for my hand. "I love my job. You know that. I love knowing that the airplanes I work on are flying all over the world and doing what needs to be done. Sure I can do this as a civilian, but I know that *because* I wear the uniform, what I do protects us and our way of life. It doesn't seem like much, but even my small contribution counts. I am studying hard to make Tech Sergeant when I test for it, and that will mean more money. The Air Force will pay for me to go to college, when I choose to. It will also afford us the ability to travel when we're ready. We don't have to worry about where we'll live – we get base housing. We live in a secure neighborhood where our daughter can play safely and freely. We have free healthcare. Tell me what other job you know of that I can do for twenty years and get a full retirement. There is none. It's not perfect, but it's not horrible, either."

He grips my hand earnestly while I search his face. "Those are great points, Rick. I know you're right – it isn't all bad. I like the security of your paycheck and a place to live. But, you were gone the first year of our marriage and then you missed a good part of Elizabeth as a baby, too. It's not easy. Remember how long it took Elizabeth to get to know you when you came home?"

He winces slightly, his jaw working. "I remember, Heather. I'm sorry about that. But that is a sacrifice that we have to make sometimes. You know that when I'm here, I'm *here*. I do my best."

"You're an incredible husband and father, and I love you. Rick, I will give anything and do anything for you. If this is what you want," I gulp. "Re-enlist."

Rick's face lights up. "You mean it? You're serious?"

"Yes, I mean it." God help me.

Rick beams and rises. He drops on his knees next to me. "I love you, Heather."

"I love you, too."

I have had a glimpse of what I will have to give up over the course of Rick's career. It scares me. But this is important to him, so it needs to be important to me, too. I've been childish and naïve thinking his choice should be simple. It's *my* choice that should be simple.

I choose him. Whatever the cost.

****

As soon as we retrieve Elizabeth, Rick, Elizabeth, and I head over to Nicole and Stan's house to say goodbye. It's nearly one o'clock.

When Nicole opens the door, she looks frazzled and her eyes are red.

"Come on in," she says hurriedly. "We're just getting his bags together."

The living room is in disarray with Stan's luggage piled close to the door. Stan is on the floor wrestling with the girls, who are giggling and laughing.

Elizabeth snatches her hand from mine, immediately joining in the fun.

"How are you?" I ask, squeezing Nicole's arm.

Nicole claps her hand over her mouth and squeezes her eyes shut, turning her back to Stan and the girls. Her face crumples and her shoulders heave. "I'm a mess."

Rick clears his throat and walks over to the sofa to sit down. Stan disentangles himself and greets him.

"I'm sorry," I say sympathetically. "I am so sorry. But at least you'll be with him in a month. It will go by quick. You'll be too busy to think about it."

Nicole squares her shoulders, collecting herself. She wipes her eyes and smiles at me. "Yes. It will go quick."

"Are you going to be okay going to the airport by yourself?"

She nods quickly. "Yeah. I'll be fine. The girls and I will be fine." She grabs me in a fierce hug. "Thank you, Heather."

"You're welcome. Can I do anything right now or later today?"

"Not that I can think of. We're all set." She turns back to her family and claps her hands. "All right, girls. We have to get moving because Daddy has to get on his plane soon."

****

The chapel service the next day is the same as I remember – comforting. There are a number of new faces while many familiar faces are absent. That's how it goes with the military – people are always coming and going.

While I am waiting to retrieve Elizabeth in the toddler room, a sharply dressed platinum blond woman approaches confidently, thrusting her retrieval slip at the attendant.

"I'm here for *Captain* Fabre's daughter, London, please."

"Mommy!" Elizabeth cries, running toward me. I pull my attention away from the blond, and bend down to scoop her up.

"Look, I made a manger!" Elizabeth cries triumphantly. She holds a piece of construction paper with popsicle sticks glued to it up for my inspection. There's a little paper baby Jesus glued above the popsicle sticks.

"That's beautiful, baby. Good job!" I collect her bag, and stroll down the hallway carrying her.

Elizabeth is still talking animatedly about her art project as we approach the foyer where Rick is talking to an older couple.

"Here's my lovely wife, Heather," Rick gestures to me when I approach. "This is our daughter Elizabeth."

"Oh, aren't you cute as a button!" the older woman exclaims, smiling at Elizabeth.

Elizabeth thrusts her art project out to the woman and proclaims, "I made a manger!"

"And what a pretty manger it is. Do you know who that is?" the older woman points to the baby.

Elizabeth nods proudly. "That's Jesus!"

"Very good! What a smart little girl you are," the older woman pats Elizabeth's back. Elizabeth beams.

"It's nice to meet you," I smile.

"This is Colonel Davies and his wife Phyllis," Rick says. I freeze. Are we supposed to be talking to them? Should I say sir and ma'am?

Noting my discomfort, Colonel Davies is quick to respond, "My name is Bill and please call me Bill. I'm only Colonel at the office. It's nice to meet you, Heather. You have a beautiful family, Rick."

"Thank you, sir. I can't agree more."

A fast clicking noise catches my attention, and I turn toward the sound. The blond woman from the nursery is approaching us as rapidly as she can in very high heels, dragging two children by the hand with a third jogging to keep up. The children look like they stepped out of a catalogue – their clothes all match, and the two girls have enormous bows in their perfectly coiffed hair. I am lucky to get a ribbon to stay in Elizabeth's hair.

"Colonel and Mrs. Davies," she gushes breathlessly as she reaches us. "It's so nice to see you two here. My, my, you are looking *so* lovely today, Mrs. Davies! Did you get your hair done this week?"

"No, Shannon, I did not," Phyllis replies, a frozen smile on her face. "But thank you just the same."

"Hello, Shannon," Bill says graciously. "It's good to see you, too. Have you met Rick and Heather?"

She turns her gaze toward us as if surprised to see someone standing there. "Oh. I'm afraid I haven't had the pleasure." She smiles broadly, thrusting her hand out to us. I put Elizabeth down in order to shake her hand. "I'm Mrs. Fabre, Captain Fabre's wife."

"It's nice to meet you," Rick replies for both of us. I am stunned into silence.

"And who is this little angel?" she gushes as she bends over to smile at Elizabeth. Elizabeth studies the woman.

"This is our daughter, Elizabeth," Rick replies.

Mrs. Fabre, aka Shannon, stands up straight and gestures to her children who obediently line up in a row, as if they've done this a hundred times. She pats each of their heads in turn as she identifies them. "These are our children. This is London, Paris, and our son Rome."

I cough and clench my jaw to keep from laughing out loud. Who names their children after cities? Rick's hand squeezes mine lightly as he remarks on the uniqueness of their names.

"Well," Shannon replies, smiling proudly. "They are our favorite places in the whole world, and these are the best children in the world. Don't we think that's true of our own children?" She laughs, looking to Bill and

Phyllis for confirmation. They smile politely and chuckle.

"Colonel Davies, I wanted to know if you would like to join us at the club for lunch today. It would be our treat and we would be thrilled to have you!" Shannon continues expectantly.

"No, I'm afraid not. We've already made plans. Thank you for the invitation, though. Perhaps some other time," Bill replies.

Shannon's face falls for a brief moment, but she recovers quickly. "I'm sure Mark will be very disappointed to hear that. Shall I give him your regards?" she asks.

Regards? People still give regards?

"Please do. You have a lovely day now," Bill replies, dismissing her.

Shannon's gaze grazes over Phyllis, Rick, and rests on me briefly. Am I being sized up?

"Thank you. Same to you. It was lovely to meet you!" She waves in our direction, gathers her children, and disappears into the crowd, the clicking of her heels eventually falling silent.

"I'm sorry, Heather," Phyllis says apologetically. "She's a climber."

My brow furrows in confusion. "I'm sorry, a what?"

"She's very ambitious to climb the ladder. Or rather, have her husband *Captain* Fabre climb the ladder. She likes to think she can help her husband's career by getting to know those that hold higher ranks."

Bill places his arm on his wife's. "Now, Phyl, don't get too worked up. She's a nice young lady, even if she is pushy."

"I don't care for her," Phyllis says.

"I know, dear. I know," Bill replies. "I think you caught on to that quick, didn't you, Rick? I noticed you didn't tell her your rank."

"I didn't think it was necessary," Rick replies. Bill chuckles and slaps Rick on the shoulder. "Good man. Never wear the rank outside the office, and especially not in God's house."

"Would you three like to join us for lunch?" Phyllis asks.

"I thought you had plans," I remark.

"Yes, our plans are *not* to eat with the Fabres," Phyllis chuckles.

"Phyl, be nice," Bill chides her, not attempting to hide a smile.

"I am being nice," she beams. "So, what do you say?"

Rick looks at me and shrugs. "What do you say?"

Mentally, I calculate the balance in our checkbook and know that we will have to be careful what we order and cut back on something else until payday if we do. "It's up to you."

"That sounds wonderful. Thank you, we would love to join you," Rick replies.

Fortunately, we go to a mid-priced restaurant. I am sure to discreetly let Rick know to only order water to drink, and Elizabeth must share our food.

Bill and Phyllis seem to be just regular folks like us. They are kind, thoughtful, and Phyllis absolutely adores Elizabeth. At the end of the meal when the server brings the checks, Bill snatches them both up and informs us that lunch is their treat.

"I'm sorry, sir. I can't let you do that," Rick protests.

"Nonsense. Believe me, I remember when I was a Second Lieutenant and we struggled, didn't we, Phyl?"

"Oh, boy did we! There were times I wasn't sure we were going to make it from one paycheck to the next," she chuckles, sipping her coffee.

"Sir…" Rick tries again, but Bill holds up his hand.

"I won't hear of it. That's an order," Bill grins and winks at Rick, places his payment in the folder and hands it to the server.

Rick looks at me, smiles and his shoulders relax. "That is very kind of both of you. Thank you very much."

"Yes, we appreciate it. You're too kind," I echo.

"You're more than welcome. I really enjoyed you kids today. This little angel is adorable, and so well behaved," Phyllis remarks.

"I do hope we'll see you next week in service?" Bill asks.

Rick looks to me, and I nod. "Yes, sir. We enjoyed it. But please don't feel in any way obligated to take us to lunch every week."

Bill and Phyllis laugh. Driving home after expressing our thanks and saying goodbyes, I am very content.

"They're such nice people. I never knew officers could be that way," I say, sharing my thoughts.

Rick chuckles. "They're people, too. There are a lot more good ones out there than bad ones."

I wrinkle my nose. "What about that Shannon person? I am sorry, Mrs. *Captain* Fabre."

Rick grins and shakes his head. "Yeah, she's a real piece of work."

I mull over that woman in contrast to Bill and Phyllis. I hope I don't run into Mrs. *Captain* Fabre again any time soon.

****

June, 1992

Time goes by quickly. Between helping Nicole get ready to move, my mother's recovery after her last round of chemotherapy, and Debbie's first prom, I barely have time to catch my breath.

The dreaded day arrives when we all have to say goodbye to Nicole. Angeline and I co-host a barbecue the day before she leaves to give her a good send-off. Of course, my family comes.

"You are looking so much better!" Angeline remarks when my mother emerges from the car, carrying a foil-covered dish, and wearing a wide-brimmed straw hat over an orange scarf. Her hair is just starting to grow back.

"I am feeling much better. The nasty cancer cells are gone, and I am alive and kicking!" Mom proclaims, grinning and accepting a hug.

"You just need to put on some weight like me," Nicole says, cradling her softly rounded midsection before coming in for a hug, as well.

"Oh, I'm keeping up. I've gained seven pounds already," Mom replies. "My taste buds are coming back. Boy, have I missed them."

"Yeah, she's been eating pretty well. You should have seen the slice of cornbread she ate last night. It was huge!" Dad smiles, placing his hand around Mom's waist.

"I'll take that over to the buffet table," Angeline says, taking the dish from Mom. "You go make yourself comfortable."

"Girls! Come back over here with that!" Nicole yells at her daughters. "Excuse me. We'll visit later."

Jeff parks his truck, an old Chevy, behind Mom and Dad's car. He bolts out of the truck, races around to the passenger side, and opens the door. His girlfriend, Cara, steps out gingerly and grins at him. Jeff beams, his neck reddening.

"Do you think this is serious?" I ask Mom quietly as I watch the interchange.

Mom shrugs. "Who knows? It seems serious enough."

"What about Debbie?"

"Oh, she's doing fine. She and Cara get along famously. Cara's a really nice young lady."

Debbie comes bounding up to us. "Where's Elizabeth?" she asks, cheeks flushed from the heat.

I shield my eyes from the sun and scan the area. "She's with Rick, right by the jungle gym in Angeline's yard."

Debbie's gaze follows where I point. With a grin, she jogs over to them.

Jeff is walking slowly across the yard holding Cara's hand. He looks both sheepish and proud. Cara is grinning, too, holding Jeff's hand in both of hers.

"Hey there, you two," I say teasingly.

"Hey, yourself," Jeff replies. "When do we eat? I am starved."

"Chris has the grill going already. Would you like to help?"

"Sure thing!" Jeff replies enthusiastically, but quickly back tracks. "If that's all right with you, Cara. You wanna help grill?" he asks hopefully.

She wrinkles her nose, and shakes her head. "You go on and go. I'll sit in the shade and watch you."

Jeff grins his big goofy grin and pecks her on the cheek, casting a quick glance at us before ducking his head and jogging over to the grill, neck crimson.

"Would you like to join us?" I ask Cara, gesturing to a group of chairs in the shade.

She smiles and nods enthusiastically. Cara thoughtfully offers the chair with the most shade to my mother before asking if Mom would like a drink.

"Why, yes, Cara. I would love some sweet tea," Mom smiles.

"Yes, ma'am. I'll be right back. Can I get you something, Heather?" she asks.

"I'll have the same. Thank you."

Cara nods and disappears.

"What a sweet and thoughtful young lady," Mom says.

"Yes, she is. Jeff has a good one right now," I reply.

"Mm hmm."

"Mom, how are you doing? Really?" I ask.

Mom reaches over, patting my leg. "I am doing just fine, sweetheart. Really. The doctor believes I'll be fine."

"Are you really gaining weight?"

"Now, do you honestly think any woman in her right mind would lie about *gaining* weight? Good heavens."

"You still look so frail, Mom."

"I know, honey. I know. But I am getting stronger every day. Don't you worry."

The barbecue is a smashing success – a number of Stan's co-workers come. There is plenty of food to go around, and the kids all have fun. At the end of the day, the remaining food is packaged and put away, the streamers and balloons are cleared, and exhausted and cranky kids are reluctantly forced to go indoors to take baths and get ready for bed.

"Will you come over in a little while? I would like to spend some time with just us one last time," Nicole says, gathering Angeline and I in a small huddle as the sun lies low in the sky, and all the other guests have gone home. She is standing next to her rental car. Her twins are strapped in their car seats, jabbering to each other excitedly.

"Of course. I have to nurse Sophia and help Chris get the kids ready for bed first. Then we'll be right over," Angeline says.

Angeline and I head over to Nicole's temporary housing in my car an hour later. Nicole passed her housing inspection last week; two days after her household goods were packed up. Her car shipped yesterday, so she is in temporary housing with a rental car. Their flight leaves early tomorrow morning, so we won't be able to see her off at the airport.

"It's better this way," she said. "I want to get all my crying out before we leave."

When we arrive at her temporary house on the other side of the base, she ushers us into the living room where she has a bottle of sparkling grape juice and three plastic cups sitting on the coffee table.

"I want to celebrate with you guys, and since I'm pregnant and you're nursing, I thought it best if we just do it with fake champagne."

She ceremoniously holds the bottle up. "This is in celebration of true friendship. You guys mean the world to me and I..." She takes a deep breath before continuing. "I just want you guys to know that. I am going to miss you more than words can say." She draws in a ragged breath and unscrews the lid, filling each cup.

She hands each of us a cup and holds it high. "To friendship."

"To friendship," Angeline and I say in unison. We tap our cups together.

We spend a little more than an hour with Nicole, crying and laughing. None of us wants to say goodbye, but we know we have to.

Nicole squeezes each of us fiercely, trembling and sobbing. "How am I going to do this without you guys?"

"Because you have to," Angeline tells her, patting her back. "Because it's what we *do*. We are military wives."

"Here, here!" I say, raising my cup again.

"At least you know Stan will be waiting for you at the airport in Germany. You'll be fine," Angeline continues.

"It stinks," I say. "I'm going to miss you and the girls so much."

"I promise I'll write you guys as soon as I can, and let you know my address. Promise you'll write back," she cries.

"You know we will," Angeline says, wiping her eyes.

When Angeline and I finally leave, the last view of my friend Nicole is of her standing in the doorway, sobbing and looking very vulnerable. I don't know if I'll ever get to see her again. I don't even know if she's having a girl or a boy. Maybe she'll have twins again. Who knows?

Such is the sacrifice we make. Such is military life.

****

July, 1992

It's difficult to see Nicole's house empty. I know that it isn't actually her house; it never was. These are military quarters. But our lives happen in military quarters. We build our families in them. Trying to explain that to an almost three-year-old is not easy; Elizabeth cannot understand why her best friends are no longer here.

"Did Hailey and Bailey go to another school?" she asks one morning, puzzled.

"Yes, sweetie. They went to a new school, and a new house that is far away," I explain, helping her with her shoes.

"Why?"

"Because the military told them it was time to move."

"Why?"

"Just because, Elizabeth. It was time."

"Are they going to come home soon?"

"No."

Elizabeth's face crumples, and she remains silent.

"Maybe some new friends will move into their old home."

Elizabeth screws up her face. "I don't want new friends. I want old friends."

"I'm sorry, baby," I say, gathering her in a hug.

Angeline and I receive postcards from her in the mail three weeks after their departure with their new military postal box and *"We're here and all right. It's crazy. I miss you guys!"* hastily scrolled on them.

Nicole's house remains empty for almost a month. There is a definite gap on our street; Angeline and I catch ourselves frequently wanting to walk over and knock, or call her to join us.

We can't. They're gone.

One bright and very hot Tuesday morning, a moving van rolls down our street and stops right in front of Nicole's house.

Just as I was about to pick up the phone and call Angeline, my phone rings.

"Look out your window!" Angeline exclaims excitedly.

"I was literally about to call you and tell you the same thing. I guess we're going to have new neighbors today. Should we make ourselves obvious and go sit out there on chairs with binoculars?"

Angeline laughs. "I wish. But I can't. I have to get to the commissary today or we're eating rice for dinner."

"Want me to watch the girls or the boys for you?"

"If you don't mind watching the boys, that would be great. I'll take Leila and Sophia with me. I will only be gone for about an hour."

"You're kidding, right? It's payday, Angeline. I expect you'll be gone for at least two."

"I'll still try to hurry."

Angeline drops the boys off ten minutes later after packing the girls up in her car. Curiosity gets the best of me; I put in a VHS tape to keep the kids occupied, and stare unashamedly out the window at the boxes and furniture being downloaded from the truck and brought into Nicole's house. My eyes dart around looking for evidence of the people that will be moving in. Most importantly, do they have children?

Aside from the three men who, from the looks of their identical brown shirts, work for the moving company, all I notice is a man with longer hair than the military allows moving in and out of the house.

"Hey! Gimme that!" Ronnie yells. I tear my attention away from the window to see Edward holding a toy above his head just out of the reach of Ronnie. "Gimme!"

I settle the squabble quickly and return my attention to the window, just in time to see the non-military approved hair man drive away in a little

Honda.

"Rats!" I mumble. The mystery will be solved soon enough, I suppose.

"Did you see anything?" Angeline asks when she picks up the boys after shopping.

"Not really. There was some guy that was there. But he can't be the one moving in. His hair was too long. So I don't know what's up."

"Hm. Well, maybe we can walk over there after dinner."

"We should let them get settled in first."

She shrugs and smiles, herding her boys out the door. "Okay. Maybe tomorrow after dinner."

Unfortunately, we don't meet our new neighbors for another week and a half. They don't ever seem to be home. The mystery man has moved in with a little boy who appears to be about seven, but we haven't seen a woman yet.

One Saturday afternoon, Angeline and I are sitting outside in the shade while our children play in the sprinkler. The now familiar Honda pulls up and parks. Angeline taps my leg, jerking her chin in that direction.

"Check it out. Maybe there is a 'she' after all," she says quietly. She and I watch as a curvy woman with a short bob of brown hair emerges from the passenger side while the now familiar man emerges from the driver's side. He retrieves a military duffel bag from the trunk while she retrieves two smaller pieces of luggage from her side. The little boy appears from the back seat, as well, and skips to the house.

Angeline and I both look at each other, puzzled.

"The plot thickens."

"No doubt," Angeline replies. "Let's end the mystery. Why don't you bake some cookies, and I'll bake banana bread. We'll take them over there tonight."

"Sounds like a plan."

When we knock on the door that night, the curvy woman answers the door with a curious smile. "Hello," she says.

"Hi! Um, we are your neighbors across the street, and we just wanted to introduce ourselves. I'm Heather, and this is Angeline," I start.

"Oh! Uh...nice to meet you. Would you like to come in?" she says, stepping aside. "Sorry about the mess. We're still settling in. I'm Allison, by the way."

"Thank you. It's nice to meet you, Allison," Angeline says, gazing around the room.

There are still a few boxes here and there and the walls are blank. The little boy is sitting in front of the television watching a cartoon. He glances up when we walk in.

"This is our son. Adam, say hello to our new neighbors. I'm sorry, what were your names again?"

"I'm Heather, and this is Angeline," I repeat.

"Hello," Adam mumbles quietly before returning his attention to the television.

The man appears from the hallway and smiles at us. He immediately approaches, holding his hand out. "Hi, I'm Jesse. Nice to meet you. Oh, treats! Nice. I'll take those." He accepts the cookies and warm loaf of banana bread, taking them to the kitchen.

"So, where did you guys move from?" Angeline asks.

"We came from England. We were there for three years," Allison answers.

"That sounds wonderful! Lucky you," I reply.

"Yeah, it was good. I had to work a lot of twelve hour shifts, but we got to travel a bit."

"You pulled twelve hour shifts?" I ask, confused.

"You're active duty?" Angeline asks.

Allison nods. "Yes. I just got home today from a school in Mississippi. Jesse and Adam had to make the move on their own."

"Oh!" I exclaim. That makes sense. That's why Jesse has that haircut. "Your husband is not military then, right?"

"No. But I feel like I am, because she is," Jesse says, emerging from the kitchen with three cookies in his hand and one in his mouth. "These are fabulous, by the way. Thank you."

"Can I have one?" Adam asks, sitting up straight.

"Sure, buddy. But just one," Allison instructs.

Adam jumps up, and runs in the kitchen.

"Believe me, we know it's hard," Angeline chuckles. "How old is your son? My two boys are six and five. Plus we have two little girls who are almost two and one. Heather has an adorable little girl, Elizabeth. She is two."

"She'll be three in October."

Allison's eyebrows rise and she addresses Angeline. "Wow! You're busy. Adam is seven and in second grade."

"Do you have any other children?" Angeline asks. I shoot her a look; that was forward.

"No. We only have Adam. He's all we need!" Allison proclaims proudly.

Jesse glances at his wife, but remains silent while he stuffs another cookie in his mouth.

"Well, we don't want to take up your time. We just wanted to introduce ourselves and let you know that we're here if you guys need anything," I say.

"Yes, we live right over there," Angeline adds, pointing to our houses. "Stop by any time."

"You probably won't see much of Allison; she deploys a lot and works long hours when she's here. Is it all right if I stop by, though? I'm sure Adam would love to play with your boys. If it makes it better, I'll even pouf up my hair and slap on some lipstick to fit in."

Jesse and Allison laugh, and we join in.

"Oh, Jesse. You're crazy! Ladies, forgive my husband. He knows he's in the minority as a civilian husband, so he tries to be one of the 'ladies'," she explains. He grins and eats another cookie.

When Angeline and I walk across the street afterward, I speak first. "Well, they're nice."

"Yeah. But," she starts before glancing at me. "Only *one* child? Don't you find that odd?"

"No, not really. I only have one child."

"True."

****

"*She's* active duty, but he's not?" Rick asks the following day over breakfast while I fill him in on the new neighbors. "That's different."

"Is that okay?" I ask, a little defensively. "What's wrong with it?"

"Nothing's wrong with it. I just wonder how he feels about that."

"How is he supposed to feel about it?"

"Heather, I just mean that it's...unusual, but not unheard of. There are a lot of women in the military. It's just unusual to find a military woman not married to a military man, that's all. I don't have a problem with it."

"Oh. Good."

Rick chuckles, and continues eating his oatmeal.

"Do you think we'll ever go to England?" I ask, blowing on my oatmeal.

Rick's head jerks up and he looks at me, surprised. "Uh, well, if you want to go we can put in for orders, and see what happens."

"I don't mean *now*. I mean, maybe sometime in the future."

"It's possible."

"I guess it would be cool to travel and see things."

Rick grins. "I would love that. I told you, I want to show you the world."

I smile. "But *you* are my world. Everything else is just extra."

****

Over the summer, Angeline and I keep in touch with Nicole. She writes us religiously every week informing us of how things are going. She is not having twins this time, and the pregnancy is going well. She lets us know the military community is very tight knit there and she's making friends easily. The girls are adjusting well, but Stan is working twelve-hour shifts with few days off, so no sight-seeing yet.

Jesse keeps his promise to bring Adam over to meet Edward and Ronnie. The first time occurs in mid-July, about a week after our introduction. Angeline and I pull up a chair for Jesse to sit in, which he gratefully accepts.

The boys are shy around each other at first before becoming fully involved in a game of cops and robbers. The only dispute arises when a decision must be made about who gets to be a cop, and who gets to be a robber. Apparently, crime is cool because all of them want to be robbers. Edward exerts his dominance – he gets to be a robber.

Elizabeth plays with Leila, instructing her on the etiquette of tea parties with dolls. Leila is content to play along, but eventually she starts sucking on the tea cups. Elizabeth has a fit.

"Mommy! She's getting slobber all over my *cups!*" Elizabeth laments. Her face puckers and she crosses her arms over her chest. "I want Hailey and Bailey back."

"I'm sorry, sweetie. But Leila is younger than you. She'll figure it out. How about you give her a cookie instead? She's not interested in the tea."

Elizabeth nods, rips the cup out of Leila's hand and gives her a vanilla cookie to suck on. Leila happily sucks away, not missing a beat.

"Sorry about that, Elizabeth," Angeline says, patting Sophia's chubby back as she sleeps draped across her mother's shoulder.

"It's all right. She'll get over it," I say.

"You ladies sure you don't mind if I join you? I could go at least put on some lipstick or something," Jesse jokes. "I mean, I don't even shave my legs."

Angeline and I both laugh. "No, you don't have to do that. It's all right to join us. I'm sure Adam will enjoy playing."

"Yeah. He needs more friends. Just having moved here is hard."

"Is he adjusting all right?" I ask.

"He's doing good. The school system here is a little off from the DoD schools he attended, but not by much." I have learned the Department of Defense runs the school system for military children overseas.

"Are you guys going to have more kids?" Angeline blurts.

I am quick to reprimand her, glancing apologetically at Jesse. "Angeline, that's not our business. I'm sorry, Jesse."

"No, no. It's all right. Well, if it's up to Allison, probably not."

"Why is that?" Angeline asks.

"Angeline!" I hiss.

"What? It's a legitimate question," she retorts innocently.

Ignoring our exchange, Jesse continues. "Because when she had Adam, she had a hard time getting the baby weight off. She had to make her weight pretty soon after he was born. So, she said she's not going to go through that again. That means no more kids."

"What? Weigh in? What?" I ask, confused.

"You know they have to maintain fitness standards, Heather. Guys and girls both do," Angeline informs me.

"Oh. Yeah, I guess I forgot about that. Rick never talks about it."

"That's because he and Chris don't have a problem with it," Angeline continues. She gestures toward her own still plump body. "Look at me. Do you think it would be an issue for *me* if I wore the uniform? Please! They'd throw me out so fast."

"They can throw you *out?*" I ask, incredulous. When Jesse and Angeline nod, I reply, "I didn't know."

"Allison actually had a promotion put on hold because she was over her weight limit. It took her eight months to get it off. So, we only have one child."

"I'm sorry," Angeline laments. "I mean, it is hard, but I wouldn't trade my babies for anything."

"You come from a large family, Angeline. I'm sure it's hard for you to imagine anything else," I reply.

"It's all right," Jesse replies, a tinge of sadness on his face. "But it's what she wants to do. She wants to stay in and go for twenty."

"What do you want to do, though?" Angeline asks.

I find her boldness jarring, but Jesse takes it in stride. "I plan to get a degree in nursing, if you can believe it. I know that sounds odd, but I like the medical field. If we can stay here long enough for me to graduate, I can make good money and go anywhere in the world with it, and take my experience along. It's a mobile career."

"That's pretty cool. I never thought of that."

"Well, I hope you're a raging success in nursing." Angeline smiles broadly at him. "More power to you!"

****

Jesse joins us regularly in the yard with Adam throughout the summer, and we enjoy his company. He eventually gets a part time job while he explores local nursing programs. Apparently, there are waiting lists to enter nursing school. We don't get to know Allison nearly as well – she does work long hours, just as Jesse predicted.

Rick and I attend services at the chapel most Sundays through the summer and into fall. Shannon begins to warm to us because of our friendship with Colonel and Mrs. Davies, until she finds out my husband is in the enlisted ranks. After that, we no longer exist. I do my best to put her out of my mind.

****

October, 1992

One warm evening, Rick and I are watching the evening news together while Elizabeth reads to her favorite dolly, Madison. She makes up stories from the pictures in books.

A disturbing image crosses the screen. The headline talks about a place called Mogadishu in Somalia, a country somewhere in Africa. There are frenzied crowds of skinny, dark-skinned Africans animatedly jumping up and down and gesturing. Some of them are standing on and in the charred remains of a helicopter. A badly wounded American soldier wearing a brown shirt similar to what Rick wears under his uniform flashes across the screen. The almost forgotten pit in my stomach reappears. Another image flashes of a dead American soldier being dragged through dusty streets. The action whips the crowd into a greater frenzy. I suck my breath in. I can't believe what I'm seeing.

"Those sons of…" Rick grits his teeth, leaving the sentence hanging. He scoots to the edge of his seat.

"What is this?" I ask breathlessly. "What's going on?"

"I don't know," he murmurs, riveted to the unfolding scene.

The horrific images disappear, and are replaced by the familiar blue curtain and podium of the President of the United States. The President appears and starts talking about condemning this attack, and how we are going to take action. A really strange name is mentioned – Mohamed Farrah Aidid – and the pit in my stomach becomes a boulder.

"Turn it off. Turn it off!" I cry.

Rick looks at me, bewildered. "What? Why?"

"Just turn it off! I don't want to see this!"

Rick mutes it, but leaves the screen on. The President's lips keep moving and he pounds the podium with a stern expression. "It's all right, Heather. Don't worry."

I shake my head rapidly, pointing a shaky finger at the television. "No. No. This is just like last time. You won't have to go anywhere, will you? Tell me this won't affect you."

He wraps his arms around me. "It's okay. Don't worry."

Elizabeth eyes us curiously.

I pull away and stare at him. "You didn't answer my question. Tell me this is not going to affect you."

Rick shakes his head slowly. "I can't say that."

"Oh, my God," I mutter, covering my mouth. I know he can't tell me that.

Rick tries to comfort me, but turns the volume back up on the television. "I need to hear this."

"I don't want to!" I cry, leaping up and hurrying into the bedroom, slamming the door behind me. I fall on the bed, covering my ears.

Rick knocks softly on the door almost twenty minutes later. "Heather? You okay?"

I sit up and look at him when he slowly opens the door, wrapping my arms around my midsection. "I don't know. Are you going to leave again?"

Rick sighs and sits down on the bed next to me. "I hope not. I don't know. I won't lie."

The phone rings at that moment and I yelp. "Don't answer it!"

Rick sighs, ignores me, and leans across the bed to pick up the phone. "Hello?" he answers gruffly. His shoulders relax instantly. "Hang on." He hands the receiver to me. "It's your father."

I grab the phone. "Hello? Dad?"

"Hey there! Did you guys watch the news?"

"Yes. We saw."

"What's going to happen with Rick? Anything?"

"I hope not, Dad."

"Ah, sweetheart. I'm sorry and I hope not, too."

"Want me to talk to him?" Rick asks, extending his hand toward me.

I hand the phone to him. Rick converses with my father, reassuring him that he'll call if anything should come up.

Two days later, it happens.

Rick comes home from work with The Look on his face and my knees go weak.

"No. Tell me no," I beg him as he approaches me, an apologetic look on his face.

"Yeah," he says before folding me in his arms.

I take a deep breath and ask, "When? How long?"

He sighs and shakes his head. "Tomorrow morning and I don't know."

"Can you at least tell me where?"

"I don't know where I'm going exactly."

Tears blur my vision. "Of course not."

"I'm glad your family is here to help."

I nod woodenly. Rick promptly calls my parents.

Elizabeth and I see Rick off in the pre-dawn hours the next morning. We drive him to the passenger terminal on base. He joins a large group of about a hundred or so other uniformed personnel. Children and spouses are all in huddles saying their goodbyes, just like us. My eye catches a particular scene that stabs my heart – a young lady dressed in BDU's holding an infant that can't be more than three-months-old. She is crying, cradling the baby tightly against her chest. A man is holding them both, his head bowed.

"Rick, is she leaving her baby?" I ask incredulously, nodding toward the little family.

Rick glances at them and nods. "Yeah. She's an airman in my shop. She just came back from maternity leave about a month ago."

"That's awful! I can't believe they would do that," I lament.

Rick shrugs. "It is hard, but she chooses to wear the uniform, so…"

I tear my attention away from that awful scene, and bury my face in Rick's shoulder. Elizabeth is asleep on his other shoulder. There's a thin line of drool pooling on his name badge.

"Promise you'll be safe."

"I will. You know I will," Rick murmurs. He squeezes me tightly.

We are forced to pull apart by an announcement that it's time to load up. Rick transfers Elizabeth to my arms after burying his face in her silky hair and kissing her head. She whimpers before going limp against my shoulder, her eyes never opening.

"Please let me know where you are as soon as you can, okay?" I beg as he gathers his bags and gear.

"I will. I'll call you as soon as possible. I promise."

An intense, muscled officer walks briskly through the crowd, clapping his hands. "Time to go!" he announces repeatedly. "Let's do this!"

"Idiot," I mutter under my breath.

Rick waves before disappearing in the sea of uniforms exiting through double doors to the still dark tarmac. My eyes unwillingly flick to the scene of the young uniformed mother. She is red-faced and openly bawling as she gently transfers her infant into her husband's arms. My tears blur the scene completely out of focus, and I quickly turn my head, unable to watch more.

When I get home, I tuck Elizabeth back into bed and return to bed myself.

Curling onto my side, I have lots of questions swimming in my head. Where is he going? Will he be in harm's way? When will he be back?

CHAPTER TWENTY ONE

Winter, 1992

Rick is gone for Elizabeth's third birthday, Thanksgiving, and Christmas.

I spend a lot of time with my family, with Angeline, and some time with Jesse, as well. Allison deployed a month after Rick did. Jesse started taking prerequisite classes for the local nursing program, so we don't see a whole lot of him. He is busy working, going to class, or doing homework. Angeline and I swap out offering to have Adam come over to give Jesse a break, for which he is grateful.

Fortunately, Chris doesn't deploy for this particular event. I am happy for Angeline. She needs him here. I need Rick, too, but I don't have four children to care for.

Mom's treatments are successful; the doctor declares her to be in remission. We heave a collective sigh of relief. I'm thankful to have that behind us. Of course, she'll have to be monitored every six months, but I am confident she'll be just fine.

She's my mother. She has to be.

I have pictures of Rick on the refrigerator, and Elizabeth and I talk to him when he's able to call. She has a concept of the whole thing, but I don't know how well she processes it. I wonder if she'll have a hard time adjusting to him when he returns, like she did last time.

"Have you heard from Nicole lately?" I ask Angeline one afternoon in early February.

"The last letter I got from her was about three weeks ago, actually," she replies, holding Sophia's hands as she toddles around my living room floor.

"The last one I got was almost a month ago," I muse, watching Sophia's unsteady but determined gait.

"She must have had the baby, you know. That's going to keep her busy."

"Do you think we'll get a birth announcement? I really miss her."

"Yeah, I know. She'll send announcements when she can. We all miss her. Does Elizabeth still ask about Hailey and Bailey?"

I shake my head. "No. Not since she found Meredith." Meredith is in Elizabeth's morning preschool class; they're inseparable at school. "Elizabeth talks about her all the time."

"I think this little girl is about ready to take off," Angeline chuckles. She plucks her fingers out of Sophia's tight grasp and places her chubby little hands on the sofa to cruise around. Sophia takes the change in stride, sticking her tongue out as she propels herself forward.

"I think she'll be walking by her first birthday."

"I don't doubt that one bit," Angeline says with a sigh, rubbing her face. "Then I'll have all four of them to chase around."

"Well, Ronnie is becoming quite the helper," I nod my chin toward Ronnie who is holding his sister Leila's hand as they emerge from the hallway. They had been playing in Elizabeth's room.

Angeline glances at them, smiling. "Yes, he is. I've had to rely on him a lot during the day, especially with Edward being in Kindergarten. I feel bad about that."

"Why? I think it teaches responsibility," I counter.

She shrugs. "Maybe, but I want him to be able to have a childhood, too."

"Don't worry, he is."

The phone rings, and I lazily reach over to answer it.

"Hello?" I sigh into the receiver.

"Honey bun? It's me. I'm coming home in about a week!" Rick crows.

I sit bolt upright, grinning. "Are you serious?" Angeline's perplexed expression comes into my field of vision. I nod and lift my hand up in celebration. Her expression morphs into confusion.

"Yes. I'll be home soon!"

I cover the receiver with my hand. "Rick will be home in a week!"

Angeline claps quietly, grinning.

"Rick, I'm so glad! When will you know exactly what day?"

"Probably in another day or two. I'll let you know when they tell me," he replies. "I can't wait to see my favorite girls! How's Elizabeth doing?"

I fill him in on her life.

"Can we have a birthday cake for her when I get back? I am really sorry I missed her birthday."

"That would be wonderful. We will have candles and hats."

"Don't tell her, though. I want it to be a surprise." He remains quiet for a moment. "Do you think she will remember me when I get home?"

"I think so. It shouldn't be like last time. She's older, and you haven't been gone quite as long."

"I hope so. That really tore me up."

"I know, sweetheart. I remember."

"I have a nice surprise for you, though."

"What is it?"

Rick chuckles. "If I told you, it wouldn't be a surprise now, would it?"

Rick comes home five days later. The homecomings aren't as large for this deployment named "Operation Restore Hope," as they were for the Gulf War, but we make it an extravagant affair – my family and Angeline's family are there with banners and balloons. The troops don't come home in the same large numbers as they did before, either. Perhaps that's why.

"Welcome home, sweetheart!" I squeal, rushing into his arms.

Rick drops his bags and nuzzles my neck, wrapping his arms around me. "It's so good to be home," he breathes. "Where's my baby girl?"

I turn to see Elizabeth standing in front of us, staring up at Rick with wide eyes.

He glances at me, I nod reassuringly, and he grins as he bends down slowly. "Hey there, sweet girl! Remember me?" he asks hopefully, holding his arms out.

She regards him for a moment, before reaching in for a hug. "You went to work," she says.

His mouth drops open. He folds his daughter in his arms and scoops her up, causing her to squeal in delight. He blows raspberries on her neck, and she descends into peels of giggles before he places her on the ground. He accepts hugs, hand shakes, and kisses from everyone. He marvels at how much Angeline's children have grown, and shakes Chris' hand.

"Wow, Louise! Your hair looks great. I'm glad it's back," Rick remarks upon seeing my mother. Her hair is long enough to wear in a fashionable short bob.

"Me, too. Although I did get pretty creative with the scarves," she replies, smiling and patting Rick's cheeks between her hands. "I'm so glad you're home, Rick. So glad."

Dad claps Rick on the back. "Welcome home again, son. Glad you're back!"

"Thank you, sir," Rick shakes Dad's hand heartily. He turns from side to side, flexing his arms. "Notice anything different?"

We all stare at him puzzled. I'm the first one to notice. I gasp. There is one more stripe on Rick's sleeve than there was before. "You made Tech Sergeant!"

Rick grins. "Yup! I put it on two weeks ago. I wanted to surprise you."

Choruses of congratulations surround him. Once it calms down, he turns his attention to Jeff and Debbie. "And who is this fine young man and lovely young lady? This can't be the little squirt, can it?"

Debbie smiles at him, appreciating the compliment. "Hi, Rick. It's good to have you home again."

"How are things at college, sir?" Rick addresses Jeff.

Jeff smiles broadly, his chest puffing up slightly. "Things are going good. Being a freshman again is hard, though."

Jeff began college in the fall, but hasn't chosen a major. Mom and Dad gave him until the end of this year to declare one, but as far as I know he has given no indication what that might be.

"Are you keeping your grades up?" Rick asks sternly.

"Yep!" Jeff replies. "All A's and B's."

"That's because he's living at home," Dad quips. Jeff shrugs and grins.

"How's Cara?" Rick asks.

"She's good. She's with her parents right now," Jeff replies. "She said to tell you welcome home, and sorry she can't be here." Jeff and Cara are still going strong. Maybe she'll be the one.

"You'll get to see her this weekend when you all come over," Mom interjects. "It's your welcome home celebration."

"Seems like we do this a lot, you know," Dad jokes. I force myself to smile and laugh. Three welcome homes in four years? I don't like this trend.

"Sounds good, but right now I'm just beat. I can't wait to be in my own home with my family again," Rick replies, resting his hand on my waist.

We thank everyone for coming, and climb into the truck to go home. Elizabeth chatters all the way home, telling Rick about her friend Meredith and regaling him with her favorite stories from the books she's begun to collect. While absorbing all of this, Rick glances over at me, most likely surprised by how much her vocabulary has grown. The two of them carry on a conversation the entire ride.

Our reunion is sweet, but I wish we didn't have them at all because I don't want him to keep leaving. I married him to be with him, not away from him. These things I hold in my heart, rather than on my tongue.

The next day after we drop Elizabeth off at preschool, Rick asks, "What kind of cake should we get her? I want to have her party tonight."

"She really likes the ice cream cakes. Mint chocolate chip ice cream with vanilla cake."

Rick opens the truck door for me, and I climb in. When he settles into the driver's seat, he adds, "Sounds great! Let's go check it out. First, I need to stop by the shop real quick, and find out my schedule."

When Rick parks the truck in front of his work building, he turns to me. "Would you like to come in with me?"

"No. I'll wait here." I feel awkward and out of place in his shop.

He sighs. "All right. I'll be right back."

Rick is gone for almost fifteen minutes. When he returns, he looks like he's thinking about something.

When he climbs in, he doesn't meet my eyes.

"Rick, what's wrong?" I ask.

He shakes his head and smiles. "Nothing. I report to work in a week. Let's go get that cake." He starts the truck and pulls out.

"Rick, is something wrong?" I press.

He glances at me as he puts the truck into gear. "Everything is fine. You said she likes mint chocolate chip ice cream?"

I search his face. Maybe I misread him. "Yes."

We aren't able to get the vanilla cake, but there is a cake in the display at the bakery with her favorite ice cream with chocolate cake. "That will be fine," I say. Rick pulls the cake out of the display, carrying it to the cheerful cashier. She passes it to another worker who writes *Happy Birthday Elizabeth* on it in pink letters.

"That small cake is eighteen dollars?" Rick asks incredulously when the cashier tells him the total.

"Yes, sir," she replies cheerfully. "It's a good one."

"It better be," Rick mutters, pulling bills out of his wallet.

We also purchase a few party hats and horns before going home, just in time to quickly put the cake in the freezer before picking Elizabeth up from preschool.

"This morning went by fast," Rick remarks.

"It usually does. It will be good when she starts Kindergarten in another year, and goes for the whole day."

"I can't believe she's close to Kindergarten. Where has the time gone?" Rick muses.

I squeeze his hand rather than reply.

****

"It's my birthday again? I thought it was done," Elizabeth remarks, seeing the cake and the silly hats on our heads.

Rick scoops her up. "Well, I wanted to have a birthday cake with you because I missed it on your birthday, and I missed you, baby girl." He showers her face with kisses until she giggles.

"Do you want to wear your hat, too?" I ask as Rick puts her feet on the floor.

She grins, and bobs her head vigorously. "Yes! Yes! Yes!" she squeals. I place the frilly hat on her head. She smiles up at Rick. "I love it!"

"You look beautiful, baby girl!" Rick grins. He grabs the matches to light the candles on her cake. Rick and I sing Happy Birthday to her. She smiles, watching us both. When we're done, she blows the candles out to our applause.

"Wait til I tell Meredith I got *two* birthday cakes!" she remarks while I slice the cake. "Bigger, mommy. Bigger!"

"You want a bigger piece than that?" I ask, pointing to the one I just placed on her plate.

She nods. "Yes! Bigger!"

"I don't want you to get a tummy ache." I slice another piece, placing it next to the first one. She grins and dives in with her fork.

"We got your favorite ice cream, but they didn't have any vanilla cake, baby girl," Rick tells her, accepting a large piece from me.

"That's okay," she says, cake crumbs decorating her mouth. "I like chocolate, too."

We devour half of the small cake and talk about her favorite parts from her birthday party in October. I'm surprised at how much detail she remembers. She's a smart girl.

When she's done, she places her hand over Rick's. "I'm sorry you missed it, Daddy."

Rick clears his throat, leaning in to kiss her forehead. "Me, too, baby girl. Me, too."

****

January, 1993

We enjoy Rick's time off before he has to report back to work, this time on night shift. Rick doesn't share this information with me until halfway through the week. That must have been what he didn't want to tell me when he stopped by his shop. At least he has Friday and Saturday nights off. He'll be able to go to the chapel with us on Sundays.

Elizabeth and I have continued to go to the base chapel, and our friendship with the Davies continues. We sit next to them every week. Phyllis always takes time to talk with Elizabeth, asking her questions and listening to her answers.

"They're such nice people, Rick. I really enjoy them." I remark the following Sunday while driving home.

Rick nods.

"People like Shannon get me upset." Shannon Fabre continues to act like we don't exist. I don't want to be friends with her, but I do wish she could at least be nice. My dislike for her came to a head when she announced at one fellowship meeting that she would like to explore the possibility of having separate Sunday school classes for the officer and enlisted children. Stunned, my jaw dropped to the floor. There were a few quiet gasps in the audience. Shannon looked triumphant and a little smug.

Fortunately, Phyllis was quick to reprimand her. She rose immediately and addressed Shannon directly, her posture commanding and authoritative.

"Young lady, there are no ranks in heaven, and there should be no ranks in God's house," she said, her voice steely. "If anyone even dreams of pursuing something so ridiculous, my husband and I will worship elsewhere, and we will strongly encourage others to do the same."

Shannon visibly blanched and sat down, her shoulders squared in defiance. She had been sharply, and publicly, rebuked. As I watched the back of Shannon's neck, it got redder and redder. The matter was dropped.

"Well, don't pay her any attention," Rick replies, interrupting my memory.

"Do you even know who her husband is?" I ask.

Rick frowns, shaking his head. "No. I can't say that I do. He must be in a different squadron."

"Good."

"Heather…" Rick warns.

I hold up my hands. "I know. I'm done."

****

Adjusting to Rick's night shift is difficult. I try to be quiet during the day so he can sleep, but it's hard to do with an active three-year-old. Thankfully, although there is a chill in the air, the sun shines most days, so Elizabeth plays outdoors. Rick goes to bed at about eight o'clock in the morning and wakes bleary-eyed between one and two o'clock every afternoon, stumbling out of the bedroom.

On the fourth day, I look up in dismay as he emerges from the bedroom, rubbing his eyes and yawning. "Rick, what are you doing up? You need to get more sleep."

He zigzags his way into the living room and plops on the sofa, resting his head back. "I know. But I just can't. My body knows it's day time."

"Those black out curtains I got don't help?"

He rubs his eyes and yawns again. "They do, but it doesn't change the time of day."

"Your eyes are blood red, Rick."

He turns toward me, looking ten years older. "I know."

"Please try to get some more sleep. You need it."

He yawns widely again before answering. "I will in a little bit."

"Daddy! Read to me!" Elizabeth runs over and climbs onto Rick's lap with a large book about bugs tucked under her arm. This book has captured her attention for the last few weeks. It has pop ups and little flaps to open.

"Sweetie, let me read to you instead. Daddy is really tired," I reply, reaching for her book.

Elizabeth frowns, but climbs off of Rick's lap and sits next to me.

"I'm sorry, baby girl. I'll read to you next time, okay?" Rick adds, yawning widely again.

"Rick, go back to bed. Seriously."

Rick sighs, drags himself up and makes his way down the hallway, softly closing the door behind him.

"Why is daddy always taking a nap?" Elizabeth asks.

"Daddy has to go to work when you and I go to sleep, so he doesn't get to sleep at night."

"Why? He should work at day time," she says matter-of-factly.

"I know. But it's not our choice. His boss said that's when he has to work."

Elizabeth scowls. "He's not a nice boss."

"Let's just read your book, sweetie." I open the book to the first page and start reading. Elizabeth quickly becomes engrossed in spiders and other creepy, crawly things.

The difficult adjustment drags on. He is weary all the time, yawning even on his days off. When he's home at night, he tries to sleep normally, so he can spend the days with us. But he awakens at least twice during the night, unable to go back to sleep. Not wanting to disrupt my sleep, he gets up and wanders the house or watches television.

Three weeks into it, I can't stand it anymore. I place my fork down next to my dinner. "Rick, why don't you just tell them you can't do this? You need to work day shift, or at least they can put you on evenings."

Rick rubs his eyes, wrapping some spaghetti around his fork. "It won't do any good, Heather. I get assigned whatever shift I get assigned. There's nothing I can do about it."

"Can't you switch with someone? I mean, there has to be *something* you can do."

"Daddy needs to work right," Elizabeth adds, her mouth smeared with sauce.

Rick glances at Elizabeth and chuckles, shoveling another bite of spaghetti into his mouth. "I'll check, Heather," he replies wearily.

I wonder if he's just telling me what I want to hear, but don't press the issue.

"I am going to take a day of leave this coming Thursday, though. You and I need to go on a date. It's been too long," Rick says, looking up with red-rimmed eyes.

I perk up. "Are we going out on Thursday?" I ask. "I'll have to check with my parents to see if they can watch Elizabeth."

He shakes his head. "No, we'll go on Friday. I already cleared it with your parents and they're excited." He turns to Elizabeth. "How does a sleepover at Grandma and Grandpa's house sound?"

Elizabeth bounces up and down in her seat excitedly. "Yay!" she cries happily.

I grin. If I were Elizabeth's age, I would probably bounce up and down in my seat, too. I choose the dignified route. "Thank you, sweetheart. I appreciate it."

He smiles lopsidedly. "I know." He leans across and kisses me lightly. "It will be fun."

****

We drop an excited Elizabeth off at my parents' house on Friday. Her toiletries, clothes, and favorite books are tucked in her pink rolling suitcase. Mom has a tea party planned; it remains Elizabeth's favorite activity.

"Where are we going?" I ask, lacing my fingers in Rick's warm hand as he backs out of my parents' driveway. He looks handsome in a blue dress shirt and slacks. I lean in and whisper seductively in his ear, "Maybe we should forget dinner and just go home." His sleep schedule isn't the only thing that has suffered because of night shift.

Rick leans in and kisses me quickly before turning his attention back to the road. "Oh, we will definitely go home, but we have reservations for dinner first."

"We are going somewhere that requires reservations?"

"Yes, ma'am. It's been a long time since we had a date, and I want it to be special."

"When did you have time to plan all of this?"

He grins. "I make time for what's important to me. You are important to me."

My heart melts. "Thank you," I squeeze his hand tightly.

The restaurant is elegant and has white linen tablecloths. Rick winks at me, both of us silently knowing the significance. We enjoy a leisurely dinner of steak, lobster, and decadent cheesecake with fresh strawberries for dessert.

Afterward, we go home and spend quite a bit of time getting to know every inch of each other all over again. The whole evening is magical. I drift to sleep that night with a very content smile on my face, my head resting on Rick's chest, listening to the strong and steady beat of his heart.

The next morning, I open my eyes to see sunlight streaming in through the blinds. Rick's limp arms are draped across me and he's snoring softly. Squinting at the clock, I see it's almost ten o'clock. I wiggle myself onto my back and rub Rick's arms lazily, enjoying the moment.

Rick stirs after several minutes. "Morning, honey bun," he whispers.

I turn and kiss him. "Morning. Did you sleep well?"

He smiles, his eyes half-closed. "Better than I have in weeks."

"You can go back to sleep. I'll get up and make coffee," I say, moving to get up.

Rick tightens his grip on me for a moment, fully awake. He's staring at me.

"What?" I ask.

He hesitates briefly before his grip relaxes. "Nothing. I'll be up in a minute."

"Okay," I reply, puzzled. "Are you sure you don't want to sleep some more? Take advantage of it while you can."

He smiles and stretches. "I feel pretty good. Much better. I'll be up in a sec."

I kiss him once more before slipping on my robe. "Take your time."

The coffee is almost fully brewed when Rick enters the kitchen, scratching his head and smiling. "That smells really good," he says, inhaling the scent of the coffee.

"Go sit down and I'll bring you a cup," I tell him.

Rick wraps his arms around me from behind, resting his chin on my shoulder. "I'll wait right here." We both watch the coffee brew until the final drips make ripples in the carafe.

When we settle on the sofa with our mugs of steaming coffee, I snuggle into the crook of Rick's arm while reaching for the television remote. Just as I click it on, Rick takes the remote from me and clicks the television off again. I turn to him, perplexed.

Rick sighs, taking a sip of his coffee. "We need to talk," he says.

I pull away and tuck my foot under my leg, turning to face him, eyebrows arching. "Talk about what? You're not being deployed again, are you?" I joke.

Rick is quick to shake his head. "No, nothing like that."

"Then what?"

Rick looks at me, searching my face. I embrace the hot mug, sipping and waiting.

"Well, uh…" he starts, dropping his gaze.

"Rick, what is it?"

He looks up sharply, brushing his hand gently across my cheek. "I think it's exciting, but I'm not sure how you're going to take it."

"What? What do you mean? Rick, out with it."

Rick heaves a huge sigh, closes his eyes for a moment before looking at me. "I got orders. We are moving to Oregon in June."

"OUCH!" I yell, leaping up from the sofa. I dropped my nearly full mug of hot coffee all over my leg. Maybe I should consider iced coffee – I always seem to have a hot cup in my hand when I hear bad news.

Rick leaps up, grabbing the toppled mug and jogging toward the kitchen. He reappears quickly with a roll of paper towels and starts wiping at the coffee still on my thigh.

"I'll get that," I reply, grabbing the towels from him. Rick takes another handful of paper towels and starts blotting the sofa. I blurt questions in rapid fire. "What do you mean we're moving to Oregon? How? Why? When did you get orders? How?"

Rick continues blotting the sofa silently for long minutes.

"Rick! Answer me!" I cry, crumpling the soaked towels in my hand.

Rick takes my wet towels, adding them to his own and disappears in the kitchen. When he returns, he looks at me sheepishly. "I found out that day I went in to the shop to get my schedule. Well," he backtracks. "they were issued a few weeks before that, but I didn't know about it until then. They held them for me until I got back."

My mouth pops open. "Three and a half *weeks*? You've known for three and a half *weeks*? Why didn't you tell me?"

Rick grimaces. "Because I knew you wouldn't like it. I didn't want to just come out and tell you like I was talking about the weather. I knew you would need time to adjust."

"But, but..." I sputter. "But...how could you get orders?" I wail.

Rick sighs and shakes his head. "It happens, Heather. We are military."

I swallow the words dangling on the end of my tongue. They're very bitter going down. "But...but...Why so soon? I mean...that's only a couple months away. How can we do this?" I am on the verge of hysterics. I turn my frenetic energy on Rick. "You put in for orders behind my back, didn't you? How could you do that?!"

Rick puts his hands up. "Whoa, whoa. I did no such thing. I would never do that, Heather, and you know it. It's five months away. It's not like we have to go next month or something."

"Then what happened, Rick? Explain this to me! How could you get orders?" I shake my accusatory finger in his face. My heart is racing.

Rick drops his hands and his eyes narrow. "Heather," he says in that low, slow voice one uses on a tantrum-throwing toddler. "Calm down. Let's sit down and talk."

With effort, I reign in my anger. Purposefully lowering my voice, I reply, "I don't want to calm down." I stare at him. "How could you do this?"

A cloud descends over his face. "Heather, I didn't *do* this. I didn't ask for this. That's not how it works."

"Then how did it happen?"

He takes a deep breath. His voice remains low and slow. "Heather, sometimes orders just come down. Oregon was on my dream sheet when I first enlisted, that's why it's still there. I can't have a blank dream sheet – there are eight slots to fill on it. That's probably how it happened. Okay? I promise I did not ask for this."

I know he's right.

Rick stares at me warily, neither of us speaking for long moments.

Gradually, powerless, the fight seeps out of me and I drop limply on the sofa with a huff. I cover my face with my hands.

"Heather, it's all right. It's just Oregon. It's not like we're going to Siberia or something," Rick attempts to soothe me.

It may as well be Siberia. We will be so far away from my family. How will we get along without them? How will they get along without *us*, especially if Mom relapses? How can I ever say goodbye to Angeline? The thought makes my heart sick. She's my next door neighbor and my best friend. She and I haven't heard from Nicole in awhile, although we both got a birth announcement. Stan and Nicole had a healthy baby boy named Robert. But we have heard nothing since – will that happen to us, too? Will we lose touch with each other?

I can't believe we have to move. I thought we'd be here longer. I am just getting used to my life and now I have to change it all. Leave my family and my friends. How can I do this?

I have to do this because I am a military wife.

CHAPTER TWENTY TWO

Spring, 1993

We are moving. We are actually leaving Texas. We are leaving my family. I always knew it could happen, someday. I never imagined someday would come so soon.

I'm not prepared.

When we told my parents, initially they were stunned into silence. But they quickly showered us with hugs and encouragement about what an adventure we are in for in the Pacific Northwest. Jeff quickly fell in line – he and Rick man-hugged each other.

Debbie took it hard. She's sixteen and riding the roller coaster of emotions her age brings. I love spending time with her. She shares her heartbreaks and teen angst with me when we go out for ice cream. She's an incredible aunt to Elizabeth, too – painting Elizabeth's nails and reading to her endlessly. When the look of shock wore off after I told her, she began to cry great big tears. I wrapped my arms around her and we clung to each other, both sobbing pitifully.

"I'm sorry, Debbie. I am so sorry, but I'll always be just a letter or phone call away," I reassured her.

She couldn't do anything other than nod and bawl.

Telling Angeline was worse. Way, way worse.

I barely got the words out before I broke down into sobs. She quickly followed my lead, and we both ended up a red-faced, swollen, snotty mess. Leila and Sophia both toddled over to their mother and patted her back while Elizabeth put her favorite dolly, Madison, on my lap. Edward and Ronnie seemingly ignored us, but cast sideways glances in our direction every few minutes while silently rearranging their cars on the floor of Angeline's living room.

"You have to leave in June?" Angeline asked incredulously, dabbing at her eyes. "That's so soon."

"I know," I said, sniffing. "I don't want to go."

"Well," Angeline replied, grabbing another tissue. "I guess we always knew it would happen to one of us sooner or later."

"I don't want it to. I hate this part of it, Angeline."

"Me, too," she said, smiling. "You're my best friend."

I sucked my lips in and took a deep breath, words failing me.

"We won't lose touch with each other. I can't imagine that happening," she said, although her eyes didn't match her words. "You know, if it weren't for the military, we never would have met. I'm thankful for that."

"Me, too. I don't want to lose touch with you, Angeline."

"We won't," she replied. We both hoped it would be true.

I'll do my best to make sure it is true.

****

June, 1993

I watch as the movers quickly and efficiently wrap, box, and tape everything that materially defines my life, calmly loading it all into the large orange and white moving van to ship to Oregon. They've only been here for four hours and the house is nearly vacant. Each time a box or piece of furniture disappears into the gaping maw that is the moving van, a little piece of my heart tears off. My life is disappearing from this place.

This is actually happening. I clap my hand over my mouth, fighting back the nausea that has been building the last few weeks. Every thought of this move makes me queasy, angry, scared, and bewildered all at the same time.

I step out of my soon-to-be vacant house and into the brilliantly hot Texas sun. It's blazing outside, but I turn my face toward the sun with closed eyes. I want to take the heat and sun with me. From what I have read, Oregon is mostly dreary, cloudy, and rainy. I am not looking forward to it.

I mutter a complaint under my breath.

"What's that?" Rick asks, trotting up the walkway with two fast food bags in one hand and drinks in a cardboard holder in the other.

I smile tightly, shaking my head. "Nothing. Need some help?"

"Sure. Do you want to sit out in the grass and have a picnic?" he asks cheerfully as another dolly loaded with boxes zips toward him on the walkway. Rick quickly sidesteps, giving the movers the right of way.

"We can borrow two of Angeline's chairs. She won't mind." I grab two chairs from her yard and haul them over. Rick hands me a drink and my cheeseburger.

We eat silently for a few minutes, me taking small bites while Rick is already onto his second cheeseburger. I fight back tears each time another load of our things disappears.

"Heather, it'll be okay," Rick says, noticing my half-eaten cheeseburger sitting ignored on my lap.

I swallow hard and nod.

"Are you going to finish that?" he asks, gesturing at my lap.

I consider the burger for a moment. "No. You can have it."

Rick takes it, finishing it in two bites. When he's wiped his mouth, he looks me over. "You feeling all right? You don't look so good."

I shrug. "I just don't want to go."

Rick crumples the wrappers and stuffs them in the bag before turning his attention to me. "I know. It'll be all right. You'll see. You'll make new friends and get involved in stuff. Just give it a chance." He covers my hand with his own, squeezing. "Please?"

I look at him sadly and nod, attempting to smile.

"That's my girl." He leans in and pecks me on the cheek.

The movers are done by three o'clock. Gaping at the lonely emptiness of our home, my knees almost buckle. Other than random dust bunnies, all that remains is what we left in the bathroom. Seasoned military folks had warned us that if it was in the house, the movers would pack it. This includes full garbage cans, purses, and refrigerated items. So we piled our luggage and other necessities into the bathtub and all over the small bathroom, firmly closing the door with a "DO NOT TOUCH!" warning sign taped on it, just in case.

Our flight leaves in four days.

Walking silently through the desolate landscape of our home and realizing the magnitude of the meaning, I promptly run for the bathroom and throw up in the sink because I can't get to the toilet. My suitcase is in the way.

We check into a TLF house that evening. It is bare bones and minimalistic with a definite military flavor to the boring furniture, but it will do for four days. It looks exactly like the one Nicole stayed in before she left for Germany.

My eyes prick with tears at the memory of her standing in the doorway of a house like this, looking so forlorn and vulnerable. I wonder how she's doing and how she did moving not just away, but across the ocean. At least I can still drive home if I really need to.

Elizabeth finds the whole business an exciting adventure. I envy her and try to take a cue from her attitude.

The house has three bedrooms, even though we only require two. Elizabeth carefully scouts her choices before selecting which room will be hers.

"I like the view here better," she proclaims, placing her pink luggage at the foot of the bed. "I'll take this one!"

"You made a good choice, baby girl," Rick replies. "Are you ready to go to Miss Angeline's house now? I'm sure she's waiting for us."

"Madison is too tired. She wants to sleep in her new room," Elizabeth says, carefully placing Madison's head on the pillow, covering her with the blanket. "She likes it bestest, too."

Once we haul our luggage into the house and place them where they need to be, we load back up in the truck for the journey to Angeline's house. I carefully avoid letting my gaze fall on what was my home. I can't bear to see it void and lifeless.

Chris and Angeline insisted on having dinner with us before we go and I, of course, want to spend as much time as possible with them before we leave.

When we arrive at Angeline's house, she's been crying – her eyes are puffy and her nose is stuffed up.

"Sorry," Chris says apologetically, hugging each of us. "She's trying, but she's a mess."

"I can't help it," Angeline says, her voice ending on a high octave. She pats her cheeks and blows her breath out. "So, let's eat."

She made a beautiful dinner. It's delicious, but it feels like rocks going down my throat. I end up pushing the food around my plate. When I glance up halfway through the meal, I see Angeline doing the same.

Chris clears his throat. "I hear it's beautiful out there. Lots of great activities to do in the summer. Very friendly people, too. The base has a great MWR. You can rent boats and stuff in the summer."

Rick smiles gratefully at him. "Yeah, that's what we've read. I think it will be nice. We can hike Mt. Hood and see the Pacific Ocean. It will be a lot of fun. You guys are welcome to visit any time."

"That would be great. That whole area is really green and the mountains are spectacular," Chris continues encouragingly.

"Yes, it will be a great place to take some awesome pictures. Don't you think, Heather?" Rick asks, nudging me with his knee.

"Yep. It will be just wonderful," I answer flatly.

Rick sighs, and spears another bite of broccoli.

****

Saying goodbye to Chris and Angeline is the second hardest thing I've ever had to do, other than saying goodbye to my own family.

Chris and Angeline, as well as my family – including Jeff's girlfriend Cara, are at the airport to send us off. There isn't a dry eye in our group. The children cry because the adults do.

Fierce hugs are exchanged all around, with the fiercest coming from Mom and Angeline.

Even my father cries. He was holding it together, joking even, until the final boarding call rang out overhead. When it came time to give him a hug, he stared at me for a moment and I watched his eyes mist, then water before his whole face crumpled. He grabbed me in a death grip of a hug, great sobs racking his body.

It was excruciating to have Dad cry like that.

"You take care of yourself, my baby girl. You take care. I love you. I love you," Dad cries into my ear.

"Honey bun, it's time," Rick whispers close by, his voice hoarse. "I'm sorry."

Dad squeezes me very hard for a second longer before pushing me back from himself. He's wearing a forced smile that looks more like a grimace.

"You guys gotta go. Don't want to miss your plane," Dad says, his voice ending stronger than when it began. "You let us know as soon as you can that you arrived safely, all right?"

The last picture in my head of this whirlwind, agonizing moment is of everyone important to me, other than my husband and daughter, standing and waving at us, their cheeks shiny. Mom has one arm around Dad and the other around Angeline, who is holding Leila. Debbie is flanked by Dad and Jeff, and Cara – all arms interlaced. Chris is holding Sophia while Ronnie and Edward stand in front of their parents, nudging each other with their hips and grinning.

This hurts. A lot. I don't ever, ever want to do this again.

It is a high cost to pay indeed.

****

The flight to Oregon is a blur. It's still daylight when we arrive, but when our impending descent into Portland is announced, I crane my neck across Elizabeth's seat and press my face into the little oval window, straining to catch a glimpse of the city. I can't see it – it's shrouded in clouds that look like dirty cotton balls.

"What do you see?" Rick asks from his aisle seat.

I sigh. "Nothing. It's covered by ugly clouds."

The engine whines and my ears pop as our plane disappears into the clouds and the view becomes obscure. The brilliant sunshine disappears and is replaced by a dim light. I feel the light in my spirit disappear along with the sun.

This is real.

Finally, we emerge from the underbelly of the clouds and I see Portland and the Pacific Northwest for the first time. My eyes scan the view. There is a river snaking its way through the city, skyscrapers and green trees everywhere. Gone are the vast open plains of Texas. I swallow hard.

"Do you see the Columbia River?" Rick asks, leaning as far over in his seat as he can.

I nod and point. "I think that's it right there."

Rick bobs his head up and down, straining to see. The plane suddenly dips down on our side as the plane turns and the city fills our window.

"Oh! There it is. I see it!" Rick exclaims excitedly.

The tiny buildings and cars become larger and more defined as we continue our descent. The streets are teeming with life – there are cars going everywhere. It's like watching some advanced species of ants in a frenzied state of activity. I have never flown before. It is amazing to see what life looks like from above.

Finally, the plane touches down on the runway and it feels like the pilot slammed on the brakes because all three of us are suddenly bending forward as we quickly lose momentum. Trepidation and excitement build.

"Is somebody going to meet us, Rick?"

"Yeah. My sponsor is supposed to be here. His name is Sergeant McPark."

"Good," I reply. That's a relief.

However, when we get off the plane, Rick scans the crowd gathered at the gate and frowns. "Maybe he's down in baggage claim," he reassures me.

When we get to baggage claim, Rick scans the crowd once more. There's no Sergeant McPark to be seen.

"Well, let's get our stuff and look around again. I know I gave him our flight info," Rick says. Once we collect our luggage, Rick directs me to wait near a row of chairs while he searches for Sergeant McPark.

Rick returns almost ten minutes later wearing a frown. "I don't think he's here."

"Rick…"

"Don't worry," Rick interrupts me. "Maybe he got stuck in traffic or something. Let's just get a rental car and a map. It'll be fine."

"I'm hungry!" Elizabeth whines, rubbing her eyes.

Rick sighs. "Let's get something to eat on the road. It's too expensive in the airport. We'll stop at a drive through. Do you want some chicken nuggets, sweet girl?" Rick asks, smiling at Elizabeth.

She smiles and nods vigorously. I open a bag of peanuts I saved from the plane and hand them to her. She munches on the peanuts, one by one.

Once Rick secures a rental car and a map, we haul our luggage out to the lot. Rick huffs placing the luggage in the trunk of our mid-sized sedan while stuffing some into the back seat, while I work to get Elizabeth's car seat installed nice and tight. It's ridiculous the amount of things we had to bring with us; I tried to keep it to a minimum, but it will take weeks before our household goods arrive.

Once we pile into the car, Rick opens the map so that it covers most of the dashboard. He searches the map for the information we need. Once he locates it, he folds it to show only that area.

"There," he says, tapping a point on the map. "There's the base. Here's the airport." He drags his finger across the map, tapping another point.

"Let's figure this out before we leave."

We search the highways and city streets, plotting our course. Once we've determined the best route, we launch our adventure into the city of Portland. The traffic is a nightmare. The streets wind and turn and there are people everywhere. Once during our journey, there is a break in the spitting rain and clouds. I notice snow-capped mountains in the background and can't believe my eyes – it's June!

"Well," Rick says, gripping the steering wheel, his eyes darting between cars. "It's not the desert of Texas."

"But snow in the mountains in June? That's crazy," I remark.

"It is quite different here. It feels fabulous outside. No more sweating!" Rick remarks cheerily.

I shrug and remain silent. I like the desert heat. It's summer. It's supposed to be hot.

"Daddy," Elizabeth whines. "I want chicken nuggets. I'm *hungry!*" Elizabeth whines.

Rick sighs. "All right, sweet girl. Heather, keep your eyes peeled and tell me where to get off."

Fortunately, there's a fast food restaurant at almost every exit from the highway, so within fifteen minutes, we are in line behind three other cars at a drive through.

Once I have Elizabeth settled in with her chicken nuggets, French fries, and milk, I turn my attention back to the map. We are back on the highway, but rush hour traffic has picked up and we are more stop than go at this point.

"*Mommy*, I have to *pee!*" Elizabeth whines twenty minutes later.

I peer at the map and compare our remaining distance to the traffic. "We better pull over again."

Rick mutters under his breath, but sighs and turns his blinker on; slowly making his way off the highway once more. Once we all go to the bathroom at a gas station, Rick asks the attendant if there's a quicker way to get to the base. The pimply faced young man with scraggly hair scratches his head and replies, "Not that I know of, dude. Traffic sucks this time of day, but I don't know any other way to get there that would be better. Sorry."

The remaining journey to the base is fraught with frustration in the front and whining in the back. It is early evening by Portland time, but approaching bed time for Elizabeth by Texas time. I go through my entire bag of tricks trying to keep her entertained, to include all of her Barney books and singing her favorite songs, but an hour and a half later she's rubbing her eyes and quietly sobbing.

Finally, we arrive at the main gate of Holtburn Air Force Base. Once we get the proper vehicle pass to get on base, the security guard gives us directions to the TLF office. While Rick makes his way onto the base, I take in the new scenery. The buildings match the weather – dreary gray and blue with large brown identifying numbers on them. I see road signs that say "Commissary" and "BX" with arrows pointing in their direction. There are other directional signs, too, but they make no sense to me – they're a jumble of letters and numbers that look more like license plates than destinations. When we finally pull into the parking lot of one of the gray and blue buildings, Rick announces, "We're here!"

"Finally," I sigh.

Elizabeth has fallen into a fitful sleep. Unfortunately, I have to wake her. She's not happy about it. She wails at first, but eventually limps along, holding my hand and carrying her dolly Madison in the other.

"Mommy, carry me!" she wails, her arms thrust upward.

"Sweetie, I can't. You're too heavy for me to carry," I reply soothingly. "Come on. We're almost done. I promise."

She throws her head back, whining, and trudges reluctantly alongside. She and I wait in some chairs in the lobby while Rick approaches the front desk. I'm anxious to get settled so I can call my parents. Elizabeth climbs onto my lap and sucks her thumb; something she hasn't done for over a year. Within minutes, she goes limp.

When Rick approaches us, he's frowning.

"Rick, please tell me they have our reservation. Please," I beg him. I'm on the verge of tears and a tantrum myself.

"Yes, they have our reservation, but we have to drive to get there."

"What? What do you mean drive to get there? We are here, aren't we?"

Rick sighs and rubs his scruffy chin. He gestures down the hall to what I thought were hotel room doors. "This is the reception desk. These rooms are all for singles, not families. We have to drive to the housing area. I got our key. Let's go."

"For the love of…" I let my sentence trail off. "Will you carry her, please? She's asleep."

I transfer Elizabeth into Rick's arms. She moans, turns her head and with a heavy sigh, goes limp over his shoulder. Madison drops to the floor. I quickly retrieve her and follow Rick out to the rental car. As soon as Rick places Elizabeth into her booster seat, she wakes up and begins to wail, loudly. I tuck Madison into her arm and climb into my own seat, slamming the door behind me.

"Heather…" Rick begins, but I cut him off with one look.

"I don't care. Right now, I just don't care, Rick. Take us to wherever the hell it is we are staying." I cross my arms and stare out the window. Elizabeth continues to wail loudly in the back seat.

I have had enough.

Finally, we pull into what I hope is the house we will be staying in. It took another thirty minutes to get there – the base is pretty spread out and the directions we were given were either lacking, or Rick got them wrong. It's almost nine thirty by the time we drag ourselves, and our luggage, into the house.

My first priority is finding which room Elizabeth is sleeping in. I quickly pull her pajamas out of her pink suitcase, help her change, brush her teeth and wash her face and hands and put her to bed. Her eyes barely open through the whole process. She moans once, rolls over, squeezes Madison, and goes soundly to sleep. There is no night light in the sparsely furnished room, so I leave her bedroom door cracked and turn the bathroom light on. If she wakes up in the middle of the night, she'll be disoriented, but I don't want her stumbling around in the dark. The room Rick and I will sleep in is right next door, so I will leave our door open, too.

"I have no doubt you'll hear her if she stirs," Rick says. "You've got the ears of a bat."

I manage a tight smile; I am not in the mood to talk. My stomach simultaneously growls while a wave of nausea pours over me. I clamp my hand to my mouth and take a deep breath.

"You okay?" Rick asks, walking past me carrying our suitcase into the bedroom.

I take another deep breath. When he returns, I nod. "Yes. I am just hungry. I need to call my parents, too."

"The phone should be in the living room," he replies. "We'll need to find the commissary tomorrow and get some groceries. I can order a pizza for now, I think. There should be a phone book around here somewhere." He looks around the sparse living room. When he spies the phone sitting on a table next to the love seat, he opens the drawer and pulls out the phone book. I explore our new temporary home for the first time while he orders the pizza. I'll call my parents when he's done.

The house is very simple and lacking in any real taste, but it will do. The kitchen is outdated, but functional and clean. The dining room set seats four around a simple round table. We have the very basics in terms of silverware, dishes, and pots and pans. I open the refrigerator – the only thing in it is a box of baking soda.

Rick's head pops around the corner. "I ordered two cheese pizzas. Is that all right for you?"

"That's fine," I reply, looking in every drawer and door. The cheap linoleum flooring has seen much better days, but I don't care. This isn't my house.

"They should be here in about half an hour," Rick says, approaching me with his arms out-stretched. "You all right? I know it's been a long day."

I give Rick a quick hug. "Yeah. I am going to call my parents. I'm sure they're worried sick." I pull away and settle myself into the love seat, picking up the phone. I call my parents collect because I don't know how to work the long distance here.

My mother answers on the first ring. "Hello?" she asks anxiously.

My eyes mist over at the sound of my mother's voice, knowing she's so far away. "Mom?" My voice is squeaky.

"Leonard! It's Heather! Are you okay, sweetheart? Did you guys make it all right?"

"We're fine. Mom…" I start to sob.

"Oh, honey. I know. I miss you, too."

I can't manage more than a squeak.

"Listen, Heather. It's going to be all right. You'll get used to it," Mom's soothing voice reaches across the miles.

Finally, I gather myself and respond coherently. "Thanks, Mom. We finally got here. It was difficult. The traffic is crazy and we had to find our own way because nobody met us at the airport."

"What? What do you mean nobody met you at the airport? Wasn't somebody supposed to?"

"Yeah, well, supposed to doesn't mean a whole lot."

"I'm sorry."

I continue to vent to her for several minutes not only about our journey but about the weather, which is too cold. Finally, a knock on the door interrupts my complaining – the pizza has arrived. My stomach growls on cue.

"Mom, I gotta go. The pizza just got here and I am starving. I don't want to drive your phone bill up too much, either."

"Oh, don't you worry about that. You can call me any time you want to. Give Elizabeth and Rick hugs and kisses from us, all right? We love you guys."

"I love you, too," I reply, eyes misting over once again. Once I hang up, I cry a few more tears before Rick appears carrying two large slender square boxes.

"Still hungry?" he asks, taking note of my wet cheeks.

I nod. "I'll get some plates."

"Don't bother dirtying up dishes we'll just have to wash. We can eat right from the box." So we do. Even though I'm ravenous, I eat two pieces and declare myself full. The nausea hasn't dissipated – I'm exhausted. I know I'll feel better after a good night's sleep. I hope the beds are more comfortable than the living room furniture.

Rick stuffs half of his fifth slice into his mouth, arching his eyebrows at me. "You sure you're full? You should be hungrier than that. There's plenty here." He pushes the box toward me.

I wrinkle my nose and push it away. "No thanks. I am just going to get ready for bed."

I quickly search through my bag, taking out only the toiletry items I need and place them in the medicine chest in the single bathroom. I robotically go through the motions, getting to bed quickly. Rick isn't far behind – he's just as tired. We barely mumble goodnight to each other before drifting off to sleep.

I didn't hear Elizabeth get up in the night. Apparently she did, though, because when I awaken in the morning she is snuggled into the crook of my arm just as I am snuggled into the crook of Rick's arm.

I lift my head and grimace at the unfamiliar surroundings. It is day time, but the sun isn't filling the room like it is supposed to. It's muted, reluctant to reveal itself. Reality dawns and I remember where I am. Heaviness falls on my heart as my head falls back on the pillow. The sun isn't out because it's a dreary, rainy day outside. I shiver and pull the covers over my shoulders.

"You awake?" Rick mumbles, rolling onto his back and stretching.

"Mm hmm," I reply quietly, not wanting to awaken Elizabeth. "When did she crawl into bed with us?"

Rick peers over my shoulder. "Oh, I didn't know she was here. I slept hard."

"Me, too," I reply, yawning widely. "What time is it?"

Rick checks the bedside clock located on his nightstand. "It's almost eight."

"That's it? It feels like it's later."

"That's because your body is on Texas time," he replies, chuckling. "I need coffee."

"I'll get up, too. Coffee sounds good, but we don't have any," I remind him.

Rick groans. "That's right. I guess I'll go get that while I get breakfast – unless you want cold pizza for breakfast. There's still half a pizza in the fridge." I wrinkle my nose in disgust. Rick knows I can't stand cold pizza. He grins. "That's what I thought. I'll throw on some clothes, and be back in a jiffy."

While Rick is gone, I peek through the blinds to see what it looks like outside behind this house. It's gray and dreary, just as I suspected. But the grass, what little there is, is vibrant green and sprinkled with pine needles. Evergreen trees are everywhere. There's a small playground not far away in a clearing. Elizabeth will have somewhere to play that doesn't require driving.

"That's a bonus," I murmur to myself. Elizabeth sighs, and I glance at her limp form. Her mouth makes little sucking motions and she turns over, still asleep. I smile and pat her bottom, covering her up before I tiptoe out of the room.

I look through all the windows that will afford me a new vantage point from this house. There is one window that offers a side view, which is of the street. Across the street are other multi-plex houses that look just like this one; we are in an end unit. The front overlooks the parking lot. The houses are arranged in a horseshoe pattern with a parking lot in the middle. There is an island of earth in the middle of the parking lot from which springs an enormous evergreen tree. The branches are so low to the ground that I know Elizabeth will want to climb it. I frown at the height, however. She could get pretty far up there.

Rick returns forty-five minutes later carrying bags of food. I really don't want to see another fast food bag again for awhile. It's making me ill. I'm sure of it.

"What did you get?" I ask, taking the drinks he's balancing.

Rick kisses me on the cheek before plopping the bags down on the dining room table. "Sausage and cheese biscuits. Plus hash browns, orange juice, milk, and coffee. I wanted to cover my bases."

"Did you remember ketchup? You know Elizabeth won't eat hash browns without it."

"Yup," he replies, pulling the packets out of one bag. "And I even got extra napkins."

I inhale deeply when I peel the lid off my coffee cup. "Ahhh, that smells heavenly."

"Oh, yes," Rick sighs, inhaling his just as deeply. "Gotta love that brew."

I unwrap my biscuit and take a large bite, feeling ravenous. Rick wolfs down two before eating a hash brown.

"How many did you buy? Be sure to save some for Elizabeth," I joke.

Rick finishes the hash brown and a third biscuit. "Don't worry, I got plenty. I even got you two, just in case." He hands me another biscuit, which I decline in favor of a hash brown.

"I wish we could have packed our bikes. I would have liked to ride around here. It may be dreary, but it's kind of pretty, too."

Rick smiles. "Yeah. That would have been nice. But our household goods will arrive before you know it and we can do just that. We will pick out some new favorite spots." He reaches over and squeezes my hand.

"Mommy? Daddy?" Elizabeth stumbles around the corner, her hair wild and her face screwed up, blinking at the bright kitchen light. She's holding tightly to Madison, whose hair is equally wild.

"Hey, there, sweet girl! You hungry?" Rick says enthusiastically, patting his knee.

Elizabeth's mouth forms a large "O" as she makes her way over to her father in a zigzag pattern. He places her gently on his knee while I unwrap a biscuit for her.

"Here you go, sweetie. Do you want orange juice or milk?" I ask.

"Juice," she says.

"What do you say?" I remind her.

"Please," she answers obediently. She finishes half of her biscuit and the entire hash brown, with ketchup. When she's all done, she perks up and looks around excitedly while sipping her juice. "Is this our new home?"

"No. This is just where we are going to stay until we find our new home," Rick explains.

Elizabeth pokes her lips out, concentrating. "Okay," she replies. "Madison says she wants a house just like our old one."

"Well, we can't have one exactly like our old one, but I'm sure it will still be great because it will be our home. We will have all our old stuff in it." Rick addresses the doll. "Is that okay, Madison?"

"Madison says that will be just fine," Elizabeth replies confidently.

****

Settling into the temporary house was easy compared to settling into the new base. Apparently, this Sergeant McPark who was supposed to be Rick's sponsor had been reassigned two weeks before we were scheduled to arrive, and we had fallen through the cracks. His new squadron never assigned him a new sponsor. I tally this latest experience on my mental list of challenges we face in the military.

We spent our first weekend at Holtburn exploring the base and unpacking our meager belongings into the house, trying to make it a home for whatever length of time we will stay there. Elizabeth spied not only the tree in the middle of the parking lot, but also the playground in the back.

Both worked as objects of bribery – I promised her playground or climbing time if she will only finish her lunch, go with Daddy and me to the commissary, bathe, or wash her hands.

I spend a good amount of time on the phone talking to my family and to Angeline. She and I both bawl at the beginning and end of our conversations. Since Sophia's birth, Angeline has never gotten a handle on her emotions. Now when she cries, I cry.

The commissary here is undergoing renovation which makes it confusing and overwhelming. The center of the commissary is completely blocked off with a floor to ceiling wall of plywood. A third of the floor space is taken up by it. We have to snake our way around it in the front and back just to get to the other side. Finding everything we need, to include salt, pepper, and facial tissue, is exhausting.

When we're done shopping almost two hours later, I turn to Rick and declare, "I am *never* shopping here again."

Rick gapes at me. "Seriously? You think we can afford to shop for groceries off base? There's no way."

"Did you see the chaos in there? Rick, I will lose my mind if I have to go in there again."

"They're supposed to be done in another month or so," the bagger informs me cheerily as he loads the groceries in the trunk of our rental car. "Did you guys just get here?"

"Yes, we did," Rick replies. "How long have you been here?"

"Oh, I retired last year. We got here about six years ago. It's a nice base. There's a lot to do and see. My wife has family in the area. Where did you guys come from?"

I bite my lip and remain silent.

"We came from Texas. My wife has family there, so it's hard." I smile quickly and hustle Elizabeth into her seat before getting in the car myself to wait for Rick.

Once the groceries are loaded and Rick slides into the driver's seat, he turns the ignition on and faces me. "That was rude," he says quietly.

I cast a glance at him. "Sorry. I didn't mean to be rude. I can't speak without crying."

Rick squeezes my hand and drops the subject.

****

"The good news is I'm not on night shift this time," Rick reports when he comes home Monday afternoon. He checked into his new squadron this morning and has been gone all day.

"What's the bad news?" I ask out of habit. There always seems to be bad news.

Rick grimaces. "Well, I am on day shift, but I have Wednesdays and Thursdays off."

I smile tightly and shove the dishtowel onto the oven handle roughly, smoothing it out. "Of course you do."

"Which would you prefer, Heather? Night shift or week days off?" he asks, an edge to his voice.

I glare at him, steel in my voice. I'm feeling very cranky lately. "Because those are our only choices, right?"

Rick presses his lips together, shaking his head. "Where's Elizabeth? Is she playing outside?"

"She's climbing that tree. She met a little boy whose family got here yesterday."

"Did you meet them yet?" he asks.

"No."

"It's good she has somebody to play with. I'm sure there will be more kids around soon. Maybe they were all out sight-seeing or something this weekend."

"Maybe," I reply sullenly.

Rick wraps his arms around me. "You'll make new friends and do new things. Just give it a chance." He kisses me softly. "Please?" He whispers and kisses me again, a little longer this time.

I pull away and search his face. "I will because I love you. I just miss my family."

"I know. But Elizabeth and I are your family, too. We are here."

"Yes." He's right. I chose Rick, now I have to walk out that choice.

That night Rick and I come together for the first time in a few weeks. There's an urgency to reconnect. We both feel it. We both need it. It's enough.

CHAPTER TWENTY THREE

Summer, 1993

The stress of the move has a huge impact on me. My appetite disappears and I am tired, even in the middle of the day. It's difficult to get a good night's sleep when the sun rises at five and sets at ten. Who would've thought just a few hours' time difference and diminished sunlight would affect me like this?

To be honest, the sun does appear. Rick makes a point of bringing it to my attention, but it's not the same. While bright, there is no heat. The Texas sun blazes on my skin, warming me through. This Oregon sun barely even registers on my skin. It's like having thirst and only being able to whet my lips. I want to drink in the heat, but it isn't there.

We spend a total of one month in the temporary house with Rick starting his new job and new shift the first week we are here. During his time off, he forces me to drive, so I'll become used to where things are on base. I hate to admit it, but it works. We even venture off base a few times, and although traffic is heavy, this place does have a certain beauty. The snow-capped mountains are breath-taking. I purchase some post cards with pictures of those mountains and send them to my family, and to Angeline. I don't bother sending them to Nicole – the last letter I sent was returned with no forwarding address. It made me very sad. I believe if she could've kept in touch, she would have. I hope they're all right.

In our month in the temporary house, Elizabeth meets, plays with, and says goodbye to ten children. She finds it bewildering.

"Mommy, why do people here come and leave so much?" she asks one evening, watching yet another friend's stuffed family car drive away.

"These are only temporary houses, Elizabeth. We are only staying in this house for a little while, too. Some families, like us, are just moving to

Oregon. Some are leaving Oregon and going to other places."

"Oh." She remains silent afterwards, lost in her own thoughts.

Our turn to pack up comes on yet another sunny but heatless day in the middle of July. The temperature never hits eighty degrees. We are able to move right into housing this time – new houses were built here in the last few years. I'm surprised, considering the President has ordered a reduction in the military budget. The houses are not what I'm used to in Texas – there is no stucco or desert landscaping. These houses have vinyl siding with grass and pine trees in the front yards. The floor plans are different, too. The bland white walls are the same. Our house has three bedrooms and two bathrooms.

While I lament about the plain white walls and boring beige carpet, Rick does his best to cheer me up.

"It will look really nice when our household goods come," he says.

They arrive a week after we move into housing, and I am thankful. We were able to borrow some really bad furniture, dented cookware, and chipped dishes from Family Services.

It was a very long week.

It made my skin crawl to sleep on a stained and used mattress, but it really bothered me to put my daughter on one, too. I splurged and bought our own bedding to include new pillows, doubling up the blankets on the naked mattress before placing the new sheets on them for both our bed, as well as Elizabeth's.

"Do you really think that's necessary?" Rick asks when he sees me working to stretch the fitted sheets over the layers of blankets.

"Did you see how stained this thing is, Rick? I am not placing a single foot in these beds without some sort of protection," I huff, pulling and tucking the sheet over the last corner.

Rick shakes his head and chuckles. "Okay, knock yourself out. I slept on worse in the dorms, you know. As a matter of fact," he glances at the furniture. "this looks a lot like what I used to have in the dorms. They probably just recycled it."

My nose wrinkles in disgust. "Ew! Are you serious?" I glance around in horror. "Do you really think they did that? I can only imagine what has happened on this…"

The thought of what may have occurred on this furniture is too much. I bolt for the bathroom to wretch.

Rick's laughter follows me all the way to the bathroom. "Heather, I am sure they've cleaned it since. It's all quite safe."

I glare at him and wretch again. Finally, when I'm emptied, Rick hands me a clean washcloth.

"Thanks," I gasp. Wiping my mouth after rinsing, I cast a sideways glance at him. He is obviously trying not to smile, but he can't hide the mirth in his blue eyes. "It's not funny, Rick. There could be all kinds of cooties in that furniture."

We argue briefly over the history and legacy of the loaner furniture until our doorbell rings. Rick looks at me quizzically.

"Expecting anyone?" he asks. I shrug and shake my head. "I'll go answer it. You finish getting cleaned up."

I cannot believe they recycled this furniture. Who does that? I grumble to myself a few moments longer before Rick returns.

"Who was it?"

"It was a neighbor kid. She wanted to know if we had any kids for her to play with."

My mood perks up. "It was a little girl? Is Elizabeth playing with her now?" I ask excitedly.

Rick nods. "Yeah. She's out front. Check it out." He slides open the little bathroom window and we peer out through the screen. Elizabeth and the little girl are sitting under the large pine tree in the front yard. Elizabeth is holding Madison and the little girl has a Barbie doll in her hand. It looks like the dolls are talking to each other.

"I'm so glad!" I exclaim. "Where does she live?"

Rick slides the window closed. "Let's get out of the bathroom first. The little girl's name is Katherine. She said she lives across the street. I don't know which house it is, though," Rick informs me while we make our way into the living room. I flinch when Rick sits on the sofa and he notices. "Heather, it's okay. I promise. You aren't going to catch anything." He pats the cushion next to him.

I carefully sit down, not letting any naked skin touch the sofa material.

Rick sighs. "You're not going to be grossed out for the whole week, are you?"

"Yes," I reply. "I am."

The next day, I solve the problem by using the bed sheets provided to us as sofa covers, much to Rick's chagrin. He thinks I'm ridiculous. I'm just being cautious.

A deep sense of relief floods me when the moving truck arrives on Wednesday morning. Rick isn't home – he and a co-worker loaded up the recycled dorm furniture into Rick's truck, which thankfully showed up a few days ago, and return it. My Honda is due to arrive the next day. We had to pull from our savings to ship my car because the military only paid to ship one vehicle. I muttered "Good riddance" when Rick and his co-worker drove off with the used furniture.

Elizabeth is bouncing up and down, excited to have her own things. "Where's my bed? Where's my kitchen?" she asks me over and over.

"Honey, they have to unload everything. We'll find them, don't worry. It's all in there." I point to the moving van.

"Do you hear that, Madison? You'll have all your clothes back, too," she tells her dolly. Madison has been forced to wear just three outfits this whole time.

The movers have been unloading and placing boxes and furniture where I tell them for almost two hours before Rick returns.

I am munching on crackers to settle my stomach while unpacking pots and pans when he finally makes his appearance. "Where have you been for so long, Rick? I thought maybe you guys had gotten lost."

Rick's face is flushed. "No, we didn't get lost. How's it coming? It looks like they're almost done."

"Yeah, they're doing well. I think I've got the boxes in the right rooms. At least I hope so. I can't make out some of the scribbles on the boxes, though. I guess we'll figure it out when we open them."

"That's good. That's good. I think I'll start in the bathrooms." Rick disappears quickly down the hall. I turn my attention back to my crackers and dishes.

The movers are finished by three. They even helped Rick assemble the beds. I quickly followed behind with freshly laundered bedding. Once the beds are made, I stand back and smile in satisfaction. We will finally sleep on our own beds. I can hardly wait. I want to crawl in mine right now and close my eyes. Instead, I drag my weary body into the kitchen to make sandwiches for dinner.

As usual, I barely finish mine before pushing it away.

"You really do need to eat more. You don't look so good lately."

I place my chin in my hand and sigh. "I know. I'm not hungry. I would rather just go to bed."

"Why don't you turn in? I'll take care of the dishes and Elizabeth."

"Okay," I reply, dragging myself off the chair. I would protest, but I'm too exhausted.

I sleep like the dead, not even stirring when Rick comes to bed. I sleep until almost ten o'clock the next morning. When I realize what time it is, I stumble into the living room and plop onto my own beautiful, clean, and comfortable sofa.

"Hey there, sleepy head," Rick says cheerily.

Elizabeth giggles. "Mommy's a sleepy head!"

I smile lopsidedly at her. "Yes, I am. I am a sleepy head."

"Want some coffee?" Rick asks, rising from his knees with a groan. He was unpacking a box. Packing material surrounds him and falls over the sides of the half empty box.

"Yes, please. Sorry to sleep so long," I yawn.

"Elizabeth and I held down the fort. Didn't we, sweet girl?" Rick smiles at Elizabeth.

She bobs her head vigorously up and down. "Yep we did!"

Once I am half-way through my steaming mug which, by the way, is my very own favorite coffee mug, I feel much better. I notice for the first time that the living room is almost completely assembled. There are even some pictures on the wall. I perk up immediately.

"You hung pictures on the wall while I was sleeping?" I ask, dumbfounded.

"Yes. Did it wake you up? I tried not to bang too loudly."

"No. No, that's the problem. I didn't hear anything."

"I'm glad you got some sleep."

"I can't believe I didn't hear you. That's crazy."

"Well, now that we are in our new home and have our own things, maybe you'll feel better. I know this move has really stressed you out."

I smile and sip coffee from my favorite mug.

"I found a good place to put my boxes," he informs me. "There's enough space in the storage room in the garage." Rick has a number of boxes that contain items I don't understand the need to keep, such as his TDY orders, some squadron coins, and old uniforms.

"Why do you want to keep those things, Rick?"

"Because they're my experiences. When I look at them, I remember."

We spend the day unpacking. By the time we fall into bed exhausted later that night, the house is completely unpacked and put together.

The next day, our phone is turned on and the cable hooked up. My first phone call is to my parents and the second is to Angeline. Rick calls his parents, as well. They're actually home in Maine for a few weeks.

It's still heart-wrenching to hear the voices of my family and Angeline knowing they're so far away. I may not be able to waltz over to Angeline's house, or drive to my parents' house, but I can still talk to them any time. I take comfort in that.

"Have you met any of your new neighbors yet?" Angeline asks.

"I met Katherine's mom briefly," I reply. "Her name is Terri. She seems nice, but she's not you."

Angeline laughs. "Well, of course she's not *me*! But that's okay. You can have other friends, too."

"She is pregnant right now, so there's always that."

"Oh, hey. That's not funny, Heather." I can hear the smile in her voice. Suddenly a scream fills the background. "Hey! Put her down! Heather, I gotta go. Love you and I'll talk to you soon!"

"Okay. Go put the fire out. Bye!" I chuckle and hang up. The last thing I hear from Angeline before the line goes dead is, "I *told* you not to hang…!"

"Oh, Angeline. You always have your hands full." I miss that chaos.

****

Unfortunately, chaos has a way of finding me. Rick brings it home a week later.

"Heather, you need to sit down," he says.

I don't like news that requires me to sit down. It is never good.

"Go ahead and tell me you're having an affair." My attempt at levity falls flat.

"Heather, please. Be serious."

"Fine. What now?" I ask impatiently, plopping onto the sofa. "Are you working days and nights with no days off?"

Rick hesitates briefly, his eyebrows meeting in the middle. "No. I am deploying to Africa."

My jaw drops. "What? Why Africa?"

"Well, if you'd been watching the news, you would know there is some serious genocide going on over there in a country called Rwanda, and we are being deployed for humanitarian purposes. No combat or anything. We will just be providing food, medical supplies, shelter, and things like that."

"How long?"

"I don't know," he shrugs. "But probably a couple of months or so."

"Great. You'll probably miss Elizabeth's fourth birthday, just like you missed her third birthday."

Rick winces. "Heather, that's not fair."

I press my lips together. "I'm sorry. That was low. It's not your fault."

Rick looks grim. "I'm sorry, too. At least it's not a combat mission. Does that make you feel any better?"

"Yes. Just a little, but I would rather you be here."

Rick swallows hard. "I know," he whispers.

He will deploy in two days. I help him pack, shed a lot of tears, and stuff the hurt deep inside. This deployment ties my stomach in knots to the point that I throw up more than I eat. Rick hasn't even been home for a full year since his last deployment.

"Are you going to be all right?" Rick asks after I throw up for the second time today. He is scheduled to leave tonight. "You really don't look well."

I wipe my mouth and shrug. "Don't worry about me. You have to go."

Rick grimaces. His eyes look hollow.

I muster a smile for him. "We will be fine."

Rick reaches for me. "I'm really sorry," he says thickly.

"I know," I sigh. "Me, too."

"Promise me you'll go to the doctor if this doesn't get better in a few days," he says sternly, clearing his throat.

"I promise." I can't be like this much longer. I have to take care of Elizabeth all by myself. It terrifies me. My family isn't here. Angeline isn't here. I have nobody I can call to help if something should happen. I'm all Elizabeth has. The realization makes my throat close.

Rick and I try to explain his leaving to Elizabeth at dinner that night. She seems to understand it, mostly. She still remembers him being gone recently, and is not happy about it.

"No, daddy. You're supposed to stay *here*," she says emphatically.

She is groggy when we say goodbye to Rick that night along with a roomful of other uniformed people. This is uncomfortably familiar. Rick squeezes Elizabeth for a long time, rocking her back and forth. His cheeks are wet when he pulls away. He kisses her hard on the cheek before putting her down to wrap his arms around me.

"I am going to miss you so much. I hope you know that," he says huskily, his breath hot in my ear.

"You're taking my heart with you," I reply, my voice quavering.

"I'm glad it's still mine."

"Always."

We kiss long and hard.

"I am leaving you the numbers of my supervisor and the First Sergeant, should you need anything. They know we just got here and don't have family or anything, so call them if you need to." He hands me a folded piece of paper.

"Thanks. I'll put it on the fridge."

His shoulders relax. "Good. I better load up," he says, swiping at his cheeks. "I love you guys more than anything."

"We love you, too. Come home soon."

"I will. I promise."

Then, he's gone. Elizabeth and I are alone.

****

"Sweetheart, you just have to find things to do and keep yourself busy," Mom encourages when I call her the next day.

"I know," I sigh. "But I just feel like poop. I'm nauseated from the stress of the move and now he's deployed. Again."

"Well, why don't you at least look into things for Elizabeth to get into? Look into preschool for her. I know she'd like to make more friends, and that's how she can do it." Katherine is Elizabeth's only friend, and she will be starting kindergarten in a few weeks. Elizabeth can't follow her.

"I will."

I find out about preschool for Elizabeth from Terri, Katherine's mother. It is at a local off-base church. They have both morning and afternoon preschool available.

"I'm not a baby anymore," Elizabeth huffs, crossing her arms. "I want to go to *real* school like Katherine."

"I know you're not a baby, but you're not old enough."

The next session of preschool starts next week. I can hardly wait. The nausea hasn't subsided much. I am a mess. I promised Rick I would schedule a doctor's appointment, but I keep putting it off. It will get better. It has to.

When Rick calls me four days after he leaves, he urges me to make the appointment.

"You promised," he reminds me.

After my third bout of vomiting the next day, I have had enough. I look up the number to the base clinic and make an appointment for the morning Elizabeth starts preschool.

Elizabeth is reluctant to go to preschool – she calls it baby school – and gives me a hard time while getting ready. She whines and flops around, almost making us late. Finally, I give her an ultimatum.

"You either get dressed and put your shoes on, or I will take Madison away for the rest of the week." That gets her attention.

When we arrive at the church, I walk a sullen Elizabeth to the preschool entrance and file in slowly with the other parents and children. There is a cheerful middle-aged woman standing at the door, greeting each child and parent with a smile and a handshake. When it's our turn, the teacher turns her sunny smile on us and introduces herself.

"Well, hello there! I don't believe we've met before! I'm Mrs. Greene and I'm your teacher." She crouches down to eye level with Elizabeth. "What's your name, beautiful?"

Elizabeth frowns and refuses to answer.

"I'm sorry. She's grouchy this morning. Her name is Elizabeth." I squeeze Elizabeth's hand gently. "Be polite and say hello to your teacher, Elizabeth."

Elizabeth responds reluctantly. "Hello," she mutters.

"Well, that's all right. I can be a little grouchy in the morning, too," Mrs. Greene says. "Why don't you come in? Mrs. Hazel will show you where your very own cubbie is, and what we're doing right now. Mrs. Hazel?"

A plump woman with skin the color of coffee ambles over, a broad smile on her mocha face. "Well, hello! I'm Mrs. Hazel. Let's go get you settled in, doll."

While Mrs. Hazel shows Elizabeth around, Elizabeth's demeanor brightens. She's eager and excited to get involved after only a few minutes. The room is large and colored in beautiful primary colors. It makes me wish I could go to preschool – there are so many things to do here.

"I think it's okay to leave her here now. She's in good hands," Mrs. Hazel pats my arm reassuringly. "We'll see you in four hours."

I smile gratefully. "Thank you so much. I love you, sweetie. You have fun!" I squeeze Elizabeth, who squeezes me back quickly before skipping off in the direction of a table set up with clay.

I feel confident leaving Elizabeth here – she's going to have a lot to tell me when I pick her up. For now, I make my way to the clinic.

The appointment doesn't take long, and I have free time on my hands before I have to pick Elizabeth up, so I clean house and call Angeline. She can't talk for more than five minutes – they were on their way out. The boys start school soon, and she needs to get to the commissary.

"I'm really sorry, Heather! I want to talk to you, but I *have* to get to the commissary before it gets too busy. It's payday, you know."

"I know. I need to go shopping there, too."

We say our hasty goodbyes with a few more apologies from Angeline. I really miss our lazy afternoons spent together in her yard or mine.

Glancing at the clock, I calculate that I should have enough time to pick up at least a few items before I have to get Elizabeth. I jot down a quick list and head out.

The commissary is still under construction. It feels like Black Friday shopping the day after Thanksgiving. I have discovered military paydays are the worst days to shop. Since everyone gets paid on the same days, everyone goes shopping on the same days – it can be a nightmare.

I pull into a parking spot of the preschool with five minutes to spare.

Elizabeth is grinning from ear to ear when I pick her up. "Mommy! Mommy! I had so much fun! I made a clay dinosaur and money and…"

"Hold on, sweetie. Hold on. You can tell me all about it on the drive home. Let's say thank you and goodbye to your teachers, okay?"

She vigorously nods and skips over to Mrs. Greene, hugging her legs.

"Oh!" Mrs. Greene laughs. "Why thank you, Elizabeth! Did you have fun today?"

"Yes! Yes! Lots and lots of fun!"

"That's wonderful!" Mrs. Greene turns to address me. "Elizabeth had a wonderful first day. She's going to do just fine here. What a smart little girl she is."

On the ride home, Elizabeth chatters on breathlessly about everything she did that morning. I don't get a word in, and I don't care. She is happier than she's been in a long time.

"It sounds like you had a lot of fun," I manage to insert when she stops to take a deep breath, sighing in pleasure.

"Yes, and I met a little girl named Brittany and she's really nice and…" She begins another long description of her new friend and what they did together.

By the time we get home, I'm exhausted from listening. Exhausted, but happy. Preschool is going to work out just fine, even if it is only three days a week.

****

Elizabeth and I are both still feeling really good about preschool the next day when the phone rings. I glance up from the book Elizabeth was reading to me – she still makes up stories from the pictures – excusing myself to answer it. It's either Angeline, Mom, or Rick. None of which I want to miss.

"Hello?" I answer, expecting a familiar voice in return.

"May I speak to Mrs. Johnson, please?" asks a young lady's voice.

I immediately straighten up. This is not a familiar voice.

"Uh...this is Mrs. Johnson."

"Hello, Mrs. Johnson. I'm Sergeant Sprecht from the clinic. How are you today?"

"I'm fine, I guess."

"I am just calling to inform you of your blood test results from yesterday. Congratulations. You are pregnant!"

"Uh...*what?* Are you kidding me?!"

She laughs. "No, ma'am. I am not kidding. You are pregnant. I would like to give you the number of the OB clinic so you can schedule your first appointment. Do you have a pen and paper ready?"

"Uh, hang on." I grab a red crayon and an envelope from today's mail. They're the closest writing utensils I can find. Good thing, too because I don't think I could hold a pen – my hand is shaking. I have to write the number twice before it's legible. I mumble thanks when the young lady congratulates me again before hanging up.

Staring into space, I try to process what I just heard.

It wasn't stress. I'm pregnant.

"Oh, God..." I cover my mouth, panic rising. How can I do this with Rick gone and me here all alone? He was gone last time, but I was with my parents. I don't have anybody.

"Mommy? Are you okay?" Elizabeth asks, peering around the corner of the dining room.

I jerk my head up and try to smooth my face. I take a deep breath and smile. "I'm fine, sweetie. Let's finish your book, all right?"

My mind whirls while Elizabeth reads. Maybe they made a mistake. It is possible, isn't it?

No. They didn't make a mistake. I am pregnant.

The nausea, the lack of appetite, it all adds up. When I filled out the questionnaire at the clinic and came to the question of when my last menstrual cycle was, I had to think because I couldn't remember. I know it was some time before we left Texas – maybe in April? Perhaps in May? I thought I skipped it because of stress.

"Mommy, you're not listening," Elizabeth scolds me.

I blink. "I'm sorry, sweetie. I'll pay better attention. Where were we?"

****

My family is elated when I call that evening. Unfortunately, there will be no cake to share the news this time. I keep my voice down, hoping Elizabeth doesn't hear. She's in her room telling Madison all about preschool. Debbie and Mom are both crying on the phone. I picture their cheeks pressed together, straining to hear me and talk at the same time.

"Mom, can you please come when it's time? Please?" I beg. I need my mother.

"You know I wouldn't miss it for anything!"

"I wanna come, too!" Debbie pleads.

"Of course I want you to come, too, Deb. I want all of you to come, but I know you can't afford that. Plus our house isn't very big."

"Debbie, you have school. Don't worry, you'll be able to see that baby soon enough," Mom pipes in.

"Aaww!!" Debbie laments. "But, Mom…"

"Deborah, not now. Now listen, Heather, you be sure to make that appointment tomorrow. You get plenty of rest when you can and eat something, too. Do you have crackers and jello on hand?"

I roll my eyes. "Yes, mother. I will make the appointment. I have crackers and jello."

Angeline actually screams when I tell her.

"Oh that's wonderful! Congratulations!!" she cries. "When are you due? What do you think you're having! Oh, I *wish* I could be there!" She starts to sob.

"Don't cry, Angeline. You're going to make me cry, too."

"Sorry, sorry." She sniffles.

"I don't know when I'm due. I literally just found out I'm…pregnant…" Wow. "…today. I will make my OB appointment tomorrow."

"Okay, well you *have* to call and let me know when you find out!"

"You know I will."

The one person I want to tell the most is the one person I can't call. I have to wait for Rick to call me. I have only been able to talk to him twice since he left. I don't know when I'll hear his voice again. How much of this pregnancy is he going to miss? How much more of our life is he going to miss?

I cry myself to sleep that night.

****

September, 1993

Rick doesn't call before I have my first OB appointment in the middle of the month. When I am done, I am thankful to have two hours before I have to pick Elizabeth up. I am stunned; I could have collected flies in my mouth. I don't remember climbing into the truck or the drive home. All I remember is sitting on the sofa, staring at the wall in silence afterward, trying to digest everything.

I'm due in January. It's a boy.

That's only four months away. How could I have missed this? My eyes flutter to my stomach and my hands slowly creep around my abdomen. I thought I just had some belly fat, but now that I am seeing myself with new, more informed eyes, there is a definite roundness there.

"This is crazy," I whisper in the silence. "How the hell could I have *missed this?* How...?" I promptly burst into tears.

I cry for a solid hour before the tears subside. Thirty minutes into it, I had gone to our bedroom, torn my clothes off and stared at my naked profile in the full length mirror. Yes, there was a definite bump there. It's not huge, but it is definitely there. When I suck my breath in, the bump looks even larger. I marvel that I haven't felt anything. The ultrasound revealed a fully formed, active little baby.

I cry to my mother, who is as shocked as I am and then to Angeline. I can barely get the words out before I cry in each conversation. It's all happening so fast. Too fast.

And Rick is not here.

****

"You're *what?*" Rick yells into the phone after a stunned, silent moment. Just like last time, I can't give him the news in person.

"I am pregnant, Rick."

"Oh, honey bun!! That's awesome!! No wonder you were so sick. It all makes sense now! Woohoo!" he chortles.

I grip the phone and close my eyes. "Rick, I'm due in January."

The silence lasts so long I think we've been disconnected. "Rick? Are you there?"

"Uh...yeah, I'm here. What do you mean you're due in January? How can that be?"

"I don't know, but I had my appointment almost two weeks ago, and that's what they said. I couldn't remember the exact date of my last period, so they did an ultrasound and that's what they dated the baby at. We are having a boy, by the way."

The strangest sound fills my ears. It takes awhile to register that Rick is sobbing. Loudly and openly.

"Rick? Are you all right?" I ask, my voice high-pitched. "Rick?"

"Yeah," Sniff. "Yeah! I'm all right. We're having a boy?" His voice ends on a squeak. I hear that same strange sobbing sound again.

"Rick, don't cry. It's all right. I...when are you coming home? I need you."

Our conversation remains stilted. Between Rick's tears and my own, we have a hard time talking. Rick isn't sure when he'll be home, and I am not sure how to do this without him.

I'm not sure how to do this without *anybody*.

****

Katherine's mother, Terri, delivers a healthy baby boy on a cold, wet and dark evening on the last day of September. Katherine spent the day with us while her parents went to the hospital. I have begun to develop a friendship with Terri and her husband, John. They're nice people, but she's not as outgoing as Angeline. I can't seem to crack her; there's a wall of separation.

One afternoon, I was feeling very alone and needed a friend to talk to in person. When I showed up at her home like I would have at Angeline's, she didn't even invite me in and it was too chilly to stay outside. I felt awkward just standing there. I haven't tried again.

It makes me lonely for Angeline's bubbly personality. I really miss her.

The clouds descend some time in late September and don't lift. The days are ridiculously short, and it's cold all the time. The rain, if you can even call it rain, sort of hangs in the air most days like it's not sure which way the ground is. Sometimes, it falls gently, but mostly it just threatens to. I spent a good deal of our savings purchasing winter clothing for both myself and Elizabeth. I didn't need to worry about that in Texas. Here, the cold air makes me tense up and suck in my breath when I open the front door. I hate it.

Everything, including my mood, is gray.

****

October, 1993

I force myself to plan Elizabeth's fourth birthday party. We invite not only Katherine, but Elizabeth's entire preschool class. Every day I hope against hope Rick will call to say he will be home. I don't want him to miss another birthday. I lose an inch of that hope as each day the sun sets – at least, it gets dark outside so I assume the sun sets even though I can't see it – and there's no news of his homecoming.

My gray mood deepens.

My next OB appointment comes and goes. The doctor was puzzled when I said I still hadn't felt the baby move, so out came the ultrasound machine. The baby was active and normal.

"Are you feeling any of this?" he asks, eyebrows arched.

I close my eyes in concentration. I did feel fluttering. Strange, I hadn't noticed it before. I open my eyes and nod mutely.

"Do you remember feeling the baby's movements before now?"

"Not really. I guess I just didn't notice."

The doctor narrows his eyes at me for a moment and writes something on the clipboard. I don't ask what it is. I just want to go home and see if Rick called.

I hurry into the house and check the machine. No messages.

"Of course not," I mutter. I lie down for a nap instead, but sleep won't come. I aimlessly flip through channels until it's time to pick Elizabeth up from preschool.

****

Elizabeth's party is in two days and I still haven't heard from Rick.

He won't make it.

Sitting in my bathrobe sipping coffee in the gray daylight that defines morning, I make myself concentrate on the party checklist I forced myself to make. I have everything I need except the cake, which I will pick up the day of the party. Seven of the eleven children in her preschool class can make it, plus Katherine. I bought enough supplies to fill the eight goodie bags with little trinkets – candy and toys.

The last thing I am in the mood for is a party, but it's her birthday and she's excited. I wish I could be. My emotions have been dulled to match the landscape. I can't shake it.

One of the preschool moms had offered her theory. "You came from sunny Texas to *this*. What did you expect to happen? Everybody gets in a funk when they first move here. Don't worry, it will pass and you'll be all right," she chuckled. "Give it a few years."

A few *years*? I don't want to give it another month.

The next day, I load Elizabeth up in the Honda for our trek to the commissary. I have learned to time my visits around payday. It took some doing, but I rearranged our pantry and our budget so I can shop a few days before payday when most people aren't there.

The renovations have finally been completed. I suppose it looks good, but I didn't see it before they began, so I have nothing to compare it to. Besides, nothing excites me anymore.

When we return, it's already getting dark even though it's not yet four o'clock. I give Elizabeth one bag with napkins and another bag with bread to carry. I grab three bags myself and head toward the door. When we're halfway up the walkway, Terri spills out of her house and yells to get my attention, waving her arms.

"Heather! Heather! Don't go in there!" she yells, panic in her voice.

I stop in my tracks. I look toward my house, scanning the exterior. Nothing seems out of the ordinary.

"What? Why?" I ask, confused.

She is almost across the street. "I saw someone go in there! I have never seen him before. I don't know if he broke in or not. I know your husband is gone, and…" She bends over to catch her breath before continuing. "My heart is racing. I was just about to call the police when I saw you come home."

Ice runs down my spine. "You saw a strange man go into *my house*? Are you sure?" I start backing away, nudging Elizabeth down the walkway with me.

She nods vigorously. "Yes! Yes! I saw him go inside. I'm sure he's still there. Unless he slipped out the back."

"Oh, my God…." I start walking faster until we get to the car. I quickly open the door and dump my groceries in the back seat, taking the bags from Elizabeth, too, and dumping them on top, not caring if I squish something or not. "Can we go to your house?"

She nods, hurrying back to her house. I grab Elizabeth's hand and we practically run across the street, stumble across her doorway, and slam the door shut behind us. My hand presses onto my chest, and I feel the rapid thumping there.

"Mommy? What's going on? Is there a bad man in our house?" Elizabeth asks, her eyes filling with tears.

"I don't know, sweetie. I don't know." I try to keep my voice even. I don't want to scare her.

"I'm calling the police," Terri says, grabbing her phone and punching numbers. She starts talking almost immediately, filling the police in on what she saw.

I plop onto an easy chair near the door that has a dish towel draped over one arm and a burp cloth draped over the other. Elizabeth climbs onto my lap, whimpering and buries her face in my shoulder.

"I want daddy," she cries.

"Me, too, sweetie. Me, too," I whisper, patting her back.

Terri hangs up the phone. "They're on their way." Suddenly a tiny wail comes from a bassinet I hadn't noticed across the room. Terri hurries over and picks up her baby, who stretches and contorts himself. His mouth is open revealing tiny gums as he grimaces. She snuggles him into her shoulder, cooing quietly. His cries stop as he finds his fist to suck on.

Two police cars show up within minutes. They pull in at angles, blocking my car and the street. One officer comes to Terri's house while three others approach my house, one going around the back.

Terri fills him in once again with what she saw and that it was only one man. No, she didn't see if he was driving a vehicle, if he got dropped off, or if he walked up to the house. She just saw him at the door and saw him go inside.

The officer addresses me. "Is that your residence, ma'am?" I nod. "Can you confirm that your husband is indeed deployed?" I nod again. "Do you have anyone staying with you or are you expecting anyone?" I shake my head.

Suddenly, there's yelling from across the street. The two officers in front have their weapons drawn and are pointing at my house, walking quickly toward it.

"Excuse me," the officer we were talking to says quickly, hurrying across to his comrades, pulling his weapon on the way. He talks into his shoulder as he goes.

Elizabeth screams and starts to cry. I pull her close to me and she buries her face in my side, quivering. Terri's baby starts to cry loudly, startled by the sound of Elizabeth's scream.

Moments later, a man emerges from my front door with his arms behind his head, slowly walking backward.

I gasp. There *was* a man in my house. My knees begin to shake. What could have happened if I had gone inside?

CHAPTER TWENTY FOUR

October, 1993

The man in the doorway of my home turns his head and addresses the police officer behind him. He continues to walk outside and lies down on the walkway, spreading his legs and arms on the cold concrete. The officer says something to his comrades, who keep their weapons trained on the man. The officer standing over the man puts his weapon away and reaches into the back pockets of the man on the ground, pulling out what looks like a wallet. He thumbs through it and pulls something out. He says something to the other officers. One more officer puts his weapon away and approaches, taking the item and examining it. Words are exchanged. I think the officer tells the man to sit up, because the man sits on the ground with his legs crossed. The second officer who approached now turns on his heel, heading toward us.

"What are they doing?" Terri asks. "I don't want that man knowing where I live."

The officer approaching us is the same officer that talked to us earlier. "Ma'am, is your name Heather Johnson?"

"Yes," I squeak.

"Come with me, please."

"What? Why?" I ask, terrified.

His face gives nothing away. "Just please come with me."

"Elizabeth, stay here with Miss Terri." I pry Elizabeth away from me, and she whimpers.

"Let her come, too. It's all right. I promise," the officer reassures me.

Elizabeth glues herself to me. We follow the officer slowly across the now darkened street and approach the scene. The officers have put their weapons away and the man is now standing on the walkway. I'm terrified to look him in the eye, but curiosity gets the better of me.

As soon as I see the face and the build of his body, I gasp and start running toward him.

"RICK!!!!" I shriek. "Rick!!" I throw myself into his arms and sob.

"Hey there, honey bun. Didn't know you wanted to get rid of me," he chuckles, slightly breathless. I can feel his heart pounding in his chest.

"Oh, my God, Rick! You're home!!" I cry.

"Daddy!!" Elizabeth cries from below.

Rick bends down, scooping her up in his arms. "Hey there, baby girl! Daddy's home!"

A throat clears, and I remember the police are standing there. "Oh! I'm sorry. This is my husband. I'm so sorry!" I sob.

The officers chuckle quietly, their postures relaxing. "No problem," one officer replies. "We are just glad everything is all right. Welcome home, sir. Sorry to have put you through that. Maybe let your wife in on it next time." He smiles.

"Yeah," Rick reaches out to shake their hands in turn. "Thanks. It's good to know my family is safe here, though. Thanks a bunch. I won't try this again." A round of laughter fills the darkness as the officers retreat to their cars.

"Is everything all right?" Terri calls, crossing the street as the officers pull away. I turn to see her walking briskly up the walkway with her baby on her shoulder.

"Yes, everything is fine. This is my husband, Rick," I say breathlessly.

"Your...? Oh boy. I am so sorry, Rick. I *swear* I didn't recognize you! If I had known... Please forgive me," she gushes, embarrassed.

Rick holds his hand up, smiling. "It's all right. Thanks for being a vigilant neighbor."

With multiple reassurances, Terri sheepishly returns to her own home. We finally come in the house, and I can't stop smiling.

"Rick, I can't believe you're here! Why didn't you call and tell me?" I ask through tears.

Rick chuckles. "I wanted to surprise you, but you surprised me first by calling the cops on me."

"How did you get here? Who picked you up?"

"Daddy! Daddy! You're home! You're here for my party tomorrow!" Elizabeth blurts excitedly.

Rick squeezes Elizabeth once more before putting her down. "Yes, I am, baby girl! I didn't want to miss your birthday party this year." He turns his attention to me. "I had one of the guys from my shop pick me up."

"How long have you known you were coming home?" I ask, wrapping my arms around his waist.

"Only for the last week. Boy, it's good to be home." His hand rubs my rounded stomach gently. "How's my boy doing?" he asks thickly.

"He's fine," I reply. Suddenly I jerk back. "Oh! The groceries are still in the car. I forgot all about them!"

Rick leans over and kisses my belly. "I'll go get them. Sit down and put your feet up."

Elizabeth looks at me puzzled. I haven't told her about the baby. "What boy? I'm a girl!" she declares emphatically.

"Go help daddy, sweetie," I answer, pushing her gently out the door with Rick. Rick turns to me, his eyebrows raised in a silent question. I shake my head and shoo them out the door.

Rick returns with Elizabeth happily in tow, both of them loaded down with bags. I stare in dismay at the bag carrying the ice cream – there's a puddle of melted ice cream in the bottom.

"Oh, no! Let me have that one," I grab the bag from Rick's hand and hurry to the kitchen, placing it carefully in the sink. Rick and Elizabeth join me, hoisting the remaining bags onto the counter.

"What's wrong?" Rick asks, peering over my shoulder while his hand creeps around my abdomen, cradling it.

"There was ice cream in there. I forgot all about it! It's ruined," I moan, tears filling my eyes.

"Hey, hey," Rick says softly, turning me to face him. "It's all right. I don't think it's all melted. It is pretty chilly out there." He peels the bag away from the ice cream and pries the lid off. "See? It's only about an inch down. We can put it in the freezer and it'll be fine." He replaces the lid, wipes it off, and puts it in the freezer.

"God, Rick," I sob. "I feel like such a failure."

Rick looks at me bewildered and silent. Elizabeth stares at us both with wide eyes.

"Uh, baby girl, why don't you go watch cartoons or play in your room? I need to talk to mommy." Elizabeth stares at us a moment longer before silently disappearing around the corner to her room.

When she's gone, Rick turns to me. "Heather, what's going on? Why are you crying over melted ice cream?"

I continue to sob, shaking my head. "I don't know. I just…I'm just…" I don't know what to say. I can't put words to the feelings bouncing around inside.

Rick sighs and folds me in his arms, patting my back like a child. Eventually, I calm down and pull away.

"I'm sorry for being such a ninny." I wipe my nose on my sleeve.

"It's okay. You can be a ninny if you want to. Maybe it's because you're pregnant."

I shrug. "Maybe. I don't know."

"Mommy, are you all right?" Elizabeth asks in a small voice, peering around the corner.

I take a deep breath and force a smile. "I'm fine, sweetie. I'm just tired."

"Let's sit down," Rick says, guiding me into the living room. "Elizabeth, we need to share some wonderful news with you. Mommy wanted to wait until I got home so we could tell you together."

When we share the news of her new baby brother, Elizabeth is beside herself with excitement. She can't wait and asks when he is supposed to come home. We tell her he will be arriving after Christmas and her brow furrows.

"That's too far away!" she laments.

Oh, sweetheart – it will be here before you know it, I want to tell her.

Although I am relieved Rick is home and sorry for the homecoming he received, I still can't shake the gray mood that has descended. I would give my right arm to see the sun and feel the heat.

Elizabeth's party is a smashing success by all accounts, her mood buoyant because of Rick's return, and the fact that she just turned into a big four-year-old. All her friends enjoy the games, eat the salvaged ice cream and cake without complaint, and squeal in delight at the contents of their goody bags. I force myself to smile for her, smile in the pictures, and smile at the people in my home. I would rather find a dark corner, cover my head, and close my eyes.

But I don't. It's Elizabeth's party.

For the next several days, Rick spends a lot of time marveling at my rounded midsection and talking to my belly. I feel bad that I can't give him more information about how active the baby is. I haven't paid much attention to him which makes me feel guilty, deepening the gray cloud in my head and heart.

"Are you..." Rick asks hesitantly one night while we are lying in bed. "Are you even excited about this new baby?"

"Yes," I reply. Aren't I? Isn't everyone excited about a new baby?

"Then how come you don't seem like it?"

I bite my lip, not having an answer. How do I explain that the clouds outside have come inside?

"I don't know. I am just overwhelmed, I think." I force some energy and joy into my voice. "Of course I'm excited! You're going to have a son."

****

November, 1993

Rick goes back to work after only a week off. He has the same schedule he had before he deployed; day shift with Wednesdays and Thursdays off. He and I have alone time on Wednesdays while Elizabeth is at preschool. Rick tries to be amorous, but I'm not in the mood. Often I beg off because I'm pregnant. Rick suspects differently, but he doesn't ask.

Every evening for the next month when Rick comes home, I am sure to have dinner cooking and the house clean. He talks to me about what's going on at work, but other than the occasional half-hearted response, I really don't engage in conversation. When he asks what I've done all day, my answers revolve around commissary shopping, cooking, cleaning, and talking on the phone to either Angeline or my parents. He encourages me to get out more, and meet some of our other neighbors.

"Just go knock on their door. Bring them some of your mom's delicious goodies – they're always a hit," he suggests cheerfully.

At the mention of my mother, I burst into tears. I haven't opened my mother's recipes in awhile. Rick's expression is one I imagine he would make if a bowling ball just crashed through our front window.

"What did I say?" he asks, bewildered. "Does baking make you upset now?"

"N-n-nothing," I blubber. What *is* wrong with me?

He continues to press the issue.

"I miss my mother! I miss my whole *family!*" I sob harder. My heart hurts terribly being so far away, especially while pregnant.

"I know and I'm sorry," he says. I know he is, but there's nothing he, or anyone else, can do about it. They can't afford to fly here, we can't afford to fly me there, and there's no middle ground. "Don't you talk to her often?"

I nod, wiping my eyes, even though the tears keep falling. "I call her once a week, but long distance is too expensive to call more often." I hiccup loudly. "Thanksgiving is next week, and we will be here all by ourselves!" I wail.

Rick hugs me tightly, cradling my head in his shoulder. "Heather, I am sorry," he murmurs. "I wish I could make this better for you."

I want to go home, I whisper in my head. I want to take you and Elizabeth and just go home. This isn't home.

Thanksgiving comes and I make the effort to cook the entire meal, struggling not to dwell on where we were last Thanksgiving, and who we were with. It's difficult. When I talk to my parents, I can hear the hustle and bustle in the background and it tears at me. Chris and Angeline are there for Thanksgiving again this year. I am so happy for them, but filled with sorrow for myself.

"They're having a get together at my supervisor's house," Rick says. "We'll go play football in the mud and watch the football game. Other families will be there, too. There will be games and things to do. What do you say?" Rick asks.

The thought of forcing myself to interact with strangers and pretend to be cheerful fills me with dread. I shrink back, shaking my head. "If you want to go with Elizabeth, sweetie, go ahead. I don't really want to."

Rick grimaces, searching my face. "I think it would be good for you," he encourages quietly.

I can't be persuaded. Rick and Elizabeth go by themselves. I take a fitful nap instead.

****

December, 1993

Rick tries his best to lift my mood, but the gray clouds continue to saturate my being just like the dreary skies I see all day, every day.

Maybe I made up the sun. Maybe it's just a half-remembered dream.

He helps me get the crib set up and some of the other necessities we will need for the baby. We're sorely lacking in little boy clothes and decor. Rick even makes a point of coming with me to my OB appointments. He remarks about seeing a new doctor each time. I don't care anymore.

I like watching the gleam in his eyes at the sound of the baby's strong heartbeat. Or the way he sits on the edge of his seat, leaning forward when they pull out the ultrasound machine and move the wand back and forth over my abdomen. The baby is very active and I am more aware of it now, in spite of the gray clouds.

Rick's excitement pierces the dullness that my life has become. Slightly.

On the way home from this last appointment, Rick squeezes my constantly cold hand. "I need to stop by the shop before we go to brunch, all right?" He told me to dress up this morning because he was taking me out afterward. He wouldn't say where, so I put forth some effort, applying a little make-up and pulling my hair up. When was the last time I did that? I don't recall.

"All right," I reply flatly, looking out the window at the dull trees against the gray backdrop. The clouds rest on top of the trees like a gossamer blanket.

When Rick pulls into the parking lot, he turns to me. "Come on inside with me. I want you to meet some of the guys I work with." I start to protest, but he pleads with me and I relent. It's not worth fighting over.

Rick comes around and gingerly helps me out of the truck – it requires more effort because of my ballooning midsection. I am due next month, after all.

"Do they know I'm pregnant?" I ask, self-conscious of my appearance.

Rick laughs. "What? Are you kidding? Of course, they know you're pregnant. I couldn't wait to tell them."

Rick leads me into the building and around the corner, stopping in front of a closed door. He knocks on it before swinging it wide open. He grins and let's me enter first.

A large group of total strangers yells, "Surprise!" in unison and I gasp in shock, clutching my chest and my stomach.

"What? What?" I ask, my eyes blinking and darting around the room trying to make sense of the scene.

"It's your baby shower, Heather. My shop is throwing you a baby shower," Rick murmurs in my ear and kisses my cheek. "Surprise!"

"My *what?*" I ask, tears that are always so close to the surface springing forth.

Every face is smiling at us and congratulating me as they slowly approach, introducing themselves. None of the names stick once they've been spoken. I notice a large mound of wrapped gifts on half of a monstrous wooden conference room table, while the other half of the table is laden with food. There's a cake in the center. The cake has little plastic blue balloons and "It's a BOY!" scrolled across the length of it.

After everyone has shaken my hand, Rick chuckles. "I think she is surprised!" Laughter echoes in the room.

"On behalf of the squadron, we want to welcome you guys and most importantly, welcome this new little guy to the world," a man says. I don't remember who he is. "Please, let's go ahead and eat, and then you can open up your presents."

There is so much food it's ridiculous. Some of it I've never seen before. Rick explains that some of the wives are from different countries, and they make different kinds of food. I am sure to get a spoonful of everything to be polite. As it turns out, the food is really good. I go back for a few more spoonfuls of some of the more exotic fare. The flavors are incredible.

Everyone is very nice, and asks me plenty of questions about everything, not just the baby. I talk at length about Texas and missing the sun and heat. One lady there is from Alaska and to her, Oregon is actually warm. Another woman is from Florida and agrees with me wholeheartedly.

When I'm sure I can't eat another bite, the same man who first spoke – it turns out he's Rick's boss – announces it's time for me to sit on my throne to open presents. Laughter rings through the room again and I look around, unsure of what to expect.

One woman enters the room on cue with an office chair that has been thoroughly wrapped in blue and white crepe paper topped off with a blue and white crepe bow on the back, streamers trailing behind.

My jaw drops and there's more laughter.

"Madam," the woman dips in an exaggerated bow and extends her arms out to the side. "Your throne."

I grin at Rick. I settle carefully into the chair, trying very hard not to rip the crepe paper.

As I open the presents one by one, read the cards, and see what amazing gifts we have gotten, I am overwhelmed. We have more than enough of everything we will need for the baby, including six packs of diapers and a $50 gift card to the commissary.

Rick hands me the last gift and says, "I think you're really going to love this one."

I take the gift and pull the card off, removing it from the envelope. When I open it and see who it's from, I cry.

"It's from her family," Rick explains to my audience. "Open it."

What's inside makes me cry even harder. It's a baby-sized quilt with a blue border and a tree in the middle. All of my family's names are on individual leaves along with Rick's family and Elizabeth. There's a blank panel awaiting the arrival of our son, whom we still need to pick a name for.

"Show everyone, Heather," Rick encourages. I had been running my fingers gently across the panels, drinking in the artistry of it.

"Oh! Sorry." I pull the quilt completely out of the box and hold it up with Rick's help. Murmurs of appreciation ripple.

Afterward, I welcome hugs and more congratulations from everyone before all of our gifts are loaded into the truck, taking up the entire bench seat area as well as the floor space at my feet.

On the way home, I ask, "How did you do that? How did you pull that off?"

He shrugs. "People were wondering where you were on Thanksgiving. I told them you'd been feeling pretty blue lately, missing your family and all. One thing led to another and we planned this shower for you."

Familiar tears spill onto my chest. "Thank you, Rick. That was so sweet." A brilliant patch of sunlight pierces the gray clouds in my head.

"You're welcome, honey bun. I just want you to be happy."

"I know. I'll try."

****

Christmas comes and we celebrate with just the three of us. Rick calls his parents, who are currently in South America, enjoying summer. They were elated to hear they'll be grandparents again, and promise to put us on their itinerary in the New Year. Their gifts arrive staggered throughout the month. Elizabeth receives some hand-crafted dolls from their travels in Brazil, Argentina, and Chile. They're absolutely beautiful and his parents insist she be allowed to play with them.

"They are not just for display," Rick's mother had said. "I want her to play with them just like the little girls do over here. That's what they're for." Elizabeth is happy Madison has some new friends.

I talk to my family, as well. I tried to replicate Christmas dinner like I would have if we were home. I even made the horrid cranberry relish that only my mother eats. To my surprise, Elizabeth gobbles it up.

****

January, 1994

I spend the next several weeks busying myself getting the nursery ready for our son, whom we will name Ethan Thomas. I do most of it while

Elizabeth is in preschool, but she likes to fold the tiny clothes and put them in the dresser, so I save that task for her. It's coming together nicely, and I like the Noah's Ark theme we've chosen. Of course, the walls remain boring white – we can't paint them.

As I tuck the baby quilt lovingly into the crib, tears blur my vision. I run my hands lightly over the names embroidered on it, missing each person as my fingers brush across the letters. Pulling the quilt off once more, I hug it to myself and sit down in the rocking chair for a good cry. That's how Rick finds me when he comes home for lunch one Monday.

"Heather, what's wrong?" he asks, dropping to his knees beside me.

"I miss my family," I whimper into the quilt, my chest heaving.

Rick's expression is pained. "I'm sorry. I'm trying my best."

"I know. I appreciate it," I say glumly, squeezing his hand.

"Is your mom going to make it?" he asks.

I nod. "Yes, she'll be here for three weeks in January. I talked to her this morning."

"That's good! Did you write down her flight information?"

I nod.

"That should cheer you up," he offers.

"Yes." It should.

****

Mom arrives exactly one week before my due date. When I see her coming off the plane, I burst into tears and sob unashamedly into her frail shoulders. She looks healthy again – the color has returned to her face and she's not as thin as she once was, but she's still just a slip of a person. I don't care who sees my raw show of emotion. She smells just like she always has – a combination of cinnamon, citrus, and just Mom, which means *home*.

"Heather, honey, are you all right?" she asks when I finally pull away. She looks questioningly between Rick and me. "Why the waterfall?"

I shake my head and wave my hands, dabbing at my eyes. I can't speak.

Rick moves in and gives Mom an enthusiastic hug. "She's really missed you guys," he replies.

"We've missed you, too, sweetheart. But I'm here now. And look at you!" She steps back and looks me up and down. "You're so big, Heather! That's going to be a strapping boy there. How are you feeling?"

"Huge," I manage to squeak.

"Let's head down to baggage claim, ladies," Rick says, smiling. "You can talk all the way home."

"Are you having any labor pains yet?" Mom asks, putting her arm around me. Her touch feels so good. The tears continue to fall, no matter how many times I swipe them away.

"No, not yet. My back hurts and I'm tired, but I'm all right."

"You look exhausted, sweetheart."

I sob a few more times before managing to collect myself. I am tired: tired of this place, tired of being away from my family. I am so very, very tired.

During the ride home, Mom shivers at the cold, gathering the collar on her coat tighter while admiring the scenery.

"Look at those mountains!" she exclaims. "Isn't that just gorgeous?"

I try to respond positively. She fills me in on everything at home. Jeff finally picked a major in college. He is studying to be an engineer. My parents are thrilled with his choice. He and Cara are still dating and doing well. Debbie is on the honor roll and playing volleyball. She isn't dating anyone seriously – her studies and volleyball consume her time.

"I'm sorry, sweetheart, this is all old news to you, isn't it? I told you about this a few weeks ago."

Did she? I don't recall. "It's okay, Mom. I like hearing old news, too."

"Dad said to tell you both he loves you and misses you. I promised everybody I would take lots of pictures, so get your smiles ready."

"Maybe you can coax some smiles out of her while you're here, Louise. She hasn't done a whole lot of that lately," Rick says, casting a sideways glance at me.

"Is that so?" she says. "Well, we'll have to figure out how to get it back, won't we, sweetheart?" She reaches up from the back seat and pats my shoulder. I grab her hand and keep it there, squeezing.

"Thanks, Mom."

****

January 22, 1994

Ethan must have been waiting for my mother's arrival as much as I was. My water breaks all over the bedroom floor the next morning when I get up. I thought I peed myself because that's what I was getting up to do. I had tossed and turned all night, attempting to get comfortable.

"I'll bet you started labor last night, Heather," Mom reprimands me. "If your back hurt bad enough to keep you awake, you should have gotten us up and yourself to the hospital hours ago. Remember when you had Elizabeth? You had horrible back pain then, too, and you ignored it."

I rub my back and pace the floor. "It didn't keep me awake, Mom. It just woke me up a few times and I couldn't get comfortable." I had forgotten about the back labor part with Elizabeth. How could I forget that?

"I didn't hear a thing," Rick says, rubbing his face. "You could have woken me up."

"For what? What could you have done?" I snap. Rick grimaces.

"Heather, don't snap at him. He just wanted to help, didn't you, dear?"

Mom interjects, rubbing Rick's arm reassuringly.

Rick offers her a half-smile.

"Is my brother coming today?" Elizabeth asks.

"I think so, sweet girl," Rick replies. "Did you get everything together to go over to Katherine's house?"

She nods, pointing to her bright pink back pack. "Yup! Madison and I are ready to go!" Her dolly is tucked securely under her arm.

"I'll be right back," Rick mumbles, ducking out the door with Elizabeth happily skipping alongside him.

"Heather, try to be nice to Rick. You've been awfully short with him."

"I know," I sigh. "I'm sorry. He's trying, but I just don't know."

"Don't know what, sweetheart?"

"I don't know…I just don't know. I don't want to be here. I love Rick, but I want my family, too."

"Oh, Heather. It's the military way. You'll have to come to terms with it."

I don't have a chance to respond because my stomach tightens and cramps, making me focus on my breathing. I place my hands on the wall like a person who's about to be arrested.

Mom's small, warm hands massage my lower back until it subsides.

"Better?" she asks.

I nod. "I think we better get to the hospital, though."

Rick returns a few minutes later and we load up in the car, Rick fussing over me while Mom double checks to be sure we have everything we need.

Halfway to the hospital, I start to moan – the cramps are getting worse. I know it will be soon. I just hope it doesn't happen as soon as we get there like it did with Elizabeth. I want an epidural this time.

Rick steps on the gas, earning some honks along the way. When we arrive and get to labor and delivery, I am immediately ushered into a triage room where I'm instructed to change into a gown that's open in the back and has slits near each breast. At least it's not a paper gown like the clinic has. Changing takes some effort – the contractions are two to three minutes apart. As soon as I am ready, Rick hurries to let someone know. Two nurses follow behind him and start an IV, while the other checks my progress.

"You're at about a five and one hundred percent effaced," she says, snapping her glove off. She glances at the monitor. "Contractions are good and strong, too."

"That's wonderful!" Mom exclaims, clapping her hands.

"Can she get her epidural soon? She really wants one," Rick says. I look at him gratefully – I am in the midst of breathing through another contraction. He squeezes my hand.

"Of course. We can get that taken care of shortly. We aren't that busy right now," the nurse replies.

I suffer through several more contractions before the doctor shows up to give me my epidural. "I'm Dr. Hanson and I'll be placing your epidural. Have you ever had one before?" she asks.

I shake my head quickly, close my eyes and begin panting as the strongest contraction yet takes over.

"It's almost peaked, it's almost peaked," Rick tells me, squeezing my hands and staring at the monitor. "There, it's heading down now. You're almost done."

Once the contraction has passed, the doctor explains the process to me. Honestly, I don't care. I just want the dumb thing *in* already.

I suffer through one more contraction that is excruciating because I'm sitting upright for the epidural placement. I scream, unable to help myself.

"That should be the last one you feel," Dr. Hanson says. She's right – it is.

Thirty minutes later, I'm sucking on ice chips and watching Oprah on television, with Rick sitting on one side, my mother on the other.

"You really aren't feeling anything at all?" Rick asks, watching the monitor needle climb higher and higher.

I glance at the monitor, pop another ice chip in my mouth, and shake my head. "Not really. I feel tingling in my stomach, but it doesn't hurt."

"Cool," he says.

The nurse bustles back into the room. "Let's check your progress. The contractions are getting closer and closer." I wiggle into position. She checks me and smiles. "Great! You're at about an eight now. It won't be long."

My eyes bug out. "Already? Wow! That was fast."

"Not really, Heather. You were most likely in labor all night, you know," Mom reminds me.

The nurse ignores the comment. "We need to go ahead and get you ready to go to the delivery room because you'll probably be complete by the time we get there."

A flurry of activity swirls in the room. Rick and Mom are both given scrubs to don over their clothes. I laugh when Rick puts the puffy blue hat on. "You look like the muffin man! Wait until I tell Elizabeth!" I crow.

A flash of light fills the room – Mom took a picture of him. "I'll show her the pictures when we get them developed. I love it!" she exclaims.

When we get to the delivery room and I am placed into position, the doctor informs me that I can start pushing. I only have to push for about an hour before Ethan makes his appearance. Rick whoops, and Mom cries at the same time Ethan does.

"Do you want to cut the cord?" the doctor asks Rick, who nods eagerly.

Once the task is complete, the doctor proclaims, "He's a healthy baby boy." He holds Ethan's bloody wet body up briefly for me to see before handing him to the nurse, who is waiting with a towel.

"Great job again, honey bun. He's beautiful!" Rick murmurs, kissing my forehead.

I smile, suddenly exhausted. I didn't feel any pain, thankfully, but I am drained.

"How much does he weigh?" Mom asks enthusiastically.

"We're doing that now," a voice replies. "He's seven pounds, nine ounces and twenty inches long." A wail fills the air. "With a healthy pair of lungs."

"That's my boy!" Rick proclaims.

When they hand Ethan to me, I drink in this new little face. He's got beautiful rounded cheeks and a full head of sandy-colored hair. "Rick, he's got your hair."

Rick grins. "So it would seem. Oh, he's gorgeous!"

"Perfect," I murmur, kissing his velvet cheek and holding him close.

The recovery time is much easier this time around – I know how to nurse, and he latches on the first time. I am thrilled to find out I only have to stay for twenty-four hours because I'm a second time mom.

"Thank *God!*" I exclaim. They also encourage Rick to stay overnight with me. I can't believe my good fortune.

"Will you be all right staying with Elizabeth, Louise?" Rick asks Mom.

"Of course. We have a lot of catching up to do. It will be fun."

Rick departs that evening to take Mom home and bring an overnight bag for himself.

Ethan and I are left alone for the first time. I prop him up on my lap after nursing him and study his tiny face carefully. He is perfectly sculpted, just like Elizabeth was. His lips are full and match the shape of Rick's mouth. I marvel at the curl of his ears, the amazing artistic details that are his fingers and toes. I can't believe how small his pinky toenail is, and tell him so. He responds by opening his mouth and sticking his little pink tongue out.

I think my heart just melted. I am head over heels in love with this little person. I gather him to my chest tenderly and rub my cheek against his velvety head. He grunts and starts rooting. Suddenly, he stiffens and passes gas loudly. I laugh heartily, which annoys him because he starts to wail.

"Sorry, little guy," I say, lying down and latching him on. He sucks heartily and settles in for a good meal.

"Honey bun? You okay? How's my little man doing?" Rick murmurs close to my ear.

I struggle to open my eyes. I scowl and blink. "What? What time is it?"

"It's almost eight," he whispers.

"Oh gosh, I guess I fell asleep," I quickly glance down to check on

Ethan. He's fast asleep, his mouth wide open. He must have fallen off my breast at some point.

"You two look very cozy there," Rick murmurs.

My stomach growls loudly. "I missed dinner?" I carefully move away from Ethan, so I don't disturb him. Rick is quick to move in, carefully sliding his hands under Ethan's tiny body and gathering him in his arms. Ethan stiffens and wiggles, but remains asleep.

"No, your tray is right here," he nods toward the domed tray on my bedside table.

"I can't believe they didn't wake me up."

"It's nice they let you sleep here. Better than last time, huh?"

"Much better." I grimace trying to sit up.

"Need help?" Rick asks.

I shake my head. "No, I'm just sore."

"I bet," he chuckles. Ethan whimpers. Rick starts gently rocking back and forth. "Come on, little man. Let's sit down and let mommy eat." Rick sits in the rocking chair in the corner.

I pull my bedside table close and take the dome off my plate. Lukewarm meatloaf, potatoes, and canned green beans greet me. There's also a roll, one pat of butter (really?), and a brownie. It is nowhere near as tasty as my mother's, but I am ravenous and devour every bite.

The night passes easily because the staff here is not intrusive, and Rick is a huge help. He and I both get a decent amount of rest; Rick sleeps on a roll away bed that was brought in for him, and I keep Ethan mostly in bed with me, switching sides throughout the night whenever he needs to nurse.

When the breakfast tray is brought in the next morning, Rick yawns widely and stretches.

"I think I'll go home and get some breakfast and a shower. Then I'll bring Elizabeth and your Mom up."

"Sounds good. We'll be waiting," I reply, removing the dome from my plate. I am ravenous again.

Rick pats Ethan's swaddled bottom in his bassinet, and kisses me quickly before packing up his overnight bag and leaving.

Mom and Elizabeth are extremely excited to see Ethan. Elizabeth settles herself into the corner rocking chair, preparing herself to hold Ethan for the first time.

"He's so little! Was I this little?" she asks, studying his tiny face.

"You were about that small when you were born, yes," Rick says. "You were cute as a button, just like him."

Mom busily snaps away with her camera. She even takes a picture of me eating lunch. "Mom," I protest, stuffing another bite of chicken breast in my mouth.

"Hey, I've got five rolls of film to fill up!" she protests, but doesn't take anymore pictures of me eating.

Once we're discharged and on our way, Elizabeth spends the entire ride home telling Ethan about his room, her room, our house, her friend Katherine and her dolly, Madison, as well as everything she's doing at preschool.

"You'll get to go to preschool when you're bigger, too. You'll have so much *fun* there!" she says.

Rick squeezes my hand. I glance at him and he smiles.

"I know," I say, smiling.

****

The euphoria I feel following Ethan's birth lasts about two weeks before the gray clouds creep back in. I can't pinpoint an exact moment when it happens, but I recognize the loss of color and brightness in the world. It's like the shades are slowly pulled down and everything dims. Emotionally, I have to squint to bring anything into focus.

"Heather, I'm worried about you," Mom says one day while I sit picking at my tuna sandwich at lunch. At least, I think it's tuna.

"Huh?" I ask, looking up.

"Honey, you're just not yourself," she says.

"What do you mean?"

"I mean," she starts. "I think you're depressed."

"I'm fine, Mom."

"No, you're not."

I pick up my sandwich and take a bite. Yes, it is definitely tuna. Mom is still staring.

"You need to make an appointment with a doctor," she continues.

"What am I supposed to say, Mom? I hate Oregon, so can you give me a pill for that?"

Mom presses her lips into a thin line. "No, Heather. It's more than that."

I close my eyes and rub my face. Ethan starts to whimper from his bassinet in the living room. "I have to go feed Ethan." I get up and walk out.

****

"Rick, you have to get her some help," Mom's soft voice carries into the bedroom. Lying down on Thursday afternoon in our bed while Ethan nursed, I slipped into semi-consciousness. At the sound of her voice, my ears perk up.

"I know," Rick sighs. "I just don't know what to do."

"You're going to have to do something. She is seriously depressed. Have you noticed how she…isn't really here anymore?"

"Yes." Rick sounds defeated.

"How long has this been going on?"

"I don't know. Probably since we moved here, I guess. I was deployed for a few months, you know. When I got back, she just…like you said, isn't here anymore. No matter what I do, it doesn't help." There's a long pause. "Maybe…maybe she should go back to Texas." His voice cracks.

"Oh, Rick. No. That won't solve anything. She's your wife. She belongs with you."

I hear Rick's ragged breathing. Is he crying? My heart picks up speed. I gently extricate myself from Ethan and creep over to the cracked bedroom door.

"I think it's what she really wants. What she really *needs*, Louise."

"Absolutely not. She needs help. I know this move was hard on her, but I would be willing to bet all those pregnancy hormones made it worse. She was pregnant before she left, but we just didn't know it. Did you know she hasn't even talked to Angeline in the longest time? That poor girl doesn't know what to think. Postpartum depression is a real medical problem, you know. We used to call them baby blues, but they know now it's a real problem. I am sure a doctor could help her."

A choked sob reaches my ear.

I silently close the door, latching it in place and return to bed. Ethan doesn't stir.

Is that what I want? Do I really want to move back to Texas? With most of my heart, yes. But I can't leave Rick here alone. I can get through this, can't I? I wonder if Mom is right – pregnancy hormones are tearing me up as much as the weather and separation from my family. I don't want to take pills.

Why am I doing this? It takes too much effort to remember.

CHAPTER TWENTY FIVE

February, 1994

Exerting so much effort feigning interest in life is exhausting, even more so than having a newborn and a preschooler to care for. Mom leaves when Ethan is three weeks old. I don't even try to keep my emotions in check for her departure. I cry on the way to the airport, and at the airport.

Mom's departing words to me were an admonition to make a doctor's appointment as soon as possible.

"Look at these three beautiful faces, Heather," Mom says, gesturing to Rick, Elizabeth, and Ethan. "They *need* you and you need them. Don't forget that."

"I won't." They are the driving force behind me continuing to breathe.

"I'll take good care of her, Louise," Rick says thickly, placing his arm around my waist.

Mom looks at Rick with such tender affection. "I know you will, Rick. I know you will." Then she is gone.

It hurts.

"Honey bun?" Rick interrupts my thoughts, or rather, lack of thoughts on the way home. I had let my head fall back and closed my eyes. I didn't want to see another dreary scene as the city whizzed by.

"Hm?" I reply, not opening my eyes.

"Please make that appointment, okay? You need to get some help."

I clear my throat and reluctantly turn toward him. "I will."

"Are you sick, mommy?" Elizabeth asks from the back seat.

"No."

"Mommy just doesn't feel good, and she needs to see a doctor to help her get better."

I shoot him a stern look, which he ignores.

"Then that means you're sick, mommy. Go see the doctor like I do when my throat hurts. Does your throat hurt?"

"No." I can't explain to a four-year-old what hurts, because everything hurts.

Rick picks up the conversation with Elizabeth. I tune them out and close my eyes.

Rick attempts to start a conversation with me that night after Elizabeth has gone to bed. I am already in bed, lying on my side while Ethan nurses. When Rick comes in, I close my eyes and pretend to be asleep. I don't want to talk. It's too much effort, and I don't have the strength. He tries to get my attention, but gives up and eventually turns the light off.

Exhaustion pulls me into bed early every night. I mechanically go through the motions of life – caring for and feeding Ethan and Elizabeth, cleaning the house, grocery shopping and cooking.

So much effort.

Too much effort.

****

"Heather, I've had enough," Rick says over lunch on Wednesday. "I made your appointment this morning. You are going to see the doctor Friday at eleven-thirty. Elizabeth will be in preschool, and I'll be home to watch Ethan."

"What?" I ask, blinking and squinting. It's so bright in here. Oh, the sun is out. I hadn't noticed.

"I made you a doctor's appointment for Friday. I wrote it on the calendar and I'll drive you there myself if I have to. You need help."

"Sure."

His eyebrows rise. "That's it? That's all you're going to say?"

I should be angry, but all I can muster is mild annoyance. Anything more is too much effort. "I guess," I sigh and rise from my chair, leaving the canned soup I heated up mostly untouched. Rick grabs my arm and stops me.

"Heather, where *are* you? It's like you're dead inside or something," he says, searching my face earnestly.

"I am," I reply mechanically, waiting for him to release my arm.

He gasps, tightening his grip. He rises and folds me in his arms. My arms hang limp. I let my eyes close. It really is bright in here.

"Heather, you don't want to harm yourself or the kids, do you?" he murmurs in my ear hesitantly.

That gets my attention. My head snaps up, and I glare at him. "I would never hurt my kids. I would never hurt myself because *that* would hurt my kids."

Rick stares at me. "What about me? Don't you think that would hurt me, too?"

"I'm not going to hurt myself, Rick. I just..." How do I put this in words? "I just don't...feel."

He looks at me questioningly, but doesn't speak. What else is there to say?

Rick drives me to my appointment with Ethan in tow. He comes into the room with me and talks with the doctor, sharing his concerns while I remain silent, detached from the conversation. When Rick finishes whatever he said – I didn't pay attention – the doctor asks him to take Ethan and wait outside. When Rick departs, the doctor turns his attention to me, asking me all sorts of questions. It's exhausting to answer. I just want to go home and sleep.

Finally, the interrogation ends. The doctor places his hand on my arm. "Mrs. Johnson, you have all the signs of severe depression. I am going to prescribe a medication for you that should help. It's safe to take while you're nursing, and it's very important you take this every day at the same time. Don't skip a dose, and don't stop taking it. I want you to come back and see me..." He goes on and on about follow-up appointments and whatever else. I don't care. His lips keep moving and I can't help but notice how thin they are. Why are his lips so thin?

"Do you have any questions, Mrs. Johnson?" he asks.

"Huh? No."

"All right," he says, scribbling on a small square pad of paper. "Go on out and have your husband come back in here, please."

I do as he says. Rick is in the doctor's office for another five minutes. When he emerges, his eyes look frightened, but he is wearing a smile, which doesn't make any sense. It doesn't matter. I just want to go home.

We get the prescription filled at the pharmacy before going home.

"Here," Rick says, handing me a glass of water and a tiny pill. "Take this now. The doctor said to go ahead and take your first dose as soon as we got it."

"Fine," I reply, taking the pill and a swallow of water. "I need to feed Ethan and then go get Elizabeth. You need to get back to work."

Rick's face looks pinched. "Yes, I do. I love you, Heather," he says, bending down to kiss my forehead before leaving. I think I heard him mutter, "I hope this works" before he left, but I'm not sure.

I don't care.

****

Over the next two weeks, my energy level and interest perk up slightly. The shades rise a centimeter. Rick ensures I take my medication every morning before he leaves for work. It's annoying, but I know he means well.

"Are you going to open any of these?" Rick asks, pointing to a messy stack of mail piled on the corner of the desk. When did the pile get so high?

"What are they?" I ask, not remembering.

Rick starts sifting through the pile. "Well, there are letters in here from Angeline, for one. Don't you want to read them?"

"I guess. Just leave them there. I'll get to it later."

Rick sighs impatiently, continuing to sift through the pile. "Heather, there are *bills* in here. Have you been paying them?"

Hadn't I? I thought so. "I think so. What's there?"

"Never mind," he says. He walks over to my purse and removes the check book. "I'll take care of it."

"I didn't mean to let that slip."

"I know. Don't worry about it. I'll take care of it until you feel better."

I hope I feel better soon.

****

My first follow-up appointment with the doctor comes. I go to the lab to have blood drawn before I see him. The doctor is pleased with the results. He asks how I'm feeling. He asks a lot more questions.

"Well, it can take up to a month before you notice a real improvement," he informs me.

"Okay," I say.

Unfortunately, I don't have that long. Rick comes home from work that night wearing a familiar look on his face. He informs me that he is deploying tomorrow morning.

I don't get angry, I don't scream or yell. It happens.

"I tried to get out of it, but I can't. I really tried. Even my supervisor went to bat for me. But with the military budget cuts, there just aren't enough people to go around. The new motto is 'do more with less.' There's nobody to take my place. We're all stretched thin."

"Of course," I reply flatly. I don't ask him where he's going, or how long he'll be gone, but he tells me anyway. It has to do with the overthrow of the President of Haiti whose name is Jean Bertand Aristade. It's very French, and that's confusing. Haiti isn't in France. This time he knows he's going to operate from the island of Cuba; apparently, we have a base on one side of the island.

I bet the sun shines there all the time.

When he's finished talking, he looks at me and the rim of fear that usually circles my eyes when he's leaving now rims his. "Heather, I am really worried about you. Can you promise me that you'll be all right? Please?" he pleads.

"Yes, I'll be fine. I promise." I cup his cheek in my hand. He covers my hand with his own and presses it there. "I'll keep taking my medication."

He nods wordlessly.

Rick leaves the next day. We embrace and say our goodbyes. Ethan is too small to know what's going on, but Elizabeth's reaction bothers me deeply. She accepts that her daddy is leaving. She accepts that we don't know how long he will be gone.

It's normal now.

Two days later, Rick calls to let me know he arrived safely, but I'm not home to answer the call. His message is short, informative, and I can tell he wants to say more. He tells me he loves me and will call as soon as he can.

Within a couple of weeks, the medicine begins to help – my energy level rises. I am able to focus more on things around me. For instance, the aqua green Geo Metro that used to park in the carport next to me has been replaced by a red Ford pick-up truck. Apparently, our neighbors moved out, and someone new moved in. Terri told me that they got out of the military due to budget cuts.

"He wanted to make it a career, but couldn't. They wouldn't let him cross-train, and his job was being eliminated, so *poof*, they're out."

"Lucky them," I murmur.

"Oh, I don't know. I mean sure, it's not an easy life, but at least we know we'll get a steady paycheck and the health care is good, right?"

"Yeah. It's just hard," I counter.

When Rick calls two weeks later, I am home. I had just put Ethan down for his afternoon nap.

"Hey," he says hesitantly. "How are you and the kids?"

"We're doing fine. Ethan is smiling a lot and making silly sounds when Elizabeth and I talk to him."

"That's good. Um…how are you doing?" he asks.

"Better. The medication is working, I think."

Rick blows his breath out. "I'm so glad to hear that. You are taking it every day?"

"Yes, Rick," I chuckle. "I take it every day."

He's silent for a long moment. "It's good to hear you laugh."

I smile. "Sorry. I'm sorry I messed up, too." We are still trying to dig ourselves out of the hole I dug by letting the bills slip.

"Don't apologize. It will be fine."

"Yeah."

I am still working my way through the stacks of mail that piled up; Rick had separated them into two piles. The smallest pile contains the bills and the other, much larger one, has cards and letters I never opened. One letter caught my attention because it had a forwarding address sticker on it. It's from Nicole – she had written me months ago apologizing for not keeping in touch, but her three kids had kept her busy. Stan was also either deployed or working twelve-hour shifts most of the time. Her handwriting was loopy and sloppy, like she was rushing to write the letter. They had gotten orders again, this time to Italy. I gasped when I read it – they were supposed to have left for Italy almost two months ago.

"Oh, no," I whisper, realizing they're long gone. I quickly pull out a note card and scribble a hasty response apologizing for not responding earlier, and urging her to write me as soon as she can. I don't know why I'm hurrying *now*, other than I feel the need to. I write her old German address on the envelope, hoping it will be forwarded.

Sifting through the remaining stack of letters, I see quite a few from Angeline. I grimace realizing how I've ignored her, too. What have I done?

"Been an idiot is what I've done," I answer myself.

I place them in order by the date stamp and read the oldest one first. As I continue to read, the tone of her letters changes. She goes from long and cheerful with lots of questions to short and informative with no questions. Chris deployed almost as much as Rick has, and it was difficult.

Her final letter brings me to tears. She and Chris got orders to England and of course they're short notice. She should have left a month ago.

"No!" I cry, leaping for the phone. I dial her number hurriedly, crossing my fingers like the fool that I am.

"I'm sorry, the number you have dialed has been disconnected or is no longer in service. Please hang up and…" The recorded message stabs through my ears and into my heart. I hang up the phone and cry.

She's gone. Angeline is gone.

Just as I did with Nicole, I write her a hasty note, hoping against hope it will be forwarded. Later that day when I drop them into the mailbox, I send up an earnest prayer that they will reach my friends. Please let them reach my friends. I don't want to lose them.

****

Two weeks later, within a day of each other, my notes are returned. They cannot be forwarded. I have lost them.

I call my mother; maybe she was able to stay in touch with Angeline.

"I'm sorry, sweetheart, but she had a hard time handling the kids with Chris being gone, so she packed up early and went home to her mother until they were ready to leave. Then she joined Chris overseas," she informs me.

"Do you have her mother's address?" Please, please, please.

"No. I'm sorry, Heather."

This is all my fault. I let everything slip through the cracks.

No amount of medication is going to deaden this pain.

When Rick calls the next two times, I ignore the phone. I just can't do this right now. I am so alone.

Weeks go by. Things go gray again. The only things in sharp focus are the faces of my children. Their faces get me up every day, get me moving every day. I pay the bills on time.

I have to keep going. I have to.

The cost is staggering.

****

April, 1994

Rick comes home to no fanfare. Those who deployed with him trickle home over several weeks, also to no fanfare. Elizabeth gives him a hug, but isn't overly excited. All Rick has done is come home from work. Ethan is three-months-old and doesn't really care who holds him or who doesn't. Rick marvels over him.

"He's got such chubby cheeks. Look at those dimples!" he exclaims, fondling Ethan's velvet cheek. Ethan smiles, enjoying this new face. Rick turns to me. "How are you doing?" he asks quietly, searching my face.

"I messed up, Rick."

He blinks a couple of times before answering me. "What do you mean?"

I tell him all about Nicole and Angeline and how I've lost them.

"I'm sorry, Heather. You couldn't help that. You weren't well."

"I should have, Rick. I should have…"

"You never know. We may run into them sometime in the future."

I nod, unable to speak.

Rick smiles and turns his attention back to the children. He makes a goofy face at Ethan then starts asking Elizabeth questions, which she is eager to answer. I take Ethan from his arms and we walk toward the truck, Rick carrying his bags.

CHAPTER TWENTY SIX

May, 1994

We will be married six years this month. It's been a long, hard six years. It's been good, too. I see that in the faces of my children. We need to celebrate *us*. I have to remind myself and Rick about us.

Adjusting to having Rick home from this deployment has been challenging. Elizabeth doesn't take instruction or correction from him as well as she does me. I have to remind her that her father needs to be obeyed, just as she obeys me. Initially, Ethan doesn't mind Rick holding him, but when he is fussy, he only quiets down when I hold him. That hurts Rick.

"I'm sorry," I lament, soothing Ethan. "He doesn't remember you. He's only a baby. Give him some time."

Rick nods, staring at his son.

With nobody to watch Elizabeth and Ethan, I settle for making our anniversary celebration a family dinner. We have another mouth to feed, and all the expenses that come with a new baby. We can't afford to go out.

I splurge and purchase T-bone steaks on sale at the commissary. They're not very thick, but they'll do. I pull out my mother's recipe book and thumb through it for ideas on what else to serve. Of course, I'll make chocolate mousse for dessert.

The day of our anniversary, Rick comes home from work with a dozen red roses and a card. I have the table set with the white linen cloth and crystal dishes I use every year.

"Happy anniversary, honey bun," Rick murmurs in my ear, embracing me tightly. "I love you."

"I love you, too," I whisper back, clinging to him. I really do.

Dinner is good. Elizabeth enjoys feeling very grown up. "It's like a restaurant in our house!" she exclaims, fingering the linen cloth and silverware.

"Yes, it is. Your mommy makes great restaurant food, too," Rick replies, raising his fork to me.

I smile and cut into my steak.

****

June, 1994

Summer comes to Oregon, or at least what passes for summer here. I still crave the Texas sun. The warmth I want doesn't come. I miss how the pavement shimmers in the summer. I miss the sharp contrast of cool pool water on my skin after letting the heat of the sun set my body on fire. It was so refreshing.

My mood brightens, and the grayness lifts. It is still hard, but I find more reasons to smile. Color returns. There is a lot of color here, even if most of it is in varying shades of green.

Rick and I pull out our bikes and take Elizabeth for a ride with us. Terri agreed to watch Ethan while we ride – he's too small to be on the back of a bike yet. He sat up for the first time only a month ago.

There are plenty of places to ride on the base and we scout beautiful areas for picnics in the future. The physical exercise and fresh air sharpen my mind and my senses. I gulp deep lungfuls of the air while we ride.

When we return, Rick heads over to Terri's to collect Ethan and I load the dishwasher while Elizabeth plays in her room.

"You seem to be feeling better, Heather," Rick says cautiously, joining me in the kitchen with Ethan in his arms. He pulls the pocket door that separates the kitchen from the living room closed to give our conversation some privacy.

"Yeah, I am."

"I'm so glad. I've missed you."

"I miss me, too."

"Was it really hard while I was gone? With the kids?" he probes, nuzzling Ethan's neck.

"The kids gave me a reason to keep going," I reply, looking up from the dishes to gaze at him. "I see your face in theirs. They remind me of the promise I made and how much I love you."

Rick's chin quivers slightly and he clears his throat. "I love you, too. I remember my promises to you, as well. Do you still want me to reconsider the military?"

I load a few more dishes before I answer. "Rick, I want you to be happy. You already re-enlisted and have ten years in. It's just…hard."

Rick shifts Ethan so that he can wrap his arm around me. "Thanks. You're an amazing woman, you know that?"

I shake my head. "No, I'm not. I really stink at this."

He pulls back, surprised. "What do you mean? You don't stink at this."

"I...Let's talk about it after the kids go to bed, all right?" I ask.

"Okay," Rick says, eyeing me.

Throughout the evening, thoughts roam through my head – at first, they're negative and I replay all of the things I dislike about military life. Eventually, more positive ones weave their way in. I recall Rick telling me the benefits of the military. He does have a steady paycheck, he can go to college basically for free whenever he wants to, and the health care is also free. It may not be perfect, but it is better than a lot of what is out there. Yes, he has to deploy – *a lot*. But there are plenty of civilian jobs that require frequent travelling, as well. Thankfully, Rick's job doesn't put him at high risk when he deploys. I am grateful for that. Living on base can be a challenge. But it is also a safe and secure neighborhood. I suppose it could be called a gated community – the thought makes me chuckle.

I share my thoughts with Rick in bed that night. He laughs at my gated community comment.

"You love your job. You are proud to serve this country. I'm proud of your patriotism. I'm sorry I haven't shared in it the way that I should," I whisper in the darkness.

Rick squeezes me. "I know it's hard, Heather. Believe me, I know. It's not easy for me, either."

I draw a ragged breath in. "Yeah."

I am beginning to realize what my mother meant when she shared her story with me about leaving dad. In my particular scenario, I am the one that needs to give up my dream to save our marriage. I will have to go through this military madness with him. I'm still not sure if I'm up to the task. I'm not sure I'm worthy of it.

Can I pay the price that is going to be asked of me? My heart of hearts tells me it will cost me dearly. I prefer not to follow that thought right now. I can't.

"I love you," Rick whispers.

"I love you, too," I reply. "I miss you every time you leave."

"I know. Even when I'm not physically here, you have to know my heart is here."

"Yes."

****

July, 1994

On a cool day late in the month (all the summer days here are cool to me), I am sitting on my front porch watching Ethan and Elizabeth play in the front yard. My thoughts turn to Angeline and our days spent outside in the glorious heat of summer. I will forever miss her.

"Howdy!" an unfamiliar voice calls out.

I jerk in surprise. I look up and blink, focusing on the woman approaching me. She has wild red hair, a freckled face and a stocky build. She exudes confidence. "Uh…hi."

"I'm Jolene. We moved in here a few months back. I think it's high time I introduced myself," she says with a flourish, thrusting her hand out for me to shake. When I place my hand in hers, she pumps it enthusiastically. "Nice to meetcha!"

"Same here," I reply, trying to get my bearings. I was in the fog of my own thoughts. "I'm Heather. These are my children Elizabeth and Ethan."

She glances at the children and grins widely. "Oh aren't they cute as little buttons! We have two boys, but they're both in summer camp right now. Their names are Beau and Brock." My eyebrows shoot up. She notices. "Yeah, they're kinda weird names, but I think they're strong sounding, don't you?"

"Uh, yes. Yes, they are." I'm not sure how to react to this woman.

"Mind if I join you?" she asks, not waiting for an answer while she pulls up another chair and plops down beside me.

"Please do," I reply, after the fact.

"How long you guys been here?" she asks, piercing me with her unusual green eyes. They're mostly green but with brown flecks in them.

"Just over a year."

"Where did you come from?"

"Texas."

"Oh, wow! What a change, huh? We came here from Guam, and let me tell you," she barks out a throaty laugh, "it is a heck of a lot better here! It's so hot in Guam; I had a hard time wanting to get dressed every day! Darn near wasn't worth it except nobody wants to see this gleaming white body in the buff!" She laughs heartily at her own joke. I smile and laugh politely.

Jolene dominates the conversation; by the time she's done, I know most of her history as well as the fact that she can't stand bologna. Apparently, she grew up eating a lot of it. Now, she refuses to buy it for her own children. She grew up in a military family, is the oldest of five children, and she and her husband have been married for almost fifteen years. She wanted to marry a military man, and so that's what she did. He is a Tech Sergeant in the security forces squadron.

"I'm sorry," she says, eyeballing me. "I just talked your ear off. So, tell me about yourself. Who's your husband and what does he do?"

I tell her about Rick and that he works on the cargo planes and he's also a Tech Sergeant.

"I think our men won't have any problem making Master Sergeant when the time comes. They've practically gutted the military, you know. Nothing but chiefs and airman left! They gotta fill out the ranks."

Jolene may be loud and read like an open book, but I think I could like her. She made the effort to introduce herself, which is more than I could say for me.

"You know, when I walked up, you looked pretty down. You okay?" she presses. "I hope I didn't interrupt you or anything. Everyone tells me I tend to be like a bull in a china shop."

"I'm all right. Just missing some friends."

"I can understand that. How many places have you all been? I imagine not many because you've only been married six years."

"Just Texas and here. Texas is my home."

"How are you holding up?"

I consider her and her question before I answer. I weigh my options and decide to just throw it out there. "I've been having a hard time. I miss my family."

"Ah, honey," she says sympathetically, her brow crinkling. "I'm sorry to hear that. It's tough, but it's good, too, right? I mean, how else can you get paid to see the world like this? Life is an adventure, and I for one plan to ride this ride to the end!"

"My husband has deployed four times since we got married, and he was in Korea the first year of our marriage."

She barks out her throaty laugh. "I hear ya. I really do. My husband has been gone a lot, too. You can imagine what with him being a cop and all. But I think it helps our marriage out – just about the time I'm sick of him leaving the cap off the toothpaste, or his socks on the floor, he goes away for a few months and we get a break. It makes our time together so much sweeter."

I chuckle. What an outlook. "I'm glad it works for you. I would rather have him here, even if he did leave the cap off the toothpaste, or his socks on the floor."

"He's gonna make this a career, right?"

"Yes."

She clucks her tongue. "You okay with that? Doesn't sound like you are."

She misses nothing. "Yes, I'm okay with it. I decided I'll do it if it's what he wants."

She frowns and places her hands on her knees, piercing me with her eyes once more. "Have you gotten involved in anything since you got here?"

"No. I was pregnant with Ethan when we got here, we moved into housing, and Rick deployed. So I haven't had the chance." Or the motivation.

"That's what you need. You don't have your family around, so you have to *make* family wherever you go. That's the secret. That's what gets you through, Heather. So listen, I belong to a supper club, and we meet once a month. It's all ladies, and they're some real characters! Would you like to come?"

"Sure. That sounds interesting."

"Good!" She slaps her thigh. "We meet in two weeks, so I'll let the gals know."

She launches into a description of how the supper club works, and I find myself getting excited. Maybe she's right – this could be just what I need.

Rick is thrilled when I tell him. He agrees with Jolene. "You need to get plugged in somewhere, Heather. It will do you a world of good."

I hope so.

****

August, 1994

Jolene instructed me to bring an appetizer to the supper club. Naturally, I flip through my mother's recipe book. I settle on bringing her stuffed mushrooms – my family always enjoyed them. At Rick's insistence, I make a double batch, leaving half at home.

There's a sharp knocking at the door promptly at six o'clock. Even Jolene's knock resonates with confidence.

"I'll get it," Rick says, rising from the sofa. I am busily securing the mushrooms on the tray with plastic wrap.

Hearing Jolene's hearty voice makes me smile. I gather the secured tray in my arm and join the conversation in the living room.

"You didn't tell me how handsome your Rick is!" Jolene exclaims. "Boy, you're a looker all right." She turns her attention to Ethan, who is propped up on the sofa, sucking on a toy. "Those girlies better watch out for you, little man. You'll have them chasing you down the street!" Ethan grins and kicks his feet.

"You guys go and have a great time. We are going to watch *Sleeping Beauty*," Rick says, rubbing his hands together. He had surprised Elizabeth with the VHS tape today. She's been eagerly waiting to watch it.

Jolene chats the entire time we drive to her friends' house, which is fifteen minutes away. We pull up to a beautiful two story home surrounded by tall, majestic pine trees. Jolene introduces me to everyone, including the hostess whose name is the only one I remember – Amber. There are twelve women in total, and the food-laden table looks amazing.

I don't need to talk very much because Jolene does it for me. I don't mind; I'm intimidated. These women all seem to be successful, and the group is so close knit, I don't know how or where to fit in. I just smile, nod, and grip my glass of iced tea.

When we've all introduced our dishes, which I have to do out loud, we pile our plates with food and take a seat at the enormous dining room table.

"So, Heather," a smartly dressed woman says. "Tell us a little more about yourself. Jolene said you have two children?"

"Yes," I quickly wipe my mouth with the napkin. "Elizabeth is four, and Ethan is six months old."

"Oh, that's a nice age gap. I had two in diapers and believe me, that was a chore," she replies. I struggle unsuccessfully to remember her name.

The other ladies continue to ask me questions. My plate of food goes relatively untouched while I try to answer everyone and satisfy their curiosity. That curiosity is finally spent when we eat dessert.

"I hope you'll all forgive me, but I don't remember your names," I say apologetically to some chuckles.

"That's all right. There are a lot of us here. Take your time," the hostess, Amber, says.

I enjoy the evening, but remain intimidated. One of the ladies is an attorney, for crying out loud. From what I can gather, Jolene and I are the only military spouses here.

A few of the ladies gather me in a hug before we leave. It's very nice.

"We hope to see you again, Heather," Amber says after hugging me. "You fit right in. Thanks for inviting her, Jolene."

While driving home, Jolene asks, "Well, what did you think?"

"They're all very nice, but I don't know that I fit."

"What do you mean?" she asks in surprise.

"Well, they are all so sophisticated and successful."

"Oh, please. We're all just women who love to eat, regardless of what we do or don't do in life. All that other stuff is left at the door."

"How did you meet these ladies? Nobody besides us in that group is military."

"In case you haven't noticed, I am a chatty person. I will talk to anybody! Shelby, the lady on the end with the beautiful black hair, remember her?" My blank look tells her I don't. "Anyway, she was sitting next to me in the salon one time when I was getting my hair done. We got to talking, and she ended up inviting me to the supper club. I think I had mentioned something about a delicious pumpkin cheesecake recipe I was reading about in *Good Housekeeping*. Or was it a squash recipe? I don't remember, but the point is that's how we met. The rest of the ladies I met when I got there. Of course, some ladies have come and some have gone, but it's a great group. They enjoyed you!"

"They were very gracious."

"Do you want to join us? Officially, I mean."

I shrug. "Sure, why not? You were right – I need to get out and get involved."

Jolene's throaty laughter fills the car as she pulls into her driveway. After hugging me fiercely, we walk to our own homes.

When I enter, Rick stops flipping through sports channels and smiles. "Hey! Did you have fun?"

I nod and smile. "It was very nice." I fill him in on the details. He agrees with Jolene about the intimidation factor.

"I'm sure it doesn't matter. Besides, you're such a great person, how could they not love you?"

I offer my empty platter. "They at least loved my stuffed mushrooms."

****

September, 1994

The skies turn gray and to my relief, my mood doesn't shift with the season this time. I have continued taking the medication, but would love not to. When I mention that to the doctor, he says he will try and wean me down slowly, starting with a smaller dose.

"Let's see how you do with that for at least two months. Then we'll talk about getting off of it," he said while scribbling some notes in my chart.

I am glad the clouds don't invade me this time; Rick's parents are supposed to visit in time to celebrate Elizabeth's fifth birthday. We don't see them often, and I want to enjoy them.

Katherine is in first grade this year, and Elizabeth is sorry to see her best friend go without her again – her birthday fell past the dead line. She will start Kindergarten next year, so for now, Elizabeth continues going to preschool.

Ethan has begun crawling and is eager to utilize this new skill every chance he gets. I caught him trying to climb out of his crib, and it scared the life out of me. His foot and arm were stuck in the rails, and he was screaming. Fortunately, he was screaming more out of frustration than pain, but the distinction didn't reach my heart in time to stop it from pounding.

"Do you think it's time to get him a toddler bed?" Rick asks.

I gape at him. "Are you kidding me? He's not even a year old. He would never stay in there."

"But if he's already trying to climb out of the crib, wouldn't it be safer? He won't get his arms or legs caught in the rails."

I called my mother to ask her advice. She told me Jeff was the same way.

"He couldn't wait to get up and get moving!" she says. "We put bells all along the side of his bed where he would get out to alert us that he was on the move. It worked like a charm. We didn't have those fancy baby monitors like you have now."

"But did you always hear them?" I ask.

"Sure. You know mommy radar never turns off, dear. But we didn't do that until he was walking. I wouldn't do it while Ethan is only crawling. Just put the mattress down farther on the crib. Put a few toys in his crib for him to play with, too. It should keep him occupied long enough for you to wake up."

Rick and I adjusted the crib mattress so that it sat lower. I still put bells around his bed, however. Just in case. Ethan is a little rascal – always thinking.

One night, Rick and I are getting amorous when the bells on his bed go off. We both stiffen, waiting. Sure enough, I hear his little hands and knees on the floor and the sound of his toys being disturbed.

Rick sighs and sits up. "I'll get him this time. You stay right here." When he returns ten minutes later, he is laughing quietly.

"That boy," he says, climbing back into bed.

"What was he doing?"

"He wanted a toy that was on his book shelf, I think. I found him trying to climb them like stairs."

That gets my attention. "He *what?*"

"It's okay. There are only two shelves. I took him down and got the toy he wanted. Plus I took everything off that top shelf so if he wants anything else, he can reach it."

"Rick, what am I going to do? He's not like Elizabeth. He's so curious and busy."

"Well, he's a boy. That's what boys do."

"Yeah, maybe. But I don't want to end up in the emergency room."

"He'll be fine. Now, where were we?" He reaches for me. The bells, in Ethan's room at least, remain silent for the rest of the night.

****

October, 1994

"Mom! Dad!" Rick yells when he spies his parents getting off the plane. His parents have flown in from Hong Kong.

"Rick!" His mother beams, waving. She and Rick's father, Skip, move as fast as they can.

"Look, Ethan, there's your Grandma Lovey," I whisper in Ethan's ear.

When they finally make it to us, they look rather fresh for such a long flight. Flying first class must be worth the money.

"Darlings!" Lovey exclaims, her eyes darting between Elizabeth and Ethan. "Oh, precious babies, you're so *big!*"

Skip and Lovey hug each of us fiercely, marveling. Rick's mother smells of gardenias, while his father smells of Old Spice.

"It's good to see you, Mom," Rick mumbles while being gathered into Lovey's arms.

Both of his parents' eyes are wet while we make our way to baggage claim, talking the whole time. Ethan allows Skip to carry him the entire way, unashamedly staring at this new face.

"I've got gifts for everyone," Lovey informs Elizabeth, gripping her hand while she walks. Elizabeth skips happily alongside.

"What did you get me?" Elizabeth asks excitedly.

"Elizabeth, don't be rude," I warn her.

Lovey waves me off. "Nonsense! I got you the most adorable doll in Hong Kong. She is wearing a beautiful silk dress, and do you know what? I got a dress made just for you that matches the doll's dress. What do you think of that?"

Elizabeth's excited response causes those around us to stare in our direction – she screams, jumps up and down, and claps her hands. Skip and Lovey only have eyes for Elizabeth and Ethan.

The chatter on the way home centers around their travels, and Elizabeth has many questions. They both answer her thoroughly and with enthusiasm. Finally, when we arrive on base, Elizabeth and Ethan are exhausted. It's close to afternoon nap time for Ethan.

"Can I pick you up, buddy?" Skip reaches his hands toward Ethan in his car seat. Ethan grins and eagerly reaches for him. Skip laughs. "I guess that's a yes! That okay with you two?"

"Sure, Dad. Go for it," Rick replies, smiling. "I'll get the bags."

Lovey retrieves the house keys from Rick, and she and Elizabeth hold hands and chatter all the way into the house. I help Rick with the bags, to Skip's protest. He offers to trade Ethan for some of the suitcases, but I decline.

"I can hold him any time. You go on ahead."

Skip bounces Ethan up and down as he heads toward our front door, close on Lovey's heels.

"I think they're going to enjoy their grandchildren," I murmur to Rick.

"Are you kidding me? They're like big kids themselves," Rick chuckles. "They're going to eat them *up*."

Skip and Lovey insisted on staying with us, even though we don't have an extra guest room.

"We don't want to miss a moment with you all!" Lovey had said. "I hope you don't mind."

Of course, we didn't. We don't get to see them very often.

We rented a queen-sized bed, and had it set up in Ethan's room. Ethan's crib is temporarily in Elizabeth's room, much to her dismay.

"I don't *want* to share my room with him! He's a baby!" she protested.

"Elizabeth, it's only for a couple of weeks. You'll be fine. Besides, don't you think your Grandma Lovey and Grandpa Skip would appreciate that?"

She agreed, but only under protest.

After showing them their room with the Noah's Ark décor and baby furniture, which they don't even bat an eye at, Rick corrals them into the living room. I close the door behind me in Elizabeth's room, attempting to calm Ethan in the quiet and semi-darkness to take his nap. Within ten minutes, he is rubbing his half-closed eyes and yawning. He dozes off just as I gently place him in his crib. He sighs, rolls over, and goes right to sleep.

I join the conversation in the living room.

"You know, Vance just made partner. We are so proud of him!" Lovey says, talking about Rick's oldest brother.

"I bet. I'm also not surprised. He worked really hard, but now he may never settle down. He won't have time."

"Honestly, I don't think he wants to settle down," Skip adds. "He's so driven. There's no time for a social life. Hey! Did our little buddy go down all right?"

"Yes, he's fast asleep," I reply. "Would you guys like anything to drink? Are you hungry?"

Lovey smiles. "I would love some iced tea, if you've got it. Sweet, of course. I remember that sweet tea at your wedding. I miss it."

"Of course I have sweet tea. I'm a Texas girl." I grin, glaring mildly at Rick for not offering his parents refreshments.

"Sorry, Mom. I didn't think about it," Rick apologizes sheepishly.

"That's all right, dear. Skip? Would you like some tea?"

"Haven't you got anything stronger?" he asks.

"I bought some whiskey for you, Dad. I remembered," Rick rolls his eyes, smiling. "It's in the cabinet above the microwave," Rick tells me.

"Good boy! Just a dab will do me in my tea."

"I'll help you, Heather," Lovey says, rising.

While we prepare the drinks, Lovey pouring a splash of whiskey in Skip's glass, she turns to me. "I am so glad to be here, Heather. Are you sure we won't inconvenience you by staying here?"

"Absolutely not. We are glad to have you. I just hope you're not inconvenienced staying here. I mean, we don't have any luxuries or anything. I won't be insulted if you'd be more comfortable in a hotel."

"Nonsense! Our room is perfectly fine. How are you guys doing? I know Rick has been away a lot."

"It's been hard, but we're managing."

"You're such a strong young lady. I hope you know we're so proud of you both."

"Thank you."

We enjoy talking with them throughout Ethan's nap. When he wakes up, it's almost dinner time.

"I planned to make pork chops. Is that all right with everyone?"

"Actually," Skip looks to his wife. "We were hoping to take you kids out for dinner. You pick the place! The sky is the limit!" He raises his empty glass.

"Well, could we do it tomorrow instead?" Rick asks. "It's just easier to plan with the kids and things. I took leave for this whole week, so we can do whatever you guys want. Heather's pork chops are amazing, by the way."

"Oh, sure, sure. I'm sorry, I didn't think about that," Skip replies. "I am sure your pork chops are delicious."

Lovey and Skip keep Elizabeth and Ethan entertained while I prepare dinner with Rick's help. I don't really need his help, but he is happy to give his parents time with the kids.

"Your parents are really sweet people, Rick," I tell him while seasoning the chops.

Rick looks up from peeling potatoes, and smiles. "I know."

I am complimented on dinner – there are no leftovers. Skip and Lovey reluctantly retire for the night by seven thirty; jet lag kicks in. Rick helps them unpack while I give Ethan a bath. His bed time is rapidly approaching, too.

"How come they're going to bed so early?" Elizabeth laments after I've put Ethan to bed. "I want to play with Grandma Lovey some more."

"They're really tired, sweetheart. They flew for a whole day to get here. Besides, they're going to be here for two weeks. You'll be able to play a lot with Grandma Lovey. She and I are going to plan your birthday party."

That perks her up.

****

When Rick's parents take us out to eat the next evening, Lovey insists Elizabeth wear her new silk dress. Elizabeth is beside herself with excitement – the dress is a beautiful turquoise blue with tiny flowers embroidered on it, just like the doll Lovey gave her.

"It's exquisite!" I exclaim when Lovey shows it to me. She carefully removes it from the box, unfolding it and removing tissue paper as the dress slowly comes into view.

"Isn't it? The tailor, Mr. Po, has amazing talent with silk. I showed him the doll and he had this dress ready two days later. Thank you for giving me Elizabeth's measurements, by the way. I had him make it a little bigger so she can grow and still be able to wear it for a long time."

At the steak and seafood restaurant – again, his parents insisted we pick a place worthy of Elizabeth's dress – Elizabeth acts like a little lady during the entire meal. She feels so grown up in that dress. I wear the beautiful Tahitian black pearl earrings and matching necklace they gave me, Rick wears his silk tie and suit. Mr. Po apparently works magic with lots of clothing items.

Ethan's gift is not something he can wear. At least, not in public. They purchased another of Mr. Po's handcrafted creations – it's a silk suit fit for an emperor. It even includes the funny little hat and shoes with a fringe on the tips of the toes. Ethan's emperor suit is of red and black silk. We promised to get pictures of Ethan in it to send to his parents. It's fantastically ridiculous.

****

Lovey insists on paying for everything to do with Elizabeth's birthday party, which apparently will include a bounce house and a clown.

"That's too much for a five-year-old," I protest in dismay. "I can't let you spend that much on this, Lovey."

"Nonsense!" It is apparently her favorite word. "You will most certainly let me spend however much I want to on my only granddaughter. I read the Grandma Manual, and it clearly states that I can spoil her if I so choose."

When I tell Rick about it, he shakes his head. "Give it up, Heather. My mother has her heart set on doing this, and I think you should let her. I never wanted a hand-out from them, but I wouldn't suggest getting in the way of my parents doing things for their grandchildren."

I relent and allow them to spend a ridiculous amount for her birthday. When Rick checks with the housing office about allowing a bounce house, there is a form he has to fill out, and we receive approval a week later.

Of course, it's drizzling on the day of her party. The caterer (caterer!) took over my kitchen and small dining room. The menu consists of child-friendly canapés. I never heard of such a thing. I have to admit, however, the food is beautiful. The caterer even made tiny little peanut butter and jelly sandwiches, artfully arranged on a silver platter. A long, rectangular table has been set up along the wall in our dining room. The food is placed in tiers with décor around it matching the theme Elizabeth chose. She wanted everything to be centered on *Alladin*. Elizabeth is dressed like Princess Jasmine. The food is placed on platters made to look like silken pillows and the table cloth is a magic carpet. Balloons and streamers, also matching the theme, are everywhere.

"Would you get a look at this?" Jolene breathes, clutching a wrapped present in her hand when she arrives. I note Beau and Brock have already made their way to the bouncy house, despite the rain. "You guys pulled out all the stops. Boy, am I glad I don't have a little girl. I could never do something like this!" Her throaty laugh rings out.

I grimace, approaching her with a golden goblet of punch. "I'm sorry. I know it's over the top."

"Over the top? This is over the *moon*!" She laughs once more. "It's awesome! How did you do this?"

A man dressed like Alladin approaches, offering her a tray of canapés. "Would you care for something to eat?"

She stares at him open-mouthed before accepting a napkin, and selecting a few of the offered morsels. "Uh, thanks."

"Honestly, I had very little to do with it. My mother-in-law insisted on this because it's what Elizabeth wanted," I tell Jolene apologetically.

She stuffs the food in her mouth, shaking her head. "I like your mother-in-law. Tell her I said hi. Where do you want me to put this?" She gestures to the present.

"Oh, that goes in the," Cough. "cave."

"The *what*?" Jolene asks.

"The cave," I reply, pointing to the little treasure cave constructed out of chicken wire and paper mache, encrusted with plastic jewels in the corner. There are already a number of presents spilling out of the opening.

"Whoa!" Jolene laughs, walking over to place her offering in the cave's mouth.

Her reaction is mirrored by the other guests as they arrive. Elizabeth beams at the attention. I hope she doesn't get used to this – we could never afford to replicate it.

The party is a hit. Elizabeth falls asleep that night with a Cheshire cat smile, grasping her golden crown firmly in her hand.

"How much did this all cost, Mom?" Rick asks his mother after the caterer and her crew have cleaned up, packed up, and left. Our house is spotless.

"Oh, Rick, you know that's not the kind of question one should ever ask," she pats his cheek.

"Yes, mother," Rick replies indulgently.

"Ah, son," Skip says. "You know your mother loves to throw a grand party. We don't get to see you guys too often, so thanks for indulging her. Elizabeth enjoyed it. I thought it was wonderful!" He pours a splash of whiskey into his punch, and settles on the sofa next to Lovey.

****

We enjoy visiting with Rick's parents until they have to go. When Rick returned to work after the first week, I take them on a short tour of the city. It helped get me not only out of the house, but off the base. Mostly they're content to visit with their grandkids, however.

They have a European cruise booked with some of their friends, and are due to board the ship the week after they leave. They plan to go home to Maine before heading to Europe.

"Go on, give them your present," I encourage Elizabeth.

She grins and hands them a square poorly wrapped in colorful paper.

"Elizabeth wrapped it herself."

"Oh, sweetie! You did a great job," Lovey says, taking the present from Elizabeth. She carefully unwraps it. Elizabeth waits excitedly.

Lovey pulls out the cardboard frame Elizabeth made in preschool – it is decorated with macaroni and plastic gems reminiscent of the ones on the treasure cave at her birthday party. In the frame is a picture of Elizabeth with Skip and Lovey at her birthday party.

"Oh, Elizabeth, this is so lovely. Thank you so much! I will put it on my bureau everywhere I go. Come and give us a hug."

Elizabeth falls into her arms.

"Don't forget me, girlie," Skip says, snatching her up and tickling her into a giggling frenzy.

"Do you really like it?" she asks breathlessly. "For real?"

Skip nods his head vigorously. "That's the best present we've ever gotten."

"It's a true treasure, sweetie," Lovely adds.

There are tearful goodbyes at the airport. When they finally disappear from view, Rick turns to me.

"That was fun, huh?" he asks.

"It was great fun. I know the kids enjoyed them. Didn't you?" I pat Ethan's back, who kicks vigorously.

"I loved, loved, loved it!" Elizabeth squeals. "I wish Grandma Louise and Grandpa Leonard could be here, too. I have the best grandmas and grandpas in the world!"

I couldn't agree more.

****

December, 1994

Life returns to normal following Skip and Lovey's visit.

I enjoy Jolene's friendship and her supper club. The ladies are genuinely friendly. If I allow myself to forget what some of them do for a living, I can look them in the eye and feel like an equal. Almost.

Jolene's outlook and advice help me a lot. She chose this life on purpose, after having been raised in it. She is naturally a very positive person and that spills over. The decreased dosage of my medication doesn't send me back into the world of gray, and so as Christmas approaches, the doctor decides to wean me off completely. I'm both excited and scared. Not just about the medication, but also because Rick tends to miss a lot of holidays with us. Will this year be any different?

Unfortunately, he gets the call in mid-December – he will be leaving the next day for at least four months and possibly up to six months. This time he's headed to a new European country called Bosnia. It used to be a part of the communist country Yugoslavia. Since the fall of the Soviet Union, it has fractured into several countries which are divided along ethnic and religious lines, all of whom are fighting for control.

"Why do they keep sending us everywhere to be peacekeepers?" I ask in frustration. "If that's what they want, why don't they send the Peace Corps instead of the Marine Corps?"

"I don't know, Heather. I just do what I'm told. I'm pretty tired of this, too. I have spent enough time in tents to last me the rest of my life. We will never go camping."

"It's one more missed Christmas," I reply sadly. "You're also going to miss Ethan's first birthday."

He grimaces. "I know. I'm sorry."

We decide to have a hasty family Christmas that night. We let the kids open their presents. I can't pull a Christmas meal together that quickly, so we opt for Christmas pizza instead. We order pizza with green peppers and pepperoni for the red and green color.

Our last night together is almost desperate. This deployment will be dangerous. There's an active war going on where he's going, even though we're technically not going to be engaged in it. I am grateful he has the job he has.

None of this makes sense. How can our government keep cutting the military budget, but then still send our troops all over the globe?

Fear and anxiety become a nasty, fermenting pit in my stomach. Rick makes me promise to stay in touch with the doctor in case I need my medication again.

"Stick close to Jolene. She's good for you. She promised me she'd look out for you," he murmurs in my ear, hugging me and the kids tightly. Ethan squirms to get out – he took his first steps a few weeks ago and hates to be still.

"I will," I promise, fighting the tears. "I hate always saying goodbye."

"I know. I do, too."

Elizabeth doesn't bat an eye as Rick disappears. Ethan doesn't care, either. He just wants to be on the move.

****

January, 1995

It's difficult juggling two children this time, especially when one of them is an active little boy. He looks at everything as a mountain to climb or conquer. That includes the book case in his room, the sofa, the recliner (which fell over once), the kitchen table, and the kitchen drawers which, when pulled out, become steps for him to climb. That's where I find him one morning in the middle of the month.

I yelp when I see him standing on the counter with one knee hoisted on the shelf, opening the cupboard for who-knows-what. The baby-proofing locks I had installed on the cupboards are strewn on the floor. They apparently can't keep this baby out.

"Ethan!" I screech, lunging for him. I snatch him off the counter, looking around at the mess he made. The drawers are mostly emptied, to include my sharpest knives, every utensil, potholders, dish towels, and Tupperware containers. I run my hands all over his body checking for blood. Finding none, I start shaking as the adrenaline cascades through my body.

I draw a ragged breath as I stumble onto a kitchen chair, clutching my son. Thoughts race through my mind about what could have happened. Thoughts about what I could have found if... I burst into tears.

Ethan must be terrified because he remains still in my arms for quite awhile. Occasionally, his chubby hands pat my back.

"My baby, my baby," I cry into his soft little hair.

"Mommy, what's wrong?" Elizabeth's sleepy face and wild hair peer around the corner.

I take another deep, steadier breath and try to compose myself. "I just found your brother on the counter trying to get into the cupboard." I jerk my chin in the direction of the crime scene. Elizabeth gazes on the mess and gasps.

"Oh, boy. Ethan you're in *big* trouble," she says.

Ethan's mouth screws up. I position him to face me and tell him in no uncertain terms that what he did was wrong. I swear he knows what I'm saying.

"You could have really hurt yourself, Ethan. Then where would mommy be without you?" I ask.

His face puckers and he buries himself in my shoulder, whimpering. Once I collect myself enough to make breakfast for the kids, I call Jolene. She'll understand this.

When I share the story with her, she laughs her throaty laugh. "Oh, Heather, all's well that ends well, right? He didn't get hurt, did he?" Her laughter fills my ear.

"Jolene, he could have killed himself, or at the very least fallen on a knife and stabbed himself," I remind her.

"Yes, but he didn't."

"What am I supposed to *do* about this boy?"

"Well, you do what you can do, and leave the rest to God. There's nothing more to be done."

"Whatever," I grumble.

"Hey, maybe I can show you a trick or two."

Her tricks include looping heavy twine through cabinet pulls and around drawer knobs to make an intricate web that locks them all closed. It's a pain in my rear end, but if it keeps him from climbing them, I'll do it.

"My mommy radar is on over-drive with this one," I tell her while she examines my twine work.

"Yeah. There's always gotta be one, don't ya know." She peers at the twine and tries to pull the drawers and cupboards open to no avail. "Good job! I think you got it. Now you just have to be sure to do this every night before you go to bed."

"I know," I moan.

When I share the experience with my mother, she clucks her tongue. "I think he'll keep you busy, Heather. He's an extremely intelligent and energetic little boy, that's for sure. I really miss him, and all of you."

"I miss you, too. How are you doing?" One of her follow-up appointments is fast approaching.

She sighs and pauses. "Pretty good, I guess. Just weary."

A chill ripples up my spine. I try to keep my voice light. "Oh? Worked too hard over the holidays?"

"Yeah, probably." She abruptly changes the subject. "Did I tell you Debbie's applying to Texas A&M? I think she may get that volleyball scholarship."

"No, I didn't know. That's awesome! Tell her congratulations for me. When will she find out?"

"Sometime in the spring. She is applying to a few other places, too, but her heart is set on that."

"How are Jeff and Cara doing?"

"Oh, they're still doing well. I think this is going to be it for Jeff. Cara is good for him, and she's such a nice young lady."

"I always liked her."

Our conversation never returns to Mom. I am okay with that.

****

April, 1995

Our lives while Rick is deployed this time are marked by the dishwasher going out, the hot water heater flooding half the house before I figure out how to turn the water off, and the truck needing a new timing belt. My Honda also finally died. It broke my heart to see it towed away for good. Now we're down to one vehicle.

Housing maintenance is slow, as usual, and I am fed up with their excuses. Also as usual, I can do nothing about it.

The timing belt incident scared me half to death – it went out while I was driving on the highway. Of course, it was cold and rainy. Fortunately, traffic wasn't too heavy, and I was able to make it over to the shoulder before the truck came to a complete stop. I sat on the side of the road for twenty minutes before someone stopped to help. That's after two sheriff's vehicles passed me and didn't stop . Both children were with me, so I didn't feel comfortable walking along the side of the highway with them in tow.

"You said *two* sheriff's cars passed you and didn't stop?" Rick asks incredulously when I fill him in on our latest misfortune. I hadn't been able to talk to him since the middle of February, a few days after I found Ethan on the counters.

"No. Finally, an older couple pulled over and gave us a ride to the service station where I called a tow truck. It was a fiasco trying to get the car seats into their old Buick. But at least they stopped. Rick, I want to look into getting one of those new cell phones. I know they're expensive, but that would be perfect for an emergency. That's all I would use it for."

He sighs. "Yeah, I would feel better knowing you could call for help if you needed to."

"Okay. Any word on when you'll be home?"

"I don't know. Probably a few more months is my guess."

"What's it like there?"

Rick tells me about the local women they've hired to clean and do laundry. Most of them, while not old in years, have been aged by their experiences. Most have bad teeth and look much older than they are. The buildings are pock marked from previous fighting in the area. He is very careful to let me know that he's not in danger where he's at. I want to believe him, so I don't press it. My sanity couldn't handle anything else.

Why else would he be getting hazardous duty pay unless he is performing hazardous duty? I can't complain too much – the loss of his food allowance during this deployment is made up for by the extra money we receive for hazardous duty. Just another oxymoron, I guess.

I pull money from our diminished savings to purchase a Motorola cell phone the following week. It takes up half my purse and is ridiculously expensive to use, but I feel safer having it. What an incredible invention.

CHAPTER TWENTY SEVEN

May, 1995

Rick returns late in the month on a rare sunny day. The skies are so blue; they don't look real against the emerald backdrop of the evergreens. I am buoyant today, probably spurred on by the weather and coming summer. It's never warm enough, but at least it's not cold and dreary.

Rick drops his bags and jogs the short distance to us, leaving his bags in a rumpled heap. He gathers me in his arms first and lifts me off the ground, spinning me around.

"Hey there, honey bun!" he laughs. "You look so good."

"Daddy!" Elizabeth cries, grabbing his legs. He drops his gaze to her and lets his mouth hang open dramatically.

"Who is this beautiful young lady? Heather," he says, turning to me. "What happened to our little girl? Where did she go?"

Elizabeth giggles. "It's me, daddy! I'm just bigger now!"

"No way! You're *this* big now?" he asks, stretching his arms out.

She grins and nods vigorously. Rick scoops her up and spins her around while she squeals. When he puts her down, his jaw genuinely drops this time when he sees Ethan.

"There's my boy," he says quietly, marveling at his sixteen-month-old son. Rick dips down slowly, getting eye level with Ethan. "Hey there, little man."

Ethan stares at him for a moment before falling into his arms, much to Rick's surprise. Rick happily scoops him up, cradling him carefully in his arms. Ethan starts to grunt, pounding Rick's shoulder with his chubby fist. Rick looks questioningly at me.

"He wants you to spin him around like you did Elizabeth."

"Oh," Rick says, obliging him. Ethan laughs and laughs.

When Rick is done, I tell him, "Trust me. You don't have to be gentle with him. I don't think he wants to be treated like a baby anymore." Much to my chagrin.

"That's my boy!" Rick declares proudly, spinning him around again and pulling him over his shoulder before flipping him back onto his feet. Ethan enjoys it immensely.

Rick transitions back into the household over the next several weeks. It takes time, as it always does. The children aren't used to their father being home; Ethan doesn't even remember him. Seeing Rick when he wakes up and when he goes to bed is disconcerting at first. He looks at Rick like he's trying to decide why he's here and doesn't go away. At least he isn't stand off-ish like Elizabeth was at that age. Rick reads with Elizabeth and wrestles Ethan on the floor, on the sofa, and anywhere else they can find.

It's hard for me to adjust to having him home, as well. I am thankful he's here, but I am not used to having someone else to care for much less someone else to help. Rick constantly reminds me of that. There are no night shifts to adjust to this time. He is working eight hour day shifts with Sundays and Mondays off.

"I can take care of the kids while you go to supper club, Heather. You don't need to find a babysitter anymore," he reprimands me quietly one afternoon.

"I'm sorry. I'm just not used to..." I leave the sentence unfinished. He knows. "Thanks."

"Don't thank me. I'm their father."

"Rick, I didn't mean..."

"Never mind," he says, ducking out of the kitchen before I can finish.

****

June, 1995

"I'm so happy for you, Heather," Mom says when I call her for my usual bi-weekly calls. "Your attitude is so much better."

"I guess I've decided to quit pushing against a mountain. I am not happy about the deployments, but being miserable isn't the answer. I am a military wife and I have to go with the flow."

"There's an incredible turn around from just a few short years ago! I'm glad to hear it. How are you feeling overall? Do you think you'll need that medication again?"

I shudder. "I don't think so. That was horrible. Ethan's seventeen months old now, so I think I'm out of the post partum stage, don't you?"

She chuckles. "Yes." She clears her throat. "Listen, my appointment went...well. But the doctor wants me to have some further tests, just to be sure. I don't want you to worry, but I just wanted you to know."

I stiffen. "What's wrong?"

"I'm *fine*. Like I said, the doctor just wants to run some tests. I'll keep you posted."

"Mom, I am not a child anymore."

"Heather," she starts before going quiet. Long seconds pass. "Heather, I'm all right. I'm just really tired. Again."

"Like last time?"

She pauses. "Yes."

"Mom…" The lump in my throat doesn't let me say more.

****

July, 1995

I close my eyes, trying to soak up what little warmth the sun offers. The sound of the Pacific Ocean waves lapping against the beach mingled with the smell of the salt air is soothing. I appreciate the distraction.

Rick has taken a week's worth of leave. He insisted we spend a day at the beach. The ocean is too cold to swim in, unlike like the Gulf of Mexico in Texas. That water is as warm as bath water.

"Daddy! Ethan is eating sand!" Elizabeth cries.

I open my eyes and squint at Ethan. He is indeed squatting on the sand, pinching the grains between his thumb and forefinger and slowly putting them into his mouth while he gazes at the water. I hear the grains crunching in his mouth.

"Ethan," Rick scolds him, opening his hands to wipe them off. "Don't eat the sand, dude. It's not good for you."

Elizabeth wrinkles her nose. "That's disgusting!"

Ethan sticks his tongue out at her, and she kicks the sand at him. He retaliates immediately by throwing a fistful of sand in her face. She screams.

"Kids! Knock it off!" I yell, my mood darkening. My mood swings lately have been scaring me. I hope I don't have to get back on the medication.

Rick is quick to intervene. "Elizabeth, get your pail and shovel and let's build a sand castle. You can help, too, Ethan. Leave your mother alone." Rick glances over at me with a look of chagrin. "Lean back and close your eyes, Heather. I got this."

I press my lips into a thin line and do as he says, feeling guilty. My temper is so short these days. I have a lot on my mind.

Sighing, I open my eyes again and address Rick. "I'm sorry, Rick. That was out of line. I just…"

"I know," he interrupts, smiling gently. "Just take it easy and enjoy the day. Relax. I got this."

Taking a deep breath, I close my eyes once more.

Mom's test results came back. The cancer returned. It's worse. Mom is sure she'll be triumphant. When she called this past week, her voice was strong and brimming with confidence.

"Good?" Ethan asks.

"It's looking really good, buddy," Rick replies.

Overhead, a seagull squawks. Another seagull answers. I wonder if they can actually talk to each other. If they do, what do they say? I wish I knew what to say to my father who broke down and cried on the phone. Or to Jeff, or Debbie. Debbie was accepted to Texas A&M, but withdrew when mother's cancer returned. Mom protested vehemently, but Debbie remained steadfast in her decision.

I don't even know what to say to myself. When I told Rick, he held me while I cried. He didn't know what to say, either.

I just wish it would go away and leave my mother, and my family, alone.

****

Fall, 1995

Mom starts her chemo. I talk to her every couple of days and sometimes every day, just to hear her voice. I don't want the particulars of the plan – it doesn't help to know.

"Well, my hair is starting to thin out again," she chuckles. "I think I'll shave it all off again like last time. No sense in hanging on to something I can't."

Her words hit me the wrong way, and I start sobbing.

"Heather, what's wrong?" Mom asks.

"I...You...I want to hang on to *you*, Mom."

"Oh, honey. I'm not going anywhere. You'll see. I am not done on this earth. I have grandbabies to watch grow up, and hopefully more grandbabies to meet!"

I take a deep, ragged breath and compose myself. "I hope so, too." There have been hints that Jeff is going to propose to Cara. It wouldn't come as a surprise to any of us. "Has Jeff said anything else?"

"Kind of, sort of. But he hasn't really let us in on too much. Cara is such a lovely young lady, Heather. Don't you think so?"

"Yes, Mom. You know I do."

"I told Jeff to seize the day. Don't waste a single moment," Mom says wistfully.

I chew on my lip and squeeze my eyes shut. "Yes."

****

October, 1995

Jeff is going to propose. We are able to be there because of Rick's parents. They know what's going on with my mother, of course. We never asked them for it, but one day four plane tickets showed up in the mail, stunning us.

"What's this all about?" I ask Rick, incredulously.

He smiles broadly at me. "Mom and Dad want us to be able to visit your family and watch Jeff propose to Cara and…see everyone."

My mouth drops and I stare at the tickets. "But…but…how? Can you get leave?"

Rick chuckles. "Yes. My leave starts next week. The tickets my parents purchased are open, so we can book them whenever we want."

"Holy moly! I…I need to call and thank them." I immediately pick up the phone and dial his parents' number. Their answering machine picks up. They must be travelling – I can't keep up. I leave a heart felt and emotional message of gratitude for them that ends with me crying and saying thank you over and over again.

When I hang up, Rick hands me a tissue. "That was sweet, Heather. They adore you, as do I."

Accepting the tissue, I dab at my eyes. "No. They're the sweet ones. Rick, you didn't ask them to do this, did you?"

He quickly shakes his head. "Absolutely not. They feel terrible for what is going on and they know how much you miss your family. This is their way of helping out."

When we arrive in Texas, it feels hot to me, even though it's October.

"You're kidding, right?" Dad asks me on the way to the car. He's wearing his Member's Only jacket while I can feel sweat beginning to bead on my neck. "It's cooled down quite a bit, you know."

Maybe I have acclimated to the Northwest more than I thought.

Mom wasn't able to meet us at the airport.

"How's she doing, Dad?" I ask quietly while he and Rick load our luggage into the trunk.

"She's bald and boney. That's what she says," he replies. "She's…tired."

Rick glances at me before ducking his head and focusing on Ethan, strapping him securely into his car seat.

When I first see my mother, she is as Dad said – bald and boney. Her head is wrapped in one of her riotously colored scarves and she struggles to a standing position when we walk in. The smile that floods her face is still hers, though, and it's radiant.

"Mom," I choke before I hug her. I want to squeeze her hard and sob, but she looks so frail. I swallow the sobs and bite my lip while she pats my back.

"I'm all right, Heather," her surprisingly strong voice fills my ear. "Everything will be just fine."

I take a deep, steadying breath and release her so everyone else can hug her, too.

"You're skinny, Grandma," Elizabeth informs her. Ethan just grins at her from Dad's arms.

"Elizabeth…" I warn her. Rick and I tried to prepare our children for what Grandma might look like. We also told them that the bad bugs were back in her body and she has to take strong medicine to get rid of them.

Mom laughs. "It's all right. Yes, I am skinny, Elizabeth. Maybe we just need to bake your first birthday cake and eat some. How does that sound?"

Elizabeth's face brightens and she nods. "My first birthday cake?" she asks, confused.

"Well, we have to make the first one to be sure we get it right before we bake the second one for the party, don't we? So let's get in the kitchen," Mom says, holding her hand out. They disappear into the kitchen, Elizabeth skipping happily.

Once again, I can't believe how much Debbie has changed. She is now nineteen. She's not my baby sister anymore.

"Hey there, squirt!" Rick says, giving her a quick hug. "Can I still call you squirt?"

She laughs. "Yes, you can call me squirt. But only when family is around, never in public."

When we embrace, we linger for a long time.

"I've missed you, Deb," I whisper.

She nods, squeezing me harder. "Me, too," she whispers back.

"How are you holding up?"

She shakes her head, not answering.

"I know."

When we pull apart, we both wipe our eyes and smile.

"When is Jeff supposed to propose?" I ask, changing the subject.

"In two days," Dad interjects. "He's made plans with her family, too. We are going to celebrate Elizabeth's birthday and that's what he told Cara it was for. So it's going to be held here, of course. He's going to pop the question at the party. I think it's pretty good cover, don't you?"

"Absolutely. I'm impressed Jeff is able to pull this off."

"He wants it to be special."

"Oh, it will be," I laugh.

It is. Cara's family arrives and we have the back yard decorated for Elizabeth's party. She opens her presents, we sing happy birthday to her, and have cake and ice cream. We filled Elizabeth in on the secret – she is now a big six-year-old and can be trusted with secrets. She didn't mind sharing her day. Elizabeth adores Cara, as does everyone.

Once the party festivities are done and everyone is gathered outside in the yard, Jeff disappears into the house and into his room, which has been stuffed with twenty helium balloons in Cara's favorite colors – pink and lavender. He instructed each of us, starting with our family, to give her a balloon before he emerges with a dozen pink and red roses – there are no lavender ones – and the jewelry box with the engagement ring in it.

Discreetly, Debbie and I disappear into the house, retrieve our balloons, and emerge to give them to Cara, who accepts them laughingly.

"What is this?" she asks, smiling.

"You'll see," Debbie replies cryptically.

As more of us slowly disappear into the house and re-emerge, handing her a balloon, she becomes increasingly perplexed.

"What's going on y'all?" she asks, still laughing. Her hands are becoming full, the balloons bouncing off of each other and swaying in the wind.

The last person to hand her a balloon is her father. He gives it to her and kisses her on the cheek before stepping aside, looking expectantly at the door. She does the same, wide-eyed and clutching the balloon ribbons tightly.

Jeff, looking handsome and so grown up, emerges wearing the biggest, but still goofy, grin I have ever seen. His cheeks are flushed. He approaches her with the bouquet of roses and takes a deep breath before dropping onto one knee.

Cara's mouth drops open. The balloons start to shake.

"Cara, you are my girlfriend and my best friend. You are my soul mate. I can't imagine my life without you. I love you with all my heart. Will you now become my wife?" He holds the open ring box up to her. The beautiful diamond sparkles in the sunlight.

We hold our collective breaths for the briefest of moments, waiting to hear her answer.

"Yes!" she screams, releasing the balloons. They flutter upward and disperse almost immediately. "Oh, no! I'm sorry!" she cries, looking heavenward and stretching her arms up.

Any words they exchange are lost – we erupt in laughter and applause. Ethan claps heartily, as well, unsure of why but if everyone else is doing it, something good must be going on.

Jeff rises and the couple engages in a passionate hug and kiss. Cara's cheeks are wet when they separate, both beaming.

Her parents are the first to close in on them in congratulations, quickly followed by the rest of us. My mother is busily snapping pictures of it all.

"Louise, get in the shot. Let me have the camera," Rick says. Mom gladly gives it to him and sidles up to Cara. Cara is flanked by my parents, while Jeff is flanked by Cara's parents. It's a beautiful picture.

It's a beautiful day.

The remaining time of our visit refreshes my spirit, and I share that with Rick.

"I know, honey bun," he replies, kissing my cheek while we pack for our flight home. "I can tell. You needed this."

"More than you can imagine," I reply, zipping up a suitcase.

****

December, 1995

Christmas approaches. It's going to be scaled down this year. We agreed to save our money so we can make it to Jeff and Cara's wedding, which is in August. I won't miss that for anything.

Later in the week, Rick comes home early for lunch and is quiet. He kisses me and loves on the children, but he avoids my gaze. Something is up.

"You're home early," I prompt him.

"Yeah."

"Okay. Not that I don't like seeing you, but why are you home so early? I know you didn't get fired, so that's not it."

"No," he chuckles with me. "But we have to talk. Sit on the back patio with me?"

I nod. "Elizabeth, we'll be right outside. Watch your brother."

She nods and continues to play in close proximity to her brother.

Rick ushers me outside and closes the sliding door behind him. We sit down on the plastic chairs and I wait.

"Well," he sighs, sitting down and rubbing his hands across his thighs nervously. "We got a memo from headquarters today, and uh…" He looks around nervously.

"Rick…"

He stands up, places his hands on his hips and looks at me with…what? Sympathy?

"I may as well throw it out there," he sighs. "The military budget cuts have gone so deep that we are going to have to get used to sustainment deployments. They're saying we should expect to be gone at the very least six months out of every year for the foreseeable future." He eyes me. "I may have to leave in January."

"Oh no…"

He rubs his face. "Yeah. I know."

"That's just perfect, you know? I mean, of course they gut the military and then expect you guys to still do everything and be everywhere." I shake my head, wrapping my arms around myself and fight tears of anger.

"I'm sorry."

I look at my husband. "Rick, I'm not mad at you. I'm just…mad. This is an insane situation and…"

"Yes, it is. There's more," he says, ducking his head and kicking the concrete.

"More? What more could there be?"

"I have to go to twelve hour shifts starting tonight."

"*Tonight?* You're working twelve hour *night* shifts?"

He nods, glancing up. "That's why they sent me home. I have to be at work at seven tonight. It's not just the deployments, either. Manning the shop here is tough, too. There just aren't enough people to go around. So twelve hour shifts it is."

I feel like I've been sucker-punched. Twelve hour night shifts *and* deployments?

"How are we going to make it?" I breathe.

Rick closes his eyes and snorts. "Because we have to, remember?"

I bend forward, placing my elbows on my knees and bury my face in my hands.

"Yeah," Rick sighs. There's nothing to say.

I throw my hands up in the air. "Well, you better get to bed, I guess."

Rick snorts again. "Like I could actually go to sleep right now. I just woke up a couple of hours ago."

"Are you going to just stay up all day and all night?"

He shrugs. "It wouldn't be the first time."

I had planned to tell him my big news tonight, but I can't now.

How are we going to keep going? Especially when he finds out.

ACKNOWLEDGEMENTS

This book has been a labor of love and tears. There are so many aspects of military life that people are unaware of. It's like anything else in life, I suppose. Going to an amusement park is nothing like working at an amusement park – so many behind the scenes activities that outsiders are unaware of.

I have to thank the military spouses who contributed their stories for fictionalization. To protect them, I am going to thank them through using their initials only – C.S., K.B., L.C., T.W., H.Z., M.C., A.C., and M.P. You are amazingly strong individuals and I appreciate your openness, your courage, your patriotism, and your honesty. There were some stories that made me cry. Not all of their stories are included here, but stay tuned – there are still two more books in this series.

Thank you to Denise Keller for being my ever patient and ever honest editor. I appreciate all your feedback! My gratitude also goes out to my friend and photographer, Susan Motluck. You are so talented and patient. You totally get what I am looking for. I appreciate both of you more than words can say.

If you enjoyed reading this book, I would like to ask two things of you:

One – consider writing a review at Amazon or your favorite retailer. Reviews are the life blood for authors such as myself and they mean a great deal.

Two – please go to www.carischaeffer.com and join my team. You'll get exclusive access to bonus material and content as they become available. You'll also be notified when I run a promotion or giveaway. When you're ready, join me!

ABOUT THE AUTHOR

Cari has worn numerous hats in her life. She proudly wore the uniform of the United States Air Force, obtained her Bachelor's degree and worked as a critical care RN for almost a decade. She also owned her own Personal Chef and Catering company for six years. After all that, she chose to turn her attention back to her family.

Closing her business hasn't made her a couch potato, however. She volunteers at her church, has volunteered her time as a Mentor Mom for two MOPS (Mothers of Preschoolers) groups, started a thriving book club a few years ago (go figure), and belongs to a lunch club. She happily spends her time entertaining people in her home and driving her kids to and from sports practices and games. She not only has a passion for writing, but also for serving. She views writing as a form of service for people from all walks of life. Jesus used story-telling to convey life principles, why can't we do the same?

She lives in southern Illinois with her ridiculously patient husband of twenty five years, three children, and her two Chihuahua guard dogs, Snoopy and Stanley McBarker. Hello and Goodbye is her second novel. The Yellow Ribbon Chronicles is her first trilogy. Faith, Hope, Love, and Chocolate was her first novel.

Cari can be found on Facebook posting pictures of her dogs and musings about life in general. Be sure to visit her at www.carischaeffer.com. **When you join her team of avid readers, you'll be automatically entered to win a FREE electronic copy of future novels weeks before they are available to the general public.**

Made in the USA
San Bernardino, CA
22 February 2016